SAVAGE GAMES

PETER BOLAND

Savage Games (John Savage Action Thriller Book 2).
Copyright © Peter Boland 2019.

ISBN: 978-0-993569-52-4

CHAPTER 1

THE BODY HAD BEEN HIDDEN in a tree, high in the branches, at least fifty feet up, where no one could see it. At that height, the tree's dense crown with its highly evolved, tight-knit matrix of branches and needles fanned out in every direction, maximising the surface area for catching sunlight. Perfect for camouflaging a body. From the ground, it was impossible to tell it had been stashed there. The two men certainly didn't know about it until it was too late.

Most people would have called them lumberjacks. But Steve and Joel were employed by the Forestry Commission and had their jobs rebranded years ago with the fancy title of 'Forest Craftsman'. The job was essentially the same: cutting down trees.

They worked in the New Forest, a vast area of ancient woodlands and damp marshes. Stretching from the edges of Southampton in the east to the borders of Christchurch in the west, the forest was nearly one thousand years old, having been planted as a giant leisure park for William the Conqueror to satisfy his lust for popping arrows into unsuspecting wild deer and pigs.

To make it easier to manage, over the centuries the forest had been divided up into a patchwork of smaller enclosures. Joel and Steve's work schedule had sent them to one of the oldest and most isolated enclosures—the macabrely named Dead Maids Wood.

"This place gives me the creeps," Steve said, as their Forestry Commission Land Rover turned into a lonely gravel car park, surrounded on three sides by dark, dense forest.

Joel shrugged. "Doesn't bother me. Just another day at the

office." He opened the door, slid off his seat and headed to the wide metal gate that prevented the public from driving into the forest. There was a small gap next to it to allow walkers through one at a time. He unlocked the gate and waved Steve through, then locked it behind him and got back in the Land Rover.

Joel wouldn't admit it, but he actually agreed with Steve; Dead Maids Wood did nothing to support the chocolate-box image of the New Forest with its roaming ponies and pretty streams and villages. A place where families could have device-free holidays, and children could run around as nature intended, building camps and having *Swallows and Amazons*-style adventures. Dead Maids Wood was more likely to give them nightmares.

As they drove along the hard-packed pebble fire road, the wizened trees looked as if they had been designed by the production team on a slasher movie. Fat, twisted trunks, claw-like branches and weary low-hanging boughs all conspired to make any visitor, even the most ardent cynic, believe in wood spirits and tree deities, or that one of the painfully gnarled limbs might suddenly reach out and ensnare them.

At first the drive was relatively smooth, but further into their journey the road gradually faded, succumbing to nature under thick wild grasses, dirt and mulch, as if the forest were trying to reclaim the road, slowly digesting it. As the Land Rover bobbed and clattered along, it was clear the forest was winning. About half an hour of off-roading later, they reached their destination according to the GPS co-ordinates printed on their shift paperwork.

Steve and Joel exited the Land Rover. The tightly packed trees around them conjured up an eerie atmosphere. Even on windy days, the air barely moved here, creating a hushed, oppressive silence that pushed against the body, hefty and suffocating. And with a dingy, muted light at any given time of day, thanks to the dense roof-like tree canopy, it was easy for a person to think they were seeing things.

Steve shivered. "Let's get on with this. I want to get out of here."

Joel made a ghostly moan. Steve shoved him and went to retrieve the clipboard from the Land Rover's cab to check their work details.

In a woodland where most of the trees had been around since men hunted with crossbows, cutting down the wrong tree was about the worst sin you could commit. There would be no such mistakes today, as the tree in question was a mere youngster. A towering Douglas fir, just over a hundred and fifty years old. Shaped like an arrow head, the monumental evergreen dwarfed the deciduous trees around it.

"Sure this is the right one?" asked Steve. It was easily a hundred feet tall with a trunk as wide as a small car.

"You having a laugh?" asked Joel. "You see any other firs around here?"

"No, but it says here," Steve licked his finger and flipped through the paperwork, "that it's diseased. Looks fine to me." Douglas firs were prone to fungal infection, turning their needles brown or stripping them altogether. As both men stared up at the dense green crown, they could see no signs of infection.

Joel shook his head, "You just want to get out of here, you big wuss."

"No, I just don't want us to fell the wrong tree."

"Ours is not to reason why," Joel replied. "This is the one on the paperwork, so this is the one coming down."

"I don't know, we should call it in. Make sure."

"No way, it'll take hours for an answer, you know how slow they are back at the office," Joel replied, circling the tree. "Besides, look here." Steve joined Joel on the other side of the tree where a big yellow X had been marked on the trunk with spray paint. "It's been marked."

"Who marks trees anymore?" Steve asked. "I thought the whole reason they brought in GPS is so we didn't have to traipse around looking for yellow X's."

"Dunno. Maybe one of the old-school managers like Fletcher, he hates change."

"I thought he'd retired."

"Who cares," said Joel, impatient to get started. "You get the gear out, I'll do the honours."

Steve returned to the Land Rover while Joel began sizing up the giant, thoughtfully twisting the bristles of his soul-patch beard below his bottom lip, considering the task ahead. Stepping back a few paces, he checked the trunk for stability and lean. The tree had grown at a slight angle, which meant any attempt to cut it down would make it more likely to fall towards that angle, putting it directly in the line of an old oak. Second deadliest sin a forestry worker could commit was cutting down the right tree, only to have it fall onto a healthy one, or worse cause a domino effect, toppling tree after tree. Luckily, there was a clearing nearby that would easily accommodate the fallen fir. Joel would have to get it through a bottleneck formed by the ugly oak to the right and a modest beech tree on the left.

Joel took his time. Like a sculptor preparing to carve a statue from solid rock, he examined the trunk from every angle, rubbing its surface to get a feel for its shape. His first series of cuts would determine the fall path of the tree. It had to be perfect.

Satisfied with his decision, Joel pulled on his helmet with its mesh visor, his ear defenders and a pair of Kevlar chaps to protect his legs. Steve had already prepared Joel's chainsaw, a Swedish-made Husqvarna, oiling and filling it with petrol. Joel fired it up, revving it a few times. He never got tired of its aggressive whine; it was the same brand as the dirt bike he loved to ride. A complete petrol head, Joel always got a warm glow in his belly whenever anything noisy and mechanical was involved, especially as this weekend he'd be getting the keys to a shiny, new pickup truck. Only one owner and less than seven thousand miles on the clock. A smile broke over his face at the thought of slinging his dirt bike in the back and going in search of new far-flung trails.

"What are you grinning at?" asked Steve.

"Nothing," said Joel, gripping the chainsaw with both hands. "Just love my job." He pulled the throttle trigger and plunged the metre-long chainsaw into the tree at a steep angle, wood chips flying everywhere, the scent of freshly cut pine mixing with the petrol stench from the engine. Joel cut a perfect arc just above the base of the tree, then retracted the chainsaw and made a horizontal incision that joined up with the one he'd just made, creating a segment of wood, like a slice of orange on its side. He let the chainsaw idle, examining the shape he'd made. It looked good, so he gave the nod. Steve came in with an axe and knocked away the segment of wood, revealing a large notch in the side of the tree like a gaping mouth. Joel circled round to the opposite side and pushed his chainsaw horizontally into the tree. Gradually the screaming chainsaw sliced almost across its entire width, stopping just a few inches short of the notch he'd made on the other side. The tree didn't budge, and it wasn't supposed to, not yet. Joel retracted his chainsaw, while Steve used the back of his axe head to hammer three plastic wedges into the cut, which would gradually force the tree to topple towards the notch. Nothing happened. Steve took a fourth wedge and hammered it in. A second later, an almighty crack came from deep within the bowels of the trunk. That was the signal. Joel and Steve edged away at a right angle to the proposed fall line, putting plenty of safe distance between them and the doomed fir. Another loud crack, this one sounding like a firework. Then another and another. The two men stood back and watched as the mighty Douglas fir lost its battle with gravity and began its descent, painfully slow at first, then gathering more and more momentum. With a loud hiss like a wave crashing on shingle, the once proud tree smashed against the forest floor.

Then they saw it.

As the tree struck the ground, from deep within its branches, as if it had been spat out, flew a large dark object, soaring high into the air, then landing heavily on the ground a few feet away.

Steve and Joel looked at each other. Partly in confusion, partly to check if the other had witnessed what had just occurred.

Simultaneously they ran and stumbled towards the lumpen dark-green mass. As they got closer, curiosity and confusion quickly turned to horror when they realised what they were looking at.

A dead body.

With its back propped up against the tree, legs out in front as if he were taking a rest or having a nap, sat a dead, white, middle-aged man, dressed in a heavy green parka and hiking boots.

Both men swore then clamped their hands around their mouths as if to stop more profanities from escaping. Eyes darting around, they desperately searched for some clue as to why the man had been up the tree. That was when they noticed hooked bungee cables, the kind you use to lash luggage to the roof of a car, scattered everywhere on the ground like dead snakes. Several were entangled around the man's chest and arms.

To add to the surrealness of the chilling discovery, a pair of in-ear headphones were plugged into the man's head, connected to an old-school Sony Walkman of the cassette variety, its casing splintered and smashed from the impact. Lengths of dark-brown magnetic tape were strewn across the man like dirty streamers.

Steve went as pale as the man lying on the ground before them, his voice quivering. "I think we just killed someone."

CHAPTER 2

S AVAGE FELT THE BLOW BEFORE he saw it. Not a good sign. Either his reactions were getting slower or hers were getting faster. He guessed it was a combination of both. She followed it up with a hard slap to his right ear, nearly rupturing his eardrum. Then a stamp to the toes of his left foot. Lucky she was wearing Doc Marten boots, the soft, air-cushioned soles taking some of the sting out of the impact. If she'd been wearing anything harder, Savage would be looking at several broken bones. It still hurt like hell. But he wasn't out of the fight yet. To ensure she'd hit her target, Tannaz had made the mistake of looking down. Only briefly. It gave Savage the split second he needed to score a double hand strike to her chest with both fists. He missed her solar plexus, a favourite target of his, striking her just below the base of the neck near her collar bone. Tannaz went flying backwards. Converting her momentum into a roll, she came right back up, onto her feet. Fists raised, she lunged for Savage then stopped short.

Savage had his hands up. "Enough," he said, in between gasps for breath.

Tannaz danced around on the balls of her feet with the energy of a caffeinated flea. "Come on, I'm ready to go again."

"Yeah, well, you're not sixty, are you?"

"Neither are you."

"I'm nearly sixty."

"Well that's not the same as being sixty, and even if you were it wouldn't matter. Stop with the self-sabotage."

Savage straightened up and stretched. A few weary joints popped. He rubbed the cheek where Tannaz had struck him.

Tannaz relaxed, dropped her guard.

Savage darted forward, snatched her left hand by the wrist, twisted it anti-clockwise forcing her to turn her back towards him. In a second he had his other arm around her neck in a choke hold. "Don't ever assume the fight is over," he said, then let her go.

"Hey, that's not fair," Tannaz protested.

"Fights aren't fair. Not real ones. Get used to it."

Tannaz sulked and flopped down on the sofa that had been pushed against one wall to make space for their sparring session. "Damn it," she complained. "I keep making dumb mistakes."

"Hey, mistakes are good. Mistakes are how you learn."

They'd been using Savage's flat for their daily fighting sessions for over a year now. It was a miracle nothing had been broken. But then there wasn't much in Savage's sparse flat to break. Five days a week, Savage taught Tannaz everything he knew about fighting or, more precisely, fighting dirty—the only way to fight, as Savage said. Tannaz's enthusiasm was insatiable. She'd wanted to train every day. Savage told her it was good to give the body time to recuperate, more for him than her—his bruises were taking a lot longer to heal than they once did.

Tannaz grumbled. Looked away. One of her moods was about to set in and he needed to snap her out of it quickly. Tannaz was a brilliant student but criticism could easily send her into a tailspin.

"One thing I will say," said Savage. "Your speed is off the chart. I'm going to start calling you Twitch."

"I'm not a titch."

Savage shook his head. "I said Twitch, not titch. As in fast-twitch muscles."

"I don't understand."

Savage sat down beside her. "Two types of muscle fibres in the body. Fast and slow twitch. Slow-twitch are responsible for endurance like long-distance running, while fast-twitch are responsible for bursts of speed. Everyone has both. I'd bet you've got loads more fast-twitch fibres than most people."

"Really?" She looked up at him, tearing her gaze away from the floor.

"Honestly, I've never seen anyone as quick as you, not on the street, not in the army. I mean it. You're going to be one hell of a fighter."

"Already am." Tannaz brightened up. Though she was prone to pessimism, she could easily flip the other way with a few choice words, going from wallowing in self-pity to overconfidence in a heartbeat.

"Don't get cocky. More fast-twitch muscles mean you tire out quicker, no good for running long distances."

"That's fine, I don't intend to sign up for the London Marathon just yet."

Tannaz got up and rifled through her leather biker jacket hanging on the back of the lounge door and pulled out a packet of cigarettes.

"Those things don't help," said Savage. "Give me a hand putting the furniture back, then you can give yourself emphysema."

"Have you given up white sugar yet?" she replied.

"No—"

"Double standards! Owned!" Tannaz shouted, doing a little victory dance.

Savage shook his head. "Nicotine is way worse than white sugar."

"White sugar kills more people, it's in everything, tobacco isn't."

"Rubbish. Cigarettes kill more people."

Tannaz stuffed the cigarette packet into the back pocket of her jeans and pulled out her smart phone. "Let's ask the Internet." She spoke into her phone's voice-activated search facility. "What kills more people, sugar or nicotine?" Tannaz scrolled through the results, frowning.

"Well, what does it say?" asked Savage.

"Inconclusive. We'll have to agree to disagree."

Savage gave a smug grin. "That's what people with weak arguments say."

"No, that's what people who don't want a load of earache say."

"I think I won that one."

Tannaz tucked her phone in her back pocket. "No way, I'll do a proper search later and prove it to you with statistics."

"Did you know eighty-five percent of statistics are made up on the spot?"

Tannaz looked at him, trying to gauge whether he was being serious. "Shut up."

Savage cracked another broad grin. He enjoyed training Tannaz, and he enjoyed her company even more, especially her feisty banter. She told it like it was, which was exactly what he needed. She reminded him of his daughter. They looked nothing like each other; his daughter Kelly had been fair with long straight hair, while Tannaz was dark with thick lustrous black curls that she mercilessly attacked with clippers up the sides of her head. However, both Tannaz and his Kelly were stubborn, wilful and clever.

"Come on, help me with the sofa," he said, standing up. "Then we'll have a cup of tea."

They each grabbed one end.

"You want hot tea after all that sweating?" asked Tannaz, as they shifted the sofa back into the middle of the room.

"Tea's good any time."

Tannaz wiped her brow. "I'd rather have an ice-cold beer."

"At eleven in the morning?"

"Beer's good any time."

"Yeah, and with the cigarettes it will slow down all that lovely speed you've got."

"Okay, I'll have a lemonade." Tannaz shrugged.

"I don't have any lemonade."

"Why not?"

"Because I'm not six years old. I'm nearly sixty."

"So you keep telling me. Stop feeling sorry for yourself, and grab that rug over there, if you can manage it at your age. And I owe you money for the fight session."

"And like I said, I'm doing this for free. It keeps me sane."

Before he'd met the young Iranian girl, Savage had attempted suicide. Post-traumatic stress had haunted him since leaving the SAS; the sheer weight of deaths pressing on his conscience. He'd always managed to keep it at bay, but after his wife and daughter died—his wife Dawn from cancer, and his daughter Kelly from a bomb in Afghanistan—things had become a whole lot worse, especially after he had retired. He'd started hearing a voice in his head, an aggravating and aggressive voice that teased, pestered and tormented him, constantly trying to persuade him to kill himself as penance for what he'd done in his career. He'd heard the voice so often that he'd even given it a name—Jeff Perkins. It had become louder and more powerful each day to the point where Savage couldn't take any more. He'd put a gun to his head at one point, nearly pulled the trigger. At the last moment sense prevailed, and he got help.

He'd met Tannaz a few months later when he needed help finding a missing girl. Her ingenuity with a computer had not only led him to the girl, it had probably saved his life. They'd become close friends, and whenever she was near, the berating voice of Jeff Perkins grew dim, skulking back into the shadows. She'd given up her job working in a seedy backstreet computer repair shop to train with Savage. He wasn't sure what she did for an income now. With her hacking skills he thought it was best not to ask.

Tannaz placed a small side table next to the sofa. "It's like a monk's funeral home, this lounge. You need more furniture."

"Then we'd have more stuff to move back each time we fight."

"Yeah, but it'd make it more homely, bit cosier. You need more colour in this room. I feel an Ikea expedition coming on."

"No. No way. I escaped Iraq on foot in the Gulf War, but could I find my way out of Ikea? Place is a maze, a flat-pack maze. Anyway, anything I need I can make myself. And I don't need anything else in my life right now, apart from a cup of tea."

The doorbell rang.

Savage went into the hall and opened the front door.

A timid-looking man in his late twenties stood on the doorstep.

Mousy bowl-shaped hair hung limply around a pale face, set in a gloomy expression like a washed-out public holiday. He fiddled nervously with the zip on his bomber jacket.

"Excuse me," he said, not making eye contact. "Are you John Savage?"

"Certainly am. Who wants to know?"

"I think you went to school with my dad, Dave Mosely. I'm his son, Luke."

Savage looked closer at the guy standing in front of him, his brain slowly catching up. Recognition dawned on him. "Oh, yes, I can see the resemblance. I did go to school with your dad. How is he?"

"Er, he died a couple of months ago."

"Oh no, I'm so sorry. How did he die?"

Luke's eyes flicked left and right. Unsure how to answer, he eventually said, "His body was found up a tree."

CHAPTER 3

S AVAGE INVITED LUKE INTO THE flat and ushered him into the lounge. He took one look at Tannaz and fixed his eyes on the carpet, clearly uncomfortable around women. He stood there awkwardly, doing that not-knowing-where-to-put-his-hands thing, changing their position every second.

"Tannaz, this is Luke," said Savage.

"Alright," said Tannaz.

Luke managed a barely audible "Hi." He still made no eye contact.

Savage gestured at the sofa, inviting him to sit.

"Luke's dad and I were good friends at school. Unfortunately, he passed away recently."

"Oh," said Tannaz. "I'm very sorry."

Luke didn't respond. An uncomfortable silence stretched out. It probably lasted only a couple of seconds but felt like a fortnight, until Tannaz said, "I'm going to nip out back for a cigarette or two, and leave you guys to it." She left the room.

"I'll make us a cup of tea," said Savage.

"Thank you," said Luke.

Savage went into the kitchen to put the kettle on, and returned with two cups of tea in his hand, giving one to Luke. "Hope that's the right colour."

"It's fine, thank you," Luke replied.

Savage sat next to him. They both took several sips, each unsure how to continue the conversation. Savage broke the silence first. "Do you mind me asking how your father died? You said he was found in a tree."

Luke swallowed a large gulp of tea, then cleared his throat. "A couple of forest workers found him. His body had been hidden, high in the branches of a large fir tree. The only reason they found him was because they cut the tree down and he fell out."

Savage wanted to remark about the weird and strange circumstances of his father's death. He held his tongue, guessing that Luke had probably heard that response from everyone he'd told, accompanied by wide-eyed expressions and gasps of disbelief. He didn't need someone else adding to his distress.

"So did he die from the impact or...?"

Luke shook his head. "No, he'd been dead for a couple of weeks. They found large quantities of Nembutal in his blood."

"Nembutal?"

"It's a drug to help you sleep. In large doses it's lethal. People take it to commit suicide because it's peaceful, like going to sleep but you never wake up."

"Is that what the police think, that it was suicide?"

"Yes."

Savage pushed his hand through his thinning hair and let out a long breath, grasping for the right words to say. There weren't any. "I can't believe it. Poor Dave. He was my best mate at school."

"He talked about you a lot," said Luke. "I mean, I didn't see him that often. He was a bit of a loner. The few times I did meet with him, your name always came up."

Savage twisted his mug of tea around and around in his hands, the guilt growing inside him. "I feel bad about not keeping in touch with him. We lost contact after I joined the army, I'm pretty certain I was his only friend. I should've made more of an effort. I didn't even realise he got married and had a son."

"Oh, he didn't. Get married, I mean. I was a bit of an accident. He met my mum one night at a gig. She was drunk and on the rebound. Dad happened to be standing next to her, and she was determined to go home with someone. I don't think he stood a chance, and I was the result. After that she didn't have anything to do with him, said it was a drunken mistake, so I never knew who he was, she didn't want him around, told him to stay away.

Brought me up on her own. So I never knew him, grew up without a dad. I mean, my mum was great, loved me to bits, but I wished he'd made an effort to see me. Even when I got in contact with him when I was older, he was pretty aloof. Uncomfortable around me. Don't know whether it was guilt or if he just didn't know how to act. Last time I saw him was when Mum died. I said we should link up on Facebook or swap email addresses. He never had a computer. Hated the things. Just liked his vinyl and record player. Real old school."

Savage smiled as sympathetically as he could.

Luke took a sip of tea and then said, "What was he like at school?"

Savage took his time and then said, "Same, really. Quiet and shy. Would have faded into the background if he could. I never really noticed him, until one day our music teacher allowed us to bring in a single to play on the school record player at the end of term. Most people brought in sappy seventies pop stuff. A few of us cool kids brought in some proper music, I think I brought in The Who, someone else brought in Led Zeppelin. You have to remember back in those days, the best band in the world, The Jam, hadn't been signed yet. When it was your dad's turn, he put on Iggy Pop's 'I Want To Be Your Dog'. I'd never heard anything like it. First time I'd heard proper punk rock. It blew me away. I wanted to know more about it. End of the lesson I went straight up to him and we got talking, became instant friends. Every break time we'd hang out and talk about music and new bands we'd heard listening to John Peel's late-night radio show; back then that was the only place you could hear alternative stuff."

Luke smiled, his face losing some of its washed-out complexion. "My dad mentioned your break-time chats. Always made him happy. And he also remembered the day you two met. It was the last time he ever got bullied, he told me. Before he met you he got picked on every day. Bullies would rip his blazer off on the way to school and rub it in dog shit. No matter how hard he washed it off in the toilet, the stink wouldn't go away, so he smelt of dog shit all day. As soon as they knew John Savage was my dad's friend, nobody ever bullied him again."

The room went silent.

Savage's mind raced back to every moment he could remember with Dave. Had every incident in Dave's life led up to the point where he'd had no choice but to take his life? Each tiny decision made, every word uttered and thought he'd had, every corner turned left instead of right, had it all conspired against him? Incremental step by incremental step, edging him closer to the inevitable. Like values being fed into a sprawling equation, each one calculated to determine his terrible fate. Or had it been with him all his life, buried deep in his DNA? A ticking genetic time bomb waiting to go off, implanted by nature to weed out the ones that simply didn't suit life. Removing him from the gene pool.

At a loss for words Savage offered his condolences once more.

Luke waved them away. "It's really not necessary, he was a stranger to me."

"Can I ask you something?"

"Sure."

"If it's uncomfortable, just tell me to mind my own business."

"Go ahead, what is it?"

"The business with the tree. Why did he commit suicide up a tree?"

"Thought you might ask that. Police said it's very rare. Some people, people like my dad, don't want anyone to know they've committed suicide. They feel ashamed, even though they can't see any other way out. They want to kill themselves but they don't want their family and friends to know, or anyone for that matter. Like you said, people like my dad just want to fade into the background, and they don't want any random dog walker or jogger to have the trauma of stumbling across their body. So, they climb a tree, strap themselves into the branches where no one can see them and kill themselves out of sight."

"Jeez, I never knew that."

"He climbed up the tree as high as he could go, secured himself to a branch with dozens of those hooked bungee cords, you know, the ones you use on roof racks. Took the Nembutal and slipped away listening to his favourite mixtape on his ancient Walkman, wearing his big old mod parka."

"That's tragic."

"His body would've stayed up there the police reckon. When the tree came down, the impact tore the bungee cords free."

Savage got up and walked around the room, trying to process the shocking information, and Savage didn't shock easily. "I suppose it makes sense. Grisly, but it makes sense. Your dad never wanted to be noticed in life and I suppose the same was true in death."

He looked out of the window. It needed cleaning, one of the many drawbacks of living in London. Even with the congestion charge, everything eventually went black. Savage turned to face Luke. "When was the last time you saw him?"

"Before Christmas. I asked him if he wanted to have Christmas dinner round my place. He said he had other plans. I'm guessing those other plans meant he was preparing to take his life."

"Did he show any signs of being unhappy or depressed?"

"Thing is, my dad always looked unhappy. His life had been a bit of a disappointment. One dead-end job after another. Then he was on benefits. Tiny room in grotty social housing. Things just didn't go his way. It was like life didn't really suit him, made him uncomfortable."

"And when did they find his body?"

"Eleventh of January. Police think he'd been dead for around seventeen days."

Savage did a quick calculation. "Oh no, so it could've been Christmas Day when he took his life?"

"That's what they think."

Savage shook his head. "Poor, Dave. I should've kept in touch with him. Met up with him for a drink now and then or gone to a gig with him. Maybe this could've been avoided."

"I don't think so. I made an effort but he didn't want to be helped. He just wanted out, you know. Some people just do."

Savage looked Luke in the eye, grabbed him by the hand and

squeezed it firmly. "Listen, Luke, if there's anything I can do for you, you name it. Anything."

Luke thought for a moment. Looked sheepish, picking at the skin around his nails. "Well, there is one thing."

"Sure, what do you need?"

Luke took a deep breath. "I need to pick some things up from my dad's flat."

Savage waited for the rest of the request, but no more came. "Really? That's it?"

Luke nodded.

"You want me to help you clear some stuff out of your dad's place?"

Luke nodded again, looking terrified, eyes rimmed with worry.

"Are you sure that's all?" said Savage, just to make sure.

"Yes. Well, it's really just his record collection, it's worth quite a bit, at least a few hundred pounds, and his record player."

"Are you sure there isn't anything else I can do for you?" asked Savage. "That doesn't sound like very much."

"Believe me, just having you with me would be enough."

"Why's that?"

"Dad's flat, I mean his room, was in a pretty horrible place called Tivoli Gardens in Thornhill, one of Southampton's worst housing estates. He always told me weird stuff went on there."

"What kind of stuff?" asked Savage.

"Wouldn't say. I know he was scared. Police won't even go there, unless they're in riot gear. I'm worried I wouldn't make it out of there alive with boxes of rare LPs under my arms."

"Well, worry no more. I've got a van outside; we can go there right now if you want."

Relief spread across Luke's face, he looked lighter somehow, as if he'd been filled with helium. "Really? Are you sure?"

"Of course," Savage replied.

"That would be brilliant. Listen, I don't have any money for petrol, but my dad had a signed copy of The Jam's first album. I know he'd want you to have it..."

Savage shook his head. "No, no way, Luke. Much as I'd love

a signed copy of *In The City*, you keep it. Besides, I've got plenty of cash. My late wife was good with money, made sure I had a nice fat pension for my retirement. I could go out and buy one tomorrow and still pay my gas bill. Driving you to Southampton is the least I can do."

"Please," Luke replied, fidgeting. "My dad would've wanted you to have it, I'm sure of it."

"Definitely not. A signed copy of The Jam's first album must be worth a few quid, that could come in handy. Put it to a holiday or something. Okay?"

Tannaz returned, rattling a creased-up carton of orange juice. "Savage, why is everything in your fridge about a year past its sell-by date?"

"Because sell-by dates are made up by big supermarkets so you throw away good food and buy more. I bet it's fine."

She held out the carton to Savage. "You drink it then."

"I'm fine. Got a nice cup of tea, thanks."

Luke's face became anxious.

"What's wrong?" asked Savage.

"Sorry," Luke said, wringing his hands. "It's just, Dad's place. The guys who live there, some of them are violent and I'm pretty sure they're all drug addicts and alcoholics, it might get... physical."

"That's okay," said Savage. "We'll take Tannaz with us."

Tannaz lost interest in the orange juice. "What's this?"

"Fancy putting your training into practice?" Savage asked.

"Hell, yeah," she replied.

CHAPTER 4

Savage's white VW Caddy slotted itself into the inside lane of the M3 as they left behind the clogged-up cholesterol lanes of London's orbital M25, a road that achieved consistent slowness regardless of the time of day. Barring any more traffic hold-ups, Southampton would only take another hour of driving.

During the journey, Luke tried several more times to push the signed Jam album on Savage. Savage was having none of it and each time Luke asked, Savage held up his hand to silence him.

Tannaz sat in the back, playing on her monstrously powerful laptop. Luke kept glancing back at her. After a while he plucked up the courage and asked, "Is that a gaming laptop?"

"Kind of," Tannaz replied, not looking up.

"Are you a gamer?" Luke asked.

"Kind of," Tannaz replied, this time giving him a cheeky smile.

Luke smiled back nervously.

"Tannaz is a computer genius," said Savage. "Built that laptop herself."

Luke suddenly lost his inhibitions. "Really?" he gushed. "That's amazing. I've never met anyone who can build computers. That's like having a superpower or something."

Tannaz laughed.

"That's not too far from the truth," Savage added. "You wouldn't believe what Tannaz can do with a computer."

"You wanna go?" Tannaz offered.

"Could I?"

"Come on, climb in the back and I'll show you some tricks."

Luke leapt out of his seat, clambered over into the van's payload and sat himself next to Tannaz, who passed the laptop to him. "Wow, it's heavy," he said.

"That's because it's a hardcore machine, built for cyber combat," Tannaz said with plenty of melodrama.

Giggles and woops of delight followed, interspersed with a geekfest of conversation about stuff that Savage didn't fully understand, as if the two of them were speaking a different language. They would have carried on forever, apart from the fact that Savage insisted on stopping for tea at Winchester services. As the three of them headed to the café, Luke broke away to visit the toilets.

Savage leant in and said to Tannaz, "I think Luke's got a little cyber crush on you."

"What's wrong with that?" she replied.

"Well, I don't know how good his gaydar is. He might not know you bat for the other team."

"Well, I have been known to cross over to the dark side, on very rare occasions," she said, playfully.

Savage stopped and stared at her. "Tannaz Darvish. I learn something new about you every day."

"Luke's cute and very sweet," she said. "Brings out my maternal instincts. Makes me want to look after him."

"Fine, just remember he's been through a lot."

"Savage, what do you take me for?"

"Just saying."

After their drinks stop, they followed the M3, turning off onto the M27 into the heart of Southampton, a city renowned for its Premier League football club, deep-water dock, overloaded container ships and Leonardo de Caprio winning passage onto the fateful *Titanic*, although that probably happened on a green screen five thousand miles away in Hollywood.

"Did you know over eight thousand Spitfires were built here during World War Two?" Savage said. "Luftwaffe bombed it to kingdom come to stop production."

"Is that why Southampton is so ugly?" asked Tannaz.

"Don't joke, Tannaz. A lot of people lost their lives when the Spitfire factory got destroyed."

"I'm not joking. I'm Iranian. We're still getting over the war we had with Iraq."

"True," said Savage. "That was a nasty war."

"So what happened after the factory was destroyed?" asked Luke.

"Production continued."

"How?" asked Tannaz.

"Blitz spirit. Spitfires got built all over the city, anywhere there was space. Garden sheds, bus stations, launderettes. Parts got taken to airfields all over the country and then assembled. Just like a giant Airfix kit."

"What's an Airfix kit?" Luke and Tannaz asked simultaneously.

Savage sighed. "Only the best part of growing up in the seventies. I'd save up my pocket money from my paper round, run down to the model shop..."

Tannaz whispered in Luke's ear, "Uh-oh, now we've set him off."

"... buy a model-airplane kit to build like a Messerschmitt 109, a Mustang P-51 or the best fighter plane in the world, the Supermarine Spitfire. Make sure I'd saved enough to buy a little tin of Humbrol to paint the underside duck-egg blue—"

Tannaz interrupted, "And then you'd have a slap-up meal in front of the TV and watch, what was that weird show you told me about, *Crackerjack*?"

"Or *Banana Splits* or *Grange Hill* or *Rentaghost*. TV was great when I was a kid."

"Didn't you say all kids' TV presenters were paedophiles when you were young?" asked Tannaz.

"Not all of them. You're spoiling the warm glow of nostalgia. Way to go, Tannaz."

Savage flicked down the indicator and took a right into the notorious area known as Thornhill, where Dave Mosely had lived out his last days.

"Bloody hell," said Tannaz as the VW pulled into the post-apocalyptic housing estate, immediately passing the black skeleton of a burnt-out car sitting in a ring of charred tarmac. It looked as if it had been there for some time, like a fossil. "I thought South London had some dodgy areas, but this makes them look like Beverly Hills."

If anyone in the future wanted to know how to create a community where crime, anti-social behaviour and childhood obesity would flourish like germs in a petri dish, Thornhill would be it. The predominant architectural style, dotted around the area like acne spots, seemed to be squat, four-storey blocks of flats, clad in dirty biscuit-coloured concrete with spindly pale blue balconies bolted to the outside. Only slightly better than scaffolding, each balcony, probably designed for the resident to access fresh air, had been adapted as a place to store rubbish and junk or washing. In between each block of flats were rows of tatty council houses where the front gardens had long since perished and become driveways of dirt, also littered with rubbish of a heavier kind—cars that didn't work, twisted-up bicycles and of course the ubiquitous dumped shopping trolley.

"Jeez," said Savage. "I can see why you didn't want to come here on your own."

Tannaz prodded away on her laptop in the back of the van. "Here's what someone posted on social media about Thornhill, 'Even the cats don't go out at night' then someone else has posted, 'Don't be daft, cats don't live long enough in Thornhill to go out at night'."

Savage glanced across at Luke, sitting rigid with fear. "Don't worry, Luke," he said. "I've been to far worse places than this, where people were trying to shoot me." Luke's expression didn't change, perhaps not considering the thought of not getting shot to be comforting.

A young teen in a black Adidas top stood beside the road waiting to cross, holding onto a scratched-up BMX with a flat front tyre. Savage slowed to a stop and waved him across. The boy walked halfway, looked towards the van and stuck up his middle finger.

"Charming," Savage remarked. "How much further?"

"Next right," said Luke, his voice small and fragile.

They passed a convenience store, its graffiti-covered metal security shutters firmly down, apart from the one over the door. Savage wondered if there was ever an occasion when it was safe enough for all its security shutters to be up.

He took the next right, into a cul-de-sac that, though an almost impossible feat, managed to look worse than the streets they had just driven down. Savage had to swerve to miss a mattress that had been dumped in the middle of the road—no doubt it would be set on fire after dark, courtesy of the local kids. Luke pointed to a large three-storey building at the end. "That's it," he said. "That's my dad's place, Tivoli Gardens."

While the rest of the buildings in Thornhill looked as if they had been built in the period when architects had decided everything should be built from brutal slabs of concrete, this building gallantly held on to its 1930s' arts-and-crafts period features. For how long was anyone's guess. As they pulled up outside, behind the one and only car on the street, Savage gave the building a quick appraisal. Being a keen DIYer, he had an eye for construction, although he didn't need to be any sort of building surveyor to tell the place should've been condemned years ago. It looked like an old battered leather suitcase about to split open and disgorge its contents. Every inch of deformed brickwork had lost its pointing, and ruptured guttering spilled green slime down the side of its walls. The roof had a hole in it that had been half-heartedly nailed over with a black tarpaulin, the edge of which flapped around lazily in the icy breeze. Each rotten window frame, the ones that weren't broken, sagged hopelessly. They looked original and he doubted if any of them closed properly. Savage felt sorry for the old three-storey pile. Probably a once splendid residence, it now reminded him of a wounded animal that needed putting down.

Savage got out of the van, followed by Luke and Tannaz. "Okay," he said. "Let's get Luke's stuff and get out of here."

Just at that moment the doors of the car parked in front of

them opened, polluting the air with dreadful high-beats-per-minute techno music and smoke of dubious origin. The car was a green modified Vauxhall Corsa. Though it was a small car with a gutless engine, the owner had added a huge exhaust the size of a bazooka in a bid to make it go faster. Savage had seen these before on tiny underpowered cars, their only function appeared to be making a racket as they drove around.

Three men got out of the Corsa, blocking their way.

The driver spat on the ground, swore at them and said, "Where do you think you're going?"

CHAPTER 5

To call them men might have been pushing it somewhat. Barely in their twenties and still in that gangly stage, each one wore training shoes and tracksuit bottoms that rode high up their lanky legs, revealing plenty of white-socked ankle. The top halves of their bodies had that hunched-over, hollow-chested look, not quite filled out yet. Immature bodies, maybe, but their faces wore permanent pinched sneers with hard unemotional eyes earned from growing up far too quickly on a rough estate. The driver of the car had odd patches of sprouting facial hair, not enough to merit having a full shave. The one from the passenger side had a painfully acned face, while the one who'd got out of the back breathed through a mouth that constantly hung open.

"Afternoon," said Savage.

"You ain't going in there, 'less you buying," said the driver with the bum fluff. They were local dealers, not the big shots by any stretch, just three low-level minions, selling on product, but dangerous none the less. Keeping their position, no matter how low on the food chain, meant enforcing it with fear and intimidation and, if needed, physical violence.

"Sorry, we're not buying," said Savage.

"Do you know who you're talking to?" said Spotty Guy. "We're legends round here. I'm the Chicken Man." Then he nodded to his mates. "That's Malarkey Shark and Bonafide Ride." They both cracked their knuckles.

"You need better gang names," said Savage. "You sound like a bunch of race horses about to enter the Grand National."

Luke sniggered. Then wished he hadn't.

Bum Fluff or Bonafide Ride, as he preferred to be called, got all up in Luke's face, trying his best to be the tough guy. "You laughing at me, boy?" Bum Fluff asked, arms wide open and waving about, trying to goad Luke into a fight. "I'll shank you. Kill your dumb ass."

Savage put himself between Luke and Bum Fluff. Then he smiled at the three thugs, not to be friendly but to show he wasn't worried in the slightest by their housing-estate hardman act—he'd seen it done a lot better, and by much more physically intimidating individuals. "Sorry, lads. We're just not buying today."

"Then you got a problem," Spotty Guy said in a fake Jamaican accent.

"It's okay," said Luke. "We can come back another time."

"That's right, you little bitch." Bum Fluff was now hitting his stride, swaggering all over the pavement, pointing in Luke's direction as if he were holding a gun sideways, gangster style. "You're a dead man. I'll come after you. Won't know what's hit you."

"Okay, guys," Savage replied calmly. "We've had a long drive from London—"

"Still not coming in," said Bum Fluff. "Not leaving neither, 'less we get paid."

Savage gestured to the guy's Corsa. "Is that your nan's car?"

Bum Fluff snapped. Started leaping around all enraged. With his long wiry frame, it just looked comedic, like he had a live rodent down his trousers. He threw a couple of F-bombs in Savage's direction.

"Good comeback," Savage replied. "You ought to do stand up." Bum Fluff spat on the ground. It landed at Savage's feet. "I presume that was supposed to land on my shoes?" asked Savage. "You should try spitting next time, not dribbling."

"I'll kill you," said Bum Fluff. He was still bouncing all over the place, unable to contain his rage, but he wouldn't engage Savage or throw a punch.

Savage's confidence radiated off him like a forcefield.

"I'm not going anywhere," said Savage, "I must warn you, I don't hit children."

Spotty Guy lunged forward. He was held back by Mouth Breather, who hadn't said anything yet. He stepped in front of his mate and approached Tannaz, eyeing her from top to bottom, finally resting his gaze on her breasts, mouth still hanging open.

"You two can kill these pricks," he said. "I'm going to have a go on her. You're well fit." He grabbed Tannaz's breasts with both hands and started fondling them.

"Please, let's go," Luke pleaded.

Savage ignored him and spoke to Mouth Breather, "I wouldn't do that if I were you."

"Why? What are you going to do—"

Before he'd finished, Tannaz grabbed Mouth Breather's hands viper-fast, thumbs on top, fingers gripping underneath, twisting his wrists outwards. A move she'd practiced a million times with Savage. Except this was no training exercise. She didn't hold back. The guy cried out in agony. She rotated his wrists past the point of no return, snapping them both simultaneously. He hadn't stood a chance.

Tannaz released her grip and the guy collapsed on the floor in the foetal position, trying to hold his arms in a way that would lessen the pain. His screams echoed off the buildings in the vicinity.

Savage turned to the guy with the bum fluff, who backed away, fearing the same would happen to him. "Do your friend a solid, put him in your little Noddy car and take him to A&E. He'll need to get his wrists set, okay?"

Bum Fluff nodded rapidly, as if his head might come off. He and the guy with the acne wasted no time, dragging their screaming friend, who was now holding his broken arms in front of him like a T-Rex, into an upright position. They shoved him into the passenger seat, then got into the Corsa.

"Bye, guys," said Savage, as they slammed the doors shut. "Make good decisions."

The little car sped off, its ridiculous exhaust sounding like an angry fog horn and spewing black smoke into the cold air.

When the car had disappeared from view, Tannaz turned to Savage and said, "Do your friend a solid?"

"What's wrong with that?" Savage asked.

"It sounds like you want him to go to the toilet."

"Really?" Savage looked at Luke for support.

"I've always thought it sounds like that too," said Luke.

"Wow," Savage said thoughtfully. "Well, I won't be requesting any solids from either of you two, then."

"That just sounds wrong," Tannaz remarked. "Come on, let's get these vinyls and go home."

They crossed the patch of dirt that used to be a front garden, walking around a rusted bike lying on its side missing a front wheel. An old armchair sat against a wall, slowly decomposing. Cigarette butts were strewn everywhere and, as they neared the entrance, Savage noticed a clutch of used hypodermic needles lying by a drain next to a mountain of empty booze bottles.

Luke stood at the front door, pushed in the key and gave it a turn. The door opened about half an inch but no more. It had swollen, and was wedged into the door frame. Savage shouldered it. The door budged a little. He gave it another shove. As it opened farther, Savage poked his head in and could see the reason for the door's reluctance to grant them access. Mountains of junk mail and takeaway leaflets, piled against the inside, acting like a barricade. One more push and it opened far enough for them to enter.

The first thing they noticed was the smell. Mould and decay, of course, mixed with rotten food and the acrid stench of urine. In the dingy light of the hallway, Savage could see the culprit. A large damp patch, presumably where a drunken resident hadn't made it to the bathroom in time and had to relieve themselves on the carpet.

"This place stinks." Tannaz pushed the door behind her. It took several attempts to close it.

Savage looked around. The hallway was narrow with a high

ceiling. He could see about six bedroom doors and a set of narrow stairs at the end, going down to a basement, and another set of stairs leading to the floors above.

"Where's your dad's room?" he asked Luke.

"Top floor, in the roof," Luke replied.

As they negotiated their way around the puddle of pee, one of the bedroom doors opened. A gargantuan figure of a man ducked under the door lintel and placed his considerable frame between them and the stairs. With a long pointy black beard and long black straggly hair, he looked like a cross between a wizard and a WWE wrestler. He was dressed in a faded black tracksuit, the hem of the top failing to contain his massive girth, revealing a sliver of white, goose-like stomach flesh. On his feet he wore strappy Velcro-fastening sandals, easily a size fourteen. He may have been overweight, but Savage could tell there was solid muscle and power beneath his doughy appearance. He approached Tannaz first, looming over her.

"Got any food?" he asked.

Adrenalin from the confrontation outside still coursed through Tannaz's veins, she was in no mood to be intimidated. "Hey, fat Gandalf," she said, fixing him with two black venomous eyes. "Back off." He stood there, impassive, like a trainee corpse, then sidestepped Tannaz to face Savage.

"Got any food?" he asked again.

Savage shook his head and smiled. "None of us have any food, my friend. Next time we're here I'll bring you a picnic hamper with some smoked salmon."

"Really?" the big guy said, eyes brightening, the sarcasm lost on him.

"Scout's honour," Savage replied. "Now, if you'll excuse us, we need to get up there."

The big guy switched his attention to Luke. "Got any food?"

Savage raised his tone, still trying to maintain a modicum of civility. "Look no one's got any food, okay my friend. Now, if you want your smoked-salmon picnic next time we come you have to move out of the way."

The big guy thought for a second then moved aside. As they climbed the stairs, Savage glanced back down. Fat Gandalf watched them every step of the way.

"How would you fight someone like that?" asked Tannaz, as they reached the first landing.

"Very carefully indeed," replied Savage.

Climbing a second flight of stairs, they reached the two rooms in the roof, separated by a small square landing covered in tattered carpet, worn through to the seams. Luke used his keys to open the door on the right.

They stepped into a strange, musty little attic room, the slanted roof and exposed rafters creating an awkwardly shaped ceiling above their heads. A single dormer window looked out over the street below where Savage's van was parked. With barely any room for furniture, a compact bed with a scruffy duvet sat at one end, while a small chest of drawers and a misshapen wardrobe, leaning over like the tower of Pisa, sat at the other. Odd clothes lay scattered here and there. An empty mug with dried-up tea in the bottom had been left beside the bed together with an old copy of *Record Collector* magazine. Savage spotted a poster on the floor face down, which had probably been stuck to the wall had it not been for the damp having other plans. Savage walked over to it and lifted it up. A young Iggy Pop stared back at him. This was definitely Dave Mosely's room.

Breathing heavily, Luke began frantically searching the space. There wasn't much to search. Panicking, he opened the flimsy drawers, which took several yanks, rifling through what few clothes his father had owned. Then he strode over to the wardrobe, flung open the door. A single item hung from a wire coat hanger, a black Harrington jacket. An assortment of scruffy shoes lay in the bottom. He slammed the door shut, got down on his knees and looked under the bed.

"They're gone!" said Luke.

"What?" said Savage.

"His records are gone."

CHAPTER 6

L UKE KICKED THE BED, TURNED and collapsed on the end, sitting with his head in his hands.

"They're gone," Luke repeated.

"Are you sure?" asked Savage.

"Positive. Last time I was here they were stacked on the floor against the wall. Next to his record player. That's gone too. I thought he might have stashed them away in the wardrobe or in his drawers."

Savage glanced in every corner of the room. An estate agent would have generously called it compact. Shoe box would have been more accurate. Not a place for playing hide and seek, or for concealing records, there just wasn't the space. Savage put a hand on Luke's shoulder and sat down next to him.

"Does anyone else have a key?" Savage asked.

"No, Dad wouldn't have trusted anyone," Luke replied.

"And there were no signs of forced entry, so that only leaves the landlord. What's his name?"

Luke raised his head, looked at Savage. "Simon Wellington. He's well dodgy; owns all the HMOs around here. Got a bad reputation."

"What's an HMO?" Tannaz asked.

"House of multiple occupancy, that's what this is," Savage answered. "Big house, lots of grotty single rooms, shared bathroom and kitchen. Cheapest, nastiest accommodation you can get—you can imagine the state of the bathroom and kitchen."

"Sounds delightful," said Tannaz.

Savage took his smart phone out. "Okay, I'm going to give this Wellington guy a call."

"No," said Luke. "What if things get nasty?"

"I'll get nasty back." Savage did a quick search and got the number for Simon Wellington Properties. After a couple of rings, a woman answered.

"Simon Wellington Properties, Vicky speaking. How can I help you?" she said, rattling the words off so quickly that they merged into one another.

"Hi," said Savage. "I'm calling on behalf of Luke Mosely, his father David Mosely used to live at one of your properties, Tivoli Gardens in Southampton. We're trying to track down some of his possessions..."

"What was the name again?" she said, cutting Savage off. He repeated the details while rapid typing came from the other end of the phone. Eventually she said, "Ah yes, David Mosely left that property quite some time ago without warning, giving us no prior notice or forwarding address. Under the Interference with Goods Act 1997 we're entitled to dispose of 'slash' sell any goods left by a tenant if we are unable to locate them. We did employ a tracing agent to locate Mr Mosely to inform him of this, but according to what's on screen we were unable to secure a positive outcome."

Savage took a deep breath. "Well, I severely doubt you did employ a tracing agent because if you did, they would have quickly discovered that David Mosely passed away recently, that's why he hasn't been living at the property. So if you don't mind, we'd like his possessions returned."

"As I said before, under the Interference with Goods Act 1997 we can dispose of 'slash' sell any goods left behind by a tenant." She didn't offer any condolences or adopt a more sympathetic tone.

"Well," Savage replied. "I think that's bull 'slash' shit. We're in David Mosely's room right now, and all his stuff is still here, apart from his record collection. So you haven't disposed of or sold his possessions, you've just come in here and taken his record collection and record player, because you knew they were worth something."

"As I said before, under the…"

"Yes, you've told me. I don't care about the Interference with Goods Act 1997. You've clearly stolen possessions from a dead man, which should rightfully go to his son. How does that make you feel?"

Silence.

"Are you still there?" asked Savage.

"As I said, under the…"

"Listen, Vicky. Is there anyone else I can talk to? Can I speak to your boss, Simon Wellington?"

"I'm afraid Mr Wellington no longer runs the company, he's retired. His son Ben Wellington is in charge now."

"Okay, can I speak to him?"

"Uh, no."

Savage waited for the rest of her answer. It never came.

"Why not?" he eventually asked.

Vicky forced a chuckle. "Ben Wellington is far too busy to get involved in a small matter like this."

"A small matter?" Savage said. "You think this is a small matter? One of your tenants has died and you've gone steaming into his room and taken everything of value. Is this how you treat all your tenants? I'm sure the local paper would be interested to hear about this."

Luke shook his head, clearly not wanting the attention of the press.

"I'm afraid we don't respond to threatening language," Vicky said, her voice suddenly serious. "If you have an issue, I suggest that you seek legal advice." And with that she hung up.

Savage looked at his phone in disgust, then put it in his back pocket. "I'm sorry, Luke. The chances of getting those records back are between none and none. The law's on their side."

"They're in the wrong," Luke said.

"Of course they are," Savage replied. "But they'll tie us up in so much red tape, we won't be able to make a move against them. These companies know what they're doing. Probably been in this situation before, dozens of times. Seizing tenants' property is a nice little sideline for them, a perk of the job. Have to face facts, those records are long gone. Probably been sold off."

"Can't you go there and bang some heads?" asked Luke.

"Believe me I'd like nothing better. It'd be my pleasure. But it wouldn't get the records back. I'd just get arrested and that wouldn't help our cause. We'd be worse off than when we started."

"What about a lawyer?" Luke asked.

"Waste of time," said Tannaz. "You'd be throwing good money after bad. End up spending more money than the records are worth."

Luke sighed heavily, swore under his breath. "I know it sounds cold, but I was going to sell the records—I could really do with the money right now. I figured Dad wouldn't have minded if I turned them into cash."

"Course he wouldn't have," said Savage. "They're rightfully yours to do whatever you want with, except that bastard Simon Wellington has taken them, or more likely one of the seedy little gits who work for him."

"Is there nothing we can do?"

"They're absolute wankers, heartless wankers," said Tannaz, standing next to Luke and resting a sympathetic hand on his shoulder. "They have the law on their side."

"She's right," Savage added. "I know it's eating you up. The best thing you can do is forget about it. Put it behind you, chalk it up to experience. Come on, let's go into Southampton and I'll buy you a posh coffee, one with all the cream and syrupy stuff."

"I prefer tea."

Savage smiled. "Now we're talking."

They drove into the city centre, left the VW in one of the many labyrinthine multi-storey car parks and strolled across a grassy area near the main library, past the monument to the engineers who lost their lives on the Titanic. Then they turned ninety degrees onto Above Bar Street, a long poker-straight medieval road. Like a corridor lined with shops and offices, it neatly divided Southampton city centre into two halves.

They stopped at a retro tearoom, made to look as if it had been frozen in time, at the point when everyone was celebrating the end of World War Two. Colourful bunting hung everywhere and waitresses in vintage frocks and 1940s' hairdos carrying big pots of tea and large slabs of comfort cake bustled between polka-dot covered tables. Big-band swing music drifted out over the sound system.

Savage told Tannaz and Luke to order him a tea, while he nipped off to the bank. When he returned, Tannaz and Luke were seated at a table by the window. Luke looked glumly into his teacup, while Tannaz sat beside him, eyes sympathetic, clearly trying to give him much-needed moral support.

Savage dumped himself down in an empty chair, then helped himself to tea from a large blue pot, pouring it into a cup sitting on a saucer. The milk was in a tiny bottle, like the ones that used to be delivered to the doorstep, back when Britain had milkmen.

"Now, that's how tea should be served," Savage said, taking a long draft. "Nothing like a cup of tea to make things better, eh?"

"Dunno," said Tannaz. "I had black coffee."

Luke managed a half-hearted smile. "Just like to thank you again for coming all this way for me. I really appreciate it."

"No need to thank me," Savage replied. "Like I said, it was the least I could do. Now, how much did you say those records were worth?"

"Not sure," Luke replied. "About three hundred."

"Let's round it up to five hundred," said Savage. He pulled a fat white envelope from his back pocket and slid it across the table to Luke.

"What's this?" asked Luke.

"Five hundred quid," Savage replied. "It's for you, to replace the records you lost, plus a bit extra."

Luke slowly prised open the top of the envelope, eyeing the contents cautiously as if they might suddenly jump out and bite him. "Oh, no," he said. "I can't accept this."

"Why not?"

"Because I can't."

Savage repeated the question. "Why not?"

Luke pushed the envelope over to Savage. "This is your money."

"And now it's yours." Savage pushed it back again. "Listen, like I said, my wife was good with money, I've got plenty, so don't worry about me. It's no skin off my nose, honestly."

"Please," said Luke. "I feel bad enough dragging you and Tannaz all this way for nothing."

"I'm the one who should feel bad," said Savage. "I was your dad's best mate at school. And I feel terrible about what happened to him. I should have kept in touch. Maybe things would have been different."

"It wasn't your fault. I don't think anyone could've done anything."

"That's no excuse. I knew your dad was a fragile guy, and I wasn't there when he needed a friend, even if he didn't want one. So giving his son five hundred quid to help him out is nothing."

Luke looked worried. The same expression his dad always had on him, like he'd eaten something that didn't agree with him. "I don't know what to say."

Savage smiled warmly. "Luke. It makes me happy to help you out. I wasn't there for your dad, but if I can go some way to making amends by being there for you, then it makes me feel a little better. So if there's anything else I can do, you call me, understand."

"Yes, thank you. I will."

"I mean it. That's not one of those empty promises people say just to sound nice."

A small tear escaped from the corner of Luke's eye. He turned his head away, ashamed, grabbed a napkin and blotted the tear. Tannaz took his hand and gave it a reassuring squeeze.

He held up the envelope of cash. "This means a lot to me. I'm going to use it for something good."

"I could build you an awesome laptop for five hundred quid," said Tannaz.

"No, but thank you," said Luke. "I'm going to use it for driving lessons. I've always wanted to drive, never been able to afford to learn. Going to get a job as a delivery driver. I love being on the move, and there's tons of work in that, nowadays. Get my life started." The sadness vanished from Luke's face as he thought about having a future, and all the possibilities that came with it. Positivity radiated off him. A man with a plan, a man who had purpose. Someone who'd had his hope restored in full.

One week later, Luke was dead.

CHAPTER 7

S AVAGE TURNED OFF THE HEFTY petrol-driven hedge trimmer, climbed down off the step ladder and stood back to survey his efforts. He'd been in the back of his tiny postage-stamp-sized garden, attacking his privet hedge, pruning it back. A glow of pride filled him as he admired the hedge's sleek rectangular shape, flat on top with sharp right-angled corners and neat vertical sides. He'd even got out his extra-long spirit level to check the sides were exactly perpendicular and that the top was as flat as Norfolk.

His hedge, or the Berlin Wall as he liked to call it, had been grown high, well over head height so he didn't have to look at his annoying neighbour or his wreck of a garden. The guy was a slob and used his outdoor space as a storage area for anything that didn't fit in his flat. Piles of bricks, stacks of wood, several car engines, a collapsed, rusting trampoline and half a motorbike that he had started to rebuild, then gave up on. Savage felt sorry for his young son who had nowhere to play and instead had to go to the local park—usually on his own.

Savage spotted a slight bulge in his otherwise pristine hedge. He picked up the trimmer and got ready to fire it up when he heard banging. It was coming from his front door, drifting along his hallway, out through his open kitchen door. Savage put down the power tool and went to investigate. As he reached the front door the banging got more intense.

Savage opened the door to see a red-faced Tannaz with one hand raised, balled into a fist for knocking and the other holding a phone. "Why haven't you been answering your phone?" she demanded. "I've been out here banging on your door for the past fifteen minutes." Without being invited in, she pushed past him.

"Tannaz, I'm kind of in the middle of something," Savage said, following her into his kitchen. "I'm doing a spot of gardening, want to help?"

Tannaz ignored him and fiddled with her phone. She looked at him, eyes brimming over with sadness. "I'm afraid I've got some bad news. Luke Mosely is dead."

"What?"

Tannaz swallowed hard and took a deep breath. "He's dead. Died a few days ago."

Savage didn't say anything. His mind processing the information like a slow computer.

"What? How?" asked Savage.

"Suicide."

"Suicide?"

Savage sat down on his little chair and table by the kitchen window. He noticed black mould peppered the skirting board, like a virus attempting to spread. "I don't believe it, are you sure?" he asked.

Tannaz sat opposite. "Positive. Saw it on a local news feed." She handed him her phone.

Savage read the article on the screen, posted the day before:

Father and son suicide tree tragedy

Police have confirmed that the body of a man found hanging from a tree in the New Forest at the weekend is that of Luke Mosely, son of David Mosely who committed suicide in the same area over Christmas. Luke Mosely's body was found by a dog walker, hanging from a low branch near to the car park at Dead Maids Wood. A typed note was found with the body, expressing how much he missed his father and wished to join him. Back in December, David Mosely also committed suicide

in Dead Maids Wood. In bizarre circumstances,
his body was discovered in January when two
forest workers felled a Douglas fir, and found
that David Mosely's body had been hidden in
its uppermost branches. Neither death is being
treated as suspicious by the police.

Savage reread the article, each time trying to make sense of it. The more he read it the more confused he became.

"I don't believe it," he said. "Luke wasn't suicidal. Nervous, maybe, and he certainly didn't miss his father. He hardly knew him. Only met him a handful of times. He wouldn't commit suicide because he missed his father."

Savage glanced at Tannaz for a reaction. She had become strangely quiet, which wasn't like her at all. She'd had more time to think about this than Savage.

"What if it was my fault?" She sniffed back a tear.

Savage got to his feet and put his arm around her shoulders. "How in the world can this be your fault?"

"Like you said, Luke wasn't suicidal, and he didn't miss his father. What if someone made it look like suicide. Killed him."

"Who would do that?"

"Those scumbag drug dealers outside Tivoli Gardens. Remember, the driver said he'd kill Luke, said he'd find him and kill him. Then I go and break his mate's wrists. Showing off my skills. What if they decided to get revenge, take it out on Luke? I went in too hard and they've killed Luke because of it."

Savage shook his head. "Rubbish. Firstly, they didn't know who he was, and secondly it was me who rubbed them up the wrong way, not Luke."

"Yeah, they wouldn't go after you or me, would they? They're too cowardly. They'd go after Luke, because he was an easy target."

"How would they find him?"

"There are ways. I'm sure a few free drugs would loosen a few tongues. They could've easily found out his dad lived there."

"Okay, let's assume you're right. Would they go to all that

trouble of making his death look like a suicide? Type up a suicide note, take him out to the New Forest and hang him from a tree? I don't think so. Not their style. Dumping his body under a bridge or in a canal is more their thing. Besides, Luke lived in London, not Southampton. They'd have to come up here, take him from his flat and then transport him back down to the New Forest. Seems like a lot of hassle."

Tannaz's eyes flitted around the kitchen, looking for answers. "I don't know, I just feel like it's my fault somehow."

"Come on, Tannaz. This is nonsense. You're not to blame here. That guy groped you, you defended yourself, that's all."

"Then why do I feel so shitty?"

"When a tragedy happens like this, it's a natural reaction. To look around for someone to blame. I should know."

"Don't you think it's weird? A week after we're there, and Luke's dead. Too much of a coincidence."

"You're right about that, definitely too much of a coincidence." Savage's voice became suddenly quiet. He slowly sat back down, as if he might collapse if the chair wasn't there.

"You okay, Savage?"

"Mmm," Savage mumbled, deep in thought. "You've got me thinking now, about what I said to Simon Wellington's receptionist."

"What about it?"

"I laid it on quite thick. Luke said Simon Wellington was dodgy, and I phoned up his office, all guns blazing, threatening to go to the press. Mentioned Luke's name and everything." Savage sighed. "When he said Wellington was dodgy, I'm wondering how dodgy? Dodgy enough to kill someone who was kicking up a fuss?"

Now it was Tannaz's turn to shake her head. "No way, not over a few records. Like you said, they're probably used to it; people phoning up, getting angry. I'm sure people get evicted from those properties on a regular basis, lose their stuff, never see it again. Desperate tenants are their bread and butter."

"Maybe. That receptionist did have all the lines well-rehearsed."

"There you go."

Her logic made sense. But Savage didn't feel any better. They stared at one another across the table. Each one thinking that they were somehow to blame. Each one feeling a cloud of guilt swelling inside them.

Savage was the first to break the cold silence. "Okay, let's get back to reality. We're just speculating here, and that's no good to anyone. Before we start condemning ourselves to a life of shame, we need to know what happened. We need intel. We need facts, otherwise we're just dealing with our own opinions, and what we believe happened. And the problem with belief is it's like clay, you can make it into anything you want. I think we can both agree that Luke's death is too coincidental. And the suicide note makes no sense. We know that for a fact. We spoke to him. He didn't miss his father because he hardly knew him. So I think we can work from the premise that someone killed him and made it look like suicide. Agreed?"

Tannaz nodded.

"So, we find out who killed him, and we make them pay. Agreed?"

"Agreed," said Tannaz. "Starting with those shitty little drug dealers."

CHAPTER 8

THEY DROVE BACK DOWN TO Southampton in silence. No stops for tea, no stopping to stretch their legs, no friendly banter. Savage was too wrapped up in his own thoughts about what had happened to Luke, churning it over in his mind, and he guessed Tannaz was too. A potent mix of guilt, disbelief, anger and confusion racked his brain, tortured him. Worst of all was the underlying feeling building inside him that by trying to help Luke, they may have inadvertently caused his death.

Normally this would be the time that Jeff Perkins would make an appearance, berating and blaming him for Luke's death, and possibly Dave's too. Jeff always raised his ugly, imaginary head when Savage had strong feelings of guilt or remorse. Thankfully, Savage had Tannaz with him, his kryptonite, keeping the irritating little prick at bay.

Savage's foot never left the accelerator, apart from when he approached a section of the motorway where he was forced to drive at forty miles an hour for no apparent reason, except that someone had placed an endless procession of orange cones there, seemingly just for the fun of it. It made him want to put his foot down even more and go ploughing into them, but he kept his cool and kept to the speed limit. Tannaz, by contrast, kept pushing out sighs between her lips, her chest heaving as she did so, as impatient as he was to get to the bottom of this.

After another hour of driving, they exited the motorway and headed towards Thornhill, arriving just after lunchtime. Turning into the estate, they weren't surprised to see the burnt-out car still there, black and skeletal. A couple of local kids who should've been in school were playing on it, as if it were a hellish climbing frame. One kid stood on the pavement, hitting the side of it repeatedly with a big stick like John Cleese in *Fawlty Towers*. Normally, this image would have made Savage smile to himself. Not today.

As they entered Tivoli Gardens, there was no sign of the silly, modified Vauxhall Corsa. Instead, parked in its place sat a large black BMW X5, the older boxier shape with blacked out windows, but still a handsome car.

"Looks like our junior drug dealers have been replaced with someone more senior," said Savage.

He swung in behind it and pulled on the handbrake. Tannaz and Savage got out and approached the BMW on the driver's side. Savage tapped on the window. With an electric whir it slid down. The car smelt of cigarettes and energy drinks. Savage clocked two substantial guys sitting in the front—heavy sections, as his old dad would've described them. Possibly in their late twenties, early thirties, the one in the driver's seat wore a black L.A. Raiders cap. Neither man deigned to look at Savage or Tannaz or speak to them, as if it were beneath them. Round here, these two probably thought they were kings. Clearly, it was up to Savage to break the ice.

"So, you a big American football fan?" Savage asked.

"Huh?" said Baseball Cap, still not looking at him.

"Your hat, L.A. Raiders, or should I say Oakland Raiders now, American Football team. Or maybe you're an Ice Cube fan?"

"Who's Ice Cube?"

"The rapper, wore a cap just like that one."

The guy just looked ahead, blanking Savage.

"Look, what you after?" asked Baseball Cap, still not bothering to look at Savage.

"We're not buying today, gentlemen," said Savage. "We just need to know the whereabouts of the guys who used to sell here."

The guy didn't answer. The window buzzed back up again. Savage clamped both his hands on the top of it. The window stopped. A furious pair of bloodshot eyes turned to face Savage. "Take your hands off my goddam window."

Savage removed his hands, holding them up in a surrender. "We just need to know where the fellows in the Corsa are. You know them?"

Nothing.

Tannaz chipped in. "They've got stupid names, Bonafide Ride or something."

"Listen. We're working here. Now if you're not buying you can go—"

"Yes, I know," said Savage. "We'll be out of your hair as soon as we know where those guys are, scout's honour."

Baseball Cap swore, the other guy sniggered, as if he couldn't believe the effrontery of Savage—or the stupidity.

"Do you know who you're talking to, asshole?" said Baseball Cap.

"No," Savage replied with as much honesty as he could muster.

"You're talking to someone who's better than you, get it?"

"Okay, got it. You're better than me," said Savage. "Now if you could just tell me where the guys in the Corsa are."

Baseball Cap shook his head then reached into his inside jacket pocket, pulled out a handgun and stuck it through the half-open window, aiming it at Savage's face.

Savage instantly recognised the weapon, a Baikal IZH-79, small, black and compact. The most popular illegal handgun on British streets, usually smuggled in from Russia where it was made.

Baseball Cap narrowed his eyes. "Now you don't listen too good, do ya, bruv?"

Savage feigned utmost terror. Face white with panic. Staring down at the barrel. It gave him the opportunity to give the weapon a once over. The gun had clearly been oiled, probably when Baseball Cap first acquired it, but it hadn't been maintained since. Lint and dust from his pocket clung to the metal, giving it a fuzzy appearance here and there. It would still fire, no problem. The Baikal was designed to be simple, designed to be reliable. It told Savage all he needed to know about its owner. No experience with weapons, just there for intimidation. Probably never been fired, wouldn't want to waste the ammunition, as it would be hard and expensive to replace.

Raising his hands even higher Savage said, "Please, please, don't shoot." A natural response. A logical response. The expected response Baseball Cap got every time he drew his piece. No doubt he enjoyed it. Revelled in it. Made him feel big. Probably even felt relaxed about it. So he didn't spot the fact that with his arms raised, Savage's hands were only a few inches away from the weapon.

In the next split second, two things happened. Blindingly fast. Savage jerked his head to the left, moving out of the line of fire. At the same time, he grabbed the barrel with both hands, twisting the whole gun around, one hundred and eighty degrees. Baseball Cap had no choice but to let go. He didn't want to of course. Body mechanics forced his hand, literally. Savage had two hands on the gun, Baseball Cap only had one. Two always beats one. If he had held onto the gun, his wrist would've snapped.

In the blink of an eye, Savage snatched the gun away. He took a step away from the car, out of Baseball Cap's reach, just to be on the safe side and ensure he didn't do the same to Savage and snatch it back, although it was highly unlikely.

Savage aimed the gun at Baseball Cap, who was still dazed by what had just happened. The guy in the passenger seat raised his hands.

"Look into my eyes," said Savage. Baseball Cap ignored him, fixated on the muzzle of the gun, probably the first time he'd had his own gun pointed at him. "I said look into my eyes." Savage said it louder this time. The guy jumped out of his trance, stared at Savage. "That's better. Now, in your opinion, do I look like the type of guy who'd shoot someone in the face?"

Baseball Cap didn't answer.

"I said—"

"Yeah, yeah you do," said the guy in the passenger seat, stuttering the words out.

"Correct. I have before and no doubt I'll do it again. Whether you two want to join the illustrious list of people whose brains I've blown out of the back of their heads is entirely up to you. I couldn't care less. Now I am going to ask a question and you are going to answer. Ready?"

They both nodded.

"Where are the guys who used to sell here? Your predecessors. The ones in the Vauxhall Corsa—"

"Mayflower Park," said the passenger, quicker than a game-show contestant anticipating a question.

"You sure?" asked Tannaz.

"I'm sure, by the skate ramps, selling weed to the skaters," said the passenger.

"Good," said Savage. Without taking his eyes off the two men, Savage stripped the handgun down to its constituent parts with the speed and dexterity of a conjuror. It took barely a second. He let the components drop to the ground where they pinged and clanged on the pavement. "You can go now," Savage said. "You never come back here, understand?"

They both nodded.

"Well," said Savage. "Go on, off you trot."

Baseball Cap hit the ignition, revved the engine. Stalled it. Tried again, and drove off, wheel-spinning all the way.

Savage scuffed the components of the dismantled handgun along the ground with his foot until they tumbled into a drain, each piece plopping as it hit the water below.

"You still need to teach me that," said Tannaz.

"It's easy, just use your foot," Savage replied.

"No. Idiot. The flippy thing with the gun. It was the first thing I asked you to teach me, remember?"

"All in good time. Come on, let's find Mayflower Park and see if we can get some answers."

As a venue for dealing drugs, Mayflower Park was an aesthetically far more attractive proposition than Tivoli Gardens. A long flat sleeve of green grass, it stretched out parallel to Southampton

Water with a wide tarmac promenade running along the water's edge. In the summer, Savage could imagine the place crowded with sightseers and sunbathers, and little families with pushchairs, dawdling along with ice creams in their hands, marvelling at the spectacle of unfeasibly large luxury liners docked in Southampton, floating cities that would take on passengers bound for the Caribbean and Mediterranean. Today, the only thing threatening to arrive on a cold weekday in early March was a spot of drizzle. The place was bleak and empty, with a handful of cars dotted around the car park, including a ridiculous modified Vauxhall Corsa with a fat exhaust pipe. They pulled up next to it. The car was empty.

Savage and Tannaz got out, looked around. It didn't take long to find their target. Off in the distance, a lonely tracksuited figure sat shivering on top of a metal skateboard ramp, eyes down on his phone, one hand punched deep into his pocket. The owner of the Corsa, the guy with fledgling facial hair, no doubt hoping to catch kids ducking out of school at lunchtime. Bonafide Ride, as he liked to call himself.

"Okay, Tannaz," Savage said. "You wait here, stay out of sight behind the van. I'll circle round and approach him from the opposite side. He'll see me coming, make a run for it back to his car, where he'll run smack bang into you."

"Sounds like a plan," she said.

Savage took a wide arc around the skate park, skirting a belt of trees that gave him some cover. He needn't have bothered. The lad never took his eyes off his screen all the while Savage was creeping up on him. Crossing the dirty concrete, stained with fading graffiti, Savage got within a few feet of him before the guy swivelled his head round, did a double take, recognised Savage and made a run for it. Savage gave chase. He had to hand it to the young guy, he could sprint and he created plenty of distance, putting on a spurt of speed as he got closer to his car. Just before he got there, he looked over his shoulder to check his pursuer, turned back and ran straight into Tannaz, who headbutted him on the nose.

CHAPTER 9

THE GUY WENT DOWN LIKE a sack of cement, landing on his back, head thumping against the ground. Clutching his face, blood spilt out of both his nostrils. Tannaz dived on top of him, fist pulled back, ready to do more damage. "Why did you kill Luke?" she screamed.

"Tannaz! Stop!" Savage got to her just before she hit him again. "We just want to talk to him, remember."

"But he killed Luke."

"Who the hell is Luke?" Bonafide Ride said, sounding nasally, as if he had a cold.

"We don't know if he killed Luke," said Savage. "Now get off him, and let's get him to his feet." Tannaz obeyed. Savage held out his hand to the guy and pulled him to his feet. Without warning, Savage then grabbed him and shoved him hard up against the back of the van, winding him. If Tannaz had been playing bad cop, then Savage was playing psycho cop.

"You are going to tell me what you did to Luke, or we'll put you in the back of this van and bury you."

"I swear, I don't what you're talking about," Bonafide Ride spluttered.

"Our friend Luke. Last time we were here you said, and these are your exact words, 'You're a dead man. I'll come after you. You won't know what's hit you,' remember?"

"I don't remember."

"Burying it is, then." Savage pulled Bonafide Ride away from the van, holding him around his neck with one arm. With his other hand Savage reached into his pocket and tossed the keys to

Tannaz. "Open the back doors." Tannaz fiddled with the keys and opened both doors wide.

"No, no!" Bonafide Ride screamed, struggling against Savage's grip. A pointless effort, as he had about as much muscle power as a stickman. Savage hurled him into the back, then climbed in after him. Savage turned to Tannaz. "Shut the doors behind me and get into the driver's seat. We're taking a trip to the forest."

The doors slammed shut. The guy started crying. "Please, please. I have no idea what you're talking about, I swear."

Savage knelt over him. "Now I would usually hit you at this point, but there's no reason to. In about half an hour, you'll be in the earth." Just at that point the engine started and Tannaz put the van in gear and drove out of the car park. Savage steadied himself, looking out of the back windows as she turned onto West Quay Road, the main drag out of Southampton.

Bonafide Ride squirmed and writhed, blood and tears splattering all over Savage's nice clean floor. Breathing spasmodically, he could hardly talk as he bargained for his life. "Please. I don't know what you're talking about. I'll tell you anything."

"You remember us?" Savage asked.

"Yes."

"You remember the guy we were with?"

"S-sort of."

"Well that guy you *sort of* remember is now dead, and you'll join him unless you give me answers."

Bonafide Ride scrambled into a sitting position, wiping his bloody nose on his sleeve, pushing his backside into the corner, as far away as he could get from Savage, which wasn't very far in the van's little cargo area. He sucked in a ragged breath. Thought hard. "I'll tell you anything. Please don't bury me."

"That's a start," said Savage. "Tell me... Tivoli Gardens, is that your regular sales base?"

"Until your girl broke my mate's wrists. We took him to A&E like you said, told them he'd fallen off a skateboard."

"Then what happened?"

"When my boss found out, he went mental. Said if we like playing with skateboards then we can work the skate parks. Split us up, put me on Mayflower Park."

"How's that a punishment?" Savage asked, although he already knew the answer.

"'Cos it don't make much. We get a cut of what we sell. I'm making a fraction of what I made at Thornhill."

"How come?"

"Thornhill's full of Simon Wellington properties. They're a gold mine. There're loads in Southampton. Full of losers, alcoholics, freaks and junkies, always buying. There's a joke that if you need to find one of Wellington's places, ask a drug dealer or a paramedic because they know the address of every one. The drug dealers for selling to junkies, and the paramedics for when they OD."

Savage shook his head in disgust. "And you're happy to be part of that little ecosystem?"

"Got no choice. No other work round here."

"And this Simon Wellington, what does he think of people selling drugs outside his properties?"

Bonafide Ride sniffed back some blood, wiped his nose again. "He takes his cut from my boss. Only guy my boss is frightened of. Everyone is, you must know that."

"I'm not from around here."

"Simon Wellington runs this city. The guy's the biggest gangster around."

"I thought his son took over, Ben Wellington?"

The guy snorted out a laugh, causing his nose to start bleeding again. "He's not in charge. If you ask me Simon Wellington still pulls the strings. They say he gets up to some weird stuff with his tenants."

"What weird stuff?"

"Don't know for sure. Just rumours. Makes them do things for him."

"What sort of things?"

"No one talks about it, they're terrified of him. Frightened he'll kick them out or worse."

"What do you mean or worse?"

"I ain't saying nothing."

Savage looked out the back windows, he could see big, ugly industrial buildings scrolling past, the kind that are quick to put up and an eyesore forever, clad in crinkly metal with no windows and big garish signs. They drove onto a flyover, and the view gave way to a large arc of Southampton Water and a muddy foreshore beside the road. The tide was out. Suddenly the view was obscured by a blur of trees, filling the back windows. They were in the forest.

Savage turned his attention back to the drug dealer. "Well, you're going to tell me because we've just entered the forest."

"Don't care. I'm dead already if Simon Wellington finds out I've been talking to you."

Savage could tell the guy wasn't lying. It was the way he answered without hesitation. Normally people who lied paused to think about their answer or looked around for clues as to what to say, or shuffled their feet. Not this guy.

"So who killed our friend Luke?"

"Not me. Not anyone I know. I swear. After that day we haven't been back to Tivoli Gardens. Was that where he lived?"

"No. He lived in London. His dad lived there. We came by to pick up some of his stuff, but Simon Wellington had already taken it. We tried to get it back, called Wellington's office, demanded they return it."

Bonafide Ride started to shake, his face switched from scared to terrified. "You did what?"

"Phoned them up," Savage replied. "Demanded they give back his dad's stuff—a record collection."

"You're joking?"

"Nope."

The guy looked around the van, as if he wanted to claw his way out of there. "Are you crazy? No wonder your mate's dead. You don't threaten Simon Wellington. Oh, man, this is bad, very bad." His breaths came rapidly, heavily; his hands trembled.

"Shit. I gotta get out of here. Gotta get away from you two. Can't be seen with you."

Bonafide Ride panicked, scrambled past Savage and tried rattling the doors, as if to try to jump out the back, even though Tannaz was doing about fifty miles an hour.

"Hey." Savage grabbed him by the arm, dragged him away from the door. "I haven't finished with you yet."

The guy shook his head back and forth manically. "If you're going to kill me you'd be doing me a favour. Don't you understand? Simon Wellington is like Keyser Söze in *The Usual Suspects*, you know the film?"

Savage nodded, surprised that he'd seen the movie or maybe he'd just heard about it from someone else.

"Wellington's the devil. Keyser Söze. Plays with people, toys with them."

"In what way?"

"I don't know. But you should leave it alone. Or we're all dead. Just like your mate. If you're looking for his killer, you can bet Simon Wellington had something to do with it."

Savage thought for a moment. "This sounds like you're spinning me an urban myth, a bogie man."

"You ask anyone in Southampton. They'll all say he's a psycho. Please, you gotta let me out."

"If that's true why hasn't he been arrested?"

Bonafide Ride looked at Savage as if he were the most naïve person in the world. "He's *smart*. He doesn't leave any loose ends, which is why I'm dead unless you let me out now." He suddenly looked very young, very scared, as if he were about to start crying for his mum. Unless he was an actor of the highest calibre, that look was very hard to fake, especially for someone who'd been trying their whole life to look mean.

"Turn the car around," Savage said to Tannaz in the front. "We're taking you back to Southampton, we'll drop you back at Mayflower Park."

"No," said the guy. "Pull over here. Now. Let me out."

"But we're in the middle of the forest," said Tannaz.

"Good. Don't want anyone to see me getting out of this van. I'll cut across the forest, safer that way."

Tannaz pulled onto a verge, halfway between Totton and Lyndhurst. Trees lined either side of the road, with deep, damp forest stretching off behind as far as the eye could see. She got out and opened the van's back doors. The guy shuffled forward on his behind, towards freedom. He leapt out of the van and sprinted across the road without looking. A second later, he was gone, as if the forest had swallowed him up.

Savage fell onto his back, lying on the van's floor, staring up at the ceiling. Tannaz perched on the edge, just above the bumper.

Savage swore. "I think my actions might've killed Luke."

"You believed that guy?" asked Tannaz.

"He wasn't lying. I know when people are lying and I know when people are scared. He was telling the truth and he was terrified."

"That doesn't mean Simon Wellington killed Luke."

Savage sat up. "Oh, come on, Tannaz. It looks pretty obvious to me. And I gave him Luke's name, spelt it out for him."

Tannaz screwed up her nose, unconvinced. "It still doesn't make sense. Why go to all that trouble to kill someone over a few records? And Luke was hardly a threat. It's not like he had some dirt on him."

"Maybe he did. Or maybe Dave did. Perhaps Wellington was being neat and tidy, like the guy just said, tying up loose ends. Worried Luke may have known what his dad knew. Who knows? Maybe Dave Mosely's death wasn't a suicide and neither was his son's."

Tannaz took a cigarette from her pocket, lit it and spoke as she blew out grey smoke. "Why go to all that trouble? Why hide Dave Mosely's body up a tree? That's got to be the most awkward way of getting rid of a body. And why fake his son's suicide? Why not just bury them both in the forest in a deep hole or throw them in the sea with some bricks? Far simpler."

"No idea. One thing's for sure, I'm on the world's worst guilt trip. Like I caused Luke's death, kick-started it."

"We don't know Luke's death had anything to do with Wellington." Tannaz paused to take a drag, then continued. "And if it did, how were you to know this would happen? You were just trying to help out a friend's kid. Do a good deed."

"It's too much of a coincidence," said Savage. "Like you said, we show up at one of Wellington's places then Luke's found hanging from a noose. I should've been more cautious. Checked this Wellington guy out, before I went in guns blazing."

"I'd hardly say you went in guns blazing. You just phoned up his office and asked for some stuff back. Not exactly World War Three. I don't feel that great either. Just headbutted an innocent guy and kidnapped him." She flicked the cigarette into the dirt and ground it out with her foot.

"I wouldn't lose any sleep over that," said Savage climbing out of the back of the van. "You headbutted and kidnapped someone who sells drugs to schoolkids and vulnerable people, whose best mate sexually assaulted you while he stood by and did nothing. I'd hardly say he was innocent."

Tannaz thought for a moment, reached into her pocket and pulled out another cigarette. "You drive back to London. I'm going on my laptop. If there's any dirt on Simon Wellington, I'll find it."

"You're not smoking in the van," said Savage. "And you dropped this," he picked up the cigarette butt and handed it to her. "This is an area of outstanding natural beauty, remember?"

"Don't like nature," Tannaz remarked. "It's too organic. Can't wait to get back to London."

"That will have to wait," said Savage. "There's something else we need to see while we're here."

CHAPTER 10

SAVAGE POINTED THE VAN IN the direction of Dead Maids Wood. It was either a murder or a suicide and, to help him determine which, Savage had to see where it had all happened. It was the starting point; the essential place to begin any investigation. Ideally, he would have liked to have seen the bodies, or at least the coroner's report. That would be out of the question. There was no way the police would let Tannaz and Savage near the bodies or their findings. Autopsy results weren't public record, and they already knew the police verdict: suicide in both cases, which meant all evidence pointed to Luke and Dave taking their own lives. But Savage and Tannaz needed to keep an open mind, be led by what they found. Not by their feelings; feelings were untrustworthy. So the next best thing was seeing where Dave and Luke both died. Not that there would be much to see; any evidence would've been bagged up and taken away. Nonetheless, in Savage's experience, everything changes once you're on the ground.

About forty minutes after they'd released the fledgling drug dealer into the wild, they pulled into the deserted gravel car park of Dead Maids Wood. The dull light threw dark ugly shapes and shadows into the dense woodland, as if the trees might come to life at any moment.

"It's like Fangorn Forest in there," remarked Savage, as he switched off the engine.

"What the hell's Fangorn Forest?" asked Tannaz.

"*Lord of the Rings*. You know, where the trees come to life?"

Tannaz shrugged, shook her head. "Never seen it."

Savage pretended to fall off his seat in shock. "You haven't read or seen *Lord of the Rings*?"

"That's what I just said."

"How come?"

"Because I'm not a geek."

"But you're in IT, aren't you all geeks?"

Tannaz looked at Savage in disgust. "We're not all into Dungeons and Dragons and comic books. Such a stereotype, I'm surprised at you."

"What was it you called that big guy at Tivoli Gardens? Fat Gandalf."

"So what? Everyone's heard of Gandalf. I'm sure you've heard of Kim Kardashian. Doesn't mean you follow her on Instagram. Anyway, you were a soldier, you're not supposed to be into all that nerdy stuff."

Savage feigned offence, mouth hanging open. "Says who? We used to watch films when we were waiting to get the green light on a job. Sometimes it took ages, so to calm the nerves we'd put on a movie or two. Sometimes we'd watch loads back to back. I guess I never got out of the habit."

"Yeah, well, you know far too much about the wrong kind of movies to make me feel comfortable about hanging out with you."

"The 'wrong kind of movies'. What's that supposed to mean?"

"You like all the corny blockbusters, the crowd pleasers. You should try watching something more challenging. Something that makes you think."

Savage snorted. "You mean arty."

"No, I mean something that's not all CGI and dumb storylines."

He pulled the keys out of the ignition. "I think you're just trying to hurt my feelings. Come on, let's take a look before it gets too dark to find our way out again. We'll finish this debate later."

Savage got out of the van but Tannaz stayed put. "I'm not going in there, it's giving me the creeps. Plus, I feel weird about seeing where Luke died."

Savage leant against the open van door. "I understand.

Painful though it is, it's always good to get a look at the murder scene, if that's what we're dealing with."

Tannaz chewed her lip, then gave a fragile smile. "You're right." She got out of the car and followed him through a narrow gap beside the wide, padlocked metal gate that barred cars from going any further. A sign bolted to it read: 'Keep Clear'. Beyond, a gravel fire road wound its way between the twisted trees.

"Jeez, this is not a place you'd want to be on your own," said Tannaz. "Oh," she said more optimistically, holding up her phone. "Well it's not that bad. I can still get a signal and WiFi."

"I worry that your wellbeing all depends on your ability to get online or not."

"That's the way of the world, Savage," Tannaz replied, ignoring the evil-looking trees closing in around her, concentrating on her phone's brightly lit screen. Savage wondered whether she really was interested in her phone or just using it to distract herself from the sinister surroundings and the fact that they were on their way to see where Luke had been found dead. Savage had to remember, he was used to people dying around him, Tannaz was not.

After a minute's stroll, barely out of sight of the car park, a lonely oak came into view with thick, low-hanging branches. As they got closer, they could see long, slender metal stakes driven into the soil around it, holding up blue-and-white police tape, most of it sagging or broken. It was the tree where Luke had been found hanging.

"So this is the place," said Savage.

Tannaz kept quiet.

"You, okay?" he asked.

"Yeah," she said, staring wide-eyed at the tree in front of them. "Just a bit numb, that's all. You know, one minute we're having tea with him and the next minute he's found hanging here."

The rope had gone, taken away for forensics no doubt, but they could see a ring worn into the branch where it had been looped around.

"I know," Savage replied. "There's nothing we can do about

that now, apart from finding what really happened to him, and his dad, and making the people responsible pay."

Tannaz nodded, shook away the sadness, and started taking shots of the tree from different angles.

Savage circled the trunk, hoping something would jump out at him. It didn't. Apart from the faint ring in the branch, there was nothing to suggest anything untoward had happened there. He turned his attention to the ground around the tree. Again, nothing but dirt and dead leaves.

"Okay," he said. "Shall we walk on, find the place where Dave's body fell out of the tree?"

Tannaz nodded again. He could see she wasn't enjoying this. She was holding onto her phone for dear life, never taking her eyes off it; her link to the virtual world more comforting than the real one.

They followed the gravel road, like Dorothy in *The Wizard of Oz* through the haunted forest. The darkness of the trees folded in around them, the stillness unnerving. The further they walked, the more the gravel road shrank until eventually it was little more than a desire line.

Up ahead Savage spotted a giant pine lying on its side, like a beached whale. Just like the tree where Luke had been found, metal stakes encircled it. However, the caution tape that had hung between each one had gone.

In this lonely part of the forest, they were surprised by the sound of footsteps. Tannaz and Savage weren't the only ones interested in the tree. They had company.

CHAPTER 11

A YOUNG COUPLE ABOUT THE SAME age as Tannaz were wandering around the fallen tree, heavy-duty cameras slung around their necks. The guy was as bald as a billiard ball and wore a long army-surplus trench coat and large circular glasses with thick black rims. The girl had a leather biker jacket, similar to Tannaz's and biker boots. In the dim light Savage could see purple dreadlocks hanging down her back.

Savage leant over and said quietly to Tannaz, "I bet they like the same movies you do."

Tannaz elbowed him in the ribs.

As they got closer, the couple didn't seem startled to hear two people approaching them. They turned and smiled, almost happy to have company.

"This is a cool place, huh," said the guy.

"If you like that sort of thing," said Tannaz.

"We do," said the girl. "There's delicious dark magic here. You can feel it." She shivered with delight.

"Hey," said the guy. "Did you see the other tree on your way here where the son was found hanging?"

"Yes," said Savage. "It's hard to miss."

"Do you know why it's called Dead Maids?" the girl asked keenly.

"No idea," said Savage.

"Well, there are two versions," she replied, relishing the thought of enlightening them. "The first is deliciously romantic. There is a legend of a highwayman around here. He had two lovers at the same time, and these women would hide him when the authorities came looking. Each woman did not know the other one existed. Both of them thought he was their one true love. They had no idea he was cheating on them. Anyway, the authorities never caught the highwayman, but they did catch the two women who harboured him. The first time they laid eyes on each other was when they met on the gallows, when they were hanged for giving refuge to a highwayman. Isn't that the most delicious story you've ever heard?"

Savage was beginning to get irritated by the girl's overuse of the word 'delicious'. Maybe it was the new hip word.

"What's the other version?" asked Tannaz.

"The realistic version is more macabre," the guy said.

"Really?" said Savage. "I thought that story was pretty macabre."

"Well, get this," the guy continued. "Apparently, in the middle ages, when families were so poor that they couldn't feed themselves, they had to make hard choices to survive. Sometimes, they would lead the oldest member of their family, usually an unmarried aunt—an old maid—deep into the forest, so deep that she couldn't find her way out and would eventually die. One less mouth to feed. This part of the forest is where they'd lead them. Hence the name, Dead Maids."

The girl couldn't contain her excitement and shook with glee. "Isn't it the most deliciously wonderful place for a suicide. Can you feel the energy here? The beauty of decay all around us. It's a deeply spiritual place. Like Aokigahara in Japan."

"What's that?" asked Savage.

"The Sea of Trees," Tannaz answered.

"That's right," the guy said. "It's this amazing forest near Mount Fuji where people go to commit suicide. The forest is so dense, sometimes the bodies aren't discovered for months. Dead Maids is like a smaller version."

"We're planning to go there next year," the girl added.

Savage should have felt angry at these two. Yes, they were annoying, and some people just had a morbid curiosity; hanging around in graveyards and being close to death. But this couple were naïve about what it really meant, no better than children playing with toys. They had probably never experienced death for themselves which is why they were beguiled by it. Savage, on the other hand, had seen enough death to last him several lifetimes. For him there was no beauty to it. It was ugly and brutal and vile and it smelt rank. It meant separation from the ones you loved. It meant pain and loss and guilt. Day in, day out.

While their enthusiasm didn't bother Savage, the same could not be said for Tannaz. Savage could feel the rage radiating off her, that temper of hers brewing like boiling acid. He grasped her hand and gave it a squeeze, as if to say, *take it easy*. She snatched it away.

"Actually," Tannaz said. "We're here because we knew one of the guys who died here. He was a friend of ours. A real nice, quiet guy. And although I didn't know him for very long, it's still very raw. We came here to pay our respects and we find you two creeps treating it like a theme park for goths. Shame on you. Luke was a real person. He had a life. His death isn't here for your amusement."

The two looked at the ground, heads bowed, humbled. "We're very sorry, we didn't know he was your friend," the girl added.

"We wouldn't have said those things, truly we're sorry," the guy added. They both went silent. Eventually the guy said, "Do you have a picture of him?"

"What?" said Tannaz.

"Could you send us one?" the girl asked. "We'd love to see what he looked like."

Savage anticipated the punch that Tannaz was about to throw and grabbed her arm before she could launch it into the girl's face.

"Get off me," Tannaz snarled. "You two are sick. If you like death so much, why don't you do everyone a favour and have a go yourselves. Two less assholes on the planet."

As Tannaz struggled against Savage, the couple stood staring at her curiously and without fear, as if she were a creature in the zoo. They both raised their cameras and started snapping off photos of her twisted angry face. Up to that point, Savage had regarded the pair as harmless idiots with a thing for gruesome details, but they had stepped over the line.

He chanced letting go of Tannaz, leaped forward and snatched the camera from the girl's hands. Quickly fiddling with it, he released the memory card from a slot in the casing.

"Hey, you can't do that," the girl said.

"Think I just have," Savage replied.

"I need the pictures. It's very important."

"Not anymore," Savage replied. He pushed the memory card into a pocket of his jeans and then handed her back the camera. Then he held out his hand to the guy, who had sensibly stopped snapping pictures. "You, Le Corbusier."

"Who's Le Corbusier?"

"Swiss architect. Invented ugly concrete buildings. Wore stupid glasses like yours. Memory card. Now."

"Please, I can't," the guy said. "I'll delete the pictures of your friend. We both will. But we need the rest of the pictures for our work."

The girl nodded rapidly. "That's right."

"Not good enough," Savage replied. "I want the memory card."

"And what if I don't," the guy replied.

"Believe me," said Tannaz. "You really don't want to go there."

The guy's shoulders dropped and he slowly pulled the small plastic memory card from his camera and passed it to Savage, who took it and pushed it into his back pocket. "Now, get lost," he said to them.

The pair looked at each other, resigned expressions on their faces. They sloped off, back along the path in the direction of the car park grumbling. "We'll have to start all over again," Savage heard one of them say.

"Sorry," said Tannaz. "Lost my temper."

"And you were quite right to," Savage replied. "Suicide is not a spectator sport."

For the next half hour, the pair of them scoured the fallen tree for anything out of the ordinary.

"Hey," said Tannaz. "There's a yellow X painted on the trunk."

"That's what lumberjacks use to identify which tree needs cutting down, so they don't accidentally fell the wrong one."

"Oh. Thought it might be a clue. X marks the spot."

"X never marks the spot, as Indiana Jones would say."

"Would you stop quoting movies at me, it's getting annoying."

"Sorry."

They continued searching. Savage pushed branches aside. They were so dense he needed to have brought a machete or even a chainsaw to cut them back. In the cold air, Savage found himself becoming sticky with sweat, dead pine needles clinging to him like little magnets.

"What are you looking for?" asked Tannaz.

"Well, assuming that Dave didn't kill himself, someone, actually more than one person, would have had to lift his body high into this tree, which is no mean feat. Dead bodies are heavy and unwieldy. They'd need pulleys or a winch, at least some climbing rope. Whatever they used would've left a mark."

Savage continued sifting through the dense network of branches but the task was pointless. A fruitless fool's errand. Many of the tree's limbs had been battered and splintered by the fall or had been crushed and then had buckled, trapped beneath the hulking trunk. Any marks left by potential killers would have been camouflaged by the damage caused by the fall.

Eventually, he satisfied himself that there was nothing to see. He joined Tannaz who sat on a stump smoking a cigarette, using a damp leaf as an ashtray. "Don't get mad at me," she said. "I'm taking the ash back with me and the butt too."

"Glad to hear it," he said, wiping the sweat from his brow. "Shall we head back?"

"If you think you're done."

"Yep, there's nothing else I need to see."

Tannaz stood up, ground out her cigarette on the leaf, scrunched it up and put it in her jacket pocket. The pair of them began the long walk back to the van.

"Well, that didn't tell us much," said Tannaz.

"On the contrary, it told us a great deal."

CHAPTER 12

TANNAZ KEPT LOOKING AT SAVAGE, eagerly waiting for his insight like a salivating dog. He seemed to be concentrating hard, his brain filtering and compartmentalising data, like a program waiting to load.

"So," said Tannaz. "What does it tell us? Don't keep a girl waiting."

"Sorry, just going over stuff, making sure my logic is sound." Savage bent down and picked up a fallen branch and started using it like a walking stick. "Okay, here we go. Now this is based on a lot of assumptions..."

"Just tell me, already."

"Our first reaction when we heard Luke was dead was that he didn't seem suicidal."

"Yes."

"Trouble is, people who often commit suicide put on a happy face to the world. Having considered suicide myself, and getting as far as putting a gun to my head and nearly pulling the trigger, I know this from first-hand experience."

Tannaz shunted Savage to a stop with both hands. "Promise if you ever feel like doing that again you call me, okay?"

"Okay, I promise."

Tannaz let go and the pair continued walking.

"Where was I?" Savage asked.

"People who commit suicide often put on a brave face."

"Yes," said Savage finally regaining his thread. "Maybe Luke was severely unhappy, and wanted to join his dad in heaven or whatever."

"But we definitely know he wasn't close to his dad."

"True. Let's say the note found on his body was correct. Maybe he also had depression, wanted to end it all, and he hid it from us very well. And he had a strong desire to join his father in the next world."

"Okay."

"If that assumption was true, why would he come all this way, and then hang himself on the first suitable tree near the car park? Surely he'd make the trek to where his dad died and carry out his final act there, so he could slip into oblivion close to where his dad departed. Or somewhere inconspicuous."

"That makes sense."

"Luke was shy, like his dad. He wouldn't want his dead body on show, just a stone's throw away from a public car park."

Tannaz nodded, lighting up another cigarette. She took a deep drag and blew it out into the still air. "Yep, Luke wasn't showy, he'd have tried to do it somewhere secluded, plus there was the risk of him being seen, being caught in the act. Unless he did it in the dead of night. I can't imagine anyone's here after dark."

"I agree," said Savage. "Now let's come at this from a different angle. Let's assume someone killed Luke and wanted to make it *look* like a suicide. That sounds easy but it isn't. Firstly, Luke lived in London. So whoever did this had their work cut out. They'd have to snatch him in London and get him down here. That poses several problems. If they kidnap him and transport him here, they have to restrain him, gag him, tie him up. All of which leaves marks on the body, defensive wounds et cetera. Marks that would show up on a medical examiner's report, pointing to the fact he struggled and therefore this was a murder made to look like a suicide. We know the police are convinced it's a suicide, so they couldn't have done that."

"So what did they do?" Tannaz asked.

"Another alternative is to drug him, to make it easier to transport him down here. Again, drugs would show up in his system, pointing to a murder."

"Okay so they didn't do it that way. How else would they do it?"

"They kill him in London. Somehow hang him behind closed doors."

Tannaz stopped, thought for a moment. "How would they do that? Lure him somewhere? That sounds hard. They'd have to avoid a struggle, marks on his body again."

Savage halted, stabbed at the ground with his stick. "True. It's tricky but not impossible," said Savage. "Let's just assume they did manage it. Now they have to transport a dead body down here."

"Why's that a problem?"

He held his stick vertically in the air. "They have to keep the body upright. If they lie the body down, say in the back of a van, all of Luke's blood will drain to the lowest part of his body and stay there." He turned the stick through ninety degrees, holding it horizontally, and ran his hand along the underside. "If they lie him on his back without a heartbeat to pump the blood around, gravity takes over and pulls all of his blood down, making it pool in his back. Like engine oil in the sump of a car. It's called livor mortis."

Tannaz shivered.

"Are you okay with all this?"

"Yep, I'm good, go on."

"So if Luke's body has livor mortis on the back, that's going to sound alarm bells ringing in a medical examiner's head. A body that's been hanged has livor mortis in the arms and legs where gravity has pulled the blood down, not the back. Our medical guy would know Luke's body's been moved and has been hung after he's dead."

"So, how would the murderers get around that?"

"Again, tricky but not impossible. They transport Luke's dead body upright. I dunno, wrap it in a carpet or blankets or bubble wrap to avoid marking the body. Then lash it to the inside panel of a van, one with extra head height. They drive it to Dead Maids car park. Unload Luke's body, still keeping it upright, and carry it through the gap beside the gate."

"That sounds really hard."

"You've hit the nail on the head. It is hard. Like I said, dead bodies are heavy and unwieldy. Even with two or three guys, carrying a dead body is hard at the best of times. They've also got to keep it upright, making it even more difficult and they've got to get it through the narrow gap, without leaving a mark on it. Once that's negotiated, they have to keep hauling the body upright, deep into the forest. Bloody difficult."

"Sod that for a game of soldiers," said Tannaz. "So they stop at the nearest, suitable tree and rehang Luke's body."

"Exactly."

Tannaz and Savage both began walking again, increasing their speed with every step, spurred on by the logic of this new deduction.

"Or maybe none of that happened," said Tannaz. "Maybe they just got him here at gun point, avoiding struggles and drugs. Sat him in the back of a car with a gun pointed at him. Drove him down here then hanged him."

"True," said Savage. "Why bring him all the way down here at gunpoint and then hang him within view of the car park, where there's a chance someone would see them?"

"Presumably, they did this is in the dead of night, when no one's around."

"We don't know the time of death, which is a bit of a handicap. Yes, you would think it was done in the dead of night, but it's still a risk to do it by the car park, even at night. There's a chance, not a big one, that someone might see them—a random car driving past. It's a risk they don't need to take. Surely anyone with half a brain would have pointed the gun and marched Luke deeper into the forest completely out of sight. Plus it looks more convincing."

The pair went silent, nothing but the sound of their feet scrunching along the pathway back to the car park. "Or maybe," Tannaz said. "Luke came here by himself intent on committing suicide near to his dad, twisted his ankle, couldn't walk any further and hung himself on the nearest available tree."

Savage blew out through his teeth. "Any of these explanations are feasible. We need more hard facts if we're going to get to the bottom of this. We could be going off at crazy tangents."

"What do you suggest?"

"We don't leave Southampton until we find the truth."

CHAPTER 13

ON THE DRIVE BACK INTO Southampton, Tannaz flipped open her laptop, and inserted the memory cards they'd taken from the goth couple with the cameras.

Savage chanced a quick glance at her screen. It was filled with hundreds of shots of trees. "Is that all that's on there?" asked Savage.

"Yep," replied Tannaz. "Just trees. Loads of them. Oh, plus a few shots of that dumb girl taken by her dumb boyfriend of her sitting on different branches. I suppose they were going to upload them to Goths Up Trees."

"What's Goths Up Trees?"

"A website where goths post pictures of themselves up trees," Tannaz said dryly.

"Really, that's a thing?"

"Yep, if you want to see goths up trees, that's the number one site to go to."

He shook his head and smiled. "There's something for everyone on the Internet."

When they got back to the city, Savage booked them into one of those budget hotel chains. It was a modern tower block near Southampton airport that resembled a pile of rabbit hutches piled one on top of the other—the embodiment of the stack-them-high-sell-them-cheap business philosophy. Corporate and soulless, it was clean and cheap and quiet. Apart from the odd plane landing and taking off, the rooms were so well soundproofed, the roar of the engines barely made it through the triple glazing.

It was dark outside. They sat in Tannaz's room. Her laptop was on the bed, and she lay on her front, fingers furiously drumming away on the keypad. "So what are we looking for?"

"Okay, so this Simon Wellington and his vile empire seem to be suspect number one. That doesn't mean he did it. Could have been someone else or someone working for him, or could be someone completely unrelated to all this. First things first, we follow the logic and find out all we can about him. One of two things will happen. We'll either find something on him and pursue it until we've got him bang to rights or we won't find anything, which means we can rule him out and move on, find who really did this."

"What's your gut telling you?"

"Simon Wellington's behind this."

"Mine too."

Tannaz pulled up a picture of Wellington on her laptop from his property company website. He had a face like a Toby jug—rosy cheeks, achingly wide smile and wavy, white, ice-cream hair, like the stuff that comes out of Mr Whippy machines. Bloated with success, the result of too many business lunches.

"He looks like he's about to sing show tunes to a room full of pensioners," said Savage.

"I know, right?" Tannaz replied. "Not exactly the Kingpin."

Savage knew not to go by looks. Most of the war criminals in Serbia had looked very similar, like kindly old uncles who did part-time work as Father Christmas during the holidays. In reality they had done despicable things to their fellow countrymen and women.

Tannaz scoured the Internet for anything else on Wellington by getting into online places where she really wasn't welcome. "Okay," she said. "Simon Wellington, born in Ireland, came over here in the nineteen seventies. Son of a plasterer. Nothing like his father. Wanted to be on the stage, as an actor. Never made it. Wife died of a heart attack when their one and only son, Ben, was about fourteen. Business-wise, he owns over four and a half thousand properties, covering Southampton, Portsmouth, Brighton and Reading, and a few in London."

"Jeez," said Savage. "The guy must be a millionaire, billionaire probably."

"I'll keep digging."

Savage opted for a more traditional route and got on the phone. He didn't know anyone in Southampton, but he knew plenty of people in London where Wellington had a number of properties; nowhere near the number he had on the south coast, but enough to need construction work now and again. And Savage knew plenty of people in London construction. One thing he knew for certain about anyone in the building industry, wherever they were, they all liked to talk. Most tradespeople could talk for England. In fact, you couldn't shut them up. On the rare occasions Savage had needed to get someone in to do work in his flat that he couldn't handle himself (usually servicing the boiler because he didn't have the right certification) he found his ear being chewed off by a plumber who felt the need to discuss everything from politics to the England football team manager. He didn't mind, that was just the way these people were. However, it did mean that Wellington's reputation would have spread far and wide, through a network of chit-chatting carpenters, bricklayers and labourers. The downside of this was he'd have to separate what was fact from fiction. There'd be enough cock-and-bull stories to fill several books.

Savage hung up on his last call, scribbling down a few words on the room's complimentary notepaper.

Tannaz sat up on the end of the bed. "Got anything?"

"Nothing that will help but I do have some good background on who we're dealing with. Better than nothing."

Savage shuffled through his notes like a newsreader and cleared his throat. "So Wellington has properties in London, and some of the guys I know have done work for him. And they've given me some good intel. Apparently, his rags-to-riches story started in the height of the eighties' property boom. He scraped enough money together to buy a cheap, ratty old B&B in Shirley, Southampton. You have to realise that property prices were out of control in the eighties. People were snapping up anything to develop so they could flip it and make a packet."

"And that's what he did?"

"Nope. Did the complete opposite. He bought the B&B and left it pretty much as it was. Decided to rent, not sell."

"Why did he do that?"

Savage fingered through his notes. "I'm coming to that. He took a massive gamble. Huge risk. Not only did he decide to rent it, he rented to the most undesirable people on the planet."

"Who?"

"The unemployed and the homeless. Most landlords want to rent to young, smart, responsible professionals. People who will look after their property and keep it nice. Wellington rented his to people that nobody else wanted. That was his masterstroke. His gamble paid off. Housing development is expensive. You have to buy the property then you have to spend a packet on doing it up before you can sell it. That eats into your profit margins. Same goes for the rental market; if you don't make the place nice nobody will want it. However, if you rent it to people who have no other choice, the homeless and the unemployed, who just need a roof over their heads, it doesn't matter."

"Beggars can't be choosers."

"Exactly. So with the first property under his belt, the rent cheques flowed in, paid directly by the local council because every tenant gets housing benefit. He bought another property. Filled that one up with the same kind of people. Then did it again and again and again. It's the perfect money-making scheme. There're more homeless and unemployed people than there is social housing. Waiting lists are endless. Councils don't have enough property to go round. So he stepped in and filled the gap. Bought up houses that nobody would buy, in areas where no one wanted to live and filled them with people that nobody likes, and the tax payer foots the bill, sending the rent money straight into his pocket. And when the recession hit in the early nineties, loads of property developers went bust. He was immune, in fact demand grew."

"Any of your contacts mention the 'weird stuff' he was into?"

"No, none at all. They all know he's got a reputation. Whatever *that* reputation is, he seems to have it all sewn up. No one talks about it because they're all frightened of him, especially his tenants." Savage paced up and down the small bedroom. Eventually he turned and faced Tannaz. "One thing we do know. We're dealing with one hell of a smart guy, who lords it over thousands of vulnerable people."

"That's not a good combination," Tannaz added. She did an image search of Wellington. Only two hits came back. One was a 'grip and grin' from the local paper years ago—him shaking hands with the head of a children's hospice, handing over a giant cheque for a new wing. The other picture was a tiny fuzzy black-and-white photograph of a young Wellington, dressed in a dinner jacket and bow tie with a dove on his arm. Half cropped out of the shot was an attractive older woman standing next to him, dressed like a Las Vegas showgirl—his assistant. He looked about nineteen, she looked in her mid-twenties.

"Click on that image," Savage asked. An archive page from the Southampton Magic Circle opened up with a large, more blurred, version of the black-and-white photograph. Next to it was an annotation that simply read: 'Simon Wellington. Award for Most Promising Young Magician, 1973'.

"Who'd have thought it?" said Savage. "Scary Simon Wellington having a sideline as second-rate David Copperfield. Desperate to be on stage, I guess."

"Magician, property magnate, gangster," Tannaz remarked. "Not four words you usually hear together."

Tannaz went back to her keyboard, hitting the buttons, sifting through page after page of Google at breakneck speed. Eventually she said: "Doesn't seem like he does the magic stuff anymore. No mention of it anywhere, just lots of stuff about him raising money for charity. Funny for someone who's clearly a bit of a performer, there being only three shots of him. Seems to have become a bit of a recluse."

"That receptionist said he's retired. Maybe that's why,

although the junior drug dealer seemed to think he was still pulling the strings in the background."

Tannaz looked up from her screen. "We should check out his son. Could be him behind all this. Not Wellington."

"Definitely. Let's find out all we can about his elusive father first, before we move onto the son. Have you got anything else?"

"Well, I checked him for a criminal record. Nothing. Guy's never even had a parking ticket. So then I hacked into the company's business bank account."

"Anything?"

Tannaz shrugged. "No. Nothing. Well there was this one thing, but it's nothing."

"Doesn't matter. Show me."

The screen showed the online bank account of Simon Wellington Properties. Columns of payments going in and out with the corresponding details of the transaction.

"What am I looking at?" asked Savage.

"This one here." Tannaz pointed to a payment made to a blacksmith called Nortoft & Sons in North Wales for five and a half thousand pounds. "It's not much. The only thing I've found that's out of place. Why the hell would they need a blacksmith— for shoeing horses?"

Savage looked at Tannaz. "You're so urban, Tannaz. Blacksmiths don't just make horseshoes, they make anything out of metal—gates, fencing, balustrades for staircases, balconies."

"Oh, okay. Now I feel really dumb."

"No, don't. This is interesting. For two reasons. Why go to a blacksmith at all? Why not go to a metal fabricator? It would be far cheaper, and why go all the way to North Wales for it?"

"What's the difference between a blacksmith and a metal fabricator?"

"You'd go to a blacksmith for something more bespoke, say a one-off item. Like a sculptural pair of gates, I dunno, like a famous musician wanting a gate made from musical notes. Metal fabrication is more straightforward, utilitarian. Boxes and fences, security grilles for shop fronts, that sort of thing."

"So he wanted something sculptural to put on one of his properties? That sounds unlikely."

"No, my guess is he got something made for his house and put it through the business to save money. Maybe gates with top hats and rabbits jumping out of them. A magical theme. Maybe this place in Wales specialises in it. See if they have a website."

Tannaz Googled the name and up popped the website for Nortoft & Sons.

"Now that is weird," said Tannaz.

Nortoft & Sons specialised in the manufacture of metal props for film and TV. The landing page of the website was covered in a grid of nasty, painful objects, ranging from swords, flails and axes to helmets and suits of armour.

"Well, you know what they say, 'you can't buy taste'. Maybe Wellington bought himself a load of suits of armour to put around his mansion. Plus a few cannons out the front of his driveway."

"With the money he's earning, he could buy the real thing."

"That's true. A man who's worth that much wouldn't buy fakes. I wonder what he ordered then."

"I'm going to find out." Tannaz grabbed her phone and punched in the contact number in the corner of the screen.

CHAPTER 14

BEFORE ANYONE AT NORTOFT & Sons had a chance to answer, Tannaz turned to Savage and asked, "What was that nasty receptionist called, the one you spoke to when we were in Dave's room?"

"Vicky."

Tannaz put the call on speaker phone so Savage could hear. It rang three times before someone answered.

"Hello." A woman with a thick Welsh accent spoke at the other end of the line. "Nortoft & Sons."

"Oh, hi, this is Vicky from Simon Wellington Properties in Southampton." Tannaz spoke in a sing-song accent, as if she were the kind of girl who read gossip magazines and watched *Magic Mike* films back to back, preferably with her girlfriends and several bottles of Prosecco.

"Oh, yes," said the woman on the phone.

"How are you today?"

"Fine, thank you."

"Good." Tannaz stretched out her vowels nearly to breaking point. "We've just had a new accounting system, and we're having a few teething problems, lost some details, so I'm just phoning around to make sure we've paid our suppliers."

Smart, thought Savage. People were always interested in getting paid.

"Oh, okay," said the woman. "Let me just open the right programme." The click of buttons filtered through the phone's speaker. "Right, go ahead."

"It's for five and a half thousand pounds from Simon Wellington Properties."

"Bear with me," the woman replied. "Ah, yes. Here it is. Our records say it's all been paid."

"Ah, wonderful. That's such a relief. So sorry to bother you."

"That's quite alright, love."

"Just one other thing. We've lost our record of what the payment was for. I don't suppose you could..."

"No problem at all. Yes, here it is. You ordered two bespoke animal cages."

Tannaz and Savage exchanged puzzled looks.

"Animal cages?" Tannaz couldn't hide the shock in her voice, her pantomime act disappearing momentarily.

"With ornate steel work," the woman continued. "First cage was small one, a metre and a half by a metre and a half. The other one, a real whopper. Nine metres by nine metres by three metres high—both cages had sides that bolted together so they could be dismantled."

Savage hurriedly scribbled the words 'for magic?' on a piece of notepaper and flashed it in front of Tannaz's eyes.

"These cages, did they have any trapdoors or hidden mechanisms, you know, for magic shows?"

"Oh, no, nothing like that. We're not allowed to do that kind of thing. Magicians have specialist contractors for that. They like to keep everything secret," she chuckled. "Ours is more props for TV and film. We did some lovely stuff for Game of Thrones, do you remember that episode..."

Tannaz quickly cut short her little anecdote. "Thing is, we've got no idea why they were ordered."

"Yes, I suppose it's a bit odd. I don't think we've ever done anything for a property company before. The only thing I can think of is maybe an aviary for the big one, to keep birds in, maybe for a retirement home."

"That makes sense," said Tannaz.

"But the small one, I couldn't hazard a guess."

"That's okay, you've been more than helpful. Could I just ask one more tiny thing? Sorry. Otherwise I'll get it in the neck from my boss. What was the delivery address for the two items?"

"Certainly. It's right here: number twenty-seven Sutton Road, Shirley, Southampton."

"Thank you so much. You've been amazing."

"Quite alright, love." The woman hung up.

Savage and Tannaz looked at each other.

"Shirley, Southampton," said Savage. "That's where Wellington bought his first property."

Tannaz shut her laptop. "This is getting weirder by the minute. Why the hell would a scumbag landlord order two animal cages?"

"Let's find out. Tomorrow morning we're heading over to twenty-seven Sutton Road."

The drive at rush hour across Southampton was nearly as bad as London. Tannaz didn't seem bothered. She had her laptop open and was using the time to find out more about Simon Wellington. Savage drummed on the steering wheel, eager to get to Shirley and find out whether this new lead would get them any closer to finding out what had happened to Dave and Luke. The satnav sent them down Shirley High Street, a clogged-up thoroughfare lined with a myriad of shopfronts, ranging from coffee chains, charity shops and budget fashion stores, to car dealers, tyre fitters and pawn brokers. Every so often, Savage's little VW van passed an empty shop or a boarded-up window, he presumed, like many retail centres, the impact of online shopping had taken its toll.

About half way down the high street, they took a right and followed a road populated with tightly packed terraced houses with front doors that spilt straight onto the narrow pavement. The road was on a bus route and Savage had been stuck behind a single decker that kept stopping to disgorge people. Finally, after another right turn, they left the bus and were into a housing estate—by no means as bad as Thornhill, but no oil painting either. Modest semi-detached homes lined up before them complete with the ubiquitous satellite dishes clinging to their walls and block-paved driveways. The grass verges lining the edges of the road had been churned up by cars parking on them, their tyres gouging deep furrows in the dirt.

Tannaz glanced up from her screen. "Are we there yet?"

"Almost," Savage replied.

"You really do take me to all the best places, doncha?"

They passed a small children's park where every inch of spare surface had been graffitied to hell and back. Beyond the park stood what looked like an abandoned property. Slightly bigger than the rest, it appeared to be two semi-detached houses that had become one property. Number twenty-seven, Sutton Road.

"I think this must be where Wellington started it all," Savage remarked.

"The B&B, you mean?"

"Looks big enough to be a B&B."

Tannaz screwed up her face. "Who the hell would want to come here for a holiday?"

"Exactly. Must have got a bargain back in the day. Why is it standing empty? Surely Wellington would want to put it to work. Get some people on welfare in there, turn a profit."

Tannaz shrugged. They pulled up outside and looked the building over from inside the van. Every window and door was sheathed in heavy-duty metal screens, presumably to prevent squatters gaining entry or vandals breaking in, although they'd had a pretty good go at the outside, using the screens as a canvas for vast artworks. Savage thought some of it was pretty good. Idiots with no talent whatsoever had then come along and sprayed squiggles and gang tags, defacing good graffiti with bad.

There was no front garden, just a low-maintenance area of dull concrete patio slabs, a checkerboard of dirty salmon pink and filthy yellow squares, like a stale Battenberg cake.

"How do we get in there without the neighbours getting nosey?" asked Tannaz.

"By hiding in plain sight and a bit of skill," said Savage. "Look in the glove compartment and hand me that black leather case. There're also a couple of hi-viz vests squashed in there."

Tannaz retrieved the small black leather case and handed it to Savage. Then she held up one of the thin nylon hi-viz vests, ringed with a couple of reflective stripes. She snorted. "I really don't do hi-viz."

"Well, you'll have to get used to it because they are extremely handy at making someone without authority, i.e. us, look like they have authority."

"Fine, I'll suffer, but it's not a good look." Tannaz shrugged on the vest. "What's in the case?"

Savage unzipped and opened it. Inside were a variety of slender metal picks, each one with a slightly different-shaped tool at the end, some no more than a hook, others, with sophisticated jagged edges.

"Oh, that is way more cool," Tannaz said, leaning in to get a closer look as if they were rare gems. "Can I have a go?"

"I'll teach you, but today we need to get in there quick so anyone looking doesn't think we're up to no good. Ready?"

"Certainly am."

"Grab the Maglite from the glove box. Oh, and a pair of nitrile gloves for both of us. Can't be too careful."

"Savage, I think you're the only person I know who actually keeps gloves in his glove box."

They exited the van and walked promptly up to the house then along the side alley to the metal screen that covered the front door. Savage went straight to work, selecting two picks and then wedging them into the lock at the top right-hand corner. A few seconds later the lock made a delicious pop. He extracted the picks, knelt down and attacked the lock in the bottom right-hand corner. That yielded a few seconds later. The screen swung open. He turned to Tannaz. "The old man's still got it."

"You are definitely teaching me that next."

"Add it to the list."

A battered, but still solid, wooden door stood before them, a single deadlock barring them from entry. Savage put the two picks back into the case. Then, like a surgeon selecting instruments for an operation, chose two different ones. Moments later, the locked clicked and they were in.

Inside the air tasted stale and old like an abandoned church. Savage tried the lights. There was no power. Tannaz flicked on the Maglite, sending a powerful flare of light around the hallway. A staircase presented itself in front of them, its treads and risers completely bare, and splattered with water stains. The floor they stood on was also bare, save for lines of paint flakes, like a gigantic case of dandruff, near the skirting board where it had parted company with the damp walls.

Savage and Tannaz moved into the front room. Same story. Naked floorboards and disintegrating paint. Something in the corner of the room caught Savage's eye.

"Shine the light over there," he asked Tannaz.

A cone of light lit up the corner. Savage bent down and picked up an ancient copy of the *Sunday Mirror* newspaper. Dated July 2011, a picture of Amy Winehouse filled the front cover. The headline simply read: 'Amy Dead'.

Savage shook his head. "Such a waste of talent."

Tannaz joined him. "Definitely." She swung the light all around the room. "So do you think this place has been empty since 2011?"

"It's starting to look like that."

They moved slowly through every room in the house. Each one empty apart from the odd piece of rubbish left behind and the fetid stench of unoccupied space. After leaving the last bedroom, Savage persuaded Tannaz to get on his shoulders. He lifted her up so she could poke her head through the loft hatch and shine the torch around in the roof space. She came back down coughing. "Nothing, just dust," she said.

Savage sighed.

"Dead end?" asked Tannaz.

"Would seem so."

"Okay, let's get out of here before anyone wonders what we're doing."

They descended the stairs and left the way they came, Savage locking the door and security screens behind him with his set of picks. They left promptly, hurrying past the grotty patio at the front of the house, towards the van parked on the road.

Savage suddenly stopped.

"Wait," he said. "We've missed something."

CHAPTER 15

S AVAGE KNELT DOWN BESIDE THE edge of the patio where the old mortar bed that held the patio slabs in place was beginning to crack and crumble.

"What is it?" asked Tannaz, studying the ground.

Savage clawed away at the brittle mortar revealing the edge of a thick, dirty black sheet, poking out from beneath one of the slabs. As he cleared more of the mortar away, it became clear the sheeting ran the length of the patio.

"What is it?" Tannaz asked again.

"It's a waterproof membrane. Stops water penetration."

Tannaz looked confused. "And why's that important?"

Savage scratched his head. "Why waterproof something that doesn't need waterproofing? It's just earth underneath."

Tannaz shrugged.

"The only reason to put in a waterproof membrane is if there's something you need to keep dry."

"Like what?" asked Tannaz.

"Like an underground room," Savage replied.

Tannaz couldn't contain her excitement. "At last," she said. "Some full-on Famous Five shit."

Fiddling with locks, Savage had them back inside within a minute. Looking around the gloomy hallway, Tannaz asked. "Where's the secret entrance?"

Savage looked blank. "I have no idea, I've never done this before. Bang on the walls I suppose, see if anything sounds hollow."

The pair of them went to it, knocking their fists along the

walls of each room, dislodging more flaky paintwork. "This feels a bit like amateur hour," Tannaz remarked.

"I know," said Savage. "We look a bit ridiculous."

One by one, each room on the ground floor was checked until they met up back in the hallway. "Nothing," said Tannaz.

"Me too," said Savage.

"Are you sure there's an underground room? Maybe that membrane thing is just to stop weeds growing through."

"True," said Savage. "That stuff's thinner, more like a fabric, lets water through but not weeds. The membrane out there is heavy-duty rubber. Made to stop water. Thing is, it usually goes under floors to stop damp rising up, so why put it under a patio? It doesn't make sense. I don't get it."

Tannaz tried her best to look sympathetic.

Savage sighed. "Well, let me just check the cupboard under the stairs then we can be on our way."

"Let me know if you find Harry Potter under there."

"I thought you didn't like mainstream films," Savage replied.

"Everyone likes *Harry Potter*, don't they?"

Savage disappeared through the small, triangular-shaped wooden door beneath the stairs. He emerged almost instantly. "One of the walls. It sounds hollow."

Quick as a rabbit down a hole, Tannaz joined him. The space beneath the stairs was big, easily big enough to accommodate a teenage wizard or two. Tannaz and Savage could both stand upright without banging their heads on the dusty stairs above.

"It's this wall here," said Savage. He pointed to the back wall, the one that formed the adjacent side of the right angle of the triangular space. Savage knocked on it, making a hollow thud. Tannaz shone the light on it to reveal a wooden panel that had been varnished rather than painted.

"How do we find out what's behind it?" asked Tannaz.

"Shine the light up here a second." In the top corner was a screw. They checked the other three corners, which also contained screws. "I'd say these screws are the only thing holding this panel in place." Savage pulled out his case of lock picks and used one shaped like a flat-head screwdriver to remove the screws one by one. When he'd extracted all four screws he placed them in his pocket. Using his fingernails he managed to get a grip on the edge of the panelling until it came away in his hands. It was light enough for Savage to lift out. As he placed it outside in the hallway, he noticed soundproofing material had been attached to the inside of it.

Savage turned to Tannaz. "Like you said, some Famous Five shit."

"I prefer the Harry Potter analogy, seeing as we're in a cupboard under the stairs. And this must be the Chamber of Secrets."

"Does that make you Hermione Granger?"

"I'm more Bellatrix Lestrange."

"Isn't she the nasty one?"

"Yeah, but she's way cooler." Tannaz shone the light into the blackness. It illuminated a set of dingy concrete steps that went down then turned at a right angle.

"That doesn't look creepy at all," said Tannaz.

Savage spotted a switch and tried it. A series of lights came on, set into the wall at regular intervals.

Cautiously, they descended the stairs, Savage going first and Tannaz following behind. At the bottom of the stairs they were confronted by another door, also with soundproofing material stuck to the outside. It was unlocked. Savage nudged it open with his fingertips. Beyond the door was a small, brightly lit hallway and a substantial metal door, held together with thick rivets. Three large hasp-and-staple brackets were bolted to the outside for securing the door with three large padlocks. The padlocks were absent and the door stood ajar.

"Shall we?" said Savage.

Tannaz nodded, noticing she was now holding the Maglite like a club.

Savage gently pulled the hefty metal door open.

In front of them was a windowless, cube-shaped room, about fifteen feet by fifteen feet, completely lined with smooth, immaculate grey concrete. Above them, set into the ceiling and protected by strong wire mesh hung a bright low-energy bulb.

Tannaz stepped in first. "What the hell is this all about, some kind of torture dungeon?"

Savage followed her in. "Certainly looks like it, minus any torture implements."

Looking around, he noticed faint circular markings on the floor about the size of a ten-pence coin. They were arranged in a square pattern in the centre of the room, little more than discolourations in the concrete.

"What do you make of this?" he asked.

"Looks like dot-to-dot marks, making up a square."

"How big would you say the square is?"

"Over a metre. Maybe a metre and a half." Tannaz's eyes went wide. "You don't think a cage has been set into that concrete? The small one from Nortoft & Sons?"

"Yes, it looks like it was here. Someone's removed it and concreted over the whole of this room. The holes where the bars were set into the floor are slightly discoloured where the concrete's taken longer to dry."

"Why would anyone put an animal cage down here?"

"I don't think it was for an animal," Savage replied. "I think someone's been held here. Kept prisoner. And look at that." Savage pointed to a small hole in the wall, high in the corner—a loose, snaking electrical wire hung out of it. Below the hole were four small screw holes.

"Maybe a light fitting was there," said Tannaz.

"Why have a light fitting and then remove it when there's already enough light from that bulb up there?"

"A camera," said Tannaz.

"That's my guess too. They wanted to keep an eye on whoever's been caged in this room."

"But they removed the cage and all the other evidence."

"Yep, they've gone to great lengths to cover it up. You can tell by the concrete everywhere."

"Why would they do that?"

"DNA. That stuff is difficult to get rid of. People think you can make it disappear with bleach or cover it up with paint, but it's still possible to get a sample. However, cement is very good at damaging DNA, makes it difficult to get a complete sample and therefore, identify anyone whose been held here."

"Or killed," Tannaz added.

Savage nodded in agreement. "Someone's covering their tracks."

"Someone like Simon Wellington?"

CHAPTER 16

AFTER LOCKING UP THE SECURITY screens at twenty-seven Sutton Road, Tannaz and Savage made their way back across Southampton towards the hotel. The rush hour was over and traffic was light, making the driving almost enjoyable, apart from the fact that the atmosphere in the van was turning confrontational. Savage could feel Tannaz's mood swinging in the wrong direction. Her laptop was propped on her thighs and she was punching the buttons with such ferocity that Savage thought her fingers might go through the keyboard.

"Surely we could go to the police now," she argued, looking at him and typing at the same time. Savage had no idea how she could concentrate on the two things at once. "That place is obviously some seedy torture dungeon, anyone could see that."

"That's an opinion, not a fact."

"Oh, come on, Savage, we know it's true."

"It's like they say in these TV courtroom dramas. It's not what you know, it's what you can prove."

"Never heard of that. Don't watch TV."

"You know what, your generation needs to watch more TV." Savage added a laugh at the end. Tannaz wasn't in a joking mood. "Look, if we go to the police, first we'd have to admit to breaking and entering—"

"We send an anonymous tip-off," Tannaz quickly countered.

"Okay, what have the police got then? A concrete basement, that's all."

"A very secure concrete basement."

Savage changed gear. "Wellington could argue it's just for storing things."

"Why all the soundproof doors?"

"Maybe he was building a recording studio down there and abandoned it half way."

Tannaz gave a false laugh. "You don't believe that."

"Course not, but it's what he could say."

"The marks where the cage was. The fresh cement to destroy DNA. It all points to something."

They stopped at a set of traffic lights. Savage pulled on the handbrake and turned to Tannaz. "Firstly, we didn't see any cage; we're just assuming that it was there. The only reason we know about it is because we hacked his account, also inadmissible. And secondly, the cement doesn't destroy DNA, it only damages it. Either way they wouldn't be able to get a proper sample of who's been down there. So they couldn't link it to anyone who's disappeared or been murdered. It's circumstantial evidence."

"Circumstantial evidence?" said Tannaz, still tapping away on her laptop. "Most convictions are based on circumstantial evidence, otherwise the only convictions that would stick would be ones where they caught the culprit red-handed."

Savage put the car in gear, released the handbrake and pulled away. "Okay, correct. What I'm saying is we need more evidence. It needs to be beyond reasonable doubt, and at the moment we're not even close. All we have are two suicides that, to the casual observer, look genuine, and a concrete basement and some cages. It's not enough to get the police interested. Plus, Wellington has a big organisation, four and a half thousand properties and goodness knows how many staff working for him. It could be someone inside the company doing this."

"I'm not so sure about that," Tannaz said, the tone of her voice suddenly becoming more optimistic.

"Why's that?"

"We know Wellington is squeaky clean. No previous convictions. I've been doing some digging, and back in 1975 a woman accused him of assault. I found a tiny article in a local newspaper archive. She told a reporter about him, said he'd, and I quote, 'treated her sadistically'."

"What's her name?"

"Jenny Hopkins. I think you need to pull over and look at her picture."

Savage turned the wheel hard without indicating and mounted the pavement, screeching to an abrupt stop. A truck passed by, beeping, the driver shaking his fist.

Tannaz turned the screen to face Savage, showing a story that only took up a single column inch. A primitively typeset headline announced: **Assistant accuses amateur magician**. Below was the same grainy picture of Wellington when he'd won young magician of the year. Standing next to him was the attractive woman dressed in a Las Vegas showgirl outfit—his assistant, Jenny Hopkins.

"We need to talk to her," Savage said.

"She's right here in Southampton. Lives in Heatherlands Nursing Home in a place called Chilworth, wherever that is."

Savage punched the address into the satnav and eased back into the traffic.

Up until then, every suburb of Southampton they had visited had either been rundown residential areas or bleak and industrial, or both. Chilworth was neither of the two and was altogether a far more genteel prospect of wide tree-lined avenues and sweeping driveways that led up to handsome properties. A desirable area populated with financially secure families. Husbands that sailed at the weekend, wives that lunched and children who would be successful.

Tannaz gave a long whistle. "Now this is more like it."

Every house they passed was beautiful.

The satnav piped up and politely told Savage that he'd arrived at his destination. In front of them a large sign announced 'Heatherlands Nursing Home'. Set in a large swath of green grass with a generous veranda that ran the length of the building, held up by a procession of columns, Heatherlands Nursing Home looked more like a posh golf clubhouse.

"Savage," said Tannaz. "When I start needing help going to the toilet, promise me you'll put me in a place like this."

"I think it'll be you putting me in a place like this, won't it?"

They got out of the van and walked into a generous reception area that resembled the lobby of a five-star hotel. A coffee machine sat purring in the corner, filling the lobby with the aroma of premium roasted beans.

A pretty nurse with glossy black hair slicked back into a ponytail sat behind a substantial curved oak desk. The name badge pinned to her well-laundered white uniform introduced her as Maria Garcia. She smiled warmly. "Can I help you?" she said in a strong Latino accent.

"We've come to see Jenny Hopkins," said Tannaz.

"Are you family?" asked Maria.

"No, friends," said Savage.

"Can I take your names please?"

They gave their names and the nurse looked doubtful. "I'm sorry, you're not on her list of approved visitors."

"How do we get on the list of approved visitors?" asked Savage.

She retrieved a form from under the desk and slid it across to Savage. "Please fill in this form, we'll submit it for security approval, takes about three days, then you can go on Jenny's list of approved visitors, and see her whenever you like. Jenny does like having visitors."

There was no way Tannaz or Savage would make it onto that list. At least the security was good in this place, but that didn't help them at this precise moment.

"That's a lovely accent you have there," said Savage. "Where are you from, Maria?"

Maria looked surprised by the unexpected question. Throwing her for a moment or two, she then said, "Madrid in Spain."

"Ah," said Savage. "That would explain the lovely rhythm your voice has. I'm told people from Madrid have the purest form of Spanish."

Maria blushed. "Gracias."

"I'm sorry," said Savage. "I've embarrassed you. I apologise."

"No, it's okay," said Maria, smiling broadly. "I don't mind."

"Well, your accent is very beautiful. Look, we only need to see Jenny for a couple of minutes. You could come with us if you like. Keep an eye on her. Tell us when we need to go. We'll only be two minutes."

The Spanish nurse eyed up Savage and Tannaz, judging whether they were genuine or not. Finally, she said picking up the phone, "Okay, let me just get someone to cover reception."

They turned away while the nurse was on the phone. Tannaz spoke quietly in Savage's ear. "Savage, you old dog. I didn't think you had it in you."

"Neither did I," Savage whispered back. "But she's not from Spain, her accent is South American. Notice how she said 'gracias' like a Brit abroad—*grass-ius*. If she was from Madrid she'd have said it with a 'th' sound, *grath-ius*. That T-H sound never made it to the new world. So why is she lying about where she's from?"

"Illegal immigrant," Tannaz proposed.

"Maybe," said Savage.

A minute later a male nurse came and took over from Maria on reception. Savage and Tannaz signed the visitors' book. Savage quickly scanned up the lines of signatures and flipped back a few pages. He subtly nudged Tannaz, who glanced down at the book. The cramped, scratchy signature of Ben Wellington, the son of Simon Wellington sat in a column beside the name Jenny Hopkins. He chanced flipping back a few more pages and there was another visit by him. Then again a week before that. Ben Wellington was a regular visitor to Jenny Hopkins.

The fake Spanish nurse showed Savage and Tannaz into a bright and airy day room full of soft pastel sofas and low coffee tables strewn with upmarket magazines, from *Horse and Hound* to *Tatler* and *Yachting Monthly*. Floor-to-ceiling windows stretched across the entire space, giving a panoramic view over the palatial grounds at the rear. With fountains and woodlands, they looked as if they went on forever.

At the far end of the room, sat a lady in a peach dressing gown in a wheelchair, with thinning wispy white hair, smiling warmly at a flat-screen TV. Maria pointed to her. "That is Jenny. I must warn you her mind is going." Then she looked at Tannaz. "She thinks every woman who visits her is her daughter Jackie."

"Really?" said Tannaz.

"Yes, so just play along. Her daughter died when she was a little girl, and she has these conspiracy theories about how she died. Just ignore them or agree. Otherwise she gets upset."

Maria ushered them to where Jenny sat, watching a movie with the sound turned down, one of the Mission Impossible franchise but Savage couldn't tell which one.

"Jenny," said the nurse, gently. "Jenny, you have some visitors. Can they join you?"

Without taking her eyes off the screen, Jenny nodded.

"Let her watch her movie to the end, then she'll talk to you," said Maria. "I'll be over there if you need me." The nurse walked to the back of the room, keeping within earshot. She began clearing empty coffee cups and plates of half-eaten biscuits in front of an elderly man who'd dozed off.

Savage and Tannaz pulled up a chair and sat down. They sat in silence watching the fast-paced action movie with its blisteringly quick jump cuts designed for short attention spans. Without the sound up, the cast seemed to be running around like headless chickens with massive anxiety issues.

Eventually Jenny said, "Is that Tom Cruise?" Her voice sounded quiet and brittle like it could crumble at any moment.

"Yes," said Savage. "I believe it is Tom Cruise."

Jenny thought for a while and then said, "He's looking old isn't he?"

"Well, I suppose he is in his late fifties now."

Jenny didn't answer, just continued to be enthralled by the onscreen antics.

After a few minutes Jenny said, "And is that Alec Baldwin?"

"Yes," said Savage. "I believe it is."

Jenny considered this and then said, "He's looking old isn't he?"

Savage decided not say anything, seeing that he was probably about the same age, and Alec Baldwin seemed to be aging far better than he was.

"And is that Simon Pegg?" she asked.

In the film, Simon Pegg sat on a chair, attempting to pass a lie-detector test with Alec Baldwin looming over him.

"Yes, that's definitely Simon Pegg," Savage replied.

"He doesn't change, does he?" Jenny said.

They sat like this for over an hour, Jenny never once looking away from the screen, commenting on every actor she recognised and how old they looked. Apart from Simon Pegg, who seemed to be the Dorian Gray of action cinema.

When the movie ended, Jenny switched off the TV with the remote and slowly swivelled around in her wheelchair to appraise her visitors. She smiled at Savage and then she looked at Tannaz and her smile grew larger and brighter. "Jackie," she said to her. "Jackie, you've come to see me. How wonderful."

"Hello... Mum," said Tannaz, going along with the charade of being her long-dead daughter.

"Jackie, you're so beautiful. Isn't she beautiful?" she said to Savage.

"Yes, very beautiful," he replied.

Jenny turned to Savage and gave him a once over, eyeing him up from head to foot. "And this must be your husband. He looks..." Jenny struggled to find a diplomatic word to describe Savage, "... sturdy."

"Hello, Jenny," said Savage. "I'm John. It's very nice to meet you. Tan—I mean, Jackie has told me so much about you. Haven't you, Jackie?" Tannaz nodded, looking unsure of what she was supposed to say.

"All good things, I hope," said Jenny.

"Very good things," Savage continued. "She tells me that you used to be a magician's assistant."

"That's right, I was very glamourous back then."

"You still are glamourous, Jenny," Tannaz said.

"Oh, you're so sweet."

Savage cleared his throat. "Were you an assistant for Simon Wellington?"

The sweet smile and glinting eyes that had graced Jenny's face suddenly fled, replaced by a hard, straight mouth and a contempt that turned her eyes small and dark. "That man is a bastard," she said, her voice gaining strength. "Cruel, sadistic. I don't care who knows. Everyone's too frightened to say anything about him. There's a conspiracy around him, a conspiracy of silence. I'm not scared of him. Not like I used to be. I'll tell it like it is and to hell with it."

"What happened?" asked Tannaz.

"You know what happened, Jackie. He tried to kill you."

"Why did he do that?" asked Savage.

"Before he had his property empire we did a magic act in clubs and pubs, to make a bit of extra money. He really wanted to be an actor. Never got anywhere. Think it made him bitter and angry. He began to get sadistic. Would do things to frighten me. He'd lock me in cabinets when we were rehearsing, and then time how long it took me to start crying to be let out. He'd write the times down and compare them. Had a little notebook full of numbers he carried around with him. Liked collecting statistics, he did. He'd even make graphs and show me how I was performing. Show me patterns emerging. Like how I lasted longer at the beginning of the week and got worse as the week went on." Jenny shivered.

"Wasn't he doing it for the act, to see how long it took you to get out?"

Jenny looked at Savage as if he were Satan himself. "No, he was not. That's just what the police said. They laughed at me. Said I needed a different job if I didn't like being locked in cabinets. So I told the local paper, they wrote a little story but nobody cared. Wellington wasn't the big shot he is today. Just a grubby little magician from Ireland with a sadistic side. But I knew what he was like. He knew it too. He did something to shut me up. Something terrible..."

CHAPTER 17

J ENNY'S EYES DARTED AT TANNAZ, confused. With a deep sadness, she took one of Tannaz's hands and gripped it hard as if she'd never let go, the thick veins standing across the back of her slender hand like scattered ropes. "He killed you, Jackie."

Savage and Tannaz exchanged confused glances.

"Wellington told me to keep quiet or I'd regret it," Jenny continued. "I refused, so he had you killed as a warning to me. A hit and run. You were just a child. Knocked you over in the middle of the street. You'd just been to the newsagent to buy sweets. Left you for dead. Said you were the first and he'd kill all my family if I didn't shut up." Jenny's expression lightened as she gazed into Tannaz's face. "I knew if I wished hard enough my little girl would come back. And here you are."

Tannaz smiled sympathetically.

Then Jenny's faced changed. A rage swept across it like she'd become possessed. "That Wellington will pay! I'll kill him myself."

"Jenny," Savage said. "Were you ever at twenty-seven Sutton Gardens in Shirley with Wellington?"

"Never heard of it," she said. "I tell you one thing for sure. I'll throttle that Wellington for what he did! You'll see. Make him pay!"

She shook and her bottom lip began to wobble, dribble escaping from her mouth. Savage feared she was having a seizure. "Nurse!" he called out.

In an instant Maria Garcia was at Jenny's side, soothing her. "Okay, Jenny," she said. "It's okay, you're safe here. It's a safe place. We need to calm down, don't we? Need to look after that heart of yours. Nice deep breaths now. Breathe out slowly."

Jenny's quivering anger slowly subsided, and her ragged, uneven breathing slowed to a more sedate pace. The nurse gently dabbed the spittle from her mouth with a tissue. "That's better, Jenny. Well done. You're doing really well."

Another nurse came over and wheeled Jenny away, back to her bedroom.

"I'm so sorry," said Tannaz. "I think we might have upset her."

"It's okay," said the nurse. "She does this quite often. Her mind's gone. It's a coping mechanism. She needs someone to blame."

"Do you think it's true? What she says about this Simon Wellington?" asked Savage.

"Who knows?"

"She seemed pretty convinced," said Savage.

"Yes, but it changes each day," the nurse replied. "Sometimes it's Richard Branson, other times it's Ricky Gervais. It changes. We have a guy upstairs thinks he's Steven Spielberg, keeps directing everyone, calling action and cut. What goes on in these people's minds is as real as you are. We just do our best to keep them comfortable."

The nurse showed Savage and Tannaz out. Nice though she was, they had a feeling they wouldn't be let back in again.

For several minutes they sat in the car park of Heatherlands Nursing Home.

"I know what you're going to say," said Savage. "And no we haven't."

"What?"

"Got enough evidence."

"I know," said Tannaz. "I feel so sorry for that poor woman, Jenny. And what she's been through. But a lady with dementia is hardly going to be a reliable witness."

"The galling thing is, I think I believe her."

Tannaz flipped open her laptop and started typing. After a few minutes, she pulled up an obituary column from the same local newspaper that had run Jenny's accusation against Wellington and said, "Well, Jenny's story checks out, she did have a daughter called Jackie who did die in a hit and run, culprit was never caught, so we know that bit is true."

"Well, if it was Wellington who was responsible, at least we're getting a strong profile of his personality. It's beginning to look like that junior drug dealer wasn't exaggerating. Wellington is sadistic and cold-hearted. Who knows how many of those little dungeons he has hidden away. And those visitations by his son, that's almost certainly to keep an eye on Jenny, make sure no one's believing her story."

"Funny she didn't mention him."

"Could be the dementia, probably forgotten he visits her every week."

The pair went quiet. Tannaz buzzed down the window and lit up a cigarette, smoking it with her head hanging out like a dog.

"A conspiracy of silence—that's what Jenny said," Savage remarked. "This is the problem. No one will talk because everyone's too afraid, apart from poor Jenny in there. And nobody's going to believe her. Plus, he's got eyes and ears everywhere, Ben Wellington for example, keeping tabs on her."

Tannaz flicked the ash off the end of her cigarette. "Well, we haven't exactly tried to question anyone in his properties yet."

"That wouldn't be a good idea. At the moment, we're still under Wellington's radar. The second we start speaking to any of his tenants one of two things will happen. They'll either clam up and the shutters will come down—the conspiracy of silence—or worse, one of them will tip off Wellington that someone's been asking awkward questions."

"So how do we get the evidence we need? Because at the moment, none of it is strong enough. No link back to Dave and Luke Mosely's deaths."

Savage sucked in a deep breath, then exhaled heavily. "I think we've been going about this all wrong."

"How so?"

"At the moment we're on the outside looking in, skirting

around the edges of something and we can't get any clarity. We need to be on the inside, so we can see it for ourselves. Experience it first-hand."

"What have you got in mind?"

"Can you hack into the welfare system, get me on housing benefit? Then hack Wellington's business and put me in one of his properties?"

Tannaz shook her head rapidly. "No way, Savage."

"Why, isn't it possible?"

"No it's a piece of cake. I just don't want you living in one of his hellholes."

"It's fine, I survived an Iraqi prison, this'll be like the Ritz."

"I don't like it."

"Aw, you gonna miss me?"

"I am actually."

Savage narrowed his eyes. "Seriously, this is the only way, if nobody's talking. I need to be on the inside. Become one of the tenants. Do a few good deeds, gain their trust, be accepted by them. Then tongues will wag. And if not, I can observe. Things will start emerging sooner or later."

"How long will that be?"

"As long as it takes."

Tannaz smoked her cigarette down to the butt then flicked it away. "Okay I'll do it, but I don't like it."

Back in Savage's hotel room, Tannaz plugged in her laptop, sat on the end of the bed and cracked her knuckles like a concert pianist about to play. "Okay, here goes."

"I'll put the kettle on," said Savage.

"Black coffee, two sugars. And I'll have a couple of those complimentary biscuits."

"Right you are," Savage said, filling up the tiny kettle. It was barely big enough to make two measly cups.

Four hours later, Savage had to physically stop Tannaz throwing her laptop out of the window like a rock star throwing out a TV. She'd wouldn't have got very far as the windows didn't open. Failing that, she would have most certainly thrown it against the wall. The benefits system was proving a lot more difficult to crack than she thought.

Savage wrestled the laptop out of her hands to prevent her doing any damage to it. Tannaz dropped a few f-bombs and kicked the wall.

"Okay, calm down," he said.

"That's easy for you to say."

"Answer me this," said Savage. "Is what you're doing possible or not."

"Yes, but—"

"Okay, what is the obstacle you're facing?"

"It's taking too long."

"That doesn't matter, Tannaz. We're not on a deadline."

"That asshole Wellington is out there swanning around while we've got two dead people, no three if you count poor Jenny's daughter..."

"If he's responsible, we'll catch him. Whether we do it today or tomorrow or in a month or a year's time doesn't matter, okay. Time is not a factor here. Don't be so hard on yourself. Just focus on what you need to do, regardless of how long it takes."

Tannaz nodded. Savage handed her back her laptop.

Two hours later, Tannaz was in the system, and Savage was on benefits.

Hacking into Wellington's systems was a far easier affair. Getting access to a database of grotty, barely habitable social housing wasn't exactly high priority to the hackers of the world. Security wasn't tight.

Tannaz looked at Savage and smiled. "Where would you like to live, sir?"

Savage rubbed his chin. "Maybe somewhere with a view of the sea, an infinity pool, concierge and walking distance to the beach, oh and a spa—one where they serve a decent cup of tea."

"Well, I can't get you that, but I can get you Dave's old room— it's still free. Actually, it seems like no one wants it."

"I'll take it."

CHAPTER 18

P EOPLE WEREN'T EXACTLY QUEUING UP to be accommodated at Tivoli Gardens, even people who really didn't have a choice. According to the database, Dave's room had been vacant ever since he supposedly committed suicide. Not many people, even someone without a roof over their head wanted to move into a room where the previous occupant had taken his own life.

"Are you sure it's a good idea putting you in Dave's room?" asked Tannaz.

"Why not?"

"You've been there before. Won't that blow your cover?"

"The only person who saw us there was the big guy with the beard."

"Fat Gandalf."

"Yeah, I think the only thing he was interested in was food. And he didn't seem like the brightest spark."

"He could say he's seen you hanging around."

"It's fine, I can just say I was having a look before I moved in. And is anyone going to really worry or take any notice? Plus, I'll be right where it all happened. If something went down there, someone might still live there who knows something. It's too good an opportunity to pass up."

"And the drug dealers outside, won't they recognise you?"

"We scared them off, took their gun. Their boss wouldn't have been happy. Probably replaced them with someone else, like he did with the three junior drug dealers. Or they'd have just moved their pitch somewhere else. Remember, Wellington has loads of properties in Thornhill and all over Southampton, plenty of places to set up shop."

"Well, if you're sure."

"I am."

"Okay, here goes." Tannaz punched a load of code into her screen. "You are now a resident of Tivoli Gardens. The minute the first housing-benefit cheque goes into Wellington's business account, you can move in."

"How long will that take?"

"A month."

"A month!"

"I thought you said we weren't in a hurry."

"We're not but I didn't think it'd be that long."

Tannaz closed her laptop. "Listen. I did that on purpose not to arouse any suspicion. One month is the average length of time it takes for a benefits claim to be processed. I could have done it quicker, got you on benefit payments instantly. That runs the risk of flagging up you've jumped the queue, and then someone at the benefits office might start taking an interest in you, which we definitely don't want."

"Okay, fair enough," Savage replied. "In the meantime, maybe I should shop for some crappier clothes so I blend in with the residents."

Tannaz eyed Savage up and down. He was wearing an old polo shirt with fledgling sweat patches under the arms, shapeless jeans and shoes that were designed for comfort rather than fashion. "Nah, I think you'll be alright."

One month later, April commenced. It should have felt like spring. The temperature didn't seem to agree. It wouldn't budge and firmly stayed a shade above freezing.

Savage called the office of Wellington Properties and arranged a time when he had to be outside his new accommodation to get given his keys. Thankfully, Vicky the receptionist did not seem to recognise his voice, and if she did, she probably wouldn't have cared anyway.

Tannaz drove Savage back towards Thornhill in his van. She dropped him off in a side road just outside the housing estate. He climbed out of the vehicle and Tannaz handed him a bulging black bin liner containing a few clothes and other bits and bobs. Savage figured someone on benefits wouldn't have luggage or matching rolling holdalls. He needed to look like someone down on his luck and nothing said that more than a bin bag full of possessions. He grasped the bag in his fist and waved Tannaz goodbye.

"Remember to update me," Tannaz said. "And if you need the cavalry to come, just call me and I'll be there."

"Certainly will," Savage replied. "Now you better leave, I need to be there by eight a.m."

"Be careful, Savage," Tannaz said.

Savage watched her drive off, back to the hotel room at Southampton Airport. Did Savage detect a modicum of sadness in her eyes? Surely not.

Throwing the bin liner over his back, he walked towards Thornhill. As he entered the estate, hordes of school kids were coming towards him, on their way to sit in stuffy overcrowded classrooms in an underfunded school full of overworked and underpaid teachers who couldn't control them. Dressed in identical scruffy uniforms, the kids looked tough and unforgiving, older than their years. Savage got jostled as he walked past them. One spat at him, another threw a stone. They all shouted expletives at him.

Normally, this would have had Savage ready to give them a piece of his mind. Not today. To all intents and purposes, he was undercover—a man relying on the state to support him, downtrodden and lacking confidence. From now on Savage would adopt a technique that he'd been trained to use, and had to rely on when he'd been captured and tortured in Iraq. He would become the 'grey man'. A persona the SAS had taught him when undergoing interrogation, when the enemy wanted information. Being the 'grey man' meant becoming bland and uninteresting, a person of no value whatsoever, with no information or opinion to offer. A nobody. A monosyllabic man of few words.

This time, once inside his new accommodation, the objective wasn't to persuade an enemy that he had no information to offer, it was to fade into the background. To be dull, boring and unremarkable. He could do dull, boring and unremarkable. All he had to do was talk about DIY and Tannaz's eyes would glaze over. He just had to crank it up a bit, or down to be more precise. He had to treat his new home like an observation post. Sit and watch. To see but not be seen.

He passed the convenience store, under siege with more school children milling around outside. They were only being let in one at a time, presumably to minimise shoplifting. Savage gave them a wide berth, crossed over to the other side of the road and kept his head down. A man who wanted to avoid trouble.

Five minutes later he stood outside Tivoli Gardens, waiting for someone from Wellington Properties to let him in. The time was eight o'clock exactly.

Twenty minutes later, Savage was still waiting outside on the pavement.

Behind him, the stiff front door opened, and out stepped a pretty young school girl about fourteen or fifteen. Dressed in uniform she had thick yellow hair tied back into a ponytail. Her worried mother swiftly followed behind, cautiously looking left and right. Never leaving her daughter's side, she hurried her along, almost as if she were trying to avoid a sniper on the roof.

Savage didn't blame her. Even though her daughter was old enough to walk to school on her own, he could tell there was no way she was letting her walk alone in a neighbourhood like this. Savage would have done the same, even though his daughter would've protested and got fed up with him for being so lame.

The woman didn't make eye contact with Savage as she passed him. She was a young mum, young enough to be her daughter's oldest sister. She was blonde too, but the years of living on an estate like this, in constant fear, had sent streaks of grey through her hair and left worry lines scarring her face.

Her daughter dawdled along behind in a dream world. Savage noticed the girl didn't have a phone. Every teenager he saw these days had a phone, and used every available moment to study them, even on the walk to school. He guessed her mum probably couldn't afford one, especially not the smart phones that chewed up expensive data by the second, and a cheap push-button phone would only invite ridicule. Better not to have one at all.

"Grace," she called to her daughter. "You're going to be late if we don't hurry."

Savage watched them disappear up the road.

It was now eight forty. Savage was worried he may have missed the person he was supposed to meet. Perhaps they had already been and left.

He knocked on the door of Tivoli Gardens. The front still a mess of dirt, old rubbish, beer bottles and rusting bikes. The discarded needles around the drain still hadn't been cleared up; in fact, there were more.

Savage knocked again and waited. No answer. He shrugged and walked back down to wait on the pavement.

The mother who had taken her daughter to school was now returning, only slightly less worried.

"Excuse me," said Savage. "I'm supposed to meet some people here from Wellington Properties..."

"Sorry, I can't help you," she said without breaking her stride. Just at that moment a dented red van pulled up with 'Simon Wellington Properties' written along the side. The woman saw it and almost sprinted towards the door. She pushed her key in the lock, but the stiff door impeded her progress.

A wiry guy with limp black hair got out the passenger side of the van. Savage noticed his long, hooked nose had been broken in two places giving it the appearance of a winding country lane. He ignored Savage and called out to the woman at the door. "Hey, Rosie. You're in a hurry. Aren't you going to say hello."

Clearly Rosie did not want to stop and say hello.

"We come and say hello to you later, Rosie, yes," he said with a distinctive eastern European accent. Rosie managed to shove the door open and disappeared inside.

He turned to Savage and said, "Women, eh? I am Vlad. To you, I am God around here, okay? You must do as I say. Otherwise, big trouble for you."

Savage guessed Vlad's accent was Romanian, possibly from the region of Transylvania.

Savage had an ear for accents. During his time as a soldier he'd worked with so many people from so many different countries in so many different regions that he'd built up a database of them in his head. Every twang, burr and inflection had been tagged and logged in his brain to the point where spotting accents had become a hobby of his, like collecting stamps.

Vlad's double broken nose wheezed and whistled every time he breathed in and out. With his Transylvanian accent, Savage decided to call him Vlad the Inhaler, but not to his face, of course.

From out of the driver's side of the van stepped an altogether scarier figure. He walked around the van and stood beside Vlad, staring blankly. About a head taller than Savage, the guy had a solid square physique with a military buzz cut, bald round the sides and about a quarter inch on top. His monobrow was in desperate need of a pair of tweezers, making his eyebrows look like two ends of a bridge attempting to meet in the middle. Though it was a chilly April morning, he wore a vest and had a St George's cross tattooed on his hairy forearm. His limbs and joints had a thickness to them, like the branches of an oak tree, apart from his neck because he didn't have one—his shoulders seemed to connect straight to his head. He too had a broken nose. This one had been really broken, pummelled flat. Savage couldn't decide whether he was an ex-boxer or an ex-rugby player. Either way, it looked like it would take a dozen men to wrestle him to the ground.

"Know who I am?" said No Neck.

Savage shook his head.

"Truck," he replied.

Savage stood there nonplussed, wondering if this was some sort of wind up or test. "Sorry?"

"Truck from *Gladiators*, the TV series. You know, Saturday nights on ITV."

"Er, I never watched it," said Savage.

"Course you did, everyone used to watch it." He went into a truck-driving pose, as if he had one hand on an imaginary steering wheel, and the other above his head pulling down on an air horn. "Parp! Parp!" he shouted. "That's my signature move." He did it again and again, his bulging midriff wobbling beneath his tight vest. Too many pies had taken their toll. "I fought with the best of them. Defeated them all. No one could beat me. Now you recognise me, right?"

Savage shrugged.

"He doesn't recognise you because you were only in it for one episode," said Vlad. "Stood in for Hunter who twisted his ankle in the last show. Then it got axed. That's why you've never heard of him."

"Hey, shut up," said Truck giving Vlad an almighty shove, sending him smashing into the side of the van. He grabbed him in a headlock, clamping Vlad around the neck so he couldn't breathe.

"Okay, I'm sorry," Vlad managed to splutter. Truck let go. Vlad straightened out his clothes and hair, nose whistling in and out. "Man, you are so sensitive."

Savage thought of about a million sarcastic remarks to say about men in fluorescent Lycra underpants who ran around TV studios play-fighting with foam bow staffs. He bit his tongue. Despite the ridiculous images of Truck forming in his head, and that he was the kind of guy who would only watch a movie if Jason Statham was in it, Truck's name suited him well. He'd be a hard guy to stop.

"I'm John Savage." Savage held out his hand for a shake, neither of them reciprocated.

"Don't care," said Truck.

"Rules here are simple," said Vlad. "You behave, you'll be

fine. You do as you're told, you'll be fine. You look after us, you'll be fine. If not..."

"Section twenty-one," said Truck, grinning wickedly.

Savage looked at them blankly.

Vlad the Inhaler wheezed heavily through his nose. "You don't know what section twenty-one is, do you, dumbass?"

Savage shook his head.

Vlad continued, "Section twenty-one is law. We throw you out, whenever we like. We don't need reason. You could be on the street again like that." He clicked his long fingers. "And there's nothing you can do, because it is law."

"This means we own you," Truck added, laughing manically.

"That's right. We own you and every loser in Wellington's properties. So you better keep us happy. Give us what we want." Vlad prodded him hard in the chest.

"We prefer cash," Truck added, rubbing his fingers together.

"I don't have any money. I'm on benefits," Savage said weakly, even though his bank balance was more than healthy, he had to play the part of a penniless no-hoper.

Truck tucked his hands into the sides of his vest. "Not our problem."

"Then we find other ways you can pay us, little tasks you do for us," Vlad said. "Otherwise, you're back on the streets. Understand?"

Savage nodded his head. He understood, all too well.

CHAPTER 19

A S SAVAGE FOLLOWED THE TWO men up to the front door of Tivoli Gardens, he wondered if they were the ones who took Dave's records. They were chancers. Parasites and scavengers. Opportunists, out to see what they could get. Preying on people who didn't have a leg to stand on. Were they also responsible for Dave's death, and Luke's? Possibly. Or maybe they carried it out, taking orders from above. Savage wasn't sure whether they were smart enough to pull off something like that. He would bide his time and find out.

Truck used the bulk of his body to shoulder open the stiff door. Inside, the hallway was just as dingy as Savage remembered and the smell of urine hadn't faded.

A door to the right of them opened and the big black-bearded wizard-looking guy stood there, still in his boat-sized sandals. "Got any food?" he asked. A flicker of recognition flashed in his eyes when he saw Savage. "Where's my smoked-salmon picnic?"

Savage ignored him.

"Get back in your room, Dink," Truck said.

Dink obeyed and closed his door.

Before they climbed the stairs, Vlad banged on the door next to Dink's, and said, "Rosie, if you need anything, you come and see us, okay."

There was no reply.

Vlad shrugged. "I guess she's not speaking to us today."

Savage followed them up the stairs, trailing cheap aftershave emanating from Vlad and a non-stop monologue from Truck about being in *Gladiators*. He gossiped about all the other guys on the show and how they were nothing but a bunch of pussies and muscle marys and gym bunnies, whereas he was the real deal. "You know," he said. "That's why I think they chose to keep me in reserve because I was too hard, too powerful, a real fighter who would've hurt the contestants. Beat them senseless."

Savage kept his mouth shut but the guy was already starting to annoy him. Nothing more tedious than a man whose one claim to fame had set sail and sunk long ago with all hands on deck. Savage could have told him what being beaten senseless was really all about. Being made to stand cold and naked in the same position for days with nothing to drink, then getting dragged into a cell and hit on the back with heavy wooden sticks by angry Iraqi guards until you weren't sure whether you were alive or dead, or in some hellish limbo in between. *Not* being hit by bouncy balls in front of a TV audience, packed with mums, dads and twelve-year-olds.

Vlad stopped at the first landing, and interrupted Truck's gladiatorial monologue. "Oh, if you see us out in Southampton, in the street or in a pub or whatever. You don't talk to us, you don't look at us, you don't come near us, okay. You're dole scum. Get it."

"Got it," said Savage.

"Good boy," said Vlad, patting him on the head. Savage could've snapped the guy's wrist in a second, hit him in the throat and sent him cartwheeling down the stairs. Savage quickly banished that little fantasy from his mind. He had to keep playing the 'grey man'.

They arrived at the top of the house, on the small square landing with the two rooms facing each other.

Truck got out a key, opened the door and walked in, followed by Vlad and Savage. The place looked just as it did before when Savage was there with Tannaz and Luke.

"This is yours," said Vlad, looking in the open wardrobe. "Looks like the loser before you left some of his crap here. Ah, a Harrington jacket, nice." Vlad lifted out the jacket and shrugged it on. His wrists protruded far out of the sleeves like a child who'd outgrown his school clothes. "Too small," he said, taking it off and dropping it on the floor.

"Tell him about the last guy," said Truck.

"Yeah, last guy in here killed himself. So sweet dreams."

"Why'd he do that?" asked Savage, tentatively.

"Look around, genius," said Vlad. "This is as bad as it gets. Skid row. Who cares, he was a nobody. Can't even remember his name."

Savage wanted to break the guy's nose, and everything else in his body. Dave was a *somebody*. Somebody who was missed. Somebody who was going to be avenged, that was for sure.

Truck held out the key to Savage. He went to take it but Truck snatched it away. "You remember to give us something each week, or it's section twenty-one for you."

"Yeah, we'll let you off this week, 'cos you're new, and we're nice guys."

They laughed again. Savage forced a smile.

Truck tossed him the keys.

Just then a small stick-figure of a man appeared at the door. He was older than Savage with a dishevelled thicket of a beard and little pebble glasses perched on the end of his red nose. A ratty navy-blue fisherman's cap drowned his pinlike head, completely covering his ears. With a dressing gown wrapped tightly around his little frame, he clutched a small bottle of vodka.

"Archie!" said Vlad warmly.

"Hello, gents," said Archie with a gravelly voice. His accent was traditional Hampshire. Someone unkind would have described him as sounding agricultural or like a pirate. "This week's payment." He held out the bottle of vodka to Truck who snatched it from his hand.

"Now this is a good tenant," said Vlad. "Pays his dues."

"Yes, sir, I do," Archie replied, cracking out a wobbly salute and standing to attention. He gave a throaty laugh that turned into a hacking cough.

"Jeez," said Vlad. "We're getting out of here before we catch something." Vlad and Truck disappeared down the stairs.

When they were out of earshot, Archie said, "Don't worry about those guys."

"Should I be worried?" asked Savage, throwing his bin liner of clothes on the bed. "They said the last guy in here committed suicide."

"Ahhh, they're just trying to scare you."

Savage was desperate to find out more and whether this Archie could shine a light on what happened to Dave. It was too early for that. He'd have to be patient. If he started asking too many questions too early on, Archie, like everyone else connected with Wellington, would join the conspiracy of silence. Better to let it happen naturally. Something was bound to slip out.

Archie said, "Just be sure you've got something to give them when they come round. Cash preferably or booze. Don't worry, though. If you're short we all try and help each other out and that. You know, look out for each other. Hey, you wanna whisky?"

"Er, it's a bit early for me yet. I'm going to make myself a tea."

Savage pulled his one luxury item out of his bin bag, something he couldn't live without, even if he was undercover—a travel kettle, along with a chipped metal mug, a gargantuan box of value teabags and a handful of small long-life milk cartons. Not as good as real milk but he didn't need to refrigerate them which meant he could keep them in his room.

"Want one?" asked Savage.

"Nah, I prefer a whisky in the morning. Kick-start the day. Come and hang out with me when you've made your tea."

"Sure," said Savage. "I'm John by the way. John Savage."

A shake of hands followed. Archie's handshake was surprisingly firm.

After making his mug of tea, Savage stepped over the small landing into Archie's room, which compared to Savage's was like an Aladdin's cave. Archie had decorated it with bits of junk and things he'd found in skips. There were old road signs, traffic cones and shelves full of empty booze bottles, some filled with stones, others filled with sand and gravel. Old air fresheners hung from the ceiling, dozens of them. To save space, Archie didn't have a bed. Instead he had a hammock slung from one wall to the other. At the far end of the room a single broken window was patched over with cardboard and Sellotape. Savage could feel an evil draft coming through.

Beneath the window was an old, tatty writing bureau with a small kettle perched on top. Archie pulled a key from his dressing gown and unlocked the wooden flap that lowered to create a desktop for writing on. Inside, instead of paper and envelopes, lined up in a row were bottles of whisky and more bottles of whisky. Savage wondered how a man on benefits could afford a drinks cabinet with such a vast array of whisky brands.

Archie selected a bottle, unscrewed the lid and took a hearty slug. "Ah, that's better," he said.

"Wow, this is quite a place you have here," said Savage. There were only two seats available. A bean bag, haemorrhaging little white polystyrene balls, and a wonky office chair, missing a wheel, both almost certainly salvaged from a skip. Savage opted for the office chair. "Shouldn't they fix that window up there, it's freezing in here."

Archie laughed and started coughing again. "Nothing gets fixed here. Besides, I've got this to warm me up." He gave the whisky bottle a shake.

"Well, you should at least try and seal it up with something better than Sellotape and cardboard. No wonder you're coughing so much."

Archie waved away Savage's concerns. "Hey, did you meet Dink on the way in?"

"Dink? The big guy?"

"Yeah, short for Dinky."

Savage couldn't see the point in shortening a name that was already fairly economic to start with.

"Ask you for food and that?"

Savage nodded.

Archie continued. "Yeah, he does that to everyone. Like a gatekeeper, that one." Archie took another slug of Scotch. "Speak of the devil."

Swivelling his office chair around, Savage took in the enormous outline of Dink standing in the open doorway. Gripping the doorframe with his shovel-like hands, the giant looked red-faced and ready to rip off Savage's head.

"Where's my smoked-salmon picnic?" he growled.

CHAPTER 20

DINK WAS TWICE SAVAGE'S SIZE. Powerful, like a grizzly bear in open-toed sandals. He could certainly do Savage some permanent damage, judging by the furious look on his face. Savage couldn't let that happen. He also couldn't jeopardise his mission here by acting like an ex-SAS operative, and pulling any slick moves. He would have to defend himself without making it look like he knew how to defend himself. Not an easy task. Savage stood up and calmly closed the door so Dink's left hand got caught in the door jamb, crushing the tips of his fingers. A deep howl came from the other side.

Archie leapt past Savage and said, "No! Stop!"

He quickly pulled the door open again, revealing the vast giant now sitting in a heap on the floor, clutching the throbbing end of his left hand. Fat tears dribbled down his face, soaked up by his sprawling black beard.

Archie put his arms around the big man. "Dink's a gentle giant, he'd never hurt anyone."

A wave of guilt washed over Savage. It was clear now that Dink was nothing more than an overgrown child.

"I'm sorry," said Savage, crouching down next to him. "I thought you were going to attack me. I got scared."

"Dink would never attack anyone," said Archie. "He just gets angry when he's hungry that's all, don't you, big guy?"

Dink rocked his head backwards and forwards, more tears dropping from his eyes.

Savage had completely misread the situation. Dink

wasn't scary or mean, but he was definitely harbouring some emotional issues.

Gasping spasmodically through his tears, Dink said, "I'm just so hungry all the time. I can't stop it."

"Even after you've eaten?" asked Savage.

"Yeah, all the time," Dink replied.

"Have you seen a doctor?" said Savage. "They can help with stuff like that."

"I don't have a doctor."

"What happens if you get ill?" Savage asked.

"My mum used to do all that for me."

"Where's your mum?"

"She died so I had to come and live here."

The wave of guilt for hurting Dink turned into a tsunami. He could see it now. Dink was a lost little boy without his mum, trapped in the body of a giant man. He needed looking after, not to be left to fend for himself in social housing.

Dink brightened a little, cuffing his damp eyes. "But it's okay, Mr Wellington's men were really kind, told me that Mr Wellington said I could live here forever, without worrying about bills."

"Really?" Savage didn't like the sound of this.

"Yeah," Dink wiped the last tear from his eye. "They said I could swap my mum's house in Chilworth for the room I've got."

"Chilworth?" asked Savage. "That's that nice area with all the big houses."

"Yes, my mum had a real big house. I didn't know how to look after it. All these bills kept coming in. Made me confused. So I gave them my mum's house so I could live here for free. No bills to worry about. I just had to sign some forms."

"Oh, jeez," said Savage, shaking his head.

"What's the matter?" asked Dink.

Savage let out a worried sigh, not exactly sure about how to respond. "Dink, I think your mum's house would have been worth far more than a room in this place, even with the bills included."

Dink looked like he was about to cry again. "Really?"

They'd taken advantage of Dink. Wellington had swindled

him out of his inheritance and all Dink had to show for it was a filthy room in a rundown HMO.

It suddenly dawned on Savage that it may have been better if Dink didn't know this. Savage quickly countered. "Then again, you don't have to worry about all those silly bills, and you don't have to fill in all those housing-benefit forms."

"Oh, they made me sign a housing-benefit form too," said Dink.

"They did what?"

"I get housing benefit too. It's paid straight to Mr Wellington."

Savage and Archie exchanged worried glances.

"What's wrong with that?" asked Dink.

Neither Savage or Archie said anything.

Dinky's eyes changed, darkening like deep tunnels. He was slow-witted but even he could see he'd been screwed over. Wellington had got his house. He was also getting his housing-benefit cheques. A double win, getting paid twice for the same thing.

Wellington was far more ruthless and evil than even Savage had imagined.

Dink's eyes glazed over. Then he said, "I want my mum." He stuck his right fist into his mouth and began gnawing the skin off it.

"It's okay, Dink," said Archie, putting his arm around him. "Come on, big guy. It's not so bad. You've got me."

"And me," said Savage.

All Dink could do was bite his knuckles in between asking for his mum. In Savage's experience there was no purer or more primal sign of unbridled fear than a grown man crying for his mother. He'd heard even the most battle-hardened soldiers dying in war zones crying for their mums. In all those scenarios, there was nothing he could do, except grip their hands and stay with them until they slipped away. But he could do something about this.

"We'll get this sorted," said Savage. "You need to stop biting your hand. You'll hurt yourself."

Dink just wanted to self-harm or overeat to make the pain go away. Savage could understand that but he had to stop it.

"Archie, have you got anything you could give Dink to eat?"

"Pot noodles."

"Take too long."

"Pork scratchings," Archie offered.

"Perfect."

Archie disappeared in his room and returned with a couple of bags of pork scratchings. Dink snatched one of the packets out of his hand, tore it open and devoured it, then the other one without taking a breath. His teeth crunched the salty snack to smithereens, crumbs tangling in his beard. Having his mouth occupied at least stopped him from biting his hand, which was now covered in small puncture wounds across the tops of his knuckles.

"I'm taking you to see a doctor right now," said Savage. "Get you some help."

"That's not a good idea," said Archie. "They'll take him away."

Dink looked worried. "I don't want to go away. Please don't make me leave."

Archie was right. There was a strong possibility he'd be held under the mental health act. Pumped full of drugs. They'd never let him out. But if he didn't get help, Dink would do himself some serious damage.

"Tell you what, Dink. Change of plan. We'll find you a support group to attend. You can talk to other people with the same problems. It's a good way of sorting out stuff in your head. Get good advice. Meet new friends."

"Will there be any food?" Dink asked.

Savage laughed. "Maybe tea and biscuits."

"Then I'll go, if you come with me."

"Of course," said Savage with slight reluctance—this wasn't a good start. Not the actions of the grey man. He was supposed to be keeping a low profile and fading into the background, not acting like a counsellor. However, he felt terrible for misreading Dink, and couldn't leave the poor fellow to face the demons in his head. He argued with himself that he was sticking to his plan, sort of—do a few good deeds, gain their trust, be accepted by them. It was just happening a lot faster than anticipated.

He turned to look at Archie who'd been strangely quiet, a bland, unreadable expression on his face, like he was weighing up whether this was a good idea or not. For a moment Savage thought he detected a fleeting concern in his expression. It vanished, and then he spoke. "Can I come?"

"Why not? We'll all go, bit of moral support," Savage replied.

CHAPTER 21

I T DIDN'T TAKE THEM LONG to walk back from the Adult Education Centre where they registered Dink for a local help group that held meetings twice a week. The centre was just a stone's throw away, in Itchen by the river. At first, Dink didn't want to go in. So, like a child, Savage had to bribe him with food and said he'd cook them all something nice and healthy the next day. Dink still wasn't convinced, balling his fists, getting ready to gnaw on them. Savage countered by saying Dink could have as much of the food he was going to cook as he wanted. He finally agreed to go in. Dink didn't utter a word as the woman at the reception area explained the purpose of the meetings and other services the centre offered. He sat mesmerised, soaking up everything that was said.

As they wandered back, Dink remained quiet. Savage was tempted to ask him what he thought. He decided not to push the guy. Baby steps, Savage thought, baby steps.

By early evening Savage, Archie and Dink were back in Tivoli Gardens.

Savage closed and locked his door and sat on his bed, reflecting on his actions so far. He really hadn't expected to be helping someone with an eating disorder. But then, out of all the missions that he'd carried out with the SAS, he couldn't think of one that had actually gone to plan. No matter how much intel they had or how much strategy they'd worked out, every mission always changed the second they were on the ground. That didn't matter. Improvise and adapt, that was the way of the SAS.

Savage picked up Dave's old Harrington jacket off the floor, the one that Vlad the Inhaler had discarded. He smoothed it out and hung it up. That was when he felt something in the pocket. A piece of folded-up paper. He opened it out to reveal a computer printout full of numbers. There were probably hundreds of them, arranged in four neat columns. Each number had three digits then a forward slash then four more digits. One of the numbers was ringed in red biro.

Savage noticed two small holes in the top left-hand corner, like tiny vampire teeth marks. Another page had been stapled to it, now missing. Savage went on a search around his room, looking everywhere to locate the missing page. There was no sign of it.

He took a shot of the page on his phone and sent it to Tannaz, together with a text:

> *Do these numbers mean anything? Found them in Dave's jacket*

> **I'll check them out. You okay?**

> *Never better*

> **How are the locals?**

> *Interesting. Not what I imagined*

> **Be careful. Don't start getting involved in anything**

Too late, thought Savage.

> *I'll take a look at the numbers too. Might be something. Might be nothing*

> **Me too. Text you when I have something. Night x**

He sat back on his bed, staring at the list of numbers, trying to make sense of them. A cacophonous noise rose up through his floorboards, a mix of sounds from every room below. A variety of thumping music, arguments and TVs turned up too loud. This certainly wasn't his quiet little flat in Camberwell.

Savage cut out all the jumble of sounds from around him and

concentrated on the list of figures. He knew Tannaz would be better at this sort of thing than him. He should let her get on with it. That would be lazy, so he started using his phone to search and play with them. Try to discover a pattern or at least what they represented. Serial numbers, perhaps? But for what?

Around one thirty in the morning, Savage hadn't got anywhere. The numbers were still a mystery and were starting to blur and dance in front of his eyes, merging into one another. He was getting sleepy. The house had quietened down, which was how he heard Archie's door open and close ever so slowly and ever so gently. The action of someone not wanting to be discovered, except the doors and walls in Tivoli Gardens were as thin as paper. Savage got up and tiptoed to his own door pressing his ear against it. He could just about hear light footsteps descending the stairs. A few second later, the stiff front door opened and closed. Savage switched off his light, went to the window and looked out.

Down on the street in front of the house, he saw the curious shape of Archie scuttling off down the street, away from Tivoli Gardens. At the corner, Archie paused briefly, his head scanning left and right, then he disappeared from view down another road. Very odd behaviour, especially considering how dangerous Thornhill was in the daytime, let alone at night, and how bitterly cold it was.

Savage made a mental note of it then went back to his numbers. He texted Tannaz to see if she'd had any luck. She too had drawn a blank.

His eyes were getting heavy and he couldn't concentrate any longer. He felt sleep coming for him. Just at that moment when consciousness began to melt away, he heard the voice. The one inside his head. Jeff Perkins, the personification of his post-traumatic stress all rolled into one irritating accuser.

"That's got to be a new low for you, Savage."

Savage sat bolt upright on the bed as if an electric shock had passed through his whole body.

Jeff spoke again, tutting. *"Hurting someone with special needs. You're really plumbing the depths now."*

Savage swore.

Jeff had always berated and tormented regularly, with the underlying aim of getting Savage to kill himself as penance for all the people he'd killed. Jeff had gone silent for a while. Now he was back.

"What are you doing here?" asked Savage.

"What I always do. I'm here to make fun of you and urge you to do the right thing. End it all. Just like your mate Dave and his son Luke. Now they had the right idea. So why is it so hard for you?"

"I don't want to do that, not anymore. I have a purpose in life. I have Tannaz, my friend."

The voice burst out laughing. *"Your friend? She's not your friend, you idiot. She's just using you for your knowledge. Once she's got what she needs she'll be off."*

"That's not true."

"Yes it is. And what happens when she gets a girlfriend? Or it might even be a boyfriend as we've just discovered. Do you think she'll want you hanging around like a creepy uncle?"

"She's my friend. People don't just give up having friends because they start going out with someone."

"She will. You mark my words."

Savage decided to go on the offensive. "You don't like Tannaz, do you?"

"Don't have an opinion on her, just stating a fact is all."

"You see, I think it's more than that. You go all quiet when she's around. Go a bit shy, don't you? And now she's not here, you suddenly make an appearance, what a surprise. You're scared of her. She's your kryptonite."

"Don't know what you're talking about."

"Oh, I think you do. You're so transparent. So easy to read. You want her out of the way, so you can come back whenever you want. Well it's not going to happen any time soon."

"That's not the reason at all. The reason I'm here is because you hit a new low. You hurt someone with special needs. How did that feel?"

A ramming punch of shame struck Savage in the gut. Made him feel sick to his core. "Stop changing the subject."

"You're the one changing the subject. You attacked someone with special needs. What's next, are you going to kick someone in a wheelchair. Tell me, what was it like? Was it like the first time you killed someone? We all remember that, don't we?"

"Shut up, Jeff."

"Your first mission as a member of an SAS in Iraq. Shall I remind you? You had to destroy that radio tower guiding Scud missiles."

Out of all the traumatic memories Savage had gathered in his time, this one stung the most. The one he'd tried to bury deep down. "You don't need to remind me, Jeff," said Savage. "It haunts me every day."

"Good. It should haunt you. So you don't need reminding of it then?"

"No, not at all. It's seared onto my brain."

"Well, tough, because I'm going to remind you anyway."

Savage lay back on his bed, scrunching his eyes up tight, as if this could block out the memory somehow.

"Should have been a straightforward mission, remember? But your intel was out of date. The Iraqis had realised just how important the tower was. They'd strengthened the garrison guarding the tower, hadn't they? Your team was outnumbered. That's what you train for in the SAS. Being outnumbered. I remember you hiding in the rocks surrounding the tower. You could see the silhouettes of dozens of Iraqi guards moving around. You had to set charges at the base of the tower but that would mean fighting through them all, then fighting back out again. Stupidly, you volunteered to go first or were you just trying to show off?"

Savage ignored the jibe. He could picture the scene like it was yesterday. The cold chill of the desert air, the vast starlight canopy above, and the enemy in front, completely unaware they were being watched.

"You were ordered to silently take out the guard closest—"

no firearms or you'd lose the element of surprise. You were supposed to knife the first guard, then like a tag team, move forward, silently taking it in turns to take out the next guard and the next, knifing them until your team silently reached the tower. You mucked it up, didn't you? Royally screwed up."

In the frigid air of his room, Savage felt hot prickles of sweat on his forehead.

"The guy you were supposed to kill first sat in a jeep, hand dangling lazily out of the window, flicking ash off the end of a cigarette. A simple kill: sidle up to the vehicle, knife ready. Pull open the door, surprise the victim, stab him in his vital organs. A quiet kill, no alarms raised. As you got close, he turned his head to blow smoke out of the window. You'll never forget the mask of sheer terror on his young face. He was barely sixteen. Even in the near darkness you could see his big innocent brown eyes and a mop of thick, black hair. An almost babyish face."

Savage groaned as he relived the moment.

"He'd never seen action and definitely never seen an enemy soldier, not this close. The boy froze at the sight of you with your knife raised. You weren't close enough to make the kill. You saw him go for his gun. You had no choice. It was either you or him. You dropped the knife, pulled out your Browning and put three rounds into him, killing him instantly.

"No time to process what you'd just done. All hell was unleashed. Your gunfire alerted every Iraqi soldier that they were under attack. A full-on fire fight. Bullets flying in every direction. The Iraqis panicked, shooting randomly into the desert night. Not like the SAS. You kept your heads, moved in, guns raised, firing only when you had to. The commotion you caused actually worked in your favour. That was lucky, wasn't it? A distraction, allowing you to get to the tower and set the charges. Getting out was harder. You fought through it and escaped with the team intact, apart from a few minor injuries. But you left dozens of Iraqis dying in the cold desert. Including that young innocent boy."

Savage swore out loud. "Shut up, shut up, shut up."

"I'm going to go now, but I'll leave you with this one thought. Your first kill is like sex, isn't it? You never forget your first time. I bet that boy never got to have sex. I bet he never got to do anything, thanks to you, Savage. Now think of all the other hundreds of people prematurely killed by your hands. All the lives you've abbreviated. Think on that, John Savage. Sweet dreams."

CHAPTER 22

A GENTLE KNOCKING DRAGGED SAVAGE FROM his sleep. It was a miracle he'd got any shut eye after the return of Jeff Perkins, and his shaming monologue. The death of that young Iraqi soldier had always haunted him. Savage had managed to push it to the back of his mind. Jeff had brought it to the forefront again, where it now sat, pecking away at his conscience like a demented bird. Savage kept telling himself that the destruction of that radio tower had saved hundreds, maybe thousands, of innocent lives and prevented missiles from reaching their target. He reminded himself of this over and over again, until it drowned out the guilt for what he'd done to that young Iraqi soldier. Gradually, the sweating and shaking stopped, and he had slipped into a short, fitful sleep, serenaded outside by car alarms, bottles being smashed and weapon dogs barking, and the couple beneath, starting up another argument. Compared to sleeping in a war zone where people were trying to put a bullet in his head, it was far more peaceful.

The knocking outside continued.

He'd fallen asleep in his clothes, so he went straight to the door and found Dink standing there.

"So we gonna make food?" said Dink, all bright-eyed like a puppy ready for a walk.

"What time is it?" asked Savage.

"Six o'clock in the morning," said Dink.

"Six? Dink, it's a bit early and we need to buy food. Nothing's going to be open yet."

"Oh," said Dink, crestfallen.

Savage rubbed his eyes. "Listen, I heard Archie go out late last night, and I never heard him come back. Do you think he's okay?"

"Oh, yeah, he's fine. Sometimes he disappears for days."

"Really?"

"Yeah, a lot of people earn extra money by doing things for Wellington."

"What sort of things?"

"Don't know. I've never been asked. Just things. Little odd jobs."

"What sort of jobs?"

Dink shrugged. "People don't talk about it, 'cos they're on benefits and I know you're not allowed to work if you're on benefits. I think Archie sometimes goes to the train station at night."

"Why's that?"

"To keep warm. Said he used to work there, as a cleaner, I think. Still knows them. They sometimes let him stay in the waiting room because it's warm and his room's freezing."

Savage remembered the loose cardboard taped over the broken window and the arctic blast coming in—the room faced north and was colder than a freezer compartment at Iceland—and the painful, hacking cough that erupted from deep within Archie's chest.

"Okay, change of plan, Dink. When Archie gets back we're going to mend his window."

Dink's face dropped. "What about the food?"

"We'll make that when we've fixed it."

"How long will that be?"

"Lunchtime, okay."

"Okay." The big man just stood there, taking up the whole of the landing and looking awkward.

"Would you like to help me fix the window?"

"Could I?"

"Why not? You go wait in your room and I'll give you a knock when we're ready."

Dink beamed, then thundered back down the stairs.

At around eleven o'clock in the morning, Savage heard Archie's door open and close. Savage was about to go knock on his door when a note slipped under his door. In shaky, spidery handwriting it read:

Wanna whiskey? Archie.

Savage noticed that whisky was misspelt with an 'e'. He scrunched up the note and stuffed it in his pocket.

Savage opened his door to see Archie with a brand new whisky bottle in his fist. A plaster was stuck to the centre of his forehead.

"What happened to your head?"

"ARI," he giggled.

"What's that?"

"Alcohol Related Injury. Walked into a door."

"You sure that's what happened? Wasn't Wellington's goons, was it?"

"No, no. They'd never hurt me. I'm always doing myself an injury and that." Archie took a slug of liquor. Savage wasn't entirely sure whether he believed him.

Archie's bedroom door was open and Savage could feel the chill breeze coming from it. "Listen, I want to fix that window of yours."

"Really. You can do that?"

"Sure."

"Won't you need new glass and that?"

"No, that would be expensive. But we can patch it up a bit better. Stop that nasty draft coming in."

Archie grinned. "What about the whisky?" he asked.

"Maybe later," said Savage. "A celebratory drink. Grab your coat, we're going on the scrounge."

They caught up with Dink downstairs, who seemed to have been sitting on the bottom step since Savage had last spoken to him. The simple idea of doing something with their day, rather than drinking or eating had energised Dink and Archie, stimulating them like they were going on an adventure, putting a bounce in their step and grins on their faces.

"What's first, boss?" said Archie.

"We need some wood from somewhere, roughly the same size as this." Savage had removed the cardboard patching from Archie's broken window to use as a template.

"How do we do that?" asked Dink.

"Find some builders who'll take pity on us."

"And then can we eat?" Dink asked.

"Once we've plugged the hole in Archie's window."

"What are we having?" asked Archie.

"It's a surprise," said Savage.

"I love surprises." Dink's big bulk quivered with joy. He still wore his open-toed sandals, while Archie and Savage were wrapped up against the biting cold.

Zig-zagging through the litter-strewn streets of Thornhill, they came across several building-contractors' vans as well as a skip outside a small block of council flats that were being renovated. There was no sign of anyone outside except for a skinny lad with a sawhorse and a stack of fencing slats. Every so often he'd stop and blow on his hands to warm them, then attempt to nail one of the thin slats onto a wooden frame to create a storage area for large communal bins. Each time he hammered a nail he'd curse and swear. Then throw the piece of wood away in disgust.

As Savage got closer, he could see the problem. Every nail he hammered in split the wood, and he'd have to start again.

The guy swore as another slat split all the way down the middle.

"Everything okay?" asked Savage.

"No, it is not," he said. "It's bloody freezing out here, and I'm not allowed to work inside until I've finished this bin store, but this cheap wood keeps splitting."

"Blunt the nail," said Savage.

"You what?" the lad replied, his eyebrows angled aggressively.

"Turn the nail on its head and tap the end a few times with the hammer to blunt it."

"You having a laugh?"

"Try it, what have you got to lose?"

The lad thought for a second, weighing up whether he was

going to be the butt of a joke. He shrugged his shoulders and did as Savage instructed, blunting the sharp end with his hammer. When he turned the nail over and struck it with the hammer it went in perfectly without splitting. "That's genius," he said. "Thanks mate."

"Could I have a bit of wood out of that skip and borrow your saw?" asked Savage.

"Be my guest," said the lad.

Savage winked at Archie and Dink, who grinned back, clearly enjoying the little mission. Savage selected a nice thick piece of exterior plywood and rested it on the sawhorse. Holding the cardboard in place, he cut around it, then held it up to examine his handiwork. Good enough.

There was a half-used tube of sealant in the skip. Savage pulled it out and asked, "Mind if I have this?"

"Listen," the lad said. "You can have whatever you like."

Dink stepped forward, eyeing the guy's sandwich box and flask. Savage knew he was going ask if he could scoff it down. Savage planted a hand on his chest just in time to stop him.

He thanked the lad and the three of them scuttled off back to Tivoli Gardens.

Back in Archie's room, Savage got Dink to use his powerful grip to squeeze globs of sealant onto one side of the wood.

"Now your turn, Archie. Just stick the wood in place over the hole, against the window frame."

Archie lifted up the plywood, his hands trembling. His whisky consumption had given him the shakes. "I'm a little wobbly," he said.

"Can I do it?" asked Dink.

"Yeah, you do it, Dink," said Archie. "You're steadier than me."

Dink took the wood and carefully positioned it perfectly square, putting all his weight behind it to secure it in place.

The effect was instant. The harsh draft ceasing immediately. "That's amazing," said Archie. "Can't feel a thing."

"Now if we really want to do a proper job," said Savage. "We need to run a thin bead of sealant all around the wood. Think you're up to it, Dink?"

Dink nodded enthusiastically.

Savage continued, "So the trick is to keep the pressure on the tube constant and move the nozzle slowly and consistently around the edge, closing off any gaps."

Dink held the tube and began feeding out sealant in a long white worm like he was squeezing toothpaste onto a brush. His tongue lolled out of the side of his mouth like a five-year-old concentrating on colouring in. As he guided the tube along the edge of the wood, the thickness of the sealant never wavered, even when he had to take it around the corners. Finally, the two ends met up.

"Excellent job, Dink," said Savage.

"Really, did I do it right?"

"Better than right," Savage replied. "That was perfect. You've got the knack. Well done."

Savage gave him a high five.

"Can we fix something else?" asked Dink, all smiley. "This is great fun."

"Sure, why not? Gives you a sense of satisfaction and achievement, doesn't it?"

"Yeah, it feels good," said Dink. "And I haven't thought about food once."

"Good for you, Dink." Savage was pleased for him, could feel the sense of pride it was giving him. A little bit of self-esteem from a job well done always worked wonders.

Savage felt a presence behind him, and turned just in time to see Truck barging into the room. He shouldered his way past the three of them, reached up and ripped the wood off the frame, then threw it on the floor.

Vlad stood in the doorway. "Who the hell told you losers you could damage Simon Wellington's property?"

The positive vibe of the room fled and turned deeply negative, and another presence made itself felt. *"Oh no,"* said Jeff Perkins inside Savage's head. *"It's Tweedledum and Tweedledickhead."*

"I said, which idiot said you could do that?" asked Vlad.

"Er, I did," said Savage, trying to feign some humility and preserve his grey-man act. A hard task with Jeff barking in his ear.

"He just called you an idiot. You're not going to stand for that are you? Grab one of Archie's booze bottles. Knock him out and that show-off from Gladiators. *I mean, how can you let a guy who used to wear Lycra hot pants on TV ruin your handiwork? Look, he's bashed up your DIY and you know how much you love DIY."*

Savage swallowed hard and tried to block out Jeff's rant. "We were just trying to fix the draft. Archie's room is really cold and..."

"Shut up, fool," said Truck, up close to Savage so their noses were nearly touching.

"He called you a fool. A fool. You're the smartest guy in the room. Look, you're close enough for a headbutt. Nice big fat one. Flatten his nose even more. Looks like a few people have done it before you, so do it extra hard, because his nerve endings might be dead."

The voice was right. Normally Savage would've stared right back at the guy before hitting him, but he had to play the grey man or all this would be for nothing.

Savage gazed at the floor. "Sorry."

"No. No. No. Savage. No. Put away the grey man. Come on, you know you want to. Put away the grey man. Put away the grey man..." Jeff chanted.

Savage stole a quick sideways glance at Dink, who looked terrified. Archie seemed numb and unreadable, mesmerised like a rabbit in the headlights.

"You'll have to pay to get this fixed properly," said Vlad.

Jeff Perkins dropped an f-bomb.

"It was already broken," said Savage.

"Tell them you'll break them."

"Doesn't matter," said Truck. "I think five hundred quid will cover it."

"Five hundred quid!"

"I haven't got five hundred quid," Savage said quietly, trying to keep a grip on reality. Savage had the money but had to keep up the pantomime of being poor.

"Then you've got a problem," said Truck.

Through all the white noise of Jeff's remarks, Savage thought of an opportunity. "I could work for it," he said. If he could get in with them, he could get closer to what was happening in Wellington's sordid little world. Maybe find out about the 'weird stuff' he made people do.

"What can a loser like you do?" asked Vlad.

"DIY, fix things up."

"That's right," said Dink, excitedly, as if he'd had too much sugar. "He can fix things, he did this magic trick with a nail and..."

"Hey, retarded hungry caterpillar," said Truck. "Shut up."

"Now that, I do agree with," Jeff said cruelly.

"Nope, I think you pay. You pay fifty a week," Truck added.

"I only get seventy a week in benefit," Savage replied.

"Not our problem. Now go get us fifty quid."

Shoulders slumped and head down, Savage shuffled out of Archie's room, back to his own. He returned and held out five ten-pound notes to Vlad.

"Don't give it to him, Savage. Are you insane? Yes, actually, you are insane, you've got me talking to you inside your head, but you know what I mean."

Vlad snatched the notes from Savage's hand and stuffed them in his pocket.

"That hole stays unfixed, understand." Truck picked up the thick square of plywood from the floor and snapped it over his meaty right thigh. He held up the two pieces and let them fall to the floor as if he were doing a mic drop. "Once when I was sparring on *Gladiators*, I snapped a bow staff in half, you should have seen the faces on all the other Gladiators. Shit scared of me they were. I think that's why I didn't get so much air time as the rest. I was too powerful."

Here we go again, thought Savage. Same ditchwater-dull story about *Gladiators*, and about how he was too powerful for the show. Savage tuned out while Truck wittered on about his fifteen minutes of fame.

"Pleasure doing business with you, Savage," said Vlad, cutting off an anecdote about Truck punching a runner on the show because he brought him the wrong flavour protein shake.

Vlad left the room. Truck stayed on to finish his boring, pointless story. "... So I thumped this guy and said next time, make sure it's strawberry." Then he left, not bothering to close the door.

CHAPTER 23

IT TOOK SAVAGE AND ARCHIE a while to stop Dink from chewing the back of his hand. The two thugs had not only destroyed the window repair, they'd broken Dink's spirit. After helping with the small job, Savage had seen a twinkle in Dink's eye, a spark of energy and purpose. Accomplishment was far better at nourishing the soul than any therapy, drugs or junk food. That was all gone now, and the low-self-esteem Dink was back again. At least Jeff Perkins had got bored and left.

They'd managed to block up the window, by stuffing it with some of Dave's old clothes he'd left behind, holding it in place with tape. It wasn't as good as a solid piece of plywood and sealant but it was far better than the cardboard. At least his room felt marginally warmer and liveable.

"Are we still having food?" said Dink desperately.

"Course we are," said Savage, trying to keep spirits up.

"You've got no cash left," said Archie. "Why don't I boil up some water and we can all have a Pot Noodle."

"Yes, Pot Noodle," said Dink, clapping his hands.

"No, we'll have something freshly cooked. It'll be better for both of you. Better for that chesty cough of yours, Archie. And Dink, this food you can have as much as you want."

Dink became a volcano of excitement. "Really? I can eat as much as I want?"

"Yep, I made a promise yesterday before the meeting. You can have as much as you like."

Dink bounced up and down on the spot making the floor shake. "Tell me what this food is. I can't wait."

"Soup," said Savage.

Dink stopped bouncing. Archie looked crestfallen. Both their shoulders slumped, as if all the air had been let out of them.

"Soup?" asked Dink.

"Vegetable soup," Savage said. "And yes, you can eat as much of it as you want. Nothing healthier than fresh vegetable soup."

"Er, I think I'll pass," said Archie, pulling a Pot Noodle from off the shelf.

"Me too," Dink added.

"Remember that warm fuzzy feeling you got from fixing the window?" asked Savage.

Dink nodded.

"You get that from making and eating your own food. Not adding boiling water to something made in a factory with dry old bits of I-don't-know-what."

Neither of them said anything. Dink looked longingly at the Pot Noodles on Archie's shelf.

"Tell you what," said Savage. "If you don't like it, you can have Pot Noodle instead."

"Okay," said Dink, some of the spark returning to his eyes. "I'll do it."

"What about you, Archie?"

"Nah, I'm good."

"Come on, Archie," said Savage. "You need good food to clear up that cough of yours."

"Don't worry," Archie said. "I eat out a lot at a local restaurant."

"Really?" asked Dink. "What's it called?"

"McDonald's." Archie's reply turned into an uncontrollable cough.

"I want to go to McDonald's," said Dink.

"Have you got any money?" asked Savage. Dink shook his head. "Then soup it is."

Savage and Dink walked to the convenience store. Dink didn't stop asking questions about the soup and how they were going to make it. He'd seemed to have blanked out the incident with Truck and Vlad.

Wandering around the aisles of the cramped and shabby little store, Savage grabbed a packet of stock cubes and filled his basket with veg, onions, potatoes, carrots, garlic, peas and anything they had that was fresh, which wasn't much. Demand wasn't high for fresh produce in Thornhill. It was more of a multi-packs-of-salty-snacks-and-cheap-beer type of place.

As they queued up to pay they noticed Rosie was having an argument with the cashier.

"I want a refund," she said holding up a reusable grocery bag, which had a hole in the bottom that she kept poking her finger through. "This is called a bag for life."

"So?" said the cashier.

"Well, it hasn't lasted for life has it. Got a hole in it, see?"

"Bag for life doesn't mean it lasts forever," the cashier replied, unconcerned. Arguing with customers was above his pay grade.

"That's false advertising."

The bag was made of canvas and clearly had "Bag for Life" printed on the side and the logo of the convenience store, together with trees and butterflies to emphasise its environmental credentials. The thing was dirty and had scuff marks all over it. Savage wondered whether Rosie had found it in the road.

"I'm sorry," said the cashier. "That bag looks well used."

Rosie's anger flared. "Course it's used," she replied. "What else am I supposed to do with it?"

"She's got a point," said Savage. Rosie swung round and glared at Savage, as if warning him to stay out of this. Maybe she wanted to fight her own battles. "A bag for life is not a bag for life if it only lasts a fortnight."

"Then it would be called a bag for a fortnight," Dink added.

"That's right," Savage agreed. "Maybe you could have a whole range depending on how long each one lasted. Bag for a month, bag for a year..."

"Bag for a short while," said Dink.

Savage laughed. "Now that would be more accurate. Bag for a short while. If you're going to call it a Bag for Life then you're really asking for trouble."

The cashier shrugged. "I'll give you a replacement bag."

"No, please," said Rosie. All the fight had gone out of her, replaced by desperation. "I need a refund. Please."

The cashier looked at Savage and Dink then back to Rosie. The hassle wasn't worth it. He opened the till and placed a pound coin on the counter. Rosie snatched it up. "Be right back." She disappeared momentarily and returned with a loaf of cheap white bread and a pint of milk. Adding the pound to a fistful of small coins, she opened her hand and spilt them over the counter. Life must be dire if she was resorting to scavenging for things to refund in a bid to feed herself and her daughter Grace.

The cashier scanned the items then counted up all the loose change. "Eleven pence short," he said bluntly.

"Are you sure?" said Rosie. "Count it again."

"Don't worry," said Savage, stepping forward. "I got it." He slapped eleven pence on the counter.

Rosie turned to fix Savage with a pair of untrusting eyes. "I'm not a charity case," she said. "Don't feel sorry for me."

"I didn't say you were a charity case," Savage replied. "And I don't feel sorry for you. I just think if our roles were reversed, you'd do the same for me."

Rosie didn't reply. She snatched up her groceries and left.

People were desperate here. Just like the estate in London where Savage grew up. They're not born this way, they're made, thought Savage. Products of their environment. If they're always watching their back, always trying and failing to make ends meet, it hardens them. No one chooses to be this way. Life's lottery shapes them.

Back at Tivoli Gardens, Dink and Savage took their bulging bag of groceries down into the kitchen in the basement.

"You're kidding me," said Savage, as he got his first look at the kitchen.

It looked worse than a war zone. Filthy plates and unwashed pans plastered in mouldy food covered every available surface, including the floor. Savage couldn't even see the sink or the cooker, they were under a pile of broken and dirty crockery. Bin bags overflowed with ancient rubbish, stinking out the place. It was a health hazard and smelt disgusting. Given a few more years, some of the organic matter would have evolved and walked out of there on its own. In one corner a rotting door leading to the rear of the house was so damp its wood was no better than cardboard.

"Jeez, we should have bought washing-up liquid and bleach," said Savage.

"I've got hand sanitizer in my room," said Dink.

"That'll have to do."

With the hand sanitizer they managed to disinfect a small rectangle of the counter on which to work. Savage managed to scrub clean a massive double-handled bucket-sized pan, together with some bowls and utensils. He used the penknife on his keychain to cut up the vegetables, while Dink peeled them. Dink had never done it before, but like his DIY skills, he had great dexterity with his hands.

"We'll use everything," said Savage. "Cook a load of it up, then we can have soup whenever we want."

Dink grinned.

Savage showed him how to fry the veg in the saucepan, then add the water, bring it to the boil, then let it simmer for ten minutes.

Dink enjoyed sprinkling in the stock cube. "And that's all we have to do?" he asked.

"Yep," said Savage. "That's it. Home-cooked soup, easiest dish to make and totally good for you."

When it had cooked and cooled, they had enough soup to feed a small school. Savage gave Dink a spoonful to try. He blew on it a few times then took a sip. His face went blank then cracked into a huge blissful smile. "Oh, that's good," he said, taking another mouthful, not waiting for it to cool. "And I can eat as much of this as I like?"

"Yeah," said Savage. "Well, within reason. There's no rubbish in that, so fill your boots. But pace yourself, I know it looks like a lot but that's got to last us." He poured some into a separate bowl—a huge one, fruit-bowl sized—and gave it to Dink, who began spooning it in his mouth like he was in an eating competition. Then Savage took a smaller bowl and filled it. "I'm going to take some up to Archie, see if I can tempt him off those instant noodles."

Dink nodded, his mouth still full.

When Savage returned, Dink stood sheepishly, leaning against the counter, like he was an errant child waiting outside the headmaster's office. He looked away and started biting his knuckles.

"Dink, what's wrong?" Savage asked as gently as he could.

Dink wouldn't say anything. Savage noticed the vast pan of soup had gone. All of it. At first he thought Dink might have wolfed the whole lot down. Even he couldn't have got through the gallons of soup they'd made in the brief amount of time Savage had been upstairs. Besides, the pan was missing.

"Has someone taken the soup?"

Dink squeezed his lips tightly together to stop the answer from accidentally slipping out, not wanting to snitch or perhaps he'd been threatened not to tell.

"It's okay," said Savage. "I won't be cross, but that's our soup. We made it. You and me. Just give me a nod. You don't have to say who it is."

Dink held his breath then slowly nodded.

"Right, you go back to your room and don't worry, okay. Everything's going to be fine."

Savage followed Dink out of the kitchen and saw him safely back into his room. Once the door was shut, Savage sniffed the air and caught the whiff of cooked vegetables. He followed it up the stairs to the next floor. There were seven bedrooms on this floor and Savage got a stronger smell of soup towards the back of the house. He came to two doors at the end of the corridor and got a waft of cooked food coming from underneath one of them. He also got the pungent aroma of strong weed.

Savage knocked on the door.

No answer.

Pot heads don't get up for much, except one thing.

Savage knocked again and said, "Pizza delivery."

CHAPTER 24

T HE DOOR OPENED A CRACK and Savage got hit by a wave of marijuana smoke mingled with shades of the soup he'd just made. A pair of sleepy half-lidded bloodshot eyes started back. Savage pushed the door, and invited himself in, past the guy who had opened the door. He wore a baggy sweatshirt and tracksuit bottoms, and his hair was thick and floppy. The room was large, with an old, battered studded sofa in the middle facing a large, broken flat-screen TV, propped against the wall. All the curtains were closed tightly and a cloud of grey-green spliff smoke hung just below the ceiling. Another guy sat on the sofa with the huge saucepan propped on a low coffee table in front of him. He spooned soup into his mouth in what looked like slow motion.

"Soup's good," said the guy who'd opened the door. "Pizza's way better. Hey, where is the pizza by the way?"

"There is no pizza," said Savage. "I just said that to get you to open the door."

"Want some soup?" said the guy on the sofa. He was similarly dressed to his friend except his greasy hair was parted in the middle.

"I do, actually," said Savage, lifting the heavy saucepan off the table. "I'll just take this, seeing as me and my friend made it."

"Oh, sure, take it, man." the guy on the sofa replied, with no malice whatsoever. "Sharing is good. Hey, wanna smoke?" He bent down and picked up a record sleeve that he was using as a tray. It was covered in weed, rolling papers and bits of torn-up cardboard for making roaches.

Savage wasn't bothered about the drug paraphernalia, it was the record cover that caught his attention. A copy of The Jam's first album, *In The City*. And it was signed.

Savage put the soup down on the floor and pulled the album from the pothead's hands, tipping his weed everywhere.

"Where'd you get this?" asked Savage.

"Oh, a guy who used to live here gave it to us," said the one who'd opened the door.

"What guy?"

"Lived on the top floor," he replied.

"Why'd he give it to you?"

The guy on the sofa started picking up weed off the floor and rolling it into a joint. "Didn't really give it to us, it was more of a trade."

"Trade for what?"

"He asked us to get him something to help him sleep."

"What was it?" Savage asked.

"Nembutal, I think."

Savage tensed. Nembutal was the drug found in Dave's blood stream, the drug that killed him. "You're sure that's what it was?"

"Yeah. He traded it for his record collection. It wasn't enough, so he went and got some cash from somewhere."

"Where'd he get the cash?" Savage asked.

The guy on the sofa shrugged and continued perfecting his rolled-up joint.

Savage examined the album closely, eyeing the black swirly signatures of Paul Weller, Rick Buckler and Bruce Foxton scrawled across the cover. "How come you didn't sell this one?"

"I quite like The Jam," said the guy on the sofa, taking a lighter from the coffee table. He lit the joint and took a long drag, holding it in. His friend sat down next to him and took the joint off him. Putting it to his lips, he inhaled deeply.

"You know that guy upstairs is dead, don't you?" said Savage.

Both men coughed out the smoke they were holding, gagging and choking at the same time. "What?" one of them said in a strangled voice.

"We didn't even notice he was gone," said the other.

"It was in the newspapers," said Savage. "Committed suicide. Know what did it? Overdose of Nembutal."

The two of them suddenly went green with nausea and wide-eyed with fear, eyes even more bloodshot than before. The effects of the marijuana probably not helping their paranoid, drug-addled brains.

"We didn't know, I swear. He said he needed the Nembutal to help him sleep," said one of them. That was probably true. He couldn't imagine Dave would go to these two jokers and tell them he needed the Nembutal so he could kill himself. Even these two dim-witted slackers wouldn't have been tempted to make that deal.

"Did you know he had a son?" asked Savage.

The men shook their head.

"He died too. Also committed suicide. Did it in the same place. That was in the news. Dead Maids Wood." If the men had been afraid before, now they were terrified, paralysed with it. "You didn't have anything to do with it, did you?"

They shook their heads furiously, so much that it looked like they were going to come off. "No way," said the one sitting nearest. "I swear, I swear, I swear. We didn't even know he had a son. Didn't even know he died."

"And you wouldn't know anyone who knows anything about it." Savage had to be careful. This was starting to sound like an interrogation. Not the actions of the grey man.

The one who'd made the joint crossed his heart. "Please, I swear, we're just a couple of stoners. We like getting high and that's about all we're good for..."

"Please, you gotta believe us," the other guy pleaded. "He just said he wanted it to help him sleep."

Savage believed them. They were far too stoned to be lying. And far too stoned to notice anything that was going on in their immediate personal space, let alone the rest of the house and the world outside.

Paranoia now gripped them. "Please don't tell the cops."

"Yeah, please. You can have all our weed and cash. We swear, he just said he wanted to get a good night's sleep. This place ain't the most peaceful. So we got him the Nembutal."

Savage thought for a moment, then said, "It's okay, I don't need your weed or your cash, but I am taking this record."

"Yeah, sure, anything you like, man."

Savage opened the door, tucked the record under his arm and picked up the soup pan with both hands. He turned just before he left. "Tell you what. You don't say anything about this conversation then I won't, okay."

They nodded. "Sure, sure. Anything you say, man."

Savage left the room. He heard the door shut and lock behind him.

A conflict arose in Savage's mind. He would be quite within his rights to go back in there and bash both their heads in with the heavy soup pan he was holding. And he might still do that. They had supplied Dave with the drug that had killed him. It wasn't as simple as that. Dave had wanted to die, that much was clear now. Savage had an inkling that had always been the case, and so had the police and his son Luke. No surprises there. It was a suicide, plain and simple. And someone who wanted to die, whether rightly or wrongly, was going to find a way, whether it was jumping in front of a train or off a tall building. Horrific ways to go. At least with the Nembutal, Dave had slipped away peacefully, like falling asleep. If anyone should be blamed for his death it should be Savage, not the ones that had supplied him the drug. Savage should have been there for Dave, to talk him out of it, to be his friend. Not leave him to die a lonely death, fifty feet up a fir tree. Perhaps Savage should be the one to be punished.

"Now, that's what I'm talking about, Savage," said Jeff Perkins, triumphantly.

Savage felt his whole body shrink.

"You should be punished. I mean that's not an enemy you killed in a war zone, that was your best friend. You weren't there for him. His death is on you. Go back to those potheads and ask them for some Nembutal, and take it yourself."

Savage ignored his jibes and took the soup back down the stairs. He was just about to give it to Dink when he thought of another idea. He knocked on Rosie's door, using his elbow.

"What are we doing here?" asked Jeff.

"Shut up," Savage said. "Just let me do this one thing first."

"What do you want?" came Rosie's voice through the door.

"It's me, John. The guy from the convenience store."

"What do you want?"

"Could you unlock the door, I'm carrying something really heavy." Savage noticed the deadlock was across but it didn't actually reach all the way into the doorframe, stopping a few millimetres short of the metal strike plate.

The door opened slightly. Rosie peered through the gap.

"What's that?" she asked.

"Soup. We made way too much, and I was just wondering if you and Grace would like it, shame for it to go to waste."

"I haven't got anything to give you."

"That's fine. I don't want anything. Look, it's yours if you want it. Made it myself. Just fresh veg and that's it. Very wholesome."

Rosie looked at him as if she was trying to get a look inside his soul, see if he was up to something. Kindness probably didn't happen around here very often. And she seemed like she wasn't sure how to respond.

"Look," said Savage. "There's nothing wrong with it, if that's what you're worried about. You saw us buying the ingredients, it's just vegetables."

After a minute of staring at him she quickly opened the door wide, took the large pot from Savage's hands and quickly slammed the door shut again.

"You're welcome," Savage said to himself.

Dink would be annoyed that Savage had given all their soup away. They could always make some more tomorrow. Besides, a single mum with a growing teenage girl to feed would need it more than they would, especially if all she could afford to buy was milk and bread.

Jeff had become strangely quiet at the sight of Rosie

but on the way back up the stairs, he piped up again. *"She's hiding something."*

"What?"

"I don't know. She has that look."

"What look?"

"The I'm-hiding-something look. You must have realised. Come on, keep up. You're slower than Dink."

"Jeff, everyone's hiding something in this place. That's why I'm here, to find out what happened."

"Nah, this is different. She's hiding something big. A big secret."

"Since when did you get so caring?"

"I couldn't care less. I'm just stating a fact. You mark my words. Didn't you see the pain behind her eyes, like a pair of dams holding back water, deep dark water."

"I thought that was just desperation."

"No, this is different. She's up to something. Something nasty."

CHAPTER 25

BACK IN HIS ROOM, SAVAGE called Tannaz, telling her they needed to meet, and that he'd had a breakthrough, of sorts. Tannaz left her hotel room immediately and picked up Savage in a quiet backstreet well away from Tivoli Gardens and the Thornhill Estate—avoiding any prying eyes.

They drove deep into the New Forest, avoiding the area of Dead Maids, to a pretty little village called Bank, just outside Lyndhurst. The village's one and only pub had a storybook appearance, nestled in the forest with an old, red phone box outside. Inside, it was everything a country pub should be—all low ceilings, exposed wooden beams and a crackling open fire with a red-nosed local propping up the end of the wooden bar. Intimate nooks and crannies were everywhere, perfect for hushed conversations over a pint. Although Tannaz's reaction was anything but intimate when Savage told her about the two drug dealers supplying Dave with the Nembutal.

"We need to give those two a serious beating," she said, taking a massive gulp of her lager.

"Keep your voice down," said Savage.

"Sorry," she replied in a quieter tone. "They killed Dave, there has to be some payback."

"And what would that accomplish?" asked Savage. "Listen, we've always known that Dave's death may have been a genuine suicide, and this confirms it. Beating the crap out of the two people who got him the drug won't change that. I mean, if he'd chosen to hang himself would you go and find the DIY store that sold him the rope, so you could beat up the cashier?"

"Nembutal is different," Tannaz protested. "It's used for suicide."

"Yep, and it's also used for insomnia. That's what Dave said it was for to the potheads."

Tannaz frowned, creases racking up on her brow. "They were naïve. That's like giving a toddler some bleach to clean their hands."

"I know this is frustrating, but we can't change the fact that Dave wanted to kill himself."

"How do you know someone didn't drive him to it?"

She had a point.

Tannaz continued, "We have the 'how', we still don't know the 'why'."

"Listen," said Savage. "I don't think there's anything suspicious about Dave's suicide. His personality, sad though I am to say it, fits the profile. What doesn't is his son, Luke. His death is still a mystery. That's what we should be concentrating on."

Tannaz thought for a moment. "Okay, but I think we should still keep an open mind about Dave. We still haven't got the whole picture."

Savage took a sip of beer. "Agreed. Any luck with the numbers found in Dave's pocket?"

"Nothing. I've put them through number-sequence software, analytical software and nothing's showing up. I've put them through prediction modelling, and serial-number search tools. Nothing's coming back. I'm stumped."

"Okay, let's keep trying, something's bound to give sooner or later."

"How's it going at Tivoli Gardens, anything emerging? Hear anything about the weird games Wellington likes to play?"

"Nothing yet. Apparently, people do disappear for a day or two, sometimes more, especially this guy Archie who's opposite me. Goes off for days now and then. Last time he came back with an Elastoplast on his head."

"Sounds dodgy."

"Said it was a drink-related injury, which could be true. I get this feeling that it could be Chinese whispers, little more than people doing cash-in-hand work for Wellington, which is why no one talks about it. It could be nothing more than people doing work on the side."

Tannaz took another large gulp of beer. "Have you questioned anyone directly, asked what's going on?"

"Too risky. I've already sailed a bit close to the wind. Need to lay low and let it happen organically."

"That could take weeks and months."

"True, but if I force it, people will clam up or worse I'll blow my cover. I think if I haven't got anywhere in a month's time I might spread the word that I need some work, see if I can get a peek behind the wizard's curtain that way."

"How will you do that?"

Savage kept his voice low. "There are a couple of goons, Vlad and Truck. Really nasty cases who look after Wellington's properties on this side of Southampton. They exploit the residents, skimming their benefits or demanding payments in booze. I think I could try and get some work out of them, although I'll probably have to pay them a percentage of it. How about you? Found anything on Wellington?"

"Nothing," Tannaz replied, retrieving her laptop from her bag and placing it on the table. "I think we got lucky with his bank account and spotting the payment to the blacksmith for the cages. That seems to be the one and only time he got sloppy. However…"

"I like howevers," said Savage.

"… His son Ben is a different matter. I wouldn't say I've found any clues or anything like that, but there's something strange going on between him and his father."

"How do you mean?" asked Savage.

Tannaz pointed to the screen and spoke quietly. "This is his bank account. Guess how much he gets paid for running his dad's property empire?"

"No idea."

"As far as I can see, twenty-eight grand."

"A year?"

Tannaz nodded.

"Is that all?"

She opened another window and typed away. "It's peanuts for such a big job. So that got me curious about other aspects of Ben Wellington's life. Check this out. He doesn't own his own house either, can't afford to. Him and his wife and their two daughters live in one of his dad's properties, a tiny two-bedroomed place in Millbrook in a road where you really wouldn't want to bring up kids, and his dad makes them pay rent. His wife works as a teaching assistant. They're skint, basically. Ben Wellington is chauffeured around in a posh Bentley Continental, but it's not his. It's owned and paid for by the company. Wellington's goons come and pick him up each day. Ferry him around."

"How strange," Savage remarked.

"Weird, right? I mean, his dad's a multi-millionaire and his son lives like a pauper, even though he's running this vast business for him."

Savage rubbed his unshaven chin, thoughtfully. "There must be some reason. I mean, why would you do such a responsible job when it pays so little? Family obviously means nothing to Simon Wellington, he's treating his son like a regular employee; worse in fact. You'd never get anyone to do that job for such low wages."

Just then something caught Savage's eye on the screen showing Ben Wellington's bank account. A monthly outgoing.

"That name sounds familiar."

"Which one?" asked Tannaz.

Savage pointed to the screen "There. A payment for the Lupin Care Group, I recognise the name from somewhere. Could you Google it?"

Tannaz opened another window, typed in a search and up popped a web page full of bright images showing happy elderly faces in a selection of care homes, one of which was Heatherlands Nursing Home.

"See, that's a bit odd. That's where Jenny Hopkins stays," said Savage. "The lady we visited who thinks Simon Wellington killed her daughter."

"Coincidence, maybe one of his relatives is staying there."

Savage shook his head. "Ben Wellington's mother died years ago and he has no aunts or uncles."

"Maybe on his wife's side?"

"I've got an idea, give them a ring and ask."

Tannaz sat back in her chair and took another sip of beer. "They're not going to give us that information, it'll be confidential."

"They will if they think we want to give them more money. Might be time to reprise your role as Vicky from Wellington Properties. Tell them you're Ben's secretary and he's asked you to enquire about moving his relative to a bigger room and would be happy to increase the monthly payments. They'll be all ears. Just claim ignorance when they ask who the relative is."

Tannaz got on the phone and put on her best Vicky telephone voice, all over-friendly and insincere. Savage moved closer so he could hear the conversation.

"Hello, Heatherlands Nursing Home. How can I help you?"

"Oh, hi. Yes, I'm calling on behalf of my boss, Ben Wellington. He currently contributes to the care of an elderly relative. He's asked me to enquire about the possibility of getting a bigger room for..." Tannaz left a big, awkward pause.

"Hello, are you still there?" said the woman at the other end of the line.

"Yes, I am so sorry. This is very embarrassing. He hasn't given me the name of his relative. I feel so stupid."

"That's okay, I can find out from the system. What did you say the name was again?"

"Ben Wellington."

"Ah, yes here it is. Oh..." The woman's voice dropped. "It's Jenny Hopkins."

"Oh, that's right. Jenny Hopkins. I'm such a dimwit." Tannaz looked at Savage and nodded her head positively.

"That's quite alright," the woman replied. "But I'm afraid it won't be possible to move Jenny to a bigger room."

"Why's that?" asked Tannaz.

"I'm very sorry to say, Jenny passed away last month."

Tannaz nearly dropped the phone. Savage felt all the blood leave his head.

"Miss, miss. Are you still there?" the woman asked.

Tannaz managed to regain a modicum of self-control. "Yes, yes. I'm here. Just shocked is all. I didn't know."

"We have notified Ben Wellington. And we will be refunding the payment that has gone out of his account this month."

"Oh, okay. I must have got my wires crossed. I feel so embarrassed."

"That's okay," said the woman. "Things like this often happen when someone passes. It can be a confusing time for everyone."

"Would you mind not mentioning this phone call to Ben? He's my boss and I feel rather silly not knowing that Jenny had passed away."

"That's quite alright, dear. Won't say a word."

Savage nudged Tannaz and mouthed some words to her, she lipread them and relayed the question to the woman on the phone. "Just one more thing," Tannaz asked. "How did Jenny die?"

"She tripped and fell."

"And when was this?"

"It happened in her room during the night of March twelfth. A nurse came in the next morning and found her on the floor. Terrible tragedy."

"Which nurse found her?"

"Maria Garcia."

Tannaz hung up, then swore. Her face went white. "Jenny died on March twelfth. Two days after we visited her. Someone killed Jenny after we questioned her. I think I'm going to be sick."

"Hold it together, Tannaz."

"That's easy for you to say. You're used to war and people dying around you."

"I am, and it never gets any easier. We can't do anything to help Jenny, but we can make the scumbags who did this pay."

"But we're responsible."

"Could be a coincidence."

Tannaz drained her pint and slammed the empty glass on the

table. "Oh, come on, Savage. First, Luke, then Jenny. Two people have died after we've talked to them."

"There could be another explanation. That nurse Maria Garcia said Jenny had been telling everyone how Simon Wellington killed her daughter. Knowing what Simon Wellington is like, I think her days were numbered. He's not the kind of gangster that leaves someone like that bad mouthing him to all and sundry, even if she did have dementia. Could just be that we showed up at the wrong time."

"Maybe," she said. "I think it's more likely we set the wheels in motion."

Savage sat back in his chair, locked his hands behind his head and breathed deeply. "You're right. Wellington probably had that place under surveillance. Ben Wellington was not only visiting her, he was paying towards her keep, possibly under the instructions of his father so he could keep an eye on her. He had free and easy access to her. His name was all over the visitors' book. Plus, there's the nurse, Maria Garcia."

"You think she's involved?"

"There's a strong possibility. Especially if she was the first person to find Jenny after she died. She might be on the Wellington payroll."

"If that's true, she could have gone straight to Wellington after we visited Jenny."

"Yep."

"And that could've kick-started his plan to silence her."

They both fell silent, contemplating the fact that by investigating one death they could've been instrumental in another.

Savage broke the silence first. "If Maria Garcia is involved, we could get answers out of her."

"How so?" Tannaz looked longingly at her empty glass.

Savage was a slow drinker. He poured some of his beer into her glass. "Her accent. She lied about where she was from, remember? If she's here illegally, we could use that as a bargaining chip. Get her to talk or threaten her with deportation."

Tannaz took a sip of beer. "Won't she go straight to Wellington, I mean, if she is involved in all this?"

"Not if we lay the threat of deportation on thick. She'll do whatever we ask, including buying her silence."

Tannaz began typing rapidly. "Okay, Maria Garcia. Let's see where you're really from."

CHAPTER 26

MARIA GARCIA STEPPED OFF THE bus and slung her bag over her shoulder, checked the road both ways and crossed Shirley High Street. She made it safely across the busy road, dodging between two badly parked cars on the other side. As she strode along the pavement, a Tesco bag swung idly by her side, scuffing against her nurse uniform she wore beneath a bland winter waterproof. Flipping up her hood, she clutched the front of her jacket tightly, hunkering down against the cold, clearly not liking the damp weather.

She was unaware she was being followed, walking home as she did every night. Tannaz tailed her on the opposite side of the road, hanging back several yards, keeping a diagonal view of Maria. It was one of the many tricks Savage had taught her, although it wasn't really necessary. Tonight, Shirley High Street was so congested with foot and car traffic that any amateur could have pulled it off. Still, she stuck with Savage's advice, following Maria at a safe distance across the road from her.

At one point, Maria Garcia stopped to look in a shop window. Tannaz just kept walking so she didn't arouse suspicion, until she found a suitable van parked up on the kerb which she stopped behind, using it to hide her presence. Tannaz sidled along the van's length, stopping just shy of its tailgate. She pulled out her phone, pretending to check her messages. From this angle, Maria would have no idea Tannaz was behind the van. Eventually, Maria lost interest in the window and resumed her walk home. Tannaz continued the pursuit.

A minute later, Maria Garcia stopped at a front door

sandwiched between a butcher's and a shop that repaired mobile phones. Tannaz sped up, increasing her pace like someone hurrying to catch a bus but not fast enough to count as a run. She crossed the road. Her timing couldn't have been more perfect. Maria Garcia pushed her key in the lock and opened the door ajar just as Tannaz passed, making it look like a chance meeting.

"Oh, hi, Maria," Tannaz said cheerfully.

Maria turned, flipping her hood down. Eyes narrowed, she scanned Tannaz's face. For a second, Tannaz thought she would feign ignorance. With her distinctive glossy black curly hair shaved mercilessly up the side and her voluptuous red lips, Tannaz was hard to forget.

"Oh, hi," Maria said weakly.

"How are you?" asked Tannaz.

Maria stared back awkwardly. "I am good. Oh, well, I better go, have dinner to make." She gestured to the shopping bag in her hand, then tried to step into her flat. Tannaz blocked her path, standing with her back to the doorway.

"Aren't you going to offer your condolences?" asked Tannaz.

Maria took a second or two to process the question. A veil of guilt passed over her face.

"Sorry?" Maria replied. "I do not know this word."

Tannaz didn't believe her but played along.

"Your condolences, you know, when someone dies. It's to say sorry, offer sympathy."

"Oh, yes. You mean Jenny. I'm sorry, I thought you had only met her once."

"Yes, that's true," said Tannaz. "But it's always upsetting when someone dies for no apparent reason."

"What do you mean?"

"I think you know."

Maria's mouth formed a hard, straight line. "Listen," she said. "I have to go. Please move out of the way."

Tannaz stood her ground. "Tell me who Sylvia Sanchez is?"

Rage flared in Maria's eyes. "I do not know who you're talking about."

"Sure you do."

"No, I don't." Maria shoved Tannaz hard in the chest, catching her off guard. Tannaz tripped over the threshold of the open door, falling backwards into a dimly lit, narrow hallway. Several bikes leant against the wall and unopened mail was scattered over the floor. Tannaz tried to get to her feet, but Maria flung the whole bag of shopping at her, hitting her square in the face. The blow bought Maria a precious second or two. She fiddled with the quick release mechanism on the frame of the nearest bike. Slid the saddle and seat post out—a firm uncomfortable racing-bike saddle—and held it high in the air. A nasty, improvised club.

Tannaz pushed her palms down hard on the floor and leapt to her feet.

Maria got ready to strike.

Tannaz's training kicked in. Savage had taught her that the most lethal part of a striking weapon was the end. It had the most velocity and therefore, the most force. The seat post was no different. Tannaz had to close the gap, minimise the distance and by doing so, the effectiveness of the weapon. Even if she got hit, the closer she was, the less it would hurt. Tannaz lunged at Maria Garcia, getting into her personal space, while bringing both arms up at an angle to protect her head. Maria swung the seat post down hard. It slid harmlessly along Tannaz's angled left forearm. Simultaneously, Tannaz rammed the heel of her right hand upwards underneath Maria Garcia's chin. Then she curled her left arm around Maria's right, the one that held the seat, tangling it up so she couldn't swing another blow. With her free right hand, Tannaz reached across and gripped the makeshift weapon, twisted her whole body round until Maria Garcia had no choice but to let go, or dislocate her shoulder.

Maria Garcia crumpled to the floor, Tannaz stood over her holding the seat post, ready to strike. Maria scooched backwards on her hands until she reached the bottom of the stairs. She fumbled with a cheap mobile phone. Big clumsy buttons and hardly any screen with a burgundy casing. It looked like a relic from the last century, probably a burner.

"Calling the police?" asked Tannaz.

Maria Garcia ignored her and thumbed the phone clumsily.

"Make sure you give them your proper name, Sylvia Sanchez."

Maria, or Sylvia as she was properly known, stopped and fixed Tannaz with a pair of terrified eyes. Sylvia was tough, and hadn't shown any fear while they were fighting. Angry and enraged, yes, but not frightened.

Now she was.

"Who are you?" she asked.

"Someone who can keep secrets," said Tannaz. "Secrets like, let's see, a Venezuelan nurse who's here illegally, pretending to be from Madrid but who can't do a Madrid accent but thinks no one will notice. And is using the false name of Maria Garcia, which is a dead giveaway because it's the most common female name in Spain, nice and bland. Bit like calling yourself Sarah Smith over here. Oh and who's also being paid on the side by Ben Wellington to keep an eye on Jenny Hopkins, and maybe had a hand in killing her."

Sylvia rapidly shook her head. "I didn't kill her, I swear on the Holy Mother."

"I'm Muslim, well ex-Muslim, so I couldn't care less about the Holy Mother."

Sylvia got to her feet. Tannaz raised the seat post higher. "Stay where you are, or I'll wrap this around your head. Then I'll call immigration and get you out of this country faster than you can say deportation order."

Sylvia laced her finger together and begged. "Please, please. I'll tell you anything, anything. Just don't get me deported, my family relies on the money I send."

Tannaz lowered the seat post. "Start from the beginning."

Sylvia's shoulders slumped and she lowered herself onto the bottom step of the stairs. "I was living in Swaythling."

"Where's that?"

"North Southampton, near the airport. I was in an HMO. Terrible place, terrible people."

"One of Wellington's places?"

"No, but just as bad. The landlord turned a blind eye to illegal immigrants, so it was all I could get. Then one day, one of Wellington's men approached me, said did I want to get out of there, live in a nice apartment. I thought he wanted me to be a prostitute. The man said no, all I had to do was work in a nursing home and keep an eye on an old lady, Jenny Hopkins."

"And you jumped at the chance."

"Of course. I'm a trained nurse in Venezuela but the only work I could do here were jobs where they ask no questions or want no work visas—picking fruit and cleaning. One of Wellington's men gave me paperwork and a fake passport, new name. Told me to apply for the job at Heatherlands. I had an interview, started working almost immediately. Meant I could rent this flat."

"Is this one of Wellington's properties?"

"No, I rent this myself from the money I earn at the nursing home. It's not much, just a bed and a room, but I have a nice job and no one bothers me."

"Apart from Wellington." Tannaz thought for a moment. "So when he said keep an eye on Jenny, what did he mean?"

"It wasn't Wellington, it was one of his men."

"Do you have a name? What did he look like?"

Sylvia shook her head. "Met him once, when he gave me this phone." She held up her mobile. "After that we would only speak on the phone."

"How long ago was that?"

"Two years ago."

"Is the phone registered in his name or yours?"

"Is disposable phone."

"A burner?"

"Yes."

"And you can't remember what he looked like?"

"Big, white, mean looking. Shaved head." Sylvia pointed to her ear. "He had a headset thing..."

"A Bluetooth."

Sylvia nodded. Could be a million guys in Southampton, Tannaz thought. "What's the number he calls you from?"

"Is withheld."

"And what did he ask you to do?"

Sylvia shifted uncomfortably. "I had to tell them things Jenny said, things she spoke about and if anyone believed her. Make sure people knew she had dementia, tell them it was all nonsense. Every Friday he'd call and I'd tell him what I'd seen during the week, and all the things she talked about. And I also had to tell him about any visitors."

"Like us you mean?" asked Tannaz.

"Yes, but I never got to tell him. Jenny died on a Wednesday and after that I got no more Friday calls from him. I guess there was no point."

"So Wellington never knew about our visit."

"No, but he did know about her one and only visitor, his son, Ben Wellington."

"Ben Wellington was the only person who visited Jenny?" Tannaz asked.

"Yes, she had no family left. They became very friendly, as far as someone with dementia can."

"Why would Wellington's son become friends with a woman his father did magic shows with years ago. To keep an eye on her?"

"I don't think so. He already had me to do that. Simon Wellington, he is a business man. He wouldn't pay for two people to do the same job."

Tannaz fitted the seat back into the bike and turned to ask, "So why would Ben visit her so much, and help pay her fees?"

Sylvia looked blank. "No idea. I think he genuinely cared for her. You can tell the people who visit because they think they have to and the ones who visit because they want to. He definitely wanted to be there."

"So his father wasn't aware Ben was visiting her until you started working there?"

"That's correct."

"And Ben didn't know his father was keeping tabs on his meetings with Jenny."

"I don't think so."

Tannaz cleared her throat. "Was Jenny murdered? Actually, I'll rephrase the question, why was Jenny murdered?"

Sylvia's big brown eyes pleaded with Tannaz. "Please don't ask me that," she gasped.

"I have to. I swear this conversation stays between us. I won't tell a soul."

Sylvia clasped her hands again. "This man, Simon Wellington, he will kill me."

"I know, that's why I won't tell him. You have my word."

Sylvia swallowed hard and took a deep, tense breath. "The day after you visited Jenny, someone called me on this phone and told me not to go near her room between the hours of one and four in the morning. I was to go in and check on her like I regularly do at seven o'clock, just before breakfast."

"And that's when you found her dead."

"Yes."

"Someone had come in the night and killed her?"

Sylvia nodded, tears falling from eyes. "Her neck was broken."

"Nobody got suspicious?"

"Many elderly people break their necks when they fall. Happens all the time."

"And do you think Simon Wellington killed her because of the things she was saying about him killing her daughter?"

She continued to nod, wiping her eyes with the heels of her hands. "At first, she never mentioned him. Then maybe once or twice, but more and more she spoke of him, and what he did. In the week before you came, she became obsessed, talked about it almost non-stop. Ranted about it to whoever would listen. I tried to calm her, keep her quiet, because I knew what would happen. Simon Wellington would shut her up." Fresh tears spilled from Sylvia's eyes.

Tannaz sat beside Sylvia on the stairs and took her by the hand. "You didn't kill her, Sylvia. That evil bastard Wellington did."

"I told him about Jenny and her outbursts."

"You had no choice."

"I could have refused. Told him I didn't want his job. Or said nothing."

"Well, then it could very well be you lying dead at the end of your bed. Thing is, Sylvia, we think Simon Wellington killed some of our friends too. And we want to make sure he doesn't do it again."

"Who did he kill?"

"Have you heard of someone called Dave Mosely?"

Sylvia shook her head.

"Luke Mosely?"

Sylvia shook her head.

Tannaz said, "We need information. We just haven't got enough to figure out what he's up to, or to prove what he's done. Do you know anything about Simon Wellington that could help us?"

Sylvia looked at the floor, clearly reluctant to answer.

"You have my word none of this will get back to him, and we won't tell the police. I swear on the Holy Mother and everything else you believe in."

Sylvia gulped back a mouthful of air and let it out slowly. "He gets people to do things for him."

"What sort of things? Things like you're doing?"

"No, I'm lucky. I've heard sometimes he forces people to do horrible things."

"What sort of things?"

"Nasty things."

"I've heard this too. I can't seem to find out what it is or why. No one talks about it."

"That's because, like me, everyone has something to lose. Like his tenants. He could make them homeless."

"Section twenty-one."

Sylvia nodded. "Yes, section twenty-one. He uses it like a weapon. They can be out, like that." She snapped her fingers. "Losing your home, no matter how bad, people will do anything to have a home, anything. Fear of living on the street, good way to keep people quiet. And even if they did say something, no one would believe them."

Tannaz smiled as reassuringly as she could, then got up to leave. "Don't worry, Sylvia. We're on your side." Tannaz held up her phone screen, showing her number. "Send me a text, then we'll have each other's numbers. You can call me if you need help or remember anything else."

Sylvia tensed up, reluctance written all over her face.

"Come on, Sylvia, you don't have many allies in this. All I'm asking for is your number, so I can contact you. Where's the harm in that? And you can call me if you need anything, or if you're worried about something."

Sylvia fidgeted, then punched Tannaz's number into her phone and sent her a text.

Tannaz's phoned pinged as the text arrived. She smiled and turned to go.

"One more thing," said Sylvia. "Simon Wellington's son, Ben. He is nothing like his father."

"Thanks, Sylvia. And if you need anything, anything at all, you call me, okay?"

Sylvia nodded. Tannaz closed the door and stepped onto the street.

Now she had Sylvia's number she could hack her phone and find out exactly who'd been calling her every Friday, and possibly the person whom Wellington had ordered to murder Jenny Hopkins.

If they could get to him, they could get to Wellington.

CHAPTER 27

T ANNAZ SAT ACROSS FROM SAVAGE in the same retro tearoom in Southampton—the place they'd drunk tea with Luke when he was still alive.

Buttery smooth big-band sounds of Glen Miller filled the bunting-strewn air. A waitress in a red wraparound dress and hair like Lana Turner, smiled and plonked a large, blue teapot in front of them. If it wasn't for the nose ring and tattoos, she'd have looked like she'd stepped straight out of the Blitz.

Tannaz rapidly relayed everything Sylvia Sanchez had said, almost word for word.

"Okay," said Savage. "So Simon Wellington had Jenny killed because of what she was saying, not because we showed up asking questions."

"Yes," replied Tannaz. "Sylvia said she had become more obsessed, ranting about Simon Wellington killing her daughter before we even visited her."

Savage poured steaming tea into his cup. "So if Wellington had Sylvia to keep tabs on Jenny, why was Ben Wellington seeing her regularly and contributing to her keep? He hasn't even got enough money for his own family."

Tannaz took a sip of black coffee. "Maybe Wellington was being thorough. Ben befriends her, gets her to open up to him, while Sylvia's there to keep an eye on her day-to-day."

Savage poured in the milk and gave his tea a stir, gazing into the swirling liquid as if the answer lay there. "Like Sylvia said, Wellington would be doubling up, two people doing the same job.

And if it was true, why would Jenny open up to the son of a man who killed her daughter?"

"Maybe she didn't know who he was."

Tannaz looked out the steamed-up window, an industrial hazard in a place where tea is served all day. She turned back to Savage and said, "Well, one good thing we've learnt, we're still under the radar as far as Simon Wellington is concerned. Sylvia never got to file the report about us sniffing around the nursing home."

"She could still say something to Simon Wellington. Rat us out."

Tannaz shook her head. "No way, she's too frightened of being deported. She won't say anything."

"Where did Sylvia's mobile phone lead you?"

"I hacked it and found the withheld number that called her every Friday, belongs to a guy goes by the name of Bluetooth, real name Kieran Preston, shaved head, always has a headset plugged into his ear. Now this guy is definitely on the payroll for Wellington. Guy never leaves his side, drives him around, kind of bodyguard slash personal assistant."

"Any pictures, background on him?"

"None. So I'm guessing Kieran Preston isn't his real name." Tannaz drained her black coffee. "So what do we do next?"

"Stick with the plan. Wait and see."

Tannaz put her cup down a little too hard, making the cutlery on the table jump. "Surely we have enough to go to the police now. We have Sylvia Sanchez. She was tipped off about Jenny's murder. Told to stay away from her room. We have Bluetooth, we can prove there's a connection between him and Sylvia. We have Ben Wellington paying for Jenny's nursing home and his visits. There's plenty of evidence. More than enough."

"It's not good enough, and it won't work."

Frustration flicked across Tannaz's face. "Why the hell not? We could put Wellington away with all that."

"Firstly, Sylvia won't testify because she's here illegally and you said it yourself, like everyone we meet, she's terrified of Simon

Wellington. Secondly, she knew something was going down with Jenny's murder, she got a tip off and she did nothing, she'd be incriminating herself, involving herself in the plot to kill Jenny. That's if the police believe there was a plot and it's not just an old lady tripping and breaking her neck in the night. Thirdly, this won't lead to Wellington being convicted. If they do prove it was murder, he'll have ring-fenced himself from all this. Wellington will have one of his low-level minions set up to take the fall."

"What about Sylvia's phone? The call records can be traced back to Wellington."

"Did Wellington give her that phone?"

"No, it was Bluetooth."

"And I'm guessing it's a burner."

"Correct."

"Then there's no connection to Wellington."

Tannaz picked up a teaspoon and gripped it hard. "We know that's a load of crap. It's obvious he was keeping tabs on Jenny to see if anyone was believing her story about him killing her daughter."

"Sure, we know that. Can we prove it? There's a motive, sure, but Wellington's smart. There are too many holes for Wellington to wriggle through."

"Like what?"

"Like his son, Ben. He's the one who visited Jenny every week, contributed to her nursing bills. Hell, knowing what Wellington's like he might even set up his own son to take the fall. Throw him under the bus if this thing comes back on him. Then there's Bluetooth, he's the one who was in contact with Sylvia, not Wellington. Remember, Wellington is a multi-millionaire, he'll have a team of elite lawyers coming up with far better arguments than this. So far he's kept his hands clean. He'll get off. I've seen it before. The chances of nailing him are slim, and that all depends on Sylvia Sanchez giving evidence, which is highly unlikely."

"Lots of people at that nursing home must have heard Jenny accusing Wellington of murder."

"They heard someone with dementia ranting about a man who killed their daughter. It's not strong enough."

They both fell silent.

Tannaz spoke, quietly with an edge of disappointment. "So what do we do?"

"Same as we've been doing. We watch and wait, gather more intel until we have enough to nail Wellington. My gut is telling me this is just the tip of the iceberg. The more we have on this guy, the more we can make it stick. If we jump the gun now, all we'll do is alert Wellington that we're on to him. What we've got at the moment is flimsy at best. Once he knows we're asking questions, it'll disappear altogether."

Tannaz slumped down in her chair, all the air leaving her lungs in one almighty sigh. "And if that fails?"

"Plan B."

"What's Plan B?"

"We take matters into our own hands."

Tannaz sat upright, more interested. "I think I prefer the sound of that. Can't we do that now?"

"Not until we know more. And Plan B is a last resort, if all else fails. We need to know everything about Wellington if we're going to outsmart him. That's the way of the SAS. Ninety-nine percent surveillance. One percent action. Minimise risk. Maximise success." Savage took a long slug of tea, gulped it down in one go. "One other thing."

"What?" asked Tannaz.

"You said that Sylvia Sanchez mentioned that Ben Wellington is nothing like his father."

"That's right."

"Do you think you'd be able to hack Simon Wellington's solicitors, get a peek at his will?"

"I'm pretty sure I could. Most wills are stored digitally these days as well as hard copy. Why do you want to see his will?"

"Might be something. Might be nothing."

CHAPTER 28

TANNAZ DROPPED OFF SAVAGE IN Northam, an industrial area near to St Mary's football stadium on the banks of the River Itchen. From there he crossed the Itchen Bridge, a slender concrete structure reaching over a mucky industrial stretch of water. In the distance he could see Fawley oil refinery, rising up like some futuristic city with the New Forest behind it.

The tide was out and even though the temperature was only a few degrees above freezing, the exposed foreshore sent a stench of effluent and rotting weeds to his olfactory nerves. As he got half way across the bridge he saw two hardy souls rowing into the wind, their sleek rowing boat doing its best to cut through the chop. The sight of the two rowers, a sport associated with private education, dreaming spires and prestigious universities, seemed at odds with the factories along the banks of the river. The area was a warren of rundown units nudging up against the filthy water to make the most of the cheap land. Their days were numbered, though. In the distance he could see cranes where the low-rent commercial properties were being swallowed up and transformed into luxury high-rise waterfront flats. Most of them probably being bought as an investment and left empty. Ironic, seeing that where he was going, people were living in HMOs packed into buildings that should've been condemned long ago.

A short walk into the cold, biting breeze and he was back in Thornhill. As he opened the front door to Tivoli Gardens, giving it a shove with his shoulder, he noticed Rosie standing in the doorway to her bedroom. She held a butter knife in her hand, attempting to use the tip as a makeshift screwdriver, attacking the screws that attached the flat metal strike plate to the doorjamb. The butter knife slipped out of her hands and Rosie swore. She stood upright, wiped her brow which was glistening with sweat even though the hallway of Tivoli Gardens held a chill. Her reddened face looked irritable and angry.

Without thinking, Savage asked, "Need a hand?" He instantly wished he hadn't because he already knew how she would answer.

Scooping up the knife from the floor, Rosie stabbed at the screws of the strike plate, trying desperately to make the blunt end find purchase on the countersunk screwheads. "Nope. I'm fine," she said abruptly, as the knife slipped out again. "Damn it!" she shouted.

"What are you trying to do?" asked Savage. "Maybe I can help."

Once more she snatched up the knife and held it threateningly, pointing outward in Savage's direction. "I said I don't need your help. I'm quite capable of doing it myself."

"Okay, fair enough," said Savage. "Whatever you're trying to do might be easier with a proper screwdriver."

"Do you have one?"

"No, but..."

"Well, you're no help. Please leave me alone now." Rosie went back to trying and failing to loosen the screws in the doorframe.

Defeated, Savage turned and climbed the stairs.

"That went well," said Jeff.

In his head, Savage told him to shut up and continued his ascent.

"Definitely hiding something, that Rosie. I'd say several things. So defensive. Didn't you see the desperation in her eyes? Like she wanted you to help but didn't at the same time. Didn't want to be in the debt of a man like you. That's understandable. I mean look at you. Such a loser. She's got you bang to rights. Poor woman is surrounded by dodgy blokes. Damaged goods. Psychos, weirdos and addicts. Bet she's scared stiff, day and night, especially with that pretty daughter of hers and all these men thinking dirty thoughts about what they'd like to do to her."

"Shut up, Jeff," Savage said.

"I will shut up. But you know it's true. I bet you've had those same thoughts."

"That's enough, Jeff! You know, sometimes I wish you were a real person."

"Why's that?"

"So I could punch you in the head until you're unconscious and dump you in that stinking river we've just crossed."

"Once a psycho, always a psycho," Jeff said triumphantly. *"You fit right in here, don't you?"*

Savage ignored him. By the time he reached the uppermost landing, Jeff had thankfully lost interest in goading him. The voice in his head fell silent and Savage breathed a sigh of relief. He pushed his key in the lock, gave it a turn and entered his tiny bedroom.

The Jam album was still lying on the bed where he left it. He swooped it up in his hands and brushed off the tiny crumbs of hash and bits of weed. Sacrilegious to use such a classic album for nothing better than rolling joints.

Savage examined the sleeve. The iconic shot of the three members of The Jam standing below the band name, graffitied on white tiles above, their faces so young, so familiar to Savage. He slid the record out of its sleeve, his fingertips holding it gently by its edges. Lifting it up to the light he expected it to be scratched or warped. Surprisingly, the pressing was still pristine. The tight black circular grooves glistened in the dull light. Something magical about vinyl. He sniffed its surface. The aroma of black plastic instantly transported him back to his teenage bedroom. The excitement of buying a new album. Slotting it onto a turntable and hearing the thump of the needle as it dropped onto the record, then the delicious crackle as it found the groove. The anticipation of waiting for the first song to start. It was a ritual, like making tea, it couldn't be hurried, and only heightened the senses.

Endless evenings spent playing albums over and over again, until he knew every chord and key change off by heart. Studying the sleeve artwork with religious adoration. The wave of nostalgia overwhelmed him. Savage only wished he had a record player to put it on. Of course, he could have used his phone to go on the Internet and download the album. But it wouldn't be the same.

For the next few days, Savage hung around Tivoli Gardens, being like all the other tenants. Doing nothing, apart from existing. Although strictly speaking, he was working. In between trying to make sense of the numbers he'd found in Dave Mosely's Harrington and making soup with Dink, he observed the comings and goings of the inhabitants of Tivoli Gardens. The people that everyone else would rather brush under the carpet and forget about, all except Simon Wellington, who had found a use for them. A sadistic use if the rumours were to be believed. Whatever use it was didn't materialise in those days. Of course, the house was a hotbed of unsociability; arguments broke out, things got broken never to be repaired, music got played too loud, and Truck and Vlad came round demanding money and booze off people who didn't really have it to give. Just business as usual at Tivoli Gardens.

A note slid under the door.

A handwritten note from Archie, which read.

Wanna whiskey?

Savage folded up the note, stuffed it in his back pocket. Yes, he would like a whisky, thank you very much. He opened the door. Archie stood there grinning, bottle in hand, two plastic cups in the other. The sticking plaster was still attached to his forehead.

"Come on in," said Savage.

Archie immediately noticed the album on the bed. "Hey, guy who used to live here had an album just like that." Archie poured a drink and shoved it in Savage's hand.

Savage thought quickly. Could be a chance to find out some information about Dave, if he was careful.

"Really? What, the guy who lived here was into The Jam?"

"Oh yeah. Had loads of records and that. All lined up on the floor. He had all The Jam stuff."

"Oh, wow. That's my favourite band. Shame I don't have a record player to put it on."

"Yeah, Dave had a record player," Archie said, picking up the album and examining the album sleeve. That was the thing about vinyl record albums, they were compelling objects, creating an irresistible urge to pick them up and scrutinise them.

"Did that annoy you, him playing his music all the time?" Savage asked.

Archie waved away the remark. "Nah, Dave was a quiet sort, considerate type. Used to use his earphones and that."

Savage thought it was safe to push it, ask a few questions without raising any eyebrows. "Those guys, Truck and Vlad, you know they said he'd killed himself. Is that true or were they just trying to put the frighteners on me?"

Archie's default cheerful face darkened. He took a long slug of whisky. "True, I'm sorry to say."

"That's horrible, poor guy. I wonder what drove him to it?"

Archie exhaled heavily. Savage got a waft of alcoholic breath over him. "Who knows what's going on in a person's mind?" Archie said.

"Guess it must have been a shock when you heard he'd killed himself."

"Not really. I know that's not a nice thing to say, he seemed the type. Quiet. Bland sort of guy. Whenever I tried to talk to him he always seemed awkward. You know, like he was wearing them smart trousers your parents would make you wear when you were little that would itch like asbestos. Always looked uncomfortable. Like I said, I wasn't surprised. People end up here 'cos they're on the skids. It's no surprise. People die in Simon Wellington properties all the time. Course, it's mostly unintended, you know, OD-ing and that. Not trekking half way across the New Forest to kill yourself up a tree."

"Someone told me his son had died in the same place."

"Terrible tragedy. Like father, like son. I guess it runs in the family."

A silence grew between them. Not an awkward one, more respectful.

"Can I ask you something, Archie?"

"Sure, go ahead."

Savage had to take care with his line of questioning. Had to couch it in the right way so it seemed like he wasn't prying. "This is purely out of self-preservation and fear I suppose…"

"Go on, spit it out."

Savage paused and then said, "Nobody here had anything to do with it, did they? I mean, are there any nutcases living here?"

Archie laughed. "We're all nutcases and that. And yes there are people who you should be careful around, especially Truck. Bit of advice, always look interested when he talks about his time on *Gladiators*. He likes to talk about it."

"I hadn't noticed," said Savage. They both grinned.

"To answer your question, did anyone in this building kill Dave? I'd say no to that. I think it's just a case of a guy at the end of his tether, hit rock bottom and couldn't come back up. Only way out for him was to end it all. I mean, I've thought about it once or twice."

"What, suicide?"

"Yeah, never had the balls to go through with it. Not like poor old Dave. We all have our cross to bear."

"What's your cross, Archie?" asked Savage.

Archie went quiet, chewed his bottom lip.

Savage held his hands up. "Oh, Archie, it's okay, if you don't want to talk about it."

"No, it's fine. Reason I drink," he said, taking another slug of whisky. "I was happy once. Very happy. Had a wife, a job. Not a great one, cleaning the trains. Enough to keep a roof over me family's head."

"You had a family?"

"Yeah, a little girl. Prettiest thing you've ever seen. Made me the happiest man in the land. Then one day I persuades the wife to go out with her friends and that. She hadn't been out since we'd had Lily—that was my little girl's name. She was two and my wife never wanted to leave her side. So I tells my wife to have a night out, see your friends and that. She didn't want to. I think she needed it. I told her not to worry. I'll feed and put Lily to bed. So she goes out and when I'm sure Lily's asleep in her cot, I run myself a hot bath, because I'd been run off me feet at work. Doorbell rings and there's some guy at the door giving me the hard sell about double glazing and that. I said there was no way we can afford double glazing, not on a cleaner's wages. This guy won't shut up, keeps giving it a load of verbal and that. By the time I get rid of him, I run back upstairs and..."

Archie's face became a mask of frozen horror.

"It's okay, you don't need to tell me," said Savage.

"I do," he said. "Lily'd climbed out of the cot. Must have thought it was bath time and fell in. Died, she did, in the scalding hot water." Archie poured a huge glass of whisky and swallowed it whole. "I killed my daughter."

"No, that was an accident."

"Everyone says that." Archie fixed him with bloodshot eyes. "But I know. I killed her. I should've been watching her. I have to live with it every day, and I would've killed myself but I was lying when I said I didn't have the balls. Suicide is too easy. Let's me off, don't it? I need to be punished. Need to stay alive so I can suffer, remembering what I done to my little girl."

A flood of tears fell from Archie's eyes, the sobs coming heavy and fast. Savage put his arm around the little man. There wasn't much else he could do. Savage knew how it felt to be responsible for the death of another human being. A life of pain is all that it offered.

Savage's phone buzzed. A text from Tannaz. Savage glanced at the screen while holding Archie's small, quivering frame.

The text read:

Sylvia Sanchez is dead.

CHAPTER 29

BACK IN THE RETRO TEAROOM, Vera Lynn was belting out 'We'll Meet Again'. The waitresses were joining in and a few of the customers too. All part of the theatrical Blitz-spirit experience. Who would've have thought nostalgia would be the future of casual dining? In uncertain times, the past was always a reassuring refuge, even if the reality was that millions of homes were destroyed and thousands of people died in the Blitz, in the most horrific ways.

The hopeful mood of the tearoom seemed at odds with Savage's. The tang of Tannaz's smoke-infused breath drifted across the table. She'd been stressed out and chain smoking, nipping outside in between necking black coffees. Her whole body jittered.

"We have to stop this investigation," she said shakily.

"Why?" asked Savage.

Tannaz swore loudly. A few customers nearby swivelled round at her outburst, bringing them out of their reminiscent fog. "Why? You have to ask why?"

"Keep it down and try to stay calm."

Tannaz lowered her voice. "Whenever we talk to anyone, they wind up dead. It keeps happening." Even though she whispered, her words were laced with rage and fear. "Luke Mosely, dead. Jenny Hopkins, dead. Sylvia Sanchez, dead. Wellington is on to us. He's killing them. Silencing them."

"That's not true."

"Course it is, we need to back off before someone else dies."

"Firstly, we still don't know it's Wellington doing this—"

"I think it's pretty damn obvious—"

Savage held up a hand to silence her. "Let me finish. Everything is pointing in that direction, I agree. However, we still need to be sure. There are too many unknowns. We haven't got enough on him. Let's just assume that it's him behind all this. Do you think Simon Wellington has a problem killing people who get in his way?"

"No, not at all."

"Then if he knows we're onto him, why not just kill us? Surely that would be easier."

Tannaz's mouthed formed an O then closed, as she struggled to find a response.

"There is a pattern emerging, and it's not to do with us. If he is killing people, he's killing them systematically. There's a logic to it. We're not sure why Dave Mosely died, probably suicide. Same with Luke, maybe, maybe not. However, it's reasonable to assume Jenny Hopkins died because she was getting more vocal about Wellington. Once Jenny was out of the way, there was no need for Sylvia Sanchez keeping an eye on her. Wellington was tying up a loose end. With hindsight we should've seen that coming. Warned Sylvia to get the hell out of Dodge. Wellington didn't have any use for her and didn't want to leave behind a witness, and we know she didn't warn Wellington about us. So that leaves us with the only logical conclusion that it's just coincidence that we talked to these people before they got killed. If he knew about us, we'd be dead now."

"I thought you didn't believe in coincidences."

"I don't. This time I think it's valid because the reasons behind the killings make sense."

"That's not quite correct."

"What do you mean?"

Tannaz fingered the screen of her smart phone, pulled up a news story and held it up for Savage to read.

He quickly scanned the article. His face dropped.

"Sylvia Sanchez was found hanging from a tree in Dead Maids?"

"Yep," said Tannaz. "Same nonsense as Luke's death. And

we're back to the same question as before, the same one we've been trying to answer all along. If Wellington had wanted her out of the way, why go to all the trouble of making it look like a suicide? Why not just dump her body in the sea between here and the Isle of Wight with a few bricks to weigh her down? And she was an illegal immigrant. Nobody was going to miss her, poor thing."

Savage read the article from Tannaz's phone again. "Says here a note found on her body said she couldn't live with the pain of Jenny Hopkins dying on her shift."

Tannaz folded her arms. "I don't believe that. Did she seem suicidal?"

"Not at all, but then neither did Luke."

"Why kill two people and leave their bodies in plain sight? Why take that risk?"

"We've still got the same conundrum as before."

"That's what I just said," Tannaz snapped. "Surely there's a connection with Wellington Properties. Both Dave and Sylvia were tenants at one time or another."

Savage shook his head. "No. Sylvia Sanchez lived in an HMO but it wasn't one of Wellington's, remember. He's covered his tracks. Picked someone unconnected to keep an eye on Jenny. We do have the phone records from Sylvia's phone to his henchman, this Bluetooth guy."

"True," said Tannaz. "But it was from a burner phone, no proof that she ever owned it. So therefore no connection to Wellington or anyone that worked for him. And I bet that burner phone has mysteriously disappeared."

Savage lifted up the teapot to pour another cup. It was empty. "I need more tea. Do you want another coffee?"

"I need something with alcohol in it," said Tannaz, defeated.

Savage grabbed the menu. Sifted through the list of drinks. There was only one thing alcoholic on the menu, right at the bottom it read: *Irish Coffee—made with finest Irish Whiskey.*

They'd spelt whisky wrong like Archie did. Savage glanced

around the room. On the blackboard was written: *Why not try our fig roll's. English tea at it's best.*

Savage shook his head, disapprovingly.

"What's up with you?" asked Tannaz.

"Cavalier use of apostrophes, as Alan Partridge would put it."

"Where?"

He pointed out *fig roll's* and *it's* on the blackboard, and also the misspelling of whisky on the menu. "Did you know there's a guy called the Grammar Vigilante? Goes round in the dead of night correcting apostrophes and spellings on signs. I think they need him in here."

"Well, I'm with you on the apostrophe, but that's not grammar is it? Surely that's punctuation, and their spelling of 'whisky' in that context is correct."

"Really, you sure?"

"Yep, in America and Ireland whisky is spelt with an 'e'."

"Well, I never," said Savage. "Tannaz, English is your second language and you have a better grasp of it than I do."

"Nah, not really. I just drink a lot of alcohol."

They both gave a restrained laugh. Humour not really appropriate at this exact time.

"So do you want one? An Irish coffee?"

Tannaz shook her head. "No, I'm good. Actually I've got something else to show you. Completely forgot after hearing about Sylvia."

"Go on."

Tannaz heaved her laptop on the table and fired it up. "Managed to hack Wellington's solicitor. Got a look at his will and guess what."

"Go on."

"Simon Wellington has left everything to his son only if he works for Wellington Properties for the rest of his life. If he leaves the company, he gets nothing. That's how he can force him to work on low wages."

"So Simon Wellington is holding his own son to ransom, making him live like a pauper?"

"Yep, and Ben Wellington *was* contributing to Jenny Hopkins' care-home bills. Goodness knows how he made ends meet. Plus, we already know that the car he drives and the house he lives in is all owned by Simon Wellington. He basically can't leave Wellington Properties or he gets nothing."

"Jeez, his father is one cold-hearted bastard."

"I know, right?"

Savage went silent. Started rubbing the bristles on his chin. He'd let his beard go for a few days. Usually, he shaved every day, like clockwork. A hangover from his army days. Being around the residents of Tivoli Gardens he thought a constant five o'clock shadow would be more appropriate. He gazed into the air in front of him.

"Savage, what are you thinking?"

"Dunno. Might be something, might be nothing."

"Spill the beans."

"First I need to head back to Tivoli Gardens."

CHAPTER 30

S AVAGE PUSHED HIS KEY INTO the front door of Tivoli Gardens, gave it a shove with his shoulder. He did it out of force of habit now. Shaking off the cold from outside he caught sight of Rosie still fiddling with the screws of the strike plate of her door, the butter knife a clumsy substitute for a proper screwdriver. Though he desperately wanted to help her, and could never resist a bit of DIY, Savage ignored the overwhelming urge and made his way up the stairs.

"Excuse me," she suddenly said.

Savage turned.

"Could you help me?" Rosie asked.

"Of course," he said, walking back down. "What's the problem?"

"The lock, it doesn't reach across to the door frame. I don't know what to do. I can't lock my door at night."

"And I suppose Wellington Properties won't come out to fix it."

Rosie snorted. "You're kidding, aren't you? As far as they're concerned, we don't exist."

"Show me," asked Savage.

Rosie closed the door and put the key in the lock, gave it a turn. The deadlock shot across the narrow gap between the door and the frame but never made it all the way, stopping short of the bolthole in the strike plate by about three millimetres.

"See what I mean, it's not reaching across."

"Well," said Savage straightening up. "If the deadbolt won't go into the strike plate, then the strike plate will have to go to the deadbolt."

"What does that mean?"

"We can fix it."

Dink's door opened. The big man stood there for a second, staring at Rosie and Savage.

"Hello, Dink," said Savage.

"Can we make some more soup?" he asked.

"Not right at this moment. We're fixing Rosie's door. Want to help?"

A big smile spread across his face. "Are you going to do another magic trick with the nail?"

"Not this time, I'm afraid. This one's a lot more straightforward. We will need to go and see the lad who we did the magic trick for. Remember the guy building the bin store?"

"Yep."

"Could you go ask him if we could borrow a screwdriver and a handful of small washers."

Dink nodded enthusiastically and scampered off like an overweight spaniel.

"Sweet guy," said Savage.

"He is," Rosie said. "I'm lucky to have him as a neighbour. He's never any trouble. Unlike some of the pricks in this place." Rosie's face became dark, worry lines popping up across her forehead.

"Everything okay?" Savage asked.

Rosie masked her gloom with a fake smile. "Everything's fine." Clearly it wasn't.

Savage took an oblique approach. "Tell me, what made you change your mind?"

"About what?"

"Me helping you. Last time I offered you nearly bit my head off, whereas now you seem more open to a bit of assistance."

Rosie shifted uneasily on her feet. Started fingering a dirty mark on the wall, of which there were many. She breathed deeply. "Someone keeps creeping into our room at night. Watching me and Grace sleep."

"You're kidding," said Savage. "Someone in here?"

She nodded.

"Why don't you call the police?"

"Don't be daft, they won't even come into Thornhill, let alone Tivoli Gardens."

"That must be terrifying."

"Luckily, my Grace sleeps through it. Doesn't know anything about it. And I want to keep it that way. I'm always awake. Just lie there scared stiff, frozen. He just sits on a chair watching us for about an hour. Then leaves."

"Is that all he does, watches you?"

Rosie looked at the floor, muttered a barely audible "no".

"What does he do?"

Rosie stuttered. "Sometimes he, you know, plays with himself."

Savage made fists with both hands, dug his fingernails into his palms. "Who is he?" he asked.

She shook her head, eyes filled with fear. "You can't do anything. It'll only make it worse. At least if the lock gets fixed he can't get in."

"Tell me who it is. I promise I won't touch him. Scout's honour."

"What are you going to do to him?"

"Nothing, absolutely nothing. I swear."

Rosie thought for a moment. "Grace will be coming out of school soon, I have to meet her."

"Don't worry, I'm not going to do anything rash."

Rosie thought for a moment, then said, "It's this slimy guy called Jezza, on the first floor. Number nine."

"Okay," said Savage. "I'll watch out for him."

An awkward silence grew while they waited for Dink to return.

"I never used to be in this position, you know," Rosie said suddenly. "Used to be happily married, had a house and a mortgage. A proud mum bringing up my young daughter while my husband worked. Then one day he disappeared. Cleaned out our bank account, left me with nothing. He's in Spain now, I think. We lost the house and had to come here."

"Guy sounds like an asshole."

"Since then I seem to be surrounded by assholes."

"We're not all bad," said Savage. The look on Rosie's face said she begged to differ.

Just then the hulking figure of Dink burst through the front door, breathless.

"Got them," he said proudly. As he approached he handed Savage the screwdriver and opened his other hand to reveal a palmful of shiny washers, like metal sweets. "He didn't know what size you wanted so he gave us lots. Did I do it right?"

"You did it perfect, Dink," said Savage. "Right, let's fix this lock."

In a second, Savage had removed the screws and prised the strike plate away from the door frame.

"How are we going to fix it?" asked Dink.

"Well," said Savage, "we simply put some of these washers underneath the strike plate, so it lifts it away from door frame, bringing it closer to the lock, like so."

Savage fitted three washers behind each of the screw holes then replaced the screws and tightened them up. The strike plate now stood slightly proud of the door frame. Closing the door gently, he made sure it didn't catch the newly raised-up strike plate, then gave the key a twist. This time the deadbolt went across and sat snugly in the bolthole, securing the door. He gave it a try, pushing against the door with all his weight. It held firm. "There," said Savage. "Safe and sound. Give it a try."

Rosie attempted to open the locked door. It wouldn't budge. A wide smile broke across her face. "Thank you so much. Thank you, thank you."

Savage handed the spare washers and screwdriver back to Dink. "Would you mind returning these to our friend on the building site, Dink?"

Dink took them and was off again, out the door.

"I must give you something," said Rosie.

"Don't be crazy, only took a minute to fix."

"Please, I insist."

"Okay then, do you have a couple of hairpins I could have."

Rosie's brow creased in confusion. "A couple of hairpins? I was thinking something more than that."

"No, really, I just need a couple of hairpins."

"Sure," she said. "I still owe you, big time." Rosie disappeared into her room and returned clutching a fistful of hairpins. "Thank you," she said.

"My pleasure." Savage turned and climbed the stairs.

"And you're not going to do anything silly, are you?" she called after him. "Jezza's dangerous."

So am I, thought Savage. "Nope, I promise I won't touch the guy." He turned and continued up the stairs.

"Done your good deed for the day, have we?" Jeff said, pouring on the sarcasm thick.

"Yes I have, actually."

"Feeling all warm and tingly, are we?"

"Why are you talking like a prick? Oh wait, you always talk like a prick. And what's wrong with helping people? And what's wrong with getting a nice feeling when you do it?"

"I suppose a bit of self-gratification isn't the problem here. The problem is, you think you've found the secret she was hiding. You're so naïve."

"So the guy creeping into her bedroom at night and jerking off while her and her daughter sleep isn't the thing that's making her scared and uptight?"

"Correct."

"So that's just a little speedbump in her life, a fly in the ointment."

"Also correct."

"Okay, astound me. What's the thing that's making her life a misery apart from living in this place, while bringing up a teenage girl and being surrounded by drug addicts, alcoholics, perverts and low lifes?"

"They're not all low lifes. You're stereotyping occupants of social housing, shame on you, I say, shame on you. Some of these people are just down on their luck. Like Archie and Dink."

"Oh so you like Dink now, do you? You implied he was a

retard the other day. That's a horrible thing to call someone with learning disabilities. Shame on you, Jeff."

Jeff didn't reply.

"Jeff, what's this amazing revelation you have then? Jeff?"

Jeff still didn't reply.

"Come on don't go all shy. What's Rosie hiding?"

"Don't know. She's still hiding something."

"Great, thanks for the heads up. That bit of information is next to useless."

"All I'm saying is, you still need to look out for her. The Jezza problem is the least of her worries. Now, on that subject, what are you going to do about Jezza? You promised not to touch him, remember."

Savage reached his bedroom door unlocked it and went in, closed the door behind him.

"I'm not going to touch him, but I am going to give him a lot to think about."

CHAPTER 31

THREE A.M. SILENCE ENVELOPED THE house. The arguments had stopped. The crashing and banging had ceased. And no music filtered up through the floorboards. The only noise came from the house itself, its weary timbers and beams calling out, popping and groaning under the strain of holding themselves together.

Savage stood outside bedroom number nine. Jezza's room. He listened with his head against the door for sounds of movement. There weren't any. Getting down on his hands and knees, he peeked under the bottom of the door, which was badly fitted and had about a half-inch gap between it and the stale carpet. Savage could see no lights on. He straightened up and gently knocked on the door. Stopped and listened. Nothing. He knocked again, this time slightly louder. No one came to the door. Jezza was fast asleep.

In the darkened landing of the first floor, Savage could vaguely make out the lock staring back at him. It didn't matter that he couldn't see it properly. He'd already checked it out during the daylight hours. Besides, Savage could pick a lock with his eyes closed, and this one didn't exactly pose a challenge. It was a cheap, unbranded pin cylinder with a latch, and unlike Rosie's, there was no deadlock. Piece of cake.

He'd already pre-shaped two of the hairpins Rosie had given him. The first one, bent at a right angle, he inserted into the base of the keyhole. This was his lever for putting pressure on the cylinder inside. The other hairpin, shaped like a hook, he pushed into the keyhole above the first hairpin. Inside the lock were five key pins he had to move out the way. Savage located the first pin, pushed it up and out of the way. As he did so he turned the lock ever so slightly with the lever, increasing the pressure to stop it from slipping back down again. He moved his hooked hairpin along ever so slightly to the next pin inside the lock, and repeated the process. After he'd pushed up all five key pins and turned the lever hairpin, the lock gave up with a satisfying click.

Extracting the hairpins, he gently pushed the door open a few inches with his fingertips. He listened. Still nothing. So far so good.

Savage opened the door just enough to put his head inside the room and get a proper look. There were no curtains, just a sheet hanging lopsided over a rail above the window. Some light from the night sky leaked in, allowing Savage to get a feel for the room. About twelve feet by twelve feet, he could make out a small bed in the middle with Jezza sleeping on his side in a T-shirt and boxer shorts without any bedclothes, despite the minimal temperature. Not much else was in the room, apart from dirty aluminium take-out trays stacked up on the floor like miniature ziggurats, clusters of beer cans and a chair piled up with unfolded clothes.

Stepping in and closing the door quietly behind him, Savage threaded his way through the remnants of take-away food to the clothes-covered chair. He tilted it forward, tipping all the clothes silently onto the floor in a heap. Lifting the chair, he placed it by Jezza's bedside, and sat down.

He watched the pervert's body rise and fall with every rhythmic breath, blissfully unaware of Savage's presence. Sleep, like death, was a great leveller, making everyone as vulnerable as a newborn baby. An apt analogy, as Jezza had a completely bald head and was overweight. Not in a Dink way, in that beer-drinker's way; arms and legs too thin to go with his bulging midriff. Savage watched him for a while then cleared his throat. Jezza didn't stir.

Savage cleared his throat again. All he got back from Jezza was a snort followed by a deep sigh.

Savage began gently tapping the bed with his foot, increasing the intensity, until Jezza started to surface. He moaned a few times, turned onto his back, licked his lips then his eyes gradually opened into lazy slits. They blinked a few times then snapped wide open when he realised someone was in his room watching him.

He sprang into an upright seated position, swore, snatched the covers and pulled them up to his chest.

"Who are you? What are you doing in my room? Get out." The words came from his mouth pea-shooter fast.

"It's okay," said Savage. "I'm just watching you sleep."

Jezza swore again. "You freaking weirdo. Get out." His voice increased in volume.

"Keep it down," said Savage. "You'll wake everyone up."

"Get out now," said Jezza, trying to muster as much machismo as he could.

"But I'm just like you, a Somnophiliac."

"What the hell's that?" Jezza asked.

"We're people who like watching others sleep. I heard you were into it too. We're likeminded you and I. So I figured, if I wanted to watch someone sleep, you'd be okay with it."

"What?" said Jezza. "It doesn't work like that."

"Oh," said Savage. "Do you mean there are rules, is there a manual?"

"No. But you can't just come in here and watch me sleep, it's—"

"Isn't that what you do? I mean, you watch that woman downstairs and her daughter. So if you're allowed to watch them, thinking about it logically, surely I'm okay to watch you, that's only fair isn't it?"

"No, no... it's totally not fair. I don't want you in my room."

"Oh, that's a bit of a setback," said Savage disappointed. "Because I plan on being here most nights to watch you. Darn it, I was really looking forward to it. So the two downstairs, do they like it when you watch them?"

"I want you out of my room now."

Savage didn't move, rubbed his chin thoughtfully. "Hey, tell you what, I can see you're a bit distressed, so how about we make a deal, work on a tit-for-tat basis. Every time you watch Rosie and Grace sleep, I get to watch you sleep for two consecutive nights."

"Wha–? No, no way. And that's not fair. Why do you get two nights?"

"Because you get to watch two people sleep, so I get two consecutive nights because there's only one of you."

"No, no. I don't want you in here at all."

Savage went quiet, then said, "Well in that case, for the deal to work you'll have to stop watching Rosie and Grace altogether."

"Yes, yes. I'll stop. Now please get out."

Savage stood up, straightened his clothes as if he'd just had a business meeting. "Okay, are you sure you won't change your mind?"

"Yes, I'm sure. Please, get out."

"Fair enough." Savage sidled over to the door and opened it, just a chink, to check if the coast was clear.

It wasn't.

The ghostly shape of Archie hurried past the landing, oblivious to Savage's gaze. As he disappeared down the stairs, Savage stepped out of Jezza's room, closing the door quietly behind him. He peeked over the bannister in time to see Archie yank open the front door and head out into the night.

Savage descended the stairs, waited a few seconds and opened the front door. In the distance the odd shape of Archie walked briskly away from Tivoli Gardens.

Closing the front door behind him, Savage followed Archie at a distance as he took an erratic route out of Thornhill housing estate, zigging then zagging down different roads. Archie strode at a hearty lick. Faster than Savage expected, especially for a guy with a whisky addiction and a hideous hacking cough. Surely the damp air would be playing havoc with it, but it didn't diminish Archie's pace.

Savage followed him for over a mile through the silent streets. Tailing someone at night had its benefits, the cover of darkness being one. It also had its drawbacks. Lack of people meant it was harder to blend in. A lone figure on a road stood out like a tree in the desert. And at that moment Savage found himself pursuing Archie along a double-yellow-lined road with shops either side, with no convenient doorways or shadowy alleyways to dart into, and no handy parked cars to hide behind.

Up ahead, Archie turned and looked behind him. He was far away enough not to recognise Savage, but not far enough that it wouldn't arouse suspicion. Why would anyone be walking the streets at this ungodly hour of the morning? Savage was completely exposed.

Thinking fast, Savage began to sway, slowly meandering from one side of the pavement to the other with uncertain steps and a sense of balance that had gone haywire. Just another drunk attempting to make it home. No threat at all. He looked more likely to hurt himself by toppling over or falling into a bush. Archie bought it and carried on walking but slowed his pace considerably. The small man began glancing up and down the road, clearly expecting something to happen or someone to appear.

Savage had no choice but to continue the charade, staggering forward, drawing closer and closer to Archie who'd now stopped altogether. By the time Savage would reach the glare of the next street light, he'd be close enough for Archie to recognise him. That couldn't happen. Savage stopped, propped himself against a shop windows and pretended to pee, buying himself some time. If that didn't buy him long enough, he also had the option to bend over and feign being sick to delay moving closer towards Archie. This reassured him. Probably the first time the thought of being sick had given him any comfort.

The smooth hum of an engine drifted up the road towards him. The only car he'd heard in a good while. He glanced over his shoulder and caught sight of a navy-blue BMW gliding past. He couldn't see who drove it, but by the way it rode low to the ground, there must have been some heavy guys inside. He memorised the licence number as it passed. Farther up the road it swung into the kerb right beside Archie.

He got in the back.

Once the car was out of sight, Savage called Tannaz.

Though it was well after three a.m. Tannaz sounded fresh and chirpy.

"What's up, Savage?" she said. He could hear her taking a drag on a cigarette.

"I need you to find the licence plate of a navy-blue BMW five series for me." He gave her the licence number. "How long do you think it will take?"

"No time at all. I know who owns it already. It belongs to Wellington Properties, one of their company cars."

"You sure?"

"Positive, thought it might be proactive to get the plates of all their vehicles, just in case."

"Good work, Tannaz. I think we might be onto something. I think Archie might be doing a job for Wellington."

CHAPTER 32

SAVAGE STOOD ON THE COLD empty street. One thing was for sure, Archie disappearing on random nights, probably wasn't to sleep in the warmth of the train station waiting room, it was to go and do something for Wellington. But what? Judging by the fresh Elastoplasts slapped across Archie's forehead it wasn't anything good. Was he satisfying Simon Wellington's perverse and sadistic desires? Getting locked up or tortured in basements like the one at the old B&B at twenty-seven Sutton Road, so he could fuel his whisky addiction? It seemed highly likely. And how many others were there like Archie, in other Wellington properties who were engaging in his bizarre games? Simon Wellington overseeing it all like some present-day Joseph Mengele. Not a totally inaccurate parallel to draw. Mengele had the whole of Auschwitz concentration camp to act out his disgusting ideas, while Wellington had his property empire, filled to the brim with vulnerable, desperate and willing people.

"So, do you want to find out where they're going?" asked Tannaz. Savage had completely forgot that Tannaz was still on the end of the phone.

"Yeah, but how?"

"The in-car navigation system. I just hacked it. They're heading out of Southampton towards the forest."

Savage nearly dropped the phone.

"Savage, you still there?"

"Yeah, just you continue to both astound and scare me with your hacking abilities. Remind me never to make an enemy of you."

"Aw, too kind. Want me to come and pick you up?"

"Definitely."

With deathly quiet streets it only took Tannaz a matter of minutes to reach Savage. The VW Caddy swung into the kerb. Tannaz got out. "Now this is what I'm talking about."

Savage looked at her confused.

"This night-time shit. Sneaking around when everyone's tucked up, following a lead."

"Well, let's find out what they're up to."

"You drive," said Tannaz. "I'll get on the laptop and track these perps."

"Perps? Archie's more like a whisky-drinking Hobbit," Savage replied, slipping into the driver's seat.

Tannaz got in and unfurled her laptop. "And we're following them into the forest. Very *Lord of the Rings*."

Savage put the VW in gear and gunned the engine, pointing the van out of Southampton.

"Is that where they're going, into the forest?" he asked.

"Last time I looked."

"Are they still moving?" asked Savage.

A simple map of the road system in and around Southampton filled her screen. A single thick black line representing the blue BMW extended across the map, growing ever longer. "Yeah, heading along the A35, through the middle of the forest. Wait, they've just turned off, going north-west towards a place called Bolderwood."

"Okay we've got some catching up to do."

Once they were clear of the city, Savage slammed the accelerator to the floor. The yellow glow of streetlights came to an abrupt end and the van plunged into the thick darkness of the forest, the road flanked by a tunnel of black trees.

"How are our targets doing?" asked Savage.

"Hold on," Tannaz replied. "They've stopped."

"You certain?"

"The black line isn't moving anymore."

"Okay, well keep an eye on them."

Tannaz groaned. "Savage, what else did you think I was going to do, start playing Candy Crush?"

"Okay, I'll admit, that was a bit patronising. Can you get more detail on where they've stopped. Anything there? Houses? Buildings?"

"Now that I can do."

The plink of rapid typing filled the front of the van.

"Anything?" asked Savage.

"Nothing."

"What 'nothing' as in you don't have details yet or 'nothing' as in there's nothing there."

"The last one, they've pulled off the road and stopped in the middle of nowhere."

"Okay, this is getting interesting. Tell me when we're within about five hundred metres of their position."

Tannaz nodded, kept her eyes on the screen.

The van went silent, apart from the drone of the engine as the ghostly forest scrolled past.

Savage turned off the A35 and headed into Bolderwood, although Bolderwood seemed indistinguishable from the area of forest they'd just driven through.

"Okay, now," said Tannaz. "We're about five hundred metres from their position."

"Hang on." Savage turned the wheel hard and the little VW left the comparative smoothness of the road and jumped onto rough ground, darting between trees. Bumping its way along, jolting both of them off their seats. The suspension complained and really wasn't up to it. Savage throttled back and came to a halt alongside some dense bushes then pulled on the handbrake.

"Good. Now we can't be seen from the road, just in case Wellington's car starts moving again and comes back this way."

"What happens now?" asked Tannaz.

"Can you get that tracking map on your smartphone?"

"Of course."

"Great. We make our way across the cover of the forest, closing in on their position. Find a good OP."

"OP?"

"Observation post, under a bush, preferably like the ones we're parked next to, make ourselves comfortable and watch."

"We're going out there, walking across the forest in pitch-black darkness to watch some guys sitting in a car?"

"Yep."

Tannaz snorted in disapproval.

"What?" asked Savage.

"I told you, I don't do nature."

"You just said you loved this night-time stuff. Sneaking around when everyone's tucked up."

"I meant more of an urban setting. You know, seedy nightclubs and bars, roughing up a few ne'er-do-wells."

Savage laughed. "Ne'er-do-wells! Is that phrase making a comeback? Because I think the last person who said that wore a top hat and breeches."

Tannaz snorted again.

"Come on, it'll be fun."

"Fun in the same way that people think camping is fun, when really it's paying to be homeless."

"Okay, you can stay here. But you may miss something. Don't you want to find out what's going on? And, I'm worried about Archie. Wellington might be exploiting him, using his drinking habit to make him do weird things for booze. I could do with some backup."

Tannaz thought for a moment, then said, "Okay, I'm coming but I'm not lying down in dirt. That's the deal."

"We need to stay out of sight."

"Savage, look around. There are about a million trees to hide behind."

"Fair enough."

They stepped out of the VW, surrounded by the dank forest air.

"You've got to be kidding me," Tannaz shrieked. "It's bloody snowing."

"Keep your voice down," Savage whispered. His tone was better suited to a shout. "I'd hardly call this snow, it's just a light flurry."

Tannaz shivered. "Two things I hate most. Nature and snow."

"Well, you're not exactly dressed for it, what have you got on under that biker jacket?"

"A T-shirt."

"A T-shirt? You're not exactly dressed for the great outdoors, are you?"

"You didn't say we'd be outdoors. You said come and pick me up."

Savage started taking off his jacket.

"What are you doing?" asked Tannaz.

"Giving you my jacket."

"Oh, no you're not," said Tannaz. "Don't give me any of that Mister Darcy crap. I'm not a helpless female. Now come on, let's do this before our targets move on." A small square of light from Tannaz's phone lit up her face. "This way."

Savage shrugged his coat back on and followed Tannaz across the leaf-strewn ground, where the snowflakes were having a hard time settling. After four or five minutes, the dark shape of a parked German car appeared out of the gloom.

Tannaz and Savage edged as close as they dared, then hid behind a tree, watched and waited. In the darkness it was difficult to tell whether anyone was in the car or not. Tannaz slotted her phone into her jacket. It was of no use now.

She nudged Savage and pointed to her wrist as if she were wearing a watch, and mouthed the words, 'How long?'

They'd only just begun to observe the car and she was already getting cold and impatient.

At that moment they heard a clunk, then several more clunks. All four car doors opened. Savage could make out the small unmistakable silhouette of Archie, and three huge figures, presumably Wellington's men. They gently closed their doors and headed into the forest, a cone of torchlight spread out in front of them, lighting their way.

Tannaz went to follow. Savage held her back. He wanted a large enough gap to open up before they went after them. In a forest in the dark, the old cliché of stepping on a branch and signalling one's position was a very real threat.

He turned to her and whispered. "They've got a light, makes them easy to follow so we can afford to hang back, reduce the risk of detection. From now on, no talking and you stay right behind me, single file. Okay? You do whatever I do. If I stop, you stop. If I dive on the ground, you dive on the ground, okay?"

"I said I wouldn't be lying in dirt, but okay."

"Good, let's go."

Up ahead the light from the torch reduced to a flicker. In the blackness of the forest it stood out like the brightest sun. Savage and Tannaz moved towards it using slow deliberate steps, carefully picking their way between tree trunks. The ground was damp and mulchy in between, the layers of decaying leaves soaking up their footsteps. Never gaining on the torchlight and never letting it get too far away, they carried on like this for about twenty minutes, the forest becoming thicker and thicker around them.

Then they saw it.

The single torchlight became two, then three, then four and finally five.

There were a group of other people up ahead. Archie and Wellington's men had rendezvoused with someone, but who and why? What they hell would anyone be doing in the deepest part of the New Forest, in the darkness, in the early hours of a freezing April morning?

Nothing good.

Savage slowed almost to a dawdle. Tannaz shunted into the back of him. They had to go dead slow now. Tales of night patrols marching unaware into enemy encampments had been drilled into him throughout his training. Their targets had torches but that didn't mean they didn't have other people out here, guarding what they were doing, unseen.

Voices drifted towards them, filtering between the trees. They were hushed, little more than whispers. Completely unintelligible. Savage needed to find out what they were saying, it was the only way to make sense of what was happening up ahead.

Tannaz and Savage pushed on, cautiously, daring to get ever closer to the strange meeting. They now moved from tree to tree, using each one as temporary cover before they felt it was safe to move to the next. Painfully slowly, they advanced on the group of people, beams of yellow light from their torches throwing sinister shapes against the trees. The voices were clearer now. Definitely men's. Savage still couldn't hear what they were saying. From the tone, the best he could deduce was that some discussion was going on. It sounded like the way that people speak when they are organising something. Not threatening, but their voices had purpose and direction.

Suddenly the voices stopped.

Savage and Tannaz froze behind the tree they'd been using for cover. Had they been discovered? Surely not. They were still too far away. And the sound of the men's chatter had been loud enough to mask any insignificant noises they had been making.

A heavy silence grew around them. Eerie and unsettling, it felt like the forest didn't want them there. That they were trespassing and night-time in this place wasn't meant for people.

The silence ended abruptly.

Rapid heavy steps. A thundering stampede approaching.

Horses? Could be. Or more likely, ponies. They roamed free in the forest.

Tannaz, spooked by the sound, went to make a run for it. Savage grabbed her jacket and pulled her back. If it was a stampede she'd be far safer behind a tree.

Louder and louder the footsteps came, until the sound was deafening.

The ground shook.

The urge to run, a primal instinct, was overwhelming. Savage held Tannaz tightly. He could feel her shaking.

Just when it seemed the din could get no louder, the stampede charged past, inches from them. A frenzied dash, forcing the still air into a breeze as it passed, swirling snowflakes everywhere. The tree behind them the only thing preventing them from being trampled flat.

But this stampede wasn't made of cattle, it was made of men.

CHAPTER 33

GLANCING LEFT AND RIGHT, SAVAGE caught sight of a blur of men sprinting either side of the tree they hid behind. Running as if the forest itself were on fire. Dozens of them, barging past.

In the dim light, there was something odd about how they ran. Unnatural and ungainly. It was too dark to make out what it was until one of the runners hit a tree, only metres away from where Tannaz and Savage stood. The man hit his forehead hard against the trunk and fell onto his back, almost at their feet, his head nearly close enough to nudge with their toes. Close enough for the fallen man to look up and see them standing above him.

The man writhed around on the floor, attempting to get up. He never saw Savage or Tannaz. He was blindfold; a thick, white handkerchief, tightly tied over his eyes. A scrape of blood just above it, where he'd bashed his head on the tree.

He scrabbled around like a tortoise on his back, taking far too long to get up. Savage thought he might still be dazed. That wasn't the reason. As he struggled to get to his feet like a newborn lamb, Savage realised the man's hands were tied behind his back.

Once up, he rejoined the other runners, following the sound of their feet.

As the last few stragglers ran past, Savage could see they were all blindfold with their hands tied behind them.

The manic footsteps subsided and the forest returned to silence.

In the darkness, Tannaz and Savage stared at each other in shock.

Savage quickly regained his senses. They needed to get out of there. They'd nearly been caught, and if the men in that bizarre ritual, or whatever it was, hadn't been wearing blindfolds the alarm would've been raised, and they'd have been outnumbered. Staying any longer would only increase their chances of discovery.

Savage pulled Tannaz by the arm and led her back to the car, taking a wide arc away from the torchlight and the runners. Every so often he would stop and listen, checking they weren't being followed or that another strange human stampede wasn't suddenly going to come crashing past. All the way they maintained complete silence, even though Savage wanted to discuss what they'd just witnessed and what the hell it all meant.

Taking a wider route back took them longer but ensured they returned to Savage's VW van without being detected. They got in. Savage started the engine and reversed it out of the dense foliage and back onto the road. Tannaz immediately put the heater on full, and put her hands over the vents to warm them up. Savage hit the accelerator and pointed the van back towards Southampton.

When he was clear of Bolderwood and back onto the A35, he flicked his headlights on.

"What the hell was all that about?" he asked. "That is the weirdest thing I think I've ever seen."

"I think I know what it was," said Tannaz.

Savage nearly crashed the car. "You do?"

"Yes. I've seen it before."

"What? Where?"

Tannaz rubbed her hands together, trying to get some heat into them. "Have you seen a film called *Intacto*?"

"Is this one of your arty-type films?"

"Kind of. It's Spanish, and it's brilliant, by the way. Pull over somewhere and I'll show you, then tell me what you think."

Savage drove until they were safely within Southampton's city limits, found a twenty-four-hour garage, and bought them tea and coffee from a machine inside. They took them back to the van parked on the forecourt. When Tannaz had warmed up she searched YouTube on her phone, found the trailer, then propped up her phone on the dashboard and hit play.

Three seconds into the trailer and there it was. The scene they'd just witnessed. Men running a race blindfolded through a forest, their hands tied behind their backs. A carbon copy of what they had just experienced, right down to one of the men running straight into a tree. The trailer continued. Savage recognised the famous actor Max Von Sydow, popping up and making various threats, interspersed with people playing Russian roulette and running across motorways, and a melodramatic voiceover. The last scene returned to Max Von Sydow, who was obviously the bad guy. He said, "If you're ready, it's time to play." Then the word *Intacto* blazed across the screen.

Savage gave a sigh. "So some guys have got together and re-enacted a scene from an obscure Spanish film."

"It's a great film and it's about people who can steal luck. Make themselves luckier than anyone else."

"Sounds like an episode of *Red Dwarf*. But this is the real world. People can't steal luck."

"I know, the film's also about gambling. Underground, illegal betting. You see, in the film, to test people's luck, they concoct more and more bizarre betting games, like the one we've just seen."

"You think what we've just seen is an illegal betting race?"

"Could be."

"And that's why Archie was there. They need participants. Nobody in their right mind is going to do something like that unless they're desperate and need the money. The kind of people who live in Wellington's HMOs, who have an addiction to feed." Savage thought of Archie and his array of whisky and the fact that he always had something to give Vlad and Truck. And how he apparently disappeared for days on end. How the last time he had returned with a plaster on his forehead. Clearly that wasn't from a drink-related injury—it was where he'd hit his head on a tree in one of these races.

Tannaz took a slurp of coffee. "We've been thinking of

Wellington as a sadist, making people suffer. What if it's more than that? What if he's running this highly illegal gambling ring? Remember what Jenny Hopkins said? That he used to note down how long she'd stay locked in the cabinet. He wrote the times down in a little book. Statistics. Odds. People who bet are obsessed with odds. I don't think it was about being sadistic. He liked collecting the stats in case he could use them in a bet."

The world shifted. Savage's mind was still playing catch up. Tannaz was onto something. It was the first time since investigating Dave and Luke's deaths that something made sense. Apart from one thing. "What has this got to do with Dave and Luke hanged in the forest?" he asked.

Tannaz thought for a moment, blew on her hot coffee and then said, "Maybe it's got nothing to do with it. Maybe that was just a scare tactic. Maybe Dave didn't want to participate, and they couldn't leave him alive with that knowledge. Did it as a warning to others, a highly visible warning. Don't do what Wellington asks and you end up hanging from a tree in Dead Maids."

"Dave went and got the Nembutal by himself, nobody forced him."

"We've only got a couple of potheads' word for that. They could be lying."

Savage stretched his arms out and yawned. "Well, at least we have some idea what Wellington's up to, and that makes him vulnerable. And we have another advantage over him."

"What's that?"

"Unlike everyone else around here, we're not scared of him."

"No. So what now? How do we use this?"

"We need to catch this asshole, and my bet, excuse the pun, is that he'll keep his hands clean. So we need hard evidence of his involvement; to find out more about his bizarre betting games. We need to catch him doing something a lot worse than making grown men race through the trees at night. We need something to put him away for good. Can you go on a fishing expedition on the dark web to see if his weird gambling games are on there, and anything else we can use? If he's organising this he'll need wealthy participants, people with lots of disposable cash, cash that can't be traced, Internet currency. So the dark web seems like the most likely place to look."

"Yep, I'm on it. What about you?"

"Don't know, I'll see if I can figure out these damn numbers." Savage pulled the printout from his coat and unfolded it. "You had any luck yet?"

"None. I'll keep trying."

"No, concentrate on seeing if Wellington is set up on the dark web, that's how we'll get him."

Savage stuffed the numbers back into his pocket, fired up the ignition and drove back towards Tivoli Gardens. Six a.m. and a dirty, grey morning light illuminated a corner of the sky, chasing the night away. As they headed through the once-empty streets, more cars began to join them. They stopped briefly at a greasy spoon to drink more tea and coffee and eat bacon sandwiches. Being out all night in the cold forest, staking out the enemy had made them ravenous.

Savage walked the rest of the way back to Tivoli Gardens, while Tannaz drove the VW van back to her hotel room by the airport.

Savage liked to walk, something about the monotony of it helped him slot things into place. Rationalise everything he'd witnessed. It was still trying to snow. Dusty little snowflakes landed on the pavement in front of him where their short lives ended as they melted into nothing. April was still firmly in the grip of winter.

By the time he reached the front door of Tivoli Gardens, the time on his phone informed him it was seven thirty. He put his key in the lock and as quietly as he could, gave the door a shove. He'd rather that no one saw him entering the house at this time so they didn't ask any questions, though he thought there'd be little danger of that at Tivoli Gardens. Apart from Rosie and Grace, the earliest any of them got up was well after ten o'clock.

He was wrong.

Every occupant in the house stood in the hallway, some of them arranged up the stairs like a wretched version of the Von

Trapp children in *The Sound of Music*, watching what was going on below. Archie was there, back from his nocturnal activities. He looked sad and worried, a fresh Elastoplast on his forehead. Looking around at the collective tenants of the house, Savage noticed they all looked unhappy, including Jezza the pervert.

Then he saw the reason. Vlad the Inhaler and Truck were standing sentry at the door to Rosie's room, grinning at the assembled audience, clearly relishing what new concoction of misery they were inflicting. Through Rosie's open door, Savage could see her and Grace busily stuffing their belongings into black bin bags. Both of them were sobbing uncontrollably.

Savage sidled over to Dink. "What's going on?" he said.

Dink had tears in his eyes. "Section twenty-one. They're throwing Rosie and Grace out on the street."

CHAPTER 34

"WHY?" SAID SAVAGE.

Dink shook his head, wouldn't answer.

"Dink, why are they throwing them out?"

Still, Dink would not answer, chewing his lips together, like he always did when he didn't want the truth to accidentally escape.

Archie appeared by his side. His eyes looked tired and Savage noticed the dirt under his fingernails.

"Archie," said Savage. "Why are they throwing Rosie and Grace out?"

Archie took his arm and led him outside through the front door, away from everything going on inside.

Savage repeated the question.

"Are you sure you want to know?" Archie said.

"Yes, I'm sure."

Archie swallowed hard, cleared his throat. "You know how, those two, Vlad and Truck skim stuff off us, money, booze and ciggies." Savage nodded. "Well, Rosie doesn't have anything to give them so, she has to..." Archie struggled to find delicate words to describe it. Savage knew what he was going to say. "... She pays them in other ways." Archie said, eyes downcast.

"She has sex with them and in return they don't throw her out?"

Archie nodded.

Savage should have known. A pretty woman like Rosie down on her luck. Easy to take advantage of. That was the secret the voice in his head was trying to tell him. Savage's anger flared and his fists clenched. "Well, we'll see about that," he said, making towards the door.

"Wait," said Archie. "There's more."

Savage spun around.

Archie looked at the ground. "The reason they're throwing her out is because they changed the deal."

"What do you mean?"

Archie looked unsure how to answer, words forming at his lips but not making them out. Eventually he said, "They upped the cost of her deal."

"Archie, spit it out. What does that mean?"

"They wanted to have sex with her daughter."

"She's barely fourteen!"

"I know," said Archie. "Rosie refused, so they're kicking her out."

Savage marched towards the front door of Tivoli Gardens. He was supposed to be undercover, investigating the death of his friend and his son, but he couldn't let a single mum and her daughter get thrown out on the streets by two foul deviants.

Time to put away the grey man.

Time to hurt bad people.

Savage kicked open the front door with such force it slammed against the inside wall. Everyone in the hallway swung their gaze onto Savage, including Rosie and Grace. Eyes red-rimmed, they stood in the hallway clutching bulging bin bags in each of their hands, their entire possessions in the world kept together by flimsy black plastic. Truck and Vlad stood behind them, in the process of escorting them out.

"Rosie," said Savage. "You and Grace go back to your room, you're not going anywhere."

"Hey," said Truck. "Shut up or we'll throw you out too."

Savage pointed at him. "The only two people leaving this place will be you two clowns." A gasp came from every one of the tenants watching, shocked that Savage would say such a thing to these two backstreet bullies. "Now you can either walk out, or you can crawl out with both legs busted. It's up to you." Savage then spoke to Rosie. "Take Grace back inside, and lock the door. I don't want you seeing this."

Vlad threw back his head and laughed, a big put-on theatrical laugh. Rosie and her daughter quickly retreated into their room and closed the door behind them.

"You!" Vlad sniggered. "You're going to throw us out? An old man with no job and no money and shit clothes is going to throw us out? How do you figure that's going to happen?"

"I have the law on my side, and I have a ton of witnesses."

"Law's on *our* side, pal," said Truck. "Section twenty-one says we can throw people out whenever we want. Don't need a reason."

"True. When did you ask her to leave?"

"Just now," Truck said, folding his thick meaty arms.

"Then under section twenty-one she has two months' notice. You can't just turf her out onto the street. You have to give her two months to find new digs."

Vlad's smile didn't diminish. He was enjoying this. Enjoying someone standing up to them. Probably liked the drama. It was safe to assume that when things like this normally happened, everyone kept their heads down, didn't make a scene. For a thug who thrived on being a bully and seeing people suffer, it probably became very boring. Everyone always capitulating.

"Not going to happen," he said with glee. "If she doesn't like it she can hire a lawyer. Oh, wait. She hasn't got enough money to feed herself, so I don't think that's going to happen. She goes now. Today." Vlad turned to the assembled tenants of Tivoli Gardens. "Let this all be a warning to you. Piss us off and you're out on the street." He turned back to Savage. "Your move old man."

No, Vlad wasn't enjoying the drama. That wasn't quite accurate. He was getting high off the power, knowing that he held the fates of everyone in Tivoli Gardens in his grubby hands. Knowing that he could have anyone out on their ear whenever the mood took him. Power always goes to people's heads, thought Savage. Well, that power was about to be challenged.

Savage took a step closer to Vlad. Met him eye to eye. "Like I said. The only two people leaving are you two clowns. Actually, I take that back, you're too dumb to be clowns. You're slower than dial-up Internet."

"No, 'cos I just bought a WiFi booster," said Vlad smugly. "Who's stupid now?"

Savage rolled his eyes. "You know, Vlad, your brain is like the TARDIS in reverse. Smaller on the inside than it is on the outside."

Truck sniggered.

Savage turned his attention to Truck. "I don't know what you're laughing at, Truck. You're as boring as Vlad is stupid. Listening to you droning on about *Gladiators*. No one cares. It's like listening to a broken hand dryer in a public toilet that won't switch off. Actually, I'd rather listen to the hand dryer, at least it's useful, has a purpose."

The dopey grin left Truck's face.

"What are you going to do, old man?" asked Vlad. "Breathe your stinky old-man breath on us and make us pass out?"

"I thought I might break something of yours, Vlad. Something important that you use a lot—obviously not your brain. Maybe your opposable thumbs. Seeing as that's about the only thing that separates you from a squirrel."

Vlad sobered up. Got serious. "Play time's over, old man."

He went for Savage, grabbed him by the neck and shoved him up against a wall, pressing his thumbs deep into Savage's windpipe. "What you gonna do now, old man?"

Savage gasped for air, tried to speak.

"What's that, old man? I can't hear you."

Savage spluttered.

Vlad released his grip very slightly to let him talk.

In a gurgled whisper, Savage said, "Changed my mind. Going to break your little fingers."

With both hands, Savage reached up and grabbed Vlad's little fingers that were still clasped around his neck. Being the weakest digits of the hand, their grip was negligible. He prised them away easily. Savage wrenched hard, bending them back on themselves, snapping them like a couple of chicken bones.

Vlad screamed. Savage still held his little fingers tightly, using them to pull his arms down by his sides, then he headbutted Vlad on his big, long nose. The thin nasal capillaries had no option but to rupture, sending torrents of blood out both nostrils.

Savage wasn't finished with the rapist yet.

He reached down and grabbed Vlad by his manhood, squeezed and twisted as hard as he could, like he was wringing out a flannel. "That's to make sure your raping days are over."

Savage felt a movement nearby. He didn't need to look round to know that in the couple of seconds it took to disable Vlad, Truck would be coming after him. Savage spun Vlad around and shoved him into the path of the oncoming Truck.

The two collided. Truck merely threw his colleague to one side, just an object in his way. Savage had known fighting Vlad wouldn't be a problem. The guy was all mouth. Truck, however, was a different matter. Solid and beefy. An unstoppable force.

With his thick, muscly arms raised in a boxing stance, Truck edged towards him. Though he'd had his fifteen minutes of fame as a TV gladiator, Truck was clearly no stranger to the ring. Savage could use this. He raised his hands, mirroring Truck's posture and movements. Familiar ground for Truck, this would make him relaxed and comfortable, just another opponent he needed to knock out with his powerful fists. Trouble with boxing, if you do a lot of it, is you expect an attack to come from the waist up, a body or head shot. Truck wouldn't be expecting an attack from below, and Savage was planning something really low.

Truck shuffled in, ready to launch a volley of punches to Savage's head. Before he had the chance, Savage kicked him with all his fury on his right shin, his leading leg.

The strike sent an electric shock through Truck's body. Nothing hurt like a kick to the shins, especially if you weren't used to it. With no muscle or fatty tissue in front of the tibia bone to cushion the blow, the kick had a direct line to thousands of nerve fibres, which right then would be lighting up Truck's brain like a Christmas tree.

A brief wave of pain shot across Truck's face, but he still kept coming.

Savage took a step back and fired another kick at the other shin.

Truck's body shuddered. The brute kept on advancing. Soon, Savage would run out of space, his back would be against the wall and he'd have no more room to launch kicks. Then it would become a fist fight, which Savage knew he wouldn't win.

He had to find another way to stop this Truck. If shin kicks wouldn't do it, Savage had to resort to something more brutal.

"Come on, old man," said Truck. "Fight properly."

Savage took two steps back, then suddenly launched himself at Truck. It took Truck by surprise. He managed to jab Savage in the face. Savage kept on moving, dodging past the guy's thick, slow frame, shoving him as he went. Truck barely moved, like shoving a standing stone. Savage made it to the stairs and ran down to the kitchen. He could hear Truck's thundering steps behind him.

"Coward", he yelled.

Savage liked to think of it as a tactical retreat, no, more like withdrawing to find a better defensive position, and better weaponry.

Making straight for the rotten back door of the dingy kitchen, Savage threw his shoulder against it. The ancient, decaying wood gave way under Savage's weight. He didn't stop, using the momentum to carry him out into the back garden—a dumping ground for piles of bin bags that had burst open, disgorging food wrappers and takeaway cartons the local foxes had picked clean.

Savage made a hard left, sprinting along the side of the house, hurdling an old rusted pram and a satellite dish that had given up clinging to the side of the house long ago.

There was a crash of footsteps behind him. Truck was out in the garden, giving chase.

As Savage rounded the front of the house, he saw what he wanted. A weapon to stop a Truck.

Bending down by the drain, he snatched up a handful of the dirty syringes. Holding them up high, like tiny daggers, needles pointing outwards, he waited at the apex of the front corner of the house.

Seconds later, Truck came charging by.

Thrusting out his arm, Savage stabbed him in the face with the dirty needles, sending them deep into the flesh of his left cheek.

Truck came to a halt. The shock of what was sticking out of his face distracting him from the chasing Savage. The hypodermics protruded from his skin, making him look like a foul pin cushion.

One by one, Truck plucked them out in horror, glaring at each grimy needle, before letting it drop to the ground.

He looked at Savage, all fight gone out of him. Then swore. "What've you done?" he said. "What have you done?"

Savage gasped melodramatically. "Oh no," he said, laying on the sarcasm thick. "I hate to think where those needles have been."

"I've probably got hepatitis now."

"Better get yourself tested. See if you've collected the full set, hepatitis A, B and C."

Truck swore again, almost crying. "You bastard."

"Well considering you're a multiple rapist, probable paedophile and exploiter of vulnerable people, I think getting stabbed in the face with dirty needles is pretty fair. You've only got yourself to blame. I did warn you. Gave you the chance to walk away."

At that moment, Vlad came spilling out of the front door, clutching his nose with both hands, his little fingers hanging limp like a couple of soggy French fries. Blood covered the front of his sweatshirt. The tenants of Tivoli Gardens cautiously followed him out, keeping a safe distance.

"Okay," said Savage. "New house rules. You two pricks aren't welcome here. If we see you here again, you'll think what's just happened is like a trip to Build-A-Bear. Now get lost and leave us alone."

Everyone stood on the dusty bowl of a front garden while the sorry sights of Vlad and Truck dawdled off the property.

"You can go a bit faster than that," someone shouted.

"Yeah, get lost, assholes." Someone threw an empty lager

can at them. Suddenly they all joined in, pelting Vlad and Truck with litter.

Savage turned away, walked back towards the house. He caught sight of Archie silently staring at him with a blank, unreadable expression. He couldn't tell whether Archie admired him for what he'd just done or thought it was reckless, putting them all in danger.

Savage ignored him, went back inside and up to his room, pulled out his phone to make a call.

"Tannaz," he said. "I think I've just mucked everything up."

CHAPTER 35

S AVAGE DOWNED HIS THIRD CUP of tea while he waited for Tannaz to join him in the retro tearoom. Noel Coward's plummy vocals crooned 'There Are Bad Times Just Around The Corner', reflecting exactly how Savage felt. To add insult to injury, Jeff Perkins wouldn't shut up.

"Well, you've really gone and done it now, Savage," he said, clearly enjoying Savage's current discomfort. *"You saved a woman you hardly know, at the expense of finding out who killed your friend and his son."*

Savage scanned the tearoom. Jeff's voice was loud and clear in his head, and he was always paranoid that others could hear him. People sitting at the tables nearby carried on chatting and blissfully dunking biscuits in tea.

Rosie's a single mum who was about to be thrown out onto the street, getting raped on a regular basis, and they were lining her daughter up next. Sorry, I wasn't going to let that happen.

"Well, it's all over now. Cat's out of the bag. So much for playing the grey man. Not getting noticed. More like the bright-pink man, waving a flag—hey, you're not the grey man, you're the gay *man. That's you, the gay man."* Jeff cackled with childish laughter.

So I'm gay now am I?

"You macho types hate being called gay. Think it's a slur on your manliness."

Jeff, I've fought alongside gay soldiers and transgender soldiers, and I'd trust them with my life, actually, I did *trust them with my life on more than one occasion. So that line of* abuse isn't going to get you anywhere. And my best friend Tannaz is gay, or bisexual sometimes—oh, who the hell cares?

"It's unnatural."

Unnatural? Oh, shut up, Jeff. Sixty years ago, writing with your left hand was unnatural. Teachers used to hit you with a ruler. You know what, you're a homophobic, transphobic racist.

"How dare you? I am not a racist."

Oh, so ethnic people are fine as long as they're straight.

"Correct."

Is that why you're scared of Tannaz?

"I'm not."

Yes, you are. You disappear whenever she's around. Ah, here she comes now.

Out on the pavement in front of the bay window of the tearoom, Tannaz bundled along, computer bag over her shoulder, leather biker jacket zipped up tight against the cold and a Doctor Who length scarf coiled round her neck. Savage really wanted to tell her to invest in a more sensible coat, but knew it would be met with a broadside of expletives.

Jeff? Jeff?

The berating voice in his head had fled now that his kryptonite was here. Savage felt mildly better.

A cold blast from outside filled the tearoom as Tannaz entered, she ordered coffee, then came and sat at Savage's table, hooking her computer bag over the chair. She fired a sympathetic look at Savage.

"Don't you dare feel guilty," she said. "You gave those raping bastards what they deserved."

"I feel like I've let Dave and Luke down," Savage replied. "I'm supposed to be playing the grey man, staying under the radar, finding out what happened to them. Now I've just sent a big rocket up into the sky."

"Have you?" asked Tannaz. "You got into a fight. I'm sure it's not the first fight that's happened in Tivoli Gardens."

"True, but I'll get evicted, sure as eggs are eggs. And there goes our inside advantage."

"Okay, fine. So you get evicted. We'll just carry on investigating from the outside. And we've already made a massive breakthrough with Wellington and his weird betting games."

"How's that going by the way?"

"Haven't found anything yet. Searching the dark web takes a lot longer than the regular one."

Savage's thoughts returned to the fight he'd just had. He slumped down in his chair. "I feel like I've blown it."

"Oh, come on, Savage, you're sounding like me. What was it you said about every SAS mission you've been on? No matter how well planned, it all goes out the window once you're on the ground and the bullets start flying. You adapt. Improvise. When things go wrong you told me to remember a technique. Breathe. Recalibrate. Deliver. So take a breath, let's regroup our thoughts and deliver what we set out to do. Nothing's changed. We might need to modify how we achieve it. That's all."

Savage studied the crumbs on the tablecloth. "I'm not sure how we do that."

"Just carry on," said Tannaz. "Go back to Tivoli Gardens, play it out. No one knows you're ex-SAS, or a friend of Dave Mosely or his son. You just had a fight is all. If you get thrown out, you get thrown out."

"Okay," said Savage. "You're right. I'm being a wuss."

"I'd hardly call you a wuss. You kicked the asses of two of Wellington's men who were asking for it. Who raped, bullied and extorted their way around Tivoli Gardens. And I'm sure that's not the only property they do that in." Tannaz paused, then said, "How did it feel?"

"What?"

"Beating the crap out of them both."

Savage smiled. "Pretty good, actually. Although, technically, I didn't beat up Truck. I stabbed him with some dirty needles."

"Even better. Prick deserved it." She shot him a warm, reassuring smile. A rare treat for Savage, as Tannaz never smiled that much. "Okay, let's stay positive. Catch Simon Wellington."

Tannaz drove Savage back and dropped him off just before the Itchen Bridge where he walked the rest of the way home. She was right. He had to just carry on. Okay, he wasn't the grey man anymore. Although, thinking about it, he hadn't done that particularly well. Being the grey man meant being featureless and bland, fading into the background. Fixing doors and the window and teaching Dink how to make soup and taking him to support groups for his food addiction and self-harming wasn't what you'd call keeping a low profile. He'd made a mark on Tivoli Gardens. It was only a matter of time before he got a knock on the door and got a section twenty-one, although Wellington Properties only used that when they didn't have a reason to throw you out. They had a pretty big reason to throw Savage out.

He was climbing the stairs back to his room, when Rosie appeared at her door. "Excuse me," she said. "I didn't get a chance to thank you. That was extremely brave what you did."

"Or stupid," he said.

"Well, I'm very grateful."

"My pleasure," he replied. "How's Grace?"

"A little shaken up. You know kids, they bounce back quickly."

"They certainly do. You take care now, Rosie."

Savage continued up to his room. Inside he sat on the bed and examined the sheet of numbers he'd found in Dave's jacket, hoping something might leap out at him. It didn't.

Outside on the landing, Savage heard the heavy footsteps of men coming up the stairs. Lots of them. Savage sprang off the bed and onto his feet. This is it, he thought. My time at Tivoli Gardens is about to come to an end. He put the sheet of numbers down on the bed and got ready to face whatever was coming through his door.

They didn't bother knocking. The door was unlocked and in trooped four big guys, dressed in black jeans and boots and various types of black bomber jacket. One of them had a completely bald head and a Bluetooth headset plugged in his ear. This must be the guy Tannaz had tracked down, Kieran Preston or 'Bluetooth'. The one who had given Sylvia Sanchez the burner phone, and possibly killed her and Jenny Hopkins.

Bluetooth had a cold, impassive face like a stone deity from Easter Island, hard and unrelenting. Savage could imagine him slitting someone's throat, then popping into M&S on his way home to pick up some bits for dinner, as if nothing had happened.

Both Bluetooth and the rest of the men radiated professionalism. Something about the way they held themselves broadcast that. Confident, calm and in control. Unlike Truck and Vlad, who were unskilled thugs, these guys definitely had brains and brawn, and that made them dangerous.

Once they'd all assembled in Savage's room, staring down at him, someone he recognised followed them in. He'd never met the man in the suit that entered his room. It was unmistakably Simon Wellington's son, Ben. He was a younger version of his old man, same wavy hair, except his was brown, not white. Same facial features, apart from the eyes. Ben's were turned down at the corners, giving them a slightly sleepy, melancholic look. Savage noticed a flicker of recognition as Ben Wellington glanced down at the list of numbers on the bed. He was definitely making a mental note of them, then he blinked and looked back at Savage.

"Please excuse us barging in like this, Mr Savage, I'm Ben Wellington." He spoke in a privately educated voice.

"I know this sounds like a cliché," said Savage. "I've been expecting you."

Ben Wellington managed a half-hearted smile. "It's okay, Mr Savage, we're not here to throw you out."

"Really? Are those guys here to do the cleaning? Make sure they wipe the sills down properly, they got missed last time."

"They're just a little security," Ben said. "You're a dangerous man by the sounds of it."

"Yes, how is Truck?"

"Oh, nothing that a few antibiotics can't cure."

"Send him my regards, everyone really misses him round here. So if you're not here to throw me out, how can I help you?"

"I've come to offer you a job."

CHAPTER 36

"**W**HAT SORT OF JOB?" ASKED Savage.

Ben cleared his throat, looked at the men behind him. Bluetooth nodded at him, as if giving him approval to continue. "Have you ever heard of bare-knuckle boxing?" he asked, the phrase not sitting well on his soft, private-school tongue.

"Of course," Savage replied.

"Well it's a bit like that. You fight an opponent. People bet on you. You get paid two thousand pounds."

"What if I lose?"

"Oh, don't worry, you still get paid."

Two thousand pounds wasn't very much for stepping into a ring without any gloves, facing an opponent he didn't know. Bare-knuckle boxers were usually paid a lot more for the risks they took.

"Make it five thousand," said Savage.

Bluetooth stepped forward, with an altogether harsher tone. "You're in no position to bargain. You're unknown so that's all you're worth. Next fight we'll think about upping the fee."

Savage thought for a moment. "And what if I don't want to fight?"

"Section twenty-one," Bluetooth replied. "You're out on your ass."

"So I really have no choice, then. I have to fight or I'm homeless."

Ben Wellington didn't say anything. His hands twitched nervously.

"It's that simple," said Bluetooth.

"Okay," said Savage. "Could I just say one thing?"

"Go ahead," said Ben.

"I'll do the fight on one condition. Rosie and her daughter Grace don't get thrown out on the street."

"Mr Savage," said Ben. "That was never our intention. Please apologise to her."

"Apologise yourself."

Ben Wellington smiled diplomatically. "From time to time, some of our employees get a little over zealous with their authority."

"Over zealous?" asked Savage. "They were going to rape her teenage daughter."

Ben Wellington winced. Looked ashamed. He seemed genuinely appalled, like bile had just crept up his throat and was burning the back of it. "Again, I'm very sorry. You have my word, Rosie and her daughter will be safe here."

"And what about Truck and Vlad the Inhaler?" Savage hadn't meant his little nickname for the rapey Romanian to slip out. A few of the henchmen chuckled quietly. Ben Wellington did not.

"They've left the organisation," he said. "They've been warned by my men not to come near Rosie and Grace or Tivoli Gardens. Like I said, you have my word."

"How good is your word?" asked Savage.

"Okay, shut up now," said Bluetooth. "You fight tonight, be ready at seven p.m."

"Tonight?"

"Yeah," said Bluetooth. "What's the matter, you got other plans?"

"Well, I had planned to take you to the vet's to get you neutered."

Unlike Truck or Vlad, the guy didn't react. After a beat he coolly said, "Just be ready at seven. Oh, one other thing. You do not talk about this to anyone. You hear? Otherwise, it's section twenty-one."

"I get it," said Savage. "First rule of Fight Club, you do not talk about Fight Club..."

"Okay, you're not taking this seriously. You're out on the street." Bluetooth and the thugs moved in on Savage, ready to take him down. Ben Wellington held up his hands, placatory.

"Gentlemen, please. Let's give Mr Savage the benefit of the doubt, shall we. He's new to this." Ben turned to face Savage, hands clasped together. "Mr Savage, you must not utter a word of this to anyone, inside or outside Tivoli Gardens, that's most important, otherwise I cannot guarantee you will have a room here, or in any Simon Wellington property."

"We can't guarantee your safety either," Bluetooth said menacingly. "I doubt anyone would miss you."

"I think threatening Mr Savage with homelessness will suffice for now," said Ben.

Savage took a deep breath. Did his best to look vulnerable and intimidated, not something that came easy to him. "I won't say a word," he said in a small defeated voice. "I don't want to go back on the street again."

"That usually does it," said Bluetooth. "Stay tight-lipped and you'll have a roof over your head and some cash in your pocket."

"Good," said Ben Wellington. "See you tonight at seven p.m."

The four big guys left the room, followed by Ben who flashed him a sympathetic smile. Savage watched from his window as they emerged outside and got into Wellington's Bentley Continental.

He called Tannaz.

"We've caught a break," he said.

"What do you mean?"

"Ben Wellington's been to see me with four of his goons. They want me to fight in a bare-knuckle boxing match. It has to be part of his father's underground betting ring. Has to be."

"Savage, are you going to be okay with that? I've heard bare-knuckle boxing is pretty harsh."

"I'll be fine. I'll just fight dirty, like I always do. It's the opportunity we've been waiting for. Get on the inside. Gather tons of intel."

"Just be careful."

"Always am. I need you to hack into the navigation system of

Ben Wellington's car, the Bentley Continental. Find out where it goes this evening and see if you can detect any video uploads. We might be able find them on the dark web."

"Already on it."

"Good."

Savage hung up. Paced the room. Now they were getting somewhere. Quite by accident. Ironic to think he was convinced he'd blown it by sticking up for Rosie when in fact it had led him deeper into the belly of the beast.

Savage needed to rest but he was too wired. He hadn't had any sleep after their night-time manoeuvres and he needed to be fresh for this fight. It'd be his second one of the day. At least this would be one on one, not two against one. Still, he needed to get a bit of shut eye and stop circling his room like a caged rat. He knew just the thing.

He knocked on Archie's door. A couple of fingers of whisky would do the trick, relax him just enough to rest without affecting his ability to fight.

No answer. He knocked again. No answer. Maybe he was asleep; probably recovering after his run through the forest.

Just then, Dink came up the stairs. "Hey, John," he said, looking like Hagrid from *Harry Potter*, his huge bulk swaying with every step.

"Hi, Dink," said Savage. "Have you seen Archie?"

"Yeah, he went out, just after you had that fight."

"Oh, know where he's gone?"

"No. He was in a hurry. Hey, do you fancy making some soup?"

"Sure, why not?" If he couldn't have a nip of whisky then maybe some hearty soup would be better, healthier. He needed to eat well if he was going to punch some random guy's head in tonight.

The two of them descended the stairs. Just as they reached the ground-floor hallway, Rosie's door opened.

"Hi," said Rosie.

"Hey," said Savage. "Are you hungry?"

"Always."

"Me too," said Dink. "We're making soup. Want to join us?"

"Yeah, okay. Why not?"

Savage killed a couple of hours with Dink and Rosie, gorging himself on too much bread and vegetable soup, enough to make him feel contented and lethargic. He made his excuses and headed back to his room where he napped a while, surfacing at about five p.m. He made himself some strong tea to wake himself up, double bagging it—two teabags, one cup for maximum potency. He'd never tried triple-bagging a cup of tea yet. He'd been tempted on a few occasions but liked the idea of having it in reserve, just in case he needed some extreme tea drinking.

At six forty-five, he was limbering up, getting some last-minute stretches in when the phone rang.

"Tannaz," said Savage, answering it. "Everything set? Are you tracking Ben Wellington's car?"

"That's what I'm calling about," said Tannaz anxiously. "Is the fight still on tonight?"

"I haven't heard anything to the contrary. Why?"

"Ben Wellington's car hasn't moved. It's still parked outside his house."

Savage paced the room, still warming up. "Maybe he's running late."

"Or maybe he's not coming at all."

"In which case, we can't track his car."

The rumble of an engine outside interrupted their conversation. Savage glanced out the window. A large black panel van came to a stop in front of Tivoli Gardens. The side door slid back and out jumped three large men, who made their way up to the front door, led by Bluetooth. Ben Wellington was not among them.

Savage relayed the licence-plate number of the van to Tannaz. "Can you track it?"

"Hold on." The clatter of high-speed typing came down the line. "One second, almost got it. Damn! It doesn't have a navigation system. Listen, it's not a problem. Just make sure you take your mobile with you. I can track its GPS."

Savage hung up. Pocketed his phone.

His door unlocked from the outside and Bluetooth invited himself in, his three henchmen in tow.

"Oh, please, come in, make yourself at home," said Savage.

"Frisk him," said Bluetooth. One of the guys obeyed, patting down Savage. He stopped when he reached Savage's trouser pocket and extracted his phone, held it up by the corner between his thumb and forefinger. "Clean," he said. "Apart from the mobile."

"Leave it here," said Bluetooth.

"Why can't I have my phone?" asked Savage.

"Because I said so. You can go on Grindr when you get back. Here, put this on him."

Bluetooth threw a black hood at one of the men, who caught it and slipped it over Savage's head, pulling a drawstring tight at the bottom.

He had no idea where they were taking him, and without his phone, neither would Tannaz.

CHAPTER 37

A CLOUD OF HIS STALE BREATH filled the bag. Savage estimated they'd been on the road for about ten minutes. From what he could tell, he was in the back of the panel van with at least two of Wellington's men. The other two had to be up front in the cab. Thankfully, they weren't the talkative types, which gave Savage the chance to listen hard to other sounds and get some idea of where they were taking him. To his left he heard the pop and clunk of a train matching them for speed. Slower than a passenger train, it sounded heavy and plodding. A freight train passing through Southampton's container port. This meant they were driving parallel to the docks. Other vehicles rushed past the van on the inside and outside lanes. A three-lane highway. That confirmed it, they were on Millbrook Road, heading out of Southampton towards the forest. Where else? Everything Wellington did seemed to involve the forest. He was obsessed with it. Or maybe it was the best place for things to happen without prying eyes.

Soon after, the noise of cars passing them on either side ceased. They were in single-file traffic, definitely on the A35—the main drag through the forest—the same road they'd taken with Bonafide Ride and when they'd followed Archie. If Savage remembered correctly, Ashurst would be the next town. It had a few nice-looking pubs with vast beer gardens. Inside the stifling hood, the thought of a cool beer made him salivate. A nice, local New Forest pale ale. He quickly dismissed the thought. Had to stop thinking like that. Had to stay sharp, focused. Couldn't lose it now. Concentrated on following the virtual map he drew in his brain.

Then it all went wrong.

The van veered sharply to the right.

They were off the main road, on something far more potholed and lumpy. A track perhaps? Could they be nearing their destination?

Suddenly the van was back on something smoother. It immediately accelerated.

From then on the van meandered, throwing Savage right and left. At one point it felt like they had driven around a circle.

Were they doing this to disorientate him? He hadn't credited them with that much foresight. It seemed he'd underestimated them.

After about twenty minutes of erratic driving, Savage had lost all sense of direction and had no idea where they were. He was sure they were still in the forest, judging by the quality of road surface, but that was all he had. The forest covered over one hundred and forty-five square miles. He could be anywhere.

The van slowed, took a sharp turn, then its wheels bumped up what felt like a kerb. The engine revved and stopped.

The woosh of a roller door closing came from behind.

The handbrake clicked on.

"Showtime," said Bluetooth.

The hood was removed. Savage gasped and took several unencumbered breaths until another hood was thrown at him. More of a mask than a hood. Bright red, it had two eye holes and laces at the back for tightening it up, like a Mexican wrestling mask.

"Take your top off and put that on your head," said Bluetooth.

Savage looked puzzled. "Who am I fighting, Nacho Libre?"

"Just put it on."

Savage removed his sweatshirt and T-shirt and put the mask on his head. One of the guys next to him went behind him to tighten and tie the laces of his mask.

"Whoa," the guy said. "Nice set of scars." He was referring

to the long, gouging wounds on Savage's back. The ones he'd received when he was captured and beaten in Iraq. "Who gave you those?"

"My ex-wife," Savage joked.

The sliding door opened and Savage was shoved out, getting his first glimpse of the fight venue.

Savage had never been to a bare-knuckle boxing match. Being from London he'd heard all about them. He expected to see an array of blokes, geezers and ne'er-do-wells, as Tannaz would have archaically described them. Men with weapon dogs smoking roll-ups or cheap cigars. Shifty types in flat caps with chalkboards taking bets with fistfuls of cash, barking out odds. And a makeshift ring made of hay bales.

There was none of that. Not many people, either. Hardly any. No sign of Ben Wellington or his father. Apart from the men he had come with and a couple of others, no one else was there. Except his opponent. He wore a blue mask. His shirt was off too. Carrying a lot of weight, the guy was out of shape, and bigger than Savage. He had at least five-inches height on him. They stared at each other for a while. Two grown men in masks with their guts hanging over their belt buckles, an absurd sight.

Savage broke the deadlock and looked away, desperately searching for any indication of where he was. There wasn't any. He was inside a large, bland, featureless metal-framed warehouse. Rough concrete floor and corrugated walls, lit with blinding fluorescent tubes. He could be on a farm or an industrial estate. Anywhere.

As Savage turned to look in the other direction, he saw a sight that made him gasp. At the other end of the warehouse was a giant cage. Its bars were swirly and ornate, almost steam-punk in design. Like a giant rectangular bird cage but instead of keeping birds this one was for fighting. This must be the one supplied by Nortoft & Sons, the Welsh blacksmiths. Wellington had it made for him bespoke—ever the showman.

Around the outside of the cage, placed at regular intervals, were six cameras on tripods.

Savage got another shock.

Adjusting one of the cameras was a face he recognised. Bald with thick-rimmed glasses, clad head to foot in black, was the goth guy Savage and Tannaz had encountered in Dead Maids with his morbid girlfriend, taking pictures of trees and wittering on about how beautiful death was. What the hell was he doing here? With his skinny, black, match-like silhouette, he looked completely out of place with Wellington's meaty goons. He was obviously being used for his filming skills.

Goth-guy finished adjusting the cameras, glanced momentarily at Savage and went and sat down behind a fold-up camping table. Placed on it was a laptop, with leads running out the back of it to each of the cameras. This guy must be controlling the upload of the fight to the dark web or wherever the hell it was going. He plugged in a headset and began typing away, focused on his work.

Savage was glad of the mask. Goth-guy would've certainly recognised him after their encounter in the forest.

Savage turned his attention back to the cage. As he looked closer, he could see hooks attached to the inside of it, with various weapons hanging from them. Big, brutal skull-crushing weapons: a length of scaffold pipe, a Japanese Samurai sword, a sledgehammer, some heavy-duty chain, a massive club, a pike staff, plus various other nasty implements.

This was not good. Not good at all.

Savage knew how to fight with his bare hands. He knew how to fight with firearms and explosives and knives. But fighting with large medieval-style hand-held weapons, he had little experience.

Savage turned to Bluetooth. "You said this was a bare-knuckle boxing match, not Thunderdome."

"I never said that," Bluetooth replied.

"Ben Wellington said it was a bare-knuckle boxing match," Savage replied.

"He didn't say it *was* a bare-knuckle boxing match. He said it was *like* a bare-knuckle boxing match. Now man up."

Savage swore. Felt uncontrollable panic rising up through his core and overflowing into his mind like a blocked drain. He had to get his mind in check. ASAP.

Breathe. Recalibrate. Deliver.

He closed his eyes momentarily. Sucked in a big gulp of air. Cleared his mind. Allowed himself to think.

This was a minor setback. He just had to adapt his strategy. This was a fight in a cage. That's all. He needed to know his parameters. Get intel.

"What are the rules?" Savage asked.

"Rules? No rules," said Bluetooth.

"Okay," said Savage. "What happens when we get in the cage? Do we get given weapons? Pick them ourselves? How does this work?"

"You ask a lot of questions," said Bluetooth. "You go in, face each other in the middle. When I yell fight, you grab a weapon, whatever you like, then you can guess the rest."

Suddenly Jeff Perkins woke up.

"My oh my, what have you got yourself into now?" he said. *"I leave you alone and then I come back and you're in some insane gladiatorial match. Nice mask by the way. At least they can't see your shame."*

Shut up, Jeff. I'm trying to think. Formulate a strategy.

"Well better hurry up, because the first round's about to begin. You could come out of this with some life-changing injuries, looking at those weapons. I really don't know why I bother trying to get you to kill yourself, you seem to be doing a really good job on your own."

Good, I'm glad you feel that way, you can leave me alone then.

"Hey, this is just like Harry Potter and The Goblet of Fire.*"*

Savage groaned inside, clearly Jeff Perkins had no intention of going away. He'd do his utmost to put Savage off. Distract him and make sure he got hurt as much as possible.

"You know, the one with Edward Cullen in it."

Cedric Diggory. Edward Cullen is from Twilight.

"Whatever. You liked The Goblet of Fire, *didn't you? Said the kids' acting got better. Of course, the adults always outshone*

the kids in Harry Potter *movies, especially Mad Eye Moody, now what's that actor's name?"*

Brendan Gleeson. Now, Jeff, I really need to get my head ready for this fight...

This was so far from where his head needed to be. He should have been forming a plan of attack, not having his brain filled with images of children in robes doing magic spells.

Jeff wouldn't shut up, keeping Savage from what he knew he needed to do, derailing his chances of winning.

"What did Madeye Moody say to Harry just before he faced the Hungarian Horntail? 'Play to your strengths.' Do you remember? Harry's no good at spells but he's good at flying. That's my favourite scene, when he summons the broomstick. Accio Firebolt! Hey, maybe you could try that, Accio chainsaw!' Doesn't quite sound right, does it? Accio chainsaw. Imagine if Harry did summon a chainsaw in that scene. Would've made it ten times better."

Savage's interest piqued.

The thing with hearing voices is sometimes they want to kill you, other times they want to help you, even if it doesn't sound like they do, even if they're not aware of it. Jeff was trying to help him, in the most roundabout, surreal way he could.

That's not a bad idea.

"What, summon a broomstick and fly out of here? Savage, you've really lost the plot."

No, the other thing you said. Play to your strengths.

"What are you going to do? Because I'm pretty sure medieval weapons weren't in your SAS training."

"You'll find out. Now shut up."

The goth guy sitting at the table gave the thumbs up. All the red lights on the video cameras around the ring came on. Bluetooth stood beside Goth-guy, looking over his shoulder at the laptop screen.

"Okay," said Bluetooth. "Gentlemen, would you like to enter the ring."

Savage followed the other masked fighter. They both climbed

in through a door in the cage, which was shut and bolted behind them.

"Stand in the middle, face to face, three feet apart."

They did as they were asked.

Savage sized up his opponent. His opponent did the same.

With the extra weight, the guy he faced breathed heavily, his big belly rising and falling with every inhalation. Good for what Savage had in mind. His opponent may have been bigger and stronger. He'd also be slower.

"Okay, gentleman. Just another minute or two, bets are still coming in."

Savage used the time to slow down his heart rate. Cool his head, and go over his strategy.

He surveyed the weapons for their usefulness. Weighed up which one would be the most effective. The pikestaff was good, great for keeping the enemy at a distance. It was also unwieldy and clumsy. He dismissed it. The scaffold pole was better, shorter, and you could still use it to keep an opponent away. However, it was heavy. Striking a blow would be slow. Same went for the chain and the sledgehammer. They relied on your opponent standing still long enough for you to hit them, and opponents, unlike fights in movies, had an annoying habit of moving when you were trying to bash their heads in.

Savage dismissed several of the other weapons, and settled on the Samurai sword. Light and devastating, it could inflict horrendous damage and keep an enemy at bay. That's what his opponent would go for, if he were smart. The guy would want to grab it first, which meant he'd go left once the signal was given.

The goth guy at the laptop gave the thumbs up again.

"Okay," said Bluetooth. "All bets are in. Gentlemen get ready. In a second I will shout 'fight', you are then free to select whichever weapon you wish from within the ring and kill your opponent."

"What?" Savage shouted.

"Didn't you know?" said his opponent, sniggering. "This is a fight to the death."

CHAPTER 38

S AVAGE RUSHED TO THE SIDE of the cage. "Hey, I didn't
sign up for this."

"Cut the cameras," Bluetooth said. All at once the red
lights on each camera flicked off. Bluetooth pulled a gun from
inside his jacket, pointed it at Savage. "Get back in position or I'll
shoot you."

Savage raised his hands. "You never told me I had to kill
someone." He could hear his opponent laughing behind him.

"Too bad. Life sucks," said Bluetooth, aiming the gun at him.
"Now get back to where you were. There's a lot of money riding
on this fight."

Reluctantly, Savage moved back to his spot in front of his
opponent. There was nothing he could do, he'd have to fight for
his life. Just like he'd been doing all his life. Business as usual.

"You know something?" said his opponent. "I'm undefeated
in this ring, already killed five guys before you."

"Tell him how many people you've killed, Savage."

Not now, Jeff. Need to concentrate.

The video cameras came back on.

"Sorry, ladies and gentlemen," said Goth-guy into his headset,
presumably apologising to all the online betters on the dark web.
"Little technical glitch but we're up and running again."

"Right," said Bluetooth. "Get ready fighters in the cage..."

Savage prepared to pounce. He had no intention of going for a
weapon. He'd play to his strengths. Go straight for his opponent.
Engage him hand-to-hand, that's what Savage was good at, and
stop him from getting his hands on that Samurai sword. Keep him

in the centre of the ring. If his opponent couldn't get a weapon, he'd have to fight Savage on his terms. Fists, feet and elbows. Savage was very good at hurting people with his fists, feet and elbows. Also his teeth, fingers and anything else he could think of.

"Fight!" shouted Bluetooth.

His opponent went right, not left, racing towards the scaffold pipe. Savage lost a valuable split second, darting the wrong way. A quick course correction and he was right behind him, chasing the guy's wide, hairy back.

His opponent was about three feet from the weapon when Savage looped his left arm around the guy's neck. He interlocked his right arm behind, almost like his arms were folded with the guy's neck trapped between them. Savage squeezed his forearms together, choking him. Simultaneously he dragged the guy back to the centre of the ring.

Blue Mask was caught off guard. But not for long.

With all his weight, his opponent tried throwing Savage off his back, tossing him left and right. He still had plenty of fight in him. The chokehold was taking too long.

Savage kicked Blue Mask hard in the back of his left heel. The guy's leg shot out from under him. Savage did the same with the right heel, kicking it out.

Both men tumbled over backwards, and that's when his opponent struck. As they fell to the floor, the other guy snapped his head back and butted Savage in the face with the back of his skull. The full weight of him landed on Savage, knocking the air out of him.

Savage was dazed and winded.

His opponent seized his chance, got to his feet and went for the scaffold pipe.

Get up! shouted a voice in his head. Not Jeff's, thankfully. More the voice of desperate self-preservation.

Savage rolled over, came to his feet, right in front of the pike staff. A big, brutal weapon.

Over his shoulder, he saw Blue Mask running at him, scaffold pole in his fists, held aloft, ready to come crashing down on Savage's skull.

No time for anything fancy. Savage gripped the end of the pikestaff and swung it around in a huge arc. His opponent was too close for the sharp metal pike to be any good, but the wooden shaft collided with the side of his midriff. Savage withdrew the pike, making sure the metal spearhead slid across the guy's ribs, slicing open a small wound.

When the pikestaff was fully retracted, Savage thrust it forward, hoping to stab his opponent in the chest. The guy was wise to this and sidestepped it. For a big guy, his reactions were quick.

His opponent came at him again, getting inside the useful striking distance of the pikestaff, making it next to useless. Blue Mask swung. Savage lifted up the shaft of his weapon to block the scaffold pole. It came crashing through, breaking his weapon in two and catching Savage on the top of his head. The shaft had taken the brunt of the blow. It still hurt like hell.

Savage sucked up the pain and with the broken end of the shaft, caught his opponent in the jaw. He followed it up by jabbing it into his gut. Savage added a shin kick for good measure.

Savage went in for another. Unlike Truck, this guy read his tactics and took a step back, giving himself room to swing the scaffold pole again.

It collided with Savage's upper arm, nearly breaking it.

Another swing. This time to Savage's head. He ducked, just a glancing blow but enough to worry Savage. This guy knew what he was doing. And he was good with his weapon of choice.

Savage kept retreating, uselessly holding two feet of broken wooden shaft in his hand. A poor weapon against five feet of thick cylindrical steel.

More blows came, thick and fast. He ducked and dodged them, one after another. Eventually, Savage's luck would run dry. He'd get knocked out and then the killer blow would come, putting him out of action for good.

Savage suppressed a tinge of panic spreading from every inch of his marrow. He'd been in worse situations than this. Had to stay positive.

Whoosh. The scaffold pole missed the tip of his nose by inches.

The tinge of panic grew in strength.

Blue Mask had Savage on the back foot. He couldn't keep retreating forever.

He needed a new tactic.

Breathe. Recalibrate. Deliver.

There wasn't much time to breathe or recalibrate. Savage thought fast, as he dodged out of the way of each new swing of the scaffold pole.

The large metal tube his opponent held was a far superior weapon than the bit of wood Savage had. He could get another weapon. Go for the samurai sword. He didn't know how to fight with a sword and this guy clearly knew how to wield a length of pipe to devastating effect. What about the other weapons? He didn't know how to use any of them. Plus, if he did try to grab a new weapon, even the split second it took could give his opponent the chance to strike.

Maybe the best weapon was already in his hands.

Where was Blue Mask vulnerable? He could only use his weapon if he could keep hold of it. His fists. Savage remembered his school days, of being rapped across the knuckles with a ruler. It was worse than being caned.

The next blow came. Savage dodged it then sprang forward and cracked his enemy hard on the right knuckle with the broken shaft. That would be his target from now on.

Another blow came. Again, Savage darted forward. Hit him across the fingers of his right hand then darted back again.

The next swing of the scaffold pipe, Savage moved sideways, allowing the pipe to catch him in the ribs. He did this on purpose, taking a hit so he could hook his left arm around the pipe, trapping it in place. With his other hand, Savage rained down blow after merciless blow on his opponent's right hand. Vicious cracks of the broken wooden shaft.

His opponent had no choice. He had to let go. The bones

of his right knuckle almost certainly crushed and crumbling. Now his opponent held the pipe with only his left hand. Fifty percent weaker.

The guy didn't give up and tried another attack. But with just one hand, his blows were slow, clumsy and predictable.

As one came down, aimed at Savage's head, he discarded his end of the broken shaft and caught the pipe with both hands. Gripping it firmly, he shrugged his opponent towards him and kicked him hard in the groin.

The guy went down on his knees.

Savage wrenched the pipe from him and struck him in the side of his head.

Blue Mask toppled over and onto his back, staring up at Savage, eyes half-lidded.

Savage stood over him, holding the pipe vertically above his opponent's face, ready to slam it down and put him out of action for good.

"Please," he said in a small, weak voice. "Please don't. I have a wife and kids. I just do this to feed them."

Savage hesitated. Didn't feel like killing the guy, even before his sob story.

He threw away the scaffold pipe, which clanged on the floor, turned and walked towards the door in the cage.

"Let me out," said Savage.

No one watching responded.

"I said, let me out."

There was a scuffle of feet behind him. Savage turned to see his opponent up and running at him. So much for his sob story.

The guy must have still been dazed because he wasn't thinking straight. He hadn't thought to pick up a weapon to fight with. "I'm gonna kill you," he shouted as he ran towards Savage.

Savage ducked low and punched him in his already injured groin. The guy crumpled. Savage straightened up and punched him again, hard in the throat, crushing his larynx. Blue Mask fell over backwards clutching his neck, gasping for air.

Savage turned to the small gathering of men. "He needs to

go to hospital. He needs an emergency tracheotomy or he's going to die."

The lights on all the cameras went off. Bluetooth approached the cage, unbolted the door and climbed in. He stood over the guy lying on the floor, painfully straining to breathe. Then he raised his boot and brought it down on the guy's throat. Once. Then twice.

Savage's opponent lay still and unbreathing. Eyes lifeless.

"He doesn't need a tracheotomy anymore," said Bluetooth coldly.

CHAPTER 39

THE MASK WAS RIPPED OFF Savage's head. The side door of the van slid back to reveal a dank, misty morning outside Tivoli Gardens. After the fight, they'd made Savage stay behind and help dismantle the giant cage. He figured they probably never used the same venue twice. It took them all night to break down the cage, unbolting it piece by piece. At least they had the civility to stop for a tea break half way through. It had been the second night without sleep for Savage. Exhaustion and pain nagged at every inch of his body.

Bluetooth stood at the door and pushed a roll of notes into Savage's hand. A bunch of twenties adding up to a couple of hundred quid.

"What happened to the two grand?" asked Savage. He had to pretend to keep up appearances, he was a desperate man on benefits.

"You didn't kill the guy," said Bluetooth. "Next time, you kill the guy, you get paid in full." Savage got shoved out onto the pavement. Just before slamming the sliding door, Bluetooth said, "Remember, keep your mouth shut about this or you'll join the guy you've just fought. We'll be in touch."

Savage watched the van accelerate away. He turned and walked slowly up to the front door, each step hurting. Now the adrenalin had worn off, the bruises were starting to make themselves known. He'd need to get some ice from the convenience store to put on them. First he needed a cup of tea, half a dozen to be honest, and he needed to call Tannaz.

Up in his room, he supped his tea and felt marginally better. Picked up the phone and called Tannaz.

"Tell me you got something," he said.

No response from Tannaz.

"Tannaz?"

"I'm here," she said. "Savage, I've got nothing."

"What?"

"Listen, I scoured the dark web for signs of a fight being broadcast live. There was nothing."

Savage swore. "How can there be nothing? I saw the guy from the forest. The goth guy who was taking pictures."

"What was he doing there?"

"He was in charge of the upload. He had cameras set up all around the ring and a laptop. And do you know what the ring was? It was that ornamental cage Wellington ordered from Nortoft & Sons, I'm sure of it. All swirly metal like a bird cage, except it was full of nasty stuff. Bits of pipes and swords and chains. And it was a fight to the death."

"What? I thought it was a bare-knuckle boxing match. Did you have to kill someone?"

"Very nearly. I refused so that guy Bluetooth, the one we think killed Jenny, stepped in and finished him off. So you can see why I'm pretty pissed off that I've just been through all that only for you to tell me you've found nothing. What the hell were you doing all night?"

"I'm sorry, there was nothing, I looked and looked."

"And we don't have the location of the fight either?"

"No, I tried tracking your phone. It just stayed put."

"They made me leave it, put a hood over my head. So basically, you got nothing out of this. A big fat zero."

"Hey," said Tannaz, her voice suddenly incendiary. "Give me a break. Do you know how hard this is? Do you? Do you think I just hit a button that says 'find bad guys'? Do you know how big the dark web is, and how difficult it is to negotiate and find what you want, and cover your tracks, so people don't get suspicious and come after you?"

Savage took a breath. Exhaled. He hadn't felt this tired for a long time. "Look, I'm sorry. I've just had a hard night. I know how difficult what you do is. I can't do this without you."

"I'm sorry too. Things sometimes don't go to plan, you said it yourself. Are you sure the fight was online?"

"Yes. The goth guy had a headset. I heard him speak to people betting online."

"Did he recognise you?"

"No. I was wearing one of those Mexican wrestler's masks."

"So Goth-guy's working for Wellington?"

"Would seem so..." The line went quiet. "Tannaz? Tannaz?"

Savage could hear her rummaging around in the background. Tannaz came back on the line. "Sorry, I was just trying to find those memory cards we took off him and his girlfriend. You know, the ones with all the pictures of trees."

"Yes, goths up trees." Savage could hear something being slotted into her laptop. Then fingers typing on a keyboard. "Tannaz, are you still there?"

"Just give me a moment."

Savage waited, serenaded down the phone by increasingly fast tapping.

"I think those pictures are about more than goths up trees," said Tannaz.

"What?"

"I've been sloppy," said Tannaz. "Real sloppy."

"Just tell me what it is."

"The photos. I didn't bother looking at them in detail. Just thought they were a bunch of stupid trees taken by two idiots obsessed with death and spooky places. Didn't look any further. I've just pulled up the metadata on each image, and something's been added."

"I thought you couldn't muck around with metadata."

"You can't. Not unless you have the right software or a high-end digital camera like those two goths."

"What did they add to the metadata?"

"A number. A three-digit number followed by a four-digit

number. Savage, they match the numbers on that list we found in Dave's jacket pocket."

"Stay where you are," said Savage. "I'm coming over to you."

Ignoring the pain signals coming from every inch of his body, he burst out of his bedroom, down the stairs and out the front door, almost bumping straight into Archie coming the other way.

"Fancy a whisky and that?" asked Archie, bottle in his hand, even though it was before breakfast. "Hey, what happened to your face?"

"Not now, Archie. Gotta run."

Savage caught a bus and was at the airport in thirty-five minutes. At the hotel he sprinted straight up to Tannaz's room, his stomach grumbled angrily through lack of food. In the last fifteen hours, all he'd had was two cups of tea.

First thing he did when he got to Tannaz's room was put the kettle on.

Tannaz had her laptop open, the screen was a grid of photos taken by the goth couple. A copy of the printout from Dave's room was beside it.

"The numbers embedded in each image," she said, "match a number on the printout. Each number corresponds with a tree in Dead Maids Woods. And you know what else I found?"

"Go on."

"Now that I know they're trees, it's narrowed down the search parameters. I know what the numbers mean. They're tree preservation orders."

"Tree preservation orders? What, to prevent them being cut down?"

"Yes. Every tree in Dead Maids Wood has a tree preservation order on it."

"And the one that's ringed on Dave's list?"

"That's the only number that doesn't have an image to go with it."

"Can you find the location of it?"

"Why?"

"Because I reckon the number ringed on that list is the tree Dave used to kill himself."

Tannaz opened up more windows on her screen, simultaneously searching several at once. Savage found it hard to keep up with what she was doing. Everything flew across the screen in a blur. She settled on one, and said, "Locations of tree preservation orders are shown by local councils on their web portals. Every tree in the country that is preserved is listed online. Weirdly, not the ones on Dave's printout. They still don't show up anywhere. That's why it was so hard for us to find out what they were. I still don't get why they're not listed online and every other tree preservation order is."

Savage thought for a moment. Paced the room, sipping his tea. "That's because it's Crown land."

"Crown land?"

"Yes, owned by the monarchy. They don't have to make anything public if they don't want to—that's why we couldn't make sense of the numbers. Unlike local government, which has to make everything public, the Crown is under no such obligation. Queen can do what the hell she wants. Eat a swan. Rob a bank."

"Rob a bank?"

"Technically she could. It's her country. Like Judge Dredd, she is the law. The prosecuting force in the UK. She can't exactly arrest herself."

"So what do we do?"

"Go to the Forestry Commission. Show them the list. Hopefully if we ask them nicely they'll tell us where this tree is." He pointed to the number that was ringed in red pen on Dave's list. "I bet this is the tree Dave used."

Tannaz nodded. "We still don't know what any of this means."

Savage said, "Well, we know Goth-guy is working for Wellington senior. Remember what he said when we took the memory cards off him? He said, 'It's for our work. Now we'll have to start all over again.' They weren't just out there on a goth jolly, snapping pictures of spooky trees. My theory is Wellington had him go there to create an image library of the trees. One of which Dave Mosely was found dead in."

"I still don't get why Wellington would do that. Why would he need pictures of preserved trees?"

"That's what we need to find out. First we go to the Forestry Commission. Confirm whether the one ringed on the list is the one Dave was found dead in, then we find out who cut down the tree. They might know something."

CHAPTER 40

THEY FOLLOWED THE A35 OUT of the city and into the forest, stopping at Lyndhurst, home to the headquarters of the Forestry Commission for the South of England. A handsomely proportioned three-storey, red-brick building with generous-sized windows, it reminded Savage of a large Victorian schoolhouse. Maybe that's what it started life as until the population of Lyndhurst grew and its children had to be educated elsewhere.

They parked up on a patch of gravel in front of the building and crunched their way towards the door marked 'Reception'. Inside was a long, plain, scrubbed wooden counter stretching across the length of a tall-ceilinged room. A computer terminal sat at one end. Educational posters covered the walls informing people to not feed the forest's wild ponies and to keep to its forty-miles-an-hour speed limit. One poster asked for volunteers to help look after the forest. Savage felt an overwhelming urge to sign up there and then. He couldn't think of a better way of spending his days than keeping an ancient forest in order, mending fences and keeping footpaths clear; of early-morning winter starts, putting his back into it and his breath condensing in front of him. First he had a psychopath to stop. Wellington.

Savage patted a gleaming brass reception bell. Seconds later, a slim, red-faced, outdoorsy type joined them, dressed in a green fleece with the Forestry Commission logo embroidered on the left side, and a name tag informing them he was called 'Trevor' pinned on the other.

Trevor smiled, his weathered face revealing a web of crow's feet around his eyes. "How can I help you?"

Savage slid the printout of numbers across the counter. "Is this one of your printouts?"

"Where did you get this?" Trevor asked, his smile disappearing.

Tannaz ignored his question. "These are tree preservation orders, right?"

Trevor eyed the list suspiciously. "The forest is Crown land. Under our protection. We don't usually give out this information to the public."

Trevor may have had the ruddy appearance of a woodsman but at heart he was a bureaucrat, a stickler for rules. Probably saw himself as some sort of defender of the realm, protecting the monarchy's land.

"We're trying to find the location of this tree." Savage pointed to the ringed number.

"We think the tree might have been cut down," said Tannaz.

Trevor didn't say anything. Stared blankly at her.

Tannaz continued, "Don't you think it's odd that a tree with a preservation order has been cut down?"

"Not really," Trevor replied. "Trees with preservation orders get cut down all the time."

"We're just concerned citizens," said Savage. "We love the forest and want to make sure the wrong tree hasn't been cut down. I mean some of those trees are over a thousand years old."

"It was a beautiful fir tree in Dead Maids. Huge," Tannaz added.

Trevor suddenly became interested. "I thought Dead Maids was all deciduous. Are you sure?"

"Positive. Maybe it's best to check."

Trevor thought for a second. Curiosity got the better of him. He reluctantly picked up the printout and moved onto the computer at the end of the counter. After a few clicks of the mouse he said, "It's a Douglas fir. They're extremely prone to disease. They have to be cut down to stop it spreading." Trevor went quiet, peered closer at the screen. "That's odd."

"What's odd?" asked Savage.

"Well, to cut a tree down, especially one with a preservation order, you have to put in a request for felling approval. Has to be authorised by a senior manager. The box here is empty, no approval's been given but the tree's been felled. That's not the way we do things round here."

"Who requested the felling approval?" asked Savage.

"One of our Forest Management Technicians, chap called Joel Diplock."

"And who cut the tree down?" asked Tannaz.

"Same person," said Trevor. "Joel Diplock."

"So we're saying that he's chopped a tree down without permission."

"Certainly seems like it," said Trevor, concern in his voice. "I really appreciate you bringing this to my attention."

"Why would he do that?" asked Savage.

"I have no idea. Staff aren't supposed to go around felling trees willy-nilly. Not on my watch."

Joel Diplock was in trouble, but Savage got the distinct impression it would be Trevor's head on the block.

"Is he in today?" asked Savage.

"No, it's his day off."

"Okay," Savage replied. "Is it possible to get an exact location of the tree? Just want to make sure it's the one we think it is. That we're not wasting your time."

"I'll send out a team of technicians to make sure."

"That sounds complicated," said Savage. "We can head over there now, check it out. Make sure it's the right one so your guys don't have a wasted journey. Plus, if it has been cut down mistakenly, you probably don't want everyone finding out. Wouldn't be good for morale or the image of the New Forest."

Trevor went quiet. Considered Savage's words. Trevor was clearly committed to the protection of the New Forest, but he was more committed to his own self-preservation. "Okay," he muttered. "Would you mind calling me and no one else. I'm here all day."

"Understood," Savage replied.

Trevor hit a few keys on the computer. A printer at the back whirred into life and spat out a single sheet. He retrieved it and stapled it on top of Savage's original list of numbers, then placed it in front of them. It was a map of Dead Maids. Covered in hundreds of black dots, each one with the tree-preservation order number beside it and its GPS co-ordinates underneath.

Trevor pointed with his pen. "Each dot represents a tree." He ringed one of them with his pen. "This is the tree Joel Diplock felled. The tree on your list. Put the GPS co-ordinates into your smart phone, and it will lead you straight to it."

"Wow," said Savage. "So every preserved tree is logged with GPS co-ordinates?"

"Correct," Trevor replied. "Makes it so much easier. We used to mark diseased trees with a yellow X for felling. Our crews had to go out hunting with their chainsaws for elusive X's marked on the trunk. Took ages. With GPS they can just go straight to them. Saves so much time."

"Wait," said Savage. "So do trees still get marked with a yellow X when they need to be cut down?"

"Not anymore."

"How long has it been like that?"

"Last five or six years."

Savage thought for a moment. "So no trees have been marked with X's since then."

"No, there'd be no point."

"Is there a chance a tree got marked the traditional way? Maybe if someone forgot," asked Tannaz.

"Possible, but highly unlikely. We used yellow to mark a preserved tree to be felled. Now we have GPS we don't bother ordering yellow spray anymore. We still use other colours for different things. Blue for a tree near a boundary, red for timber harvesting. But not yellow, just don't have it in our stores."

"Thank you, Trevor," said Savage. "You've been extremely helpful. One other thing, has a goth couple been in asking about this area?"

Trevor looked puzzled and shook his head.

"Okay, thanks," said Savage.

"Make sure you contact me when you find the fir," Trevor said. "Here's my number." He scribbled down his mobile number on the top of the printout.

"Will do."

Tannaz and Savage returned to the VW van. "Okay," said Savage, starting up the engine. "So I have another theory."

"Go on."

"We thought Dave selected a tree that would suit his needs. Scoped it out alone, then went back later and killed himself up it."

"Isn't that what happened?"

"No." Savage held up the two printouts. The original list of numbers, plus the location map stapled to it. "I think someone gave this to Dave, told him which tree he needed to use for his suicide. Ringed it and maybe gave him a location map, exactly like this one. Remember the list had staple marks in it. Except the location map and the list became separated. I think Dave took the map with him to find his way through Dead Maids. Left the list of numbers behind in his room because he didn't need it."

"Okay, plausible," said Tannaz. "Even with the map of GPS locations it doesn't help him find the tree."

"Why not?"

"Because Dave was a complete technophobe. Luke said he didn't have a computer, he hated them so we can safely assume he didn't have a smart phone, and the GPS co-ordinates would be useless to him. If someone picked the tree for him, how was he going to find the right one?"

"So the map gets him in the right area, then all he needs to do is find the tree marked with a yellow X, old-school style. He doesn't need a smart phone. And if they used yellow, that points the finger at a forest worker still following tradition. A tree which he later fells without permission."

"You think this Joel Diplock did it? And what does this have to do with Wellington and all those trees?"

"Don't know. Joel Diplock is now suspect number one. Has to

be. First we go to Dead Maids. Confirm these co-ordinates. Check we're not barking up the wrong tree."

Tannaz groaned at his pun.

"Sorry, that wasn't intended. After that, we find Joel Diplock. And get answers."

CHAPTER 41

J UST AFTER LUNCH, SAVAGE'S VW van pulled into the car park at Dead Maids Wood. They both got out. Seconds later, another car entered the car park and pulled up nearby. A fairly new Toyota estate with two child seats in the back, no doubt covered in crumbs and indelibly stained with sticky baby food and dried up puddles of juice. The only occupant of the car stepped out of the driver's side. A spectacled man, possibly mid-thirties, he was tall and greying at the sides, his back slightly hunched, his shoulders sloping, the result of hours and hours slumped at a boring desk job, no doubt. Dressed in outdoor walking gear; powder blue hiking jacket and brown walking boots, he slung a rucksack over his shoulder and disappeared into the forest before Savage had a chance to say 'afternoon'.

"He's in a hurry," said Tannaz. "Maybe he didn't like the look of us."

"Nah, guy's got young kids. See the car seats? This is his day off and he probably just wants a bit of alone time in the forest."

"Well, he'll certainly get that in Dead Maids."

"Too right," said Savage. "Come on, let's make sure this is the tree on Dave's list, then we can question this Diplock fellow."

Tannaz punched the GPS co-ordinates into her smart phone and off they trekked.

About an hour later, they came in sight of the felled Douglas fir, still lying helplessly on the ground. A defeated giant. Exactly the same one they'd seen last time they were here.

"Well, there's no doubt about it. This is definitely the tree ringed on Dave's list," said Tannaz.

"Good. Now we can confront Diplock and get to the bottom of why he cut it down."

They turned tail and began walking back to the car. "Seems like a bit of a waste of time, doing this," said Tannaz. "It was a pretty fair guess that it would be the one."

"One thing I've learnt in all my years," said Savage. "Never assume anything. What if the co-ordinates were for a different tree, and we went off to accuse Joel Diplock? We'd look pretty stupid. Always check the facts, no matter how tedious or obvious things look. That reminds me." Savage kept his word to Trevor and texted him to say they'd positively identified the tree.

They headed back. After ten minutes Tannaz stopped for a cigarette.

"I thought you were in a hurry with this investigation?" Savage asked.

"Yes, but I need to feed my addiction." She sat down on a tree stump and sparked up the end of a Marlboro. "Don't worry, I'll take the butt and ash home with me," she selected a large damp leaf off the ground and used it as a makeshift ash tray.

After her last puff, she ground out the cigarette on the leaf, wrapped it up and put it in the pocket of her biker jacket.

"Hey, do you want to hear a joke?" asked Savage. He didn't wait for her reply. "Did you hear about the man who had a dog with no legs?"

Tannaz rolled her eyes, and reluctantly shook her head, disinterested.

"He called it Cigarette because every night he'd take it out for a drag."

She tried to keep a straight face but couldn't stop a smile from forming.

"Hey, you laughed at one of my jokes."

"Smiled, not laughed," she corrected him. "Hey, what's that over there?"

"What's what?"

Tannaz pointed. "That blue thing through the trees."

Savage turned and looked, eyes squinting. "I can't see anything."

"Wait, it keeps disappearing."

Savage kept staring.

Sure enough, a blurry slice of blue appeared, way off in the distance, between the trees. Amongst the forest's muted palette of greens, browns, burgundies and mustard yellows, it stood out like a neon light.

Then it was gone again.

"I saw it," said Savage. "A blue shape, about head height, sort of hovering."

"This is freaky," Tannaz replied, getting to her feet. "Let's get out of here, this place gives me the creeps."

"Not just yet. Let's take a look."

"Savage, we've got work to do. Bad guys to catch."

"Bad guys aren't going anywhere."

Savage headed in the rough direction of where the blue shape had appeared, followed by Tannaz grumbling behind. A second later, it flashed into view again, then disappeared. It kept doing this with regular frequency. Appearing and disappearing.

Savage quickened his pace, wanting his curiosity satisfied. As they trudged through the mulch the ground became damp and squelchy.

"Savage, this is not doing my Doc Martens any good," Tannaz complained.

"So you can clean them later. Or I'll buy you another pair—"

Savage didn't get to finish his sentence.

He broke into a sprint, almost as if hit by a bolt of electricity.

"Savage, what is it?" Tannaz cried.

The blue shape emerged, and now they were close enough to see what it truly was.

It belonged to the man they had seen in the car park. He was still wearing his blue walking jacket and the reason it kept disappearing and reappearing from view was because he kept swinging backwards and forwards from a noose attached to the low bough of an oak tree. A human pendulum slowly swaying, the rope creaking eerily like the rigging of the *Marie Celeste*.

"Tannaz, help me!" cried Savage. He reached the guys legs, which hung roughly at chest height. Grasping them in a bear hug, Savage hoisted up the man's body, attempting to take the strain off his neck.

Tannaz caught up seconds later, swore rapidly and panicked. "What do I do? What do I do?"

"Reach into my jacket pocket. Grab my keys. There's a Swiss Army knife on the keyring. Climb up the tree and cut him down."

Tannaz followed Savage's instructions, swearing with every breath.

"Hurry, Tannaz," said Savage. "There's a chance we can still save him."

Tannaz ran for the tree, held onto the nearest branch and pulled herself up. Savage watched the soles of her boots slipping as she scampered higher, his arms and shoulders burning under the strain of the hanged man.

"One day, Savage, all this could be yours."

Savage cursed. Jeff Perkins was back and it seemed his kryptonite, Tannaz, wasn't keeping him at bay.

"I'm going as fast as I can," said Tannaz, assuming the profanity was aimed at her.

"I dream of seeing you up there one day, Savage, swaying gently in the breeze, the noose crushing your neck, squeezing the life out of you."

Savage didn't respond. Just concentrated on keeping the dying man aloft, if indeed he was still alive.

"You should just let him die, you know. That's what he would've wanted. If you save him, he's going to be really annoyed at you two. Nobody likes their suicide being interfered with. And if you're wondering how I can be here even though Tannaz, your little good-luck charm, is here too, it's because you're on my home turf—suicide. If we're going with the Superman analogy, and Tannaz is my kryptonite, then suicide is my yellow sun, makes me stronger."

In his mind, Savage urged Tannaz to go quicker. Moments later, she was on the branch the man hung from. She unfolded the main blade on the Swiss Army knife, which Savage kept fiercely sharp, and began to saw at the rope, panting heavily. Several strokes later it gave way, and the man and Savage tumbled into a heap on the ground. Savage loosened the noose from around the man's neck and checked for a pulse on his carotid artery just below his jawline. It was weak and erratic. Still alive.

"Oh no," said Jeff. "*He's still alive, and now you're going to ruin it all by bringing him back to life. Why do you always have to be a hero? It's selfish. You're denying him his miserable death.*"

Savage ignored the voice in his head. Pumped hard on the man's chest with the heels of his hands. Tannaz climbed down from the tree, joining him beside the walker.

Over and over Savage pushed down on the man's rib cage, hoping to force the life back into him, stopping only to breathe air into his mouth.

After several minutes, panting heavily, Savage stopped to check the man's pulse.

"He's gone," said Savage.

"*Hooray,*" said Jeff. "*Music to my ears. Another one bites the dust, or should I say leaves, and best of all you couldn't do anything about it.*"

Once again, Savage wished more than anything that Jeff Perkins was real so he could punch him repeatedly in the face.

Tannaz stared at the dead body, her mouth open. Mesmerised by the sight of death. Savage spoke softly, "We did everything we could. We just got here too late."

Tannaz didn't reply, her face in shock, stuck on pause.

"Come on," he said. "We need to get out of here."

This shook her out of her trance. "Wait," said Tannaz. "We need to call the police, the ambulance."

"And we will, but not here."

She grabbed his arm. "You're just going to leave him here?"

"*That's it, run away, Savage, like you always do.*"

"Tannaz, if we're here when the police show up, they'll ask us lots of questions. Awkward questions. Why are you here? What are you doing in Southampton? Where are you staying? We'll have to do lots of lying. Make stuff up. Despite what people think, the police aren't stupid. They'll think we're an odd couple. A young computer hacker and an ex-captain in the SAS with a busted-up face in the middle of a forest where people are committing suicide. They won't buy our story. Then we'll be on their radar. It'll be more hassle than it's worth."

Savage knelt down by the body and pulled out the guy's wallet.

"Shame on you, Savage, stealing from a dead man."

He slid out the guy's driver's licence. "Samuel Thwaite, from Doncaster." He slotted it back in and pulled out another, a printed security-access card. "Worked in a place called Leadman's Accountants, also in Doncaster."

"How can you be so calm about all this? He's just died right in front of us."

"That's because Savage is already dead inside. Run, Tannaz, run."

"Believe me, I'm anything but calm," said Savage. "What I'm saying is we can't help this guy anymore. Have to suck it up and get on with it. I realise this is a shock to you; let's go back to the hotel. Maybe it'd be a good thing if we take a break."

Determination came back into Tannaz. "No, we carry on."

"Are you sure?"

"Positive, let's get back to the van, and find this Joel Diplock character."

CHAPTER 42

A S THEY TRUDGED BACK TO the car park, the voice of
Jeff faded. Putting distance between them and the
suicidal man made him lose his potency. Although he
had definitely rattled Savage. The voice had never been that loud
before. Maybe Jeff was right about one thing. Being so close to a
suicide gave him power and strength, which he fed off, growing
fatter like a character in a Roald Dahl story.

When they were in the van and had put a few miles between
themselves and Dead Maids, Tannaz pinged an anonymous email
to the police, informing them of the suicide victim they'd found.

As Savage drove, Tannaz punched the keys of her laptop
furiously.

"What are you doing?"

"Trying to find a connection between this Samuel Thwaite
and Wellington. Everyone who's wound up dead in that forest
has had something to do with Simon Wellington."

"Anything?"

"Nothing. Nothing at all so far. Thwaite was born and bred in
Doncaster. Lived there all his life. As far as I can tell he's never
even been to Southampton. Oh, crap."

"What?"

"I've just found his Facebook page, his last post reads: 'Have
made up my mind. All the sadness will be over soon. I'm taking
my final trip today.'"

"Can Facebook posts be faked?" asked Savage.

"Easily," Tannaz replied. "Someone could have made it look

like a suicide. But we saw him in the car park. No one was forcing him to kill himself."

"There are other ways to coerce someone. Blackmail, threats to his family. Kill yourself or we'll make your kids suffer. He had kids, we saw the car seats."

"There are pictures on his Facebook page. Two girls. If Wellington had targeted him, I can't see the connection."

"Maybe that's just it," said Savage. "Maybe he had to change the pattern. Say he's got a sadistic thing for making people hang themselves at Dead Maids, the next one needed to be random, nothing to do with him. So he shut his eyes and flicked through the phone book and picked this guy."

"Or, it's a genuine suicide. He heard about this place and came here to end it all like others before him, maybe it's becoming the mecca for suicide, the UK's version of the Sea of Trees."

Savage groaned. "Is it possible that this is what Wellington wants to create, another Sea of Trees?"

"He'd have to be an absolute sick psychopath."

"I thought that was abundantly clear already. Park it for now, a connection with Thwaite and Wellington may emerge. First we find this Joel Diplock. I need an address."

"Already on it."

Two minutes later, Tannaz said, "Turn the van around, we're going the wrong way. Joel Diplock lives in Ringwood. About eighteen miles south-west of here."

"Right you are."

Savage pulled a massive, screeching U-turn in the middle of the forest and accelerated towards Ringwood.

"Can you hack his bank account?" asked Savage. "Look for anything irregular."

Frighteningly fast, Tannaz was into Diplock's personal account and read out a history of the guy's purchases. "Gets paid monthly by bank transfer. Shops at Tesco. Subscription to Netflix. Subscription to *Top Gear* magazine. Member of a local gym. Goes to the pub Saturday night and Sunday lunchtime.

Occasionally does paintball. Oh, his car insurance has gone up massively. Almost ten times as much."

"When?"

"January."

"That's when Dave's tree got felled. Why has his insurance gone up?"

"Let me see." More typing. "Okay, I'm into his insurance. It's because he went from a ten-year-old Honda Civic to a year-old Ford Ranger four-wheel-drive pickup."

"I wonder where he got the money for that? Any tax rebates, Christmas bonuses, large sums of money being deposited in his accounts from loan companies or pay-outs?"

"No, nothing. Just his monthly salary."

"So our man gets a big load of cash from somewhere and buys himself a new truck. Interesting. If in doubt, always follow the money. It never lies."

Joel Diplock lived on a modest new estate on the outskirts of Ringwood. By the look of the place, it had been built in the early eighties when designers had learnt lessons from the mistakes of the seventies and had made pathetic attempts to soften the look of housing estates, by giving them pointless mock period features like dormer windows with false leading and minuscule white wooden porches. They weren't fooling anyone. Like one of those posh burgers with all the trimmings that come in a brioche bun, it was still just a burger. And a housing estate with a bit of tat nailed onto it was still just a housing estate.

Joel Diplock was easy to find. His truck dwarfed the tiny driveway it sat on. Next to it on the small patch of grass that formed his front garden, a sparkling Husqvarna dirt bike was propped up on its kickstand, recently washed, presumably by the substantial pressure washer standing next to it. Heavy-metal music thumped out the truck's car stereo, which the neighbours must have loved.

Savage parked up opposite the house. He and Tannaz both exited the van and casually walked over to Joel Diplock.

He was busying himself, making the Ford Ranger spotless, buffing it with a chamois leather. He was a big guy, broad shouldered, straight hair down to his shoulders that looked like it had been coloured to give it a surfie beach-blonde appearance. Beneath his lower lip he sported a soul-patch beard.

"Nice truck," said Savage. "How much did that set you back?"

Nothing got a man's attention like being paid a compliment about the vehicle he drove.

Joel turned and smiled proudly. "What this bad boy? Set me back just over nineteen grand."

Savage blew out through his teeth in amazement.

"I'll take you for spin in it if you want," Joel said, ignoring Savage and talking directly to Tannaz. "It's a hell of a buzz, off-roading in that beast." He winked at her.

Tannaz began smoking a cigarette with as much nonchalance as she could muster. "I don't like being outdoors. Don't like pickup trucks either. They're usually driven by redneck pricks with small brains and tiny dicks."

Joel's face dropped.

"So where'd you get nineteen grand to pay for your truck, Joel?" asked Savage.

"How do you know my name?"

Savage ignored the question and continued, "I'm guessing it was paid for in cash, and I'm sure you declared that money. I mean, it'd be difficult to hide it from the taxman, a big four-wheel-drive vehicle like that sitting in your driveway. You know that's how the tax office catches most tax dodgers, when they suddenly get something expensive out of the blue—acquisition of an unexplained asset they call it—bit hard to cover that one up. So you must have declared the money, no one's that stupid."

Joel didn't say anything.

"Oh no," said Savage. "You are that stupid. You haven't declared the money you earned have you? Oh dear, well, being conscientious citizens we'll have to call the tax office."

Joel's worry turned to fear, then to anger. Brow furrowed, eyes pinched around the edges. He straightened up in an attempt to make himself look more intimidating. He threw his chamois leather on the floor in anger.

"You've lost your rag," said Savage.

Tannaz laughed.

"I knew it," said Savage. "She pretends not to like my jokes, but I know she loves them."

Joel raised his fists, limbered up his shoulders. Ready to fight.

"Really?" said Savage. "You want to fight?"

"Damn straight," said Joel. "You don't come on my property and threaten me."

Savage yawned. Two nights without sleep catching up on him. "Look, I'm too tired for fighting."

"I'll fight him," said Tannaz. "I need the practice."

"I'm not fighting a girl," said Joel.

"You're going to regret saying that," said Tannaz, grinding her cigarette out on the driveway and squaring up to him.

"Listen, Joel," said Savage. "We've had quite a traumatic day already. Seen some things we really didn't want to see. So let's make this easy. No need for fisticuffs. You wouldn't win anyway. Just tell us who asked you to fell the tree in Dead Maids, and we won't grass you up to the taxman. Or did you do it of your own volition?"

"I don't know how you know my name or who you are. Like I said, no one comes on my property and threatens me."

"Just tell us why you cut the tree down. No need for anyone to get hurt."

"You'll be the only ones getting hurt," Joel replied.

"Tannaz?" said Savage. "Drop this fool."

"I'm not fighting a chick," said Joel. Then without warning, he swung a right hook at the side of Tannaz's face. With her lightning speed, she dropped low, avoiding the blow, and gave him an uppercut to the groin. He doubled over instantly. A gasp of pain escaping from his mouth like a burst balloon. Then she grabbed him tightly by both ears and headbutted him, making blood run all down his face, turning his soul patch red.

Joel collapsed in a heap on his driveway, curling into a ball.

"You're getting good at those headbutts," Savage remarked, then he crouched beside Joel. "Okay, fella. Just breathe. Get some oxygen in your lungs. Pain will go soon."

They gave Joel a few minutes. Eventually he sat up wiped his nose and sniffed back the blood.

"Better?" asked Savage.

He nodded.

"The Douglas fir in Dead Maids," said Savage. "Why did you cut it down?"

Joel took a breath, then said, "Some guys came here a few months ago in a blue BMW, I think. Heavy-duty looking guys, dressed in black. One of them was bald with a Bluetooth."

Definitely Wellington's men.

"The guy with the Bluetooth, did he ask you to cut the tree down?"

"No, there was another guy with them. They were like his minders."

"And what was he like?"

"Posh. Smartly dressed, suit and tie. Had brown wavy hair. Looked a little unsure of himself."

"How do you mean?" asked Tannaz.

"Kind of depressed. Like he didn't want to be there."

A perfectly accurate description of Ben Wellington, thought Savage. "And he asked you to cut the tree down?" asked Savage.

"Yeah. First, I had to mark it with an X, like we used to do in the old days with a spray can."

"When did they ask you to mark the tree?"

"December, just before Christmas. They gave me the exact co-ordinates in Dead Maids, a Douglas fir. Then I had to cut it down in January."

"Did you ask why?"

"No, they wanted to pay me ten grand. Five up front and then five when the job was done. I wasn't going to start getting nosey."

"And when the body came out of the tree..."

Joel's eyes turned icy with fear. "Listen, I had nothing to do with that. You gotta believe me. I didn't know that body was up there, would never have done it if I did."

"It's okay, we believe you," said Savage. "Look, we're not after you, just the people who organised this." Savage turned to Tannaz. "Okay we've got what we need." He turned back to Joel. "No mention of our little visit, okay? Not to anyone, unless you want the taxman to come calling."

Joel nodded eagerly.

Savage stood up and stretched out his hand to Joel. He took it and Savage hoisted him to his feet.

"One other thing," said Joel.

"Yes?" Savage replied.

"Are you two an item?"

"No," said Tannaz. "More of a partnership."

"Oh, okay."

"Why do you ask?" said Tannaz.

Joel went a tad shy, eyes down. "I was just wondering if you might want to go out some time."

"Joel," said Tannaz. "I just punched you in the groin and headbutted you to the ground."

"Yeah, I know." He grinned impishly, unsure how to form his next few words. "I guess, if I'm honest, I kind of liked it."

Tannaz turned on her heel. "Bye, Joel." Savage followed her.

Joel called after her, "If you change your mind you know where I am. I think you're great. A badass Asian Wonder Woman."

They got into the van and drove off.

"Hear that?" said Tannaz. "I'm a badass Asian Wonder Woman."

"You know that's your new nickname now," said Savage. "Badass Asian Wonder Woman."

Tannaz groaned, "No, I don't want you calling me that. I'm changing the subject. What's our next move?"

"I think we need some facetime with Ben Wellington, preferably without his minders around."

"How are we going to do that?"

"I think this is a job for Badass Asian Wonder Woman."

"I said don't call me that."

CHAPTER 43

S AVAGE HAD A SAYING—ROUTINE MAKES you vulnerable. Doing the same thing day in, day out, repeating the same pattern every week makes you open to attack. House burglars use it to great effect, watching and learning a person's weekly comings and goings then striking when they know there's no chance of them being in. There was a famous British comedian who did a live show on TV in the eighties on a Saturday night. Twice in a row his flat got burgled while he was on TV, the robbers knowing he was on stage and not at home. Probably the first time a TV schedule had been used to pull off a theft.

In the case of Ben Wellington, it wasn't about knowing his weekly routine so Savage could break into his house, it was watching him so he could get him alone. Whenever he went out, his minders would go with him. Even on the weekends, his ever-present bodyguards would shadow him, making sure he'd come to no harm, although Savage suspected it wasn't just about keeping him safe. More about ensuring he didn't do anything stupid.

Savage and Tannaz observed his activities for the next two weeks. Following the Bentley at a discreet distance to get an idea of his every movement, every day of the week. The bodyguards never left him, they'd even park outside his house, keeping an eye on him at night. They'd change shift, of course, every five hours. 24/7 Ben Wellington was never alone, apart from Saturday morning.

At nine thirty a.m. on Saturdays, Ben Wellington would take his two girls swimming. Pretty as a summer's day, they'd skip up to his car, blonde ponytails swishing from side to side, colourful rucksacks strapped to their backs. Ben would drive with one bodyguard in the passenger seat and three more following along behind in the navy-blue BMW. It seemed like a lot of security to take a man and his daughters swimming.

They'd park up, while Ben took his girls to the pool. The security detail stayed outside with the cars, leaning on bonnets, chatting and drinking coffee and sucking on vape machines. Bluetooth was not amongst them, but if he had been, Savage was sure he'd have reprimanded them for letting their mark out of sight.

Ben Wellington sat in the stands, close to the side of the pool watching his daughters jump in off the side, giving them little comments of encouragement. He seemed like a good father.

Savage slotted himself next to him. "Hello, Ben."

Ben swung round, horror on his face.

"Relax," said Savage. "I just want to talk. No funny business."

"What do you want?"

"Just to talk. Oh, by the way, thanks for sending me into the lion's den a few weeks ago. You said it was a bare-knuckle boxing match. I had to fight for my life."

"Look, I'm really sorry. Really I am."

"Apology accepted. The way I figure it, you owe me one."

Ben went silent. Gazed at his girls splashing in the pool. Eventually he said, "What do you want?"

"Just information."

"You're taking an awful risk talking to me," he said dramatically. "I have my men outside. Very nasty men."

"Well, they're not much good outside, are they. See, that's the thing, you say 'my men' but I get the impression they're not your men, they're your dad's. First, I thought they were to protect you from any lowlifes you might encounter, like me. There must be a lot of them in Wellington properties and each time one of them gets chucked out on the street, I guess that makes them a risk. There's the odd chance someone might want to even the score with the son of the man who's made them homeless. Hence, all the security around you. That's not their only job, is it? They're here to supervise you. Make sure you do what you're told. I guess your old man still pulls the strings."

"You're still taking an awful risk talking to me. If he finds out you're here, we're both in trouble."

"Did you kill Jenny Hopkins?"

Ben's eyes narrowed. "No, I did not."

"Then why did you visit her, contribute to her care home bills, even though your dad pays you a pittance?"

"How did you know...?"

"You were keeping an eye on her, weren't you? Making sure nobody believed her stories about your father killing her daughter."

Ben snapped, "You haven't got a clue about Jenny Hopkins, have you?"

"Then set me straight."

Ben paused, thought for a moment, then said, "I liked her, that's all."

Savage gave a fake laugh. "Oh, come on, you expect me to believe that? That you had a soft spot for your dad's stage assistant from a magic show he did years ago. There's something you're not telling me."

"I can't say."

"Why not?"

"You do know who my father is, what he's like?"

"Yeah, I think he kills people for fun."

Ben stared down at the floor. Nudged a discarded Elastoplast with the toe of his smart Oxford shoes.

"You're scared of him, aren't you?" Savage said. "Did he kill my friend, Dave Mosely? He used to live at Tivoli Gardens, found dead up a tree in Dead Maids Wood, until it got cut down."

Ben remained silent.

"I know you paid off the guy to cut the tree down..."

"I was just following my father's orders."

"That's what they said in Nazi Germany."

Ben turned to Savage. "Listen, do you think I enjoy this, do you think I want to be part of my father's twisted empire?

Going around pretending to intimidate people. I'm not that kind of person."

"So leave."

"I can't."

"Why not?"

Savage knew the answer. If he left he'd get nothing. His family would be destitute, out on the street. But that wasn't the main reason.

"I'm terrified of my father. Everyone is. You know they call him Keyser Söze round here? You know, the villain from *The Usual Suspects*."

"I know that movie well," said Savage.

"Remember that scene, when Keyser Söze's family are held hostage, guns at their heads? Keyser Söze shoots his own family rather than submit to the hostage-takers. Well, that's what my father is like. If we walked away, knowing what we know about his operation, he wouldn't just kill me, he'd kill my wife and my daughters. And I'd do anything to protect my family, they're all I care about."

"Ben, you don't know he'd do that," said Savage.

"I do know that, he's done it before."

"What?"

"He killed my sister."

CHAPTER 44

SAVAGE THOUGHT THEY'D DONE THEIR homework on Ben Wellington. Clearly they hadn't.

"You had a sister?" Savage asked. "I thought you were an only child?"

"I was," Ben replied. "Until my father had an affair with Jenny Hopkins and they had a child, she was called Jackie."

"Jackie was your half-sister?"

"Yes. At first, I didn't know about her. Jenny reached out to me, without my father knowing, introduced me to my half-sister. Being an only child, I loved having a sister. She was a lot younger than me, of course. I liked being the big brother. Used to go see her all the time, until my father had her killed. Ran her over in the middle of the street."

"Was he behind the wheel?"

"Don't know, probably not. Likes to keep his hands clean, probably got one of his thugs to do it. Of course, he completely denied it. I felt terrible. Awful. Still do, that my father could do that to his own flesh and blood. Least I could do was look after Jenny, make sure she was okay."

"She didn't blame you?"

"Yes, she did. Didn't want to see me. Hated me because I was my father's son. But I persevered. Had to. I owed it to her. Swore I'd look out for her, even if she hated my guts. Soon we became friends, until my father ended her life too."

"I'm sorry."

"So you see, Mr Savage. I'm in a no-win situation. I have to do these vile things because otherwise my family will end up like Jackie and Jenny. And I can't let that happen."

"I can help you."

"No one can help me. I'm stuck with this wretched life of constant fear. I'm used to it."

"I'll put it another way, I can take your father out of the equation. Put him away. He'd never know you had anything to do with it. No one would know."

"Put him away?" Ben chuckled. "Not good enough. My father needs to be wiped off the face of the earth. No one's safe until that happens. Not me, not you, not my family and not the people unfortunate enough to be living in his properties." Ben stood up and called to his children. "Five more minutes, girls." He sat down and turned back to Savage. "I think we're done here."

"Just give me one more bit of information."

Ben took a deep breath. "What do you need?"

"His underground gambling ring. Bizarre games in the forest, underground torture chambers, fights to the death et cetera. We thought it was run over the dark net. My IT expert couldn't find it anywhere."

"I'm not involved in any of that. He doesn't trust me enough. Just makes me round up suitable candidates to be in his strange betting shows. I know it's international. Big billionaire players from around the world. Very secretive."

"That's what we figured. The uploads don't appear anywhere in cyberspace. And there's no sign of how he communicates with them."

"Maybe you need a better IT guy."

"Believe me, I have the best, and it's not a guy it's a girl."

"Like I said, I have no idea about all that. I'm sorry I can't help you." Ben Wellington stood up, leant over the handrail. "Okay, girls, time's up." Groans of disappointment flew back at him from the pool edge. He turned back to Savage. "There was one thing I kept hearing when he was setting this all up. Got him all excited."

"Yes?" said Savage.

"Decentralised network."

"What's that?"

"I have no idea."

Back in her room, Tannaz had used the hotel's printer to run off various Google images, which she'd Sellotaped to one wall. An impromptu evidence board of what they had so far.

Savage walked in the door to see Tannaz stepping back to admire her handiwork. "Looks a bit pathetic," she said. "They always look a lot more impressive on TV."

Savage had to admit, there wasn't much to go on. There was the map from the Forestry Commission showing the dotted GPS locations of every tree in Dead Maids Wood. Next to that, to represent Wellington's betting ring, was a shot of a full-size roulette table, seen from above. Alongside it, she'd stuck a gruesome image of somebody hanged in the Sea of Trees in Japan, the man's face was pixelated out, signifying the suicides at Dead Maids, if that's indeed what they were. Above these were the names of the deceased who'd been found at Dead Maids. Each name printed on a single sheet: Dave Mosely, his son Luke Mosley, the nurse Sylvia Sanchez and the hiker Samuel Thwaite. To the left of these was another sheet with Jenny Hopkins' name, and on the right, sitting alone, was a screen grab of Monty Python's Michael Palin in a red checked shirt singing the 'Lumberjack Song'.

"Don't tell me," said Savage. "Michael Palin's supposed to represent Joel Diplock, the guy who cut Dave's tree down."

"Yeah."

Above all these names, as if sitting at the top of the pyramid was the blurred and grainy bloated face of Simon Wellington, enlarged and copied from the Internet.

"I think this is the sorriest-looking evidence board, I've ever seen," Tannaz remarked.

"Any evidence is good evidence, no matter how sparse."

"See, if this were TV or a movie, it'd now cut to a montage of us wracking our brains, writing stuff down then screwing up bits of paper, and having heated debates and looking moody while pointing at our evidence wall with pens, and drinking endless cups of coffee. Then suddenly one of us would look to camera. The montage would stop, and one of us would announce a breakthrough."

Savage chuckled. "Yeah, I can't see any of that happening. I still don't get any of this, or what the connection is, apart from Wellington bumping off people who had dirt on him, which then begs the question, why kill them in such a bizarre, overt way?"

"Maybe sending a message to his rivals?"

"He doesn't have any."

"How did you get on with Ben Wellington?"

Savage filled her in, recounting everything he'd said word for word.

"Wow," said Tannaz. "Wasn't expecting Jenny Hopkins' daughter to be Ben's half-sister. I suppose it explains a lot—I'll have to do a print out of that with a red line going from Ben to Jenny. Ben and Jenny's, like the ice cream. Hey, I made a pun."

"Yeah, not a very good one," said Savage.

Tannaz threw the Sellotape at him. Savage caught it, started to pick at the end with is fingernail. "I think we might have an unlikely ally in Ben Wellington," he said. "The guy's a totally dedicated father. Would do anything to protect his family. Feels the biggest threat to their safety is his own dad. Terrible state to be in."

"I suppose he could be lying."

"Can't see why. He'd have to be a hell of a good actor."

"Maybe he's trying to get your trust. So he can tell his father what we're up to. I mean, you've let the cat out of the bag now. What's to stop him blabbing to Simon Wellington about us? Talking to him was a bit of a risk, wasn't it?"

"Yes, but one we could afford to take. Ben Wellington bribed that forestry worker; we've got something on him now, so he has to be careful. He did give us one other bit of information about the betting ring, he said something about a 'decentralised network', does that mean anything?"

"What did you say?"

"Decentralised network."

Tannaz dropped enough f-bombs to flatten a city and started violently punching herself in the head. "Stupid, stupid, stupid, stupid, idiot!" she screamed.

Savage grabbed her wrists to stop her giving herself concussion. "Tannaz, stop it, calm down."

Tannaz snatched her hands away from Savage's grip.

"Tannaz. Remember our little SAS mantra—Breathe. Recalibrate. Deliver."

She sat on the end of the bed, took in a lungful of air and let it out slowly.

"Now tell me. What's a decentralised network?"

"It's so simple. I am such a moron."

"Look, stop berating yourself. Just tell me."

Tannaz stood up and grabbed a marker pen, started drawing lots of little boxes on the wall.

"Er, isn't that a permanent marker?" asked Savage.

Tannaz shot him a venomous look.

"Okay, doesn't matter. There goes my deposit."

She linked all the boxes with lots of little lines. "Imagine all these boxes are computers, servers and printers. When they're all connected up it's called a network. That's what the Internet is, just on a massive scale. Millions of devices all linked up, so they can share stuff. A network that covers the entire world. Okay?"

"Okay."

"The software on all these different devices allows them to talk to each other." Tannaz drew a little 's' in each of the boxes to represent software. "That was the dream of the Internet—free, open access to information. Everyone linked up, no boundaries. Sharing stuff. All good. The trouble is people like me. Hackers. I can hack computers and servers on this network, and get round security, exploit all these links."

Tannaz drew a little curly haired stick figure, presumably herself, with little arrows coming out of her body, going into the computers.

"So it's the age-old dilemma of the Internet: access versus

security. How do you have complete freedom over a network to do and say what you want, without people like me or the authorities sticking their nose in?"

"Don't know," said Savage.

"You create your own network." Tannaz started drawing a circle of boxes off to the right of the one she'd already drawn. Inside each box she wrote a 'd'. Savage shuddered for whoever was going to have to clean it all off. "D for decentralised network," she continued. "Completely separate from the Internet. Also known as a peer-to-peer network because it runs on people's smartphones and laptops, there are no servers, just personal devices making up the network. Not any old Tom, Dick and Harry can join it. You have to be invited. Totally private. That's what Wellington's using for his little betting ring. That's why we can't find it."

"How do you get onto it?"

"We can't. A decentralised network has its own bespoke software. Someone has to give you the software to put on your device. A highly bespoke encrypted software."

"But you're a brilliant hacker."

"Thanks, but I still can't get in. Look at this." She slipped the hotel room's key card out of her back pocket, held it up in front of her. "This lets me into my room. Now imagine you come along and try to break into my room with your little pouch of lock picks. Doesn't matter how brilliant you are at picking locks. It's not going to work because—"

"It's a completely different system."

"Now you're getting it."

"So is there a way to get on it?"

"Maybe. It's a big maybe. Each member of Wellington's international betting ring will have been given this software at some point, to put on their device. We get one of those devices I might be able to copy it, crack the encryption, and hopefully get us in. Trouble is, we don't know who's on his little betting network."

"We do know one person."

"Who?"

"Simon Wellington."

CHAPTER 45

A FEW DAYS LATER, SAVAGE CALLED Ben Wellington to ask for one last favour. When he was certain that Ben couldn't be overheard by his father's goons, Savage asked him to snatch his father's phone, and get it to them, so Tannaz could crack the encryption.

Without any hesitation, Ben Wellington refused. No amount of persuasion would make him do it, and Savage could understand why. If he got caught he'd be signing his family's death warrant. But he did give them something else, almost as good.

Monday, Tuesday and Wednesday, with religious regularity, Simon Wellington was chauffeured from his mansion in the outrageously posh town of Esher in Surrey, to his outrageously posh club in London—the Cygnet Club in Mayfair. He'd spend all day there, sipping brandy, reading the paper, having lunch, and then snoozing the afternoon away in a wing chair, until his chauffeur picked him up at four p.m., before rush hour properly started, and ferried him back home. Ben told Savage that his father's alcohol-induced afternoon snooze would be the best time to lift his smart phone.

There was just one problem.

Like all exclusive gentleman's clubs that had been established over two hundred years ago, getting in was virtually impossible. Becoming a member was virtually impossible too. Even if you had money, that was no guarantee. You had to know the right people and be from the right family with the right heritage. Simon Wellington had neither, which meant the only other option was that he had some dirt on someone at the club and had bribed them to get in.

"That's the only drawback to our plan," said Tannaz. "Getting in."

Tannaz had managed to get hold of the schematics to the building. Savage was poring over them on her laptop screen. "It's not the getting in. It's the staying in. I've no doubt I could get in through the delivery entrance, do the usual, show up with a fake delivery et cetera, et cetera, but after that, trying to get close to Wellington, I'd stick out like a sore thumb."

"Ben Wellington says he takes his snooze in the library."

"Yep."

"What about if you pretended to be a waiter or something?"

Savage smiled. "That sort of thing works in movies, not in real life."

"If the only way to get in is be a member. Why don't I hack their system, put you on the membership?"

"It's not that kind of place. These old clubs still use ledgers and fill in membership applications with ink and quills, probably..."

"And a sorting hat." Tannaz laughed.

"Don't laugh, that's not a million miles away from the truth. We're talking old-school tradition here. Arrogant, rich, entitled people that belong there, and know they do."

"So how do we get in and stay in?"

Savage paced the hotel room, decided to make a cup of tea. He filled the kettle and flicked the switch to boil. "You know, there was this one woman my wife used to work with. Would come in late every single day. Never ever got told off or disciplined. Used to drive my wife nuts."

"So how did she get away with it?"

"Every morning, she'd burst through the door, stomp her way to her desk, a mass of different work bags slung over her shoulder, phone wedged in her neck, bollocking some supplier or other, shouting at the top of her voice. Thing is, it was all a smokescreen, pretending she was busy and important to distract from the fact that she was always late."

"So, are you saying we make a big song and dance of going in there, like we own the place, no one will challenge us?"

Savage stopped pacing. "That's exactly what I'm saying. And the best way to look like you own the place is to make big loud entrance, like my wife's work colleague."

"How do we do that?"

"We show up outside the front door in a convoy of posh cars with blacked-out windows—like bonafide VIPs."

Savage went for his phone, speed-dialled a number. "Hello, Harry. It's John Savage." The guy on the other spoke so loudly it was as if he were on speaker phone.

"Savage, I thought I recognised those Dorset tones."

"It's dulcet, Harry. Dulcet tones."

"Whatever. Hey, I was just thinking about you. I was in the bogs in King's Cross station and saw your name and number written on the wall in the last cubicle." A hacking laugh came from the other end of the line that made the fillings in Tannaz's teeth ache.

"What were you doing in the bogs at King's Cross station, meeting a client?"

More throaty cackling. Tannaz rolled her eyes.

"How's business, Harry?"

Harry Preston was an old mate who had started a prestigious chauffeur company a few years ago, with one limo and one driver—himself. Things went well and before long he had a fleet of five limos and a roster of regular drivers, mostly friends. Things were looking up for the fledgling business, apart from the fact that success breeds resentment, and in Harry's case his rivals had tried to put him out of business by sending round thugs to smash headlights, pull off wing mirrors and scare the drivers away. That was until one by one, the thugs got put out of action by a mysterious guy who'd follow them home after the pub and hurt them, not badly, just so they couldn't work. A broken finger here, a fractured jaw there. This kept happening until the rival company got the message that there was space in the market for another chauffeur company. From then on, Harry had owed Savage, big time.

"Business is good, great in fact," Harry blurted out. "Thank God for the Russians and Chinese. Paranoid, they are. Frightened someone wants to assassinate them. Always want to be driven around in bulletproof cars when they come and visit their empty properties in London. We got seven of them now, put in an order for three more."

"Listen, that was what I was going ask you about, Harry. I need to cash that favour. I need to borrow five black Range Rover Sentinels."

"Five? Five!"

The line went quiet.

"Harry, you still there?"

"Yep, just got up off the floor in shock. I think I'm okay now. What the hell do you want five bulletproof Range Rovers for? Not thinking of storming an embassy, are you?"

"No, just need to make a good impression."

"Well if you want to do that you need to stop buying your clothes at Poundland."

Tannaz laughed.

"Please, Harry. It's important. And I need drivers too—big, smart guys who look like they work for the FBI. Shades and good haircuts."

"How is your hair by the way? Still like the ice caps—rapidly receding." More guttural laughter. "Jeez, you want the moon on a stick."

"I only need them for half an hour, just to drop me and my partner at a posh club. It's important Harry."

"When do you need them?"

"As soon as."

"Look, I can do you two Range Rover Sentinels, plus a bulletproof Jaguar XJ-L but tomorrow's the only day I can do. After that, every vehicle's spoken for."

Savage thought for a moment. Tomorrow was Wednesday.

"You know, that might be even better. The Jag in the middle, a Range Rover front and rear."

"Classy, eh? Where do you want picking up?"

"Outside Victoria station, around lunchtime. I'll text you an exact time."

"Right you are."

"Thanks, mate."

Savage hung up.

Tannaz looked serious, eyes unblinking. "What did you mean by me and my partner?"

"You're coming with me."

"But the Cygnet Club's a bastion of misogyny."

"Nope. It's one of the few clubs that allows women in."

Tannaz looked disgusted. "Wow, I feel so privileged to rub shoulders with a load of old, sexist imperialists who still wish it were the nineteen thirties." Tannaz slammed her laptop lid down hard.

"This is probably not a good time to bring this up," said Savage. "I need you to pretend to be my PA."

"Why can't you be my PA?"

"Because, like you said, they're a bunch of old, sexist imperialists. Although this place admits woman, it's still backward. A place where white, bigoted male dinosaurs are still allowed to roam free. No one's going to bat an eyelid if you're my PA. They will if it's the other way round. Remember, we're just doing it to get in there and get Wellington's device. Bit of role playing, that's all."

Tannaz stared at him, fire burning in her eyes. "Okay, fine, but I don't like it." She got up and headed to the door.

"Where are you going?"

"To get some printouts from the hotel's printer. Floorplans of the Cygnet Club. We need to memorise them so we know where we're going, otherwise we'll look like a couple of idiots who've just snuck in."

She slammed the door shut behind her.

CHAPTER 46

T HEY SPENT WEDNESDAY MORNING IN Southampton, Tannaz being Savage's personal shopper attempting to make him look the part of a filthy rich, hereditary land owner who went to a posh school, where the uniform alone would cost more than most people made in a year. To pull this off, Savage had to act upper class, and that meant behaving like he never did anything for himself because he could pay other people to do it for him. For such a resourceful, practical person as Savage, this was going to be tricky. So getting the look right was going to be everything.

In the end they settled on a pure wool tweed jacket with clean simple lines and a subtle brown overcheck with a matching waistcoat and a light blue shirt. Trousers were dark brown needle cords with brown leather brogues.

Tannaz went for a simple black pencil skirt, matching jacket with a white blouse underneath. She slicked her hair back and added black-rimmed glasses with clear lenses, even though she didn't wear glasses, to give her that studious look. Shoes were a problem. She refused to wear anything with a sharp heel, and argued with Savage about wearing a pair of comfortable black Doc Marten shoes instead. Savage argued that it would make her look more like a nurse about to go on duty than a high-powered PA. In the end they compromised on a smart pair of ballet shoes. To finish the look, Tannaz added a sleek black leather computer bag with a shoulder strap.

Two and half hours later they stepped off the train and onto the platform at London Victoria, the capital's second busiest station after Waterloo. Throughout the whole journey they had sat silently, going over the plan in their heads, even though they knew it backwards, and could have still pulled it off even if they were floating in zero gravity.

Stepping outside the train station, they were confronted by a line of three glossy black vehicles parked up on the opposite pavement, even though to do this risked incurring the wrath of every traffic warden in London.

Just as Harry had promised, a sleek black Jaguar XJ-L, bookended by two intimidatingly large Range Rover Sentinels. The drivers sat ready with the engines running, while a second man stood beside each vehicle, decked out in plain black bomber jackets and dark glasses. All three men were well-groomed and had muscular frames.

Tannaz and Savage hurried across the congested lanes of traffic that continually orbited the station like the rings around Saturn. Horns blasted as they crossed.

When they reached the Jag, the man standing beside the car turned and opened the rear door for them. Harry had even gone as far as to give each man an earpiece with a curling lead that disappeared down the back of their necks. They did indeed look like they were about to storm an embassy. Tannaz and Savage climbed in the back seats of the sumptuous car. Tannaz's right knee began bobbing up and down nervously. Savage steadied it with his hand. "Calm thoughts," he said.

"Good afternoon, sir, madam," said the driver.

"I've never been a madam before," Tannaz replied.

"Just to confirm our itinerary today, sir," said the guy in the passenger seat. "We are en route to the Cygnet Club on St James's Street. Estimated journey time of fifteen minutes. Is that satisfactory?"

"Correct," said Savage. "When we get there, I want all three cars to mount the pavement and stop outside the entrance."

The guy in the passenger seat turned around. "Sir, that's a very dangerous thing to do, especially in London with all the terrorist attacks. It might be better to pull up beside the pavement."

"Not good enough," Savage replied. "I need you to drive up onto the pavement and come to an immediate halt outside the club. We need to get their attention. Make them think that we're important. So important that we can park on the pavement."

"Very good, sir."

"One other thing. I want you and two of your colleagues to escort us into the building."

"Okay, sir."

"You've done this before?"

"Yes, sir."

"Good," said Savage. "There's a long entrance hall leading up to a reception desk. You and your men can turn and leave once we're safely past the desk. You'll need to walk us up that entrance hall like we're high-value individuals. Standard bodyguarding wedge formation. One up front, two at the rear. You and your men familiar with that?"

"Yes, sir."

"Good. Now can you relay those instructions to your colleagues?"

"Will do."

The guy got on his phone and confirmed Savage's instructions with the men in the other two vehicles.

Just as the guy had predicted, fifteen minutes later, they were skirting the edge of Green Park, a name that had always baffled Savage—what other colour would a park be? Past the Japanese Embassy, they took a right onto St James's Street, a wide, elegant thoroughfare lined with four- and five-storey buildings, like palaces that had been nudged together, shoulder to shoulder. Clad in fine grey Portland stone and with pleasing Greek proportions, each one typified the British Regency style, a layered cake of ornate cornices, porticos and fluted columns with fairy-tale balconies supported by vast bay windows.

The street was home to the oldest and most prestigious clubs in London—Boodle's, Brooks's, White's (Savage wondered whether it had that name because they were the only people it allowed in), the Carlton Club and the Cygnet Club, where a certain Simon

Wellington would hopefully be sleeping off a rich three-course lunch, and one-too-many brandies.

"We're here, sir," said the guy in front. The cars slowed and then mounted the wide accommodating pavement. Several pedestrians darted to the edge, eyeing them warily, as if they were terrorists about to mow them down. They were the wrong type of vehicles. Terrorists didn't usually use bulletproof executive cars to cause murder and mayhem, they hired cheap budget trucks or vans. The pedestrians relaxed and went about their business. All three cars came to a stop outside the entrance, and within view of the club's generous windows.

The guys in the passenger sides of the cars stepped out first, dark glasses on, playing their parts perfectly. They scanned the street, searching for threats. Not that there would be any, but they had to keep up the pantomime for the Cygnet Club's CCTV cameras that would certainly be catching all this. At that moment, someone inside would be alerting the staff that someone incredibly important was about to pay them a visit.

Savage and Tannaz got the nod that it was safe to get out. Savage turned to her and said, "Remember, act arrogant. Like everyone's beneath you."

"Already do," said Tannaz, winking.

As they got out, the three security guys fell into place just as Savage had asked. Two behind, one in front. Standard bodyguarding wedge formation.

The little entourage marched up the steps and into the Cygnet Club.

Tannaz supressed a gasp as they entered the cathedral-like entrance hall. A long processional space, barrel-vaulted ceiling held up by a series of white marble columns, ending in a grand staircase covered in a blood-red carpet that just needed a Disney Princess to come sweeping down it.

Held in place with brass stair rods as long as spears, the red carpet led up to a vast landing where the staircase split in two, and continued up to a galleried first floor.

Barring their way to the staircase sat a huge polished oak

desk, behind which sat two men, who immediately got to their feet and straightened their jackets. A good sign, a deferential sign, Savage hoped, which meant they'd grant him and Tannaz access without question.

The guy at the front of their bodyguarding wedge, the one who'd been in the passenger seat of the Jag, marched purposefully towards the men at the desk, an intimidating sight with his broad shoulders and muscular neck. Just as he got to the desk, he turned and ignored the men standing behind it, as if they weren't there. The move couldn't have been more perfect. Looking back down the hallway, he held his wrist mike up to his mouth and said, "Assets safe. Returning to vehicles." Savage and Tannaz breezed past him, and the men at the desk, making a beeline for the stairs. Their bodyguarding escorts turned and left.

By the time Tannaz and Savage had reached the first landing, one of the men at the desk, said, "Er excuse me."

Tannaz turned on her heel, fixed the man with a look that could've incinerated granite. "Tea in the library. And a pot of black coffee, and make sure it's extra strong and extra hot. Last time I was here it tasted like dirty bathwater." She turned to carry on up the stairs. Then turned back to the men at the desk. "And don't disturb us."

She caught up with Savage, who whispered, "Next time you demand free hot beverages somewhere posh, don't forget biscuits."

On the first-floor landing the walls were covered in vast portraits the size of ping-pong tables. The aristocratic, oil-painted images of former members throughout the ages, stared back at Tannaz and Savage with apparent disapproval. As they passed each one, the canvasses grew in size, presumably each member trying to outdo the next by commissioning a larger portrait than their predecessor.

"All that money and they still look miserable," Tannaz remarked.

Dead ahead of them was a wide wood-panelled door with a simple polished brass sign engraved with the word 'Library'. They pushed it open and quietly went in.

The same thick, dark-red carpet covered the floor. Every wall was taken up with bookcases that stretched to the ceiling, which was easily twenty-feet high. At regular intervals along the far wall, a series of floor-to-ceiling windows looked out onto St James's Street below. Clusters of studded leather chairs were arranged around low coffee tables. A gentleman peered around his copy of the *Telegraph* at them, then went back to reading. Another two sat together, talking in hushed tones. And right by one of the windows, his hands clasped across his small midriff, his eyes firmly clamped shut, sat the devil himself, Simon Wellington, in a post-lunch slump. He looked smaller than Savage imagined and older compared to the photos they'd seen online. He'd lost a lot of weight too. The pudgy face had gone, replaced by something more shrivelled and birdlike. He still had that wavy, white, ice-cream hair combed across his head. Dressed in a navy-blue pinstripe suit, he snoozed contentedly, an empty brandy glass on the table in front of him and, more importantly, his mobile phone. Lifting it might be a lot easier than they thought.

Savage and Tannaz sat down two tables away from him. The plan was simple. Tannaz would take his phone, head to the toilets and copy it. Then she'd return, slipping it back on the table. If Wellington happened to wake up to find his phone missing, she'd return to the library and announce that she'd found someone's phone on the floor outside and hand it back to him. In his post-nap wakefulness, he'd be unlikely to question it. Then they'd get the hell out of there.

Savage gave her the nod. Tannaz was just about to get to her feet and snatch the phone when the door opened and a waiter brought in a tray with their drinks and placed them on the table in front of them. When he'd left and closed the door behind him, Tannaz silently got to her feet and casually walked past Wellington, sweeping his phone off the table and into the pocket of her jacket. She turned sharply and headed for the door. Just as she reached it, four men came through it, barring her way. One of them Savage recognised. It was Bluetooth.

Savage looked across at Wellington who now had his eyes wide open and was smiling at him like a demon.

CHAPTER 47

BLUETOOTH HELD OUT HIS HAND.

Tannaz glared back at him. "What?"

"You know what. Give me Mr Wellington's phone."

"Why don't you try taking it off me. I'll break both your wrists before you can say dumb, bald idiot in a headset."

Bluetooth smiled. "That might work on a silly little drug dealer, but not me."

"Give it to him," said Savage. "We're outnumbered."

"Listen to your friend, Miss Darvish," said Wellington, his Irish accent was soft and lyrical, completely at odds with who he was. He turned to address the other three members in the library. "Excuse me, gentlemen. May we have the room?"

The men immediately obeyed, standing up and walking out.

Wellington's henchmen escorted Tannaz back to the table where she sat beside Savage. Simon Wellington got up and joined them. His eyes bright and full of life, there was something familiar about them but Savage couldn't quite figure out what.

Almost as if reading his mind, Wellington said, "Have we met before?"

"No, I think I would have remembered," Savage replied.

Wellington smiled to himself. This seemed to amuse him. His henchmen encircled the table, watching over Savage and Tannaz.

"Is there something I can get you?" asked Wellington.

"Do they do Novichok sandwiches?" asked Savage.

"Why, do you feel like taking your own life?"

"No, I thought I'd force feed it to you."

Wellington chuckled. "I seriously doubt that's going to

happen. Look around you. Now why are you trying to steal my phone, Miss Darvish?"

"I found it on the floor. Finders keepers. It's mine now. Hand it back."

"So feisty in the face of overwhelming odds. I like that."

"Yes, you like a good bet don't you, Wellington," Savage added.

"I do. I do indeed. Actually it's the reason I joined this particular club. Have you heard the story about the two gentlemen who put wagers on everything? Even down to two raindrops racing down a window, betting on which one would reach the windowsill first?"

"I have heard that story," Savage replied.

"It happened right here. In this very room. Amazing, eh?"

"Why did you kill my friend Dave Mosely?" asked Savage.

Wellington arched his eyebrows. "I did no such thing. That man wanted to die and would have found a way if I hadn't helped him."

"So you did kill him."

"No. He needed money to buy Nembutal. I merely gave him the extra money he needed. Well, my men did, I'd actually never met him."

"In return for what?" asked Savage.

"He wanted to die up a tree out of sight, away from the public. I merely did a trade. I gave him the extra money he needed for his death drug but I got to choose which tree he used. He agreed, and the rest is history." Wellington casually waved his hand, as if it were nothing.

"You had the tree chopped down, why?"

Wellington folded his arms. "That's where our little show and tell must end I'm afraid. I'm not one of those Bond villains about to reveal his secret plans to you."

"You've just told me you helped a man take his life. I believe assisted suicide is still illegal in this country."

"It is, but who's going to believe you? It's your word against mine. Plus, I have lots of lovely dirt on you both."

"Like what?" asked Savage.

"I have a video of you killing a man in a fighting cage."

"A fight that you organised, and I didn't kill him, Bluetooth over there did that."

Wellington smiled. "We won't show that part of the tape. Edit it out."

"I was wearing a mask, no one would know it was me."

"You have some very distinctive war scars on your back, almost as distinctive as a fingerprint, and we film everything in HD, doesn't miss a thing. They'll match up nicely when we send the footage to the police. Plus, we'll tip them off to where the body is hidden, it'll be covered in your blood and DNA. So you see, you have to do as I say. And you Miss Darvish, Savage's head of tech support, aren't blameless either. You've been hacking into my accounts and my business systems." Wellington made tutting sounds. "And you've just tried to steal my phone. Why is that, Miss Darvish?"

Tannaz threw him a vicious look. "You know why. Your little gambling ring is on a decentralised network, no one can get into it and see what you're up to."

"And that's the way it's staying," said Wellington. "None of this evidence is relevant anymore. You thought you were going to just swan in here and take my phone without there being consequences. You're so naïve."

Savage cursed himself for putting his trust in Ben Wellington. He was the only one who knew they were onto his father. "Who tipped you off about us coming here?" he asked. "Was it your son, Ben?"

"Nobody tipped me off. Certainly not Ben. The boy's soft like his mother. A wet blanket. Not much good for anything. Sure, I use him for a few things, try and toughen him up; my men have to keep an eye on him, though, make sure he does what he's told. But to answer your question, the only person who tipped me off was you, Mr Savage."

"Me? I find that a bit difficult to believe."

Wellington sat back in his winged chair. "No, it's not difficult to believe. I take an interest in anyone who takes an interest in me, no matter how trivial. You called my office on your cell phone, laying down the law about getting Dave Mosely's things back."

"I never said who I was."

"Oh, Tannaz," said Wellington. "How do you put up with him? Mobile phones are so easy to trace. I found out who you were, checked your background. Very impressive, I must say. Then I made it my business to keep an eye on you. When your name flagged up as being on our system, well, I knew you were up to something. Why would anyone hack into our system so they could get a room in Tivoli Gardens of all places? And why the hell did you use your own name? So sloppy. Anyway, so I've been keeping tabs on you, playing with you a like a mouse in a trap."

Savage felt his stomach lurch. All this time they thought they'd been under Wellington's radar when he'd been following their every move. No matter. Just because an enemy knew what you were up to, didn't mean you couldn't snatch victory from them. He'd done it before, and he could do it again.

"Yes," said Savage, confidently. "I heard you like playing games with people."

"Oh yes, I do. And the people who live in my properties are such good sports, so willing. That's the thing about desperate people, they'll do anything to keep a roof over their heads. And about ninety-nine percent of them are addicted to something. Drink, drugs, food. You dangle those carrots in front of them and they dance a merry dance for you. The other thing about them is they make terrible witnesses. Nobody believes them. They can complain, and no one listens, they can accuse you of not fixing their window and no one listens, hell, they could accuse you of murder and no one listens. They are perfect. It's like having a great big toy basket, and I've got hundreds, no thousands of toys to play with. There are so many of them. And they just keep appearing, like second-hand copies of *Fifty Shades of Grey* in a charity shop. And if someone does, on the rare occasion, take them seriously, I make them disappear. No one comes looking for them. Well, apart from you two."

"Is that why you killed Dave's son Luke, because he spoke to us?" asked Tannaz.

"Like I said, this is not James Bond. I'm not going to confess then leave you to die in some bizarre shark tank so you can escape. But there are consequences for what you've just tried. I'm afraid this is the end of the road for you..."

Bluetooth stood at Savage's right shoulder and slipped out a handgun fitted with a silencer from his inside jacket pocket, holding it by his side. It really didn't matter that Wellington had dirt on them. They were to be executed, bumped off in the library. It sounded like the start of a farcical 1920s' murder-mystery. Wellington certainly had a flair for the theatrical.

"What's going on at Dead Maids? Why are you hanging people there?" asked Savage.

"You'd love to know, wouldn't you?" Wellington grinned. "It's eating you alive that you can't figure it out. And I'm not going to tell you because I know how much you want to know. I will let you in on one little secret. A secret that will shock the pants off you."

"I don't shock easily."

"Oh, I think this will do it." Wellington took some bent pebble glasses from his jacket pocket and fitted them around his face. From another pocket he pulled an old blue fisherman's hat and slipped it on his head. "Now imagine me with a bushy beard." Wellington dropped his native Irish accent, and put on a rural Hampshire one. "Fancy a whisky and that? It's me, your old pal, Archie."

CHAPTER 48

S AVAGE STUDIED THE MAN IN front of him, his brain filling in the gaps. Recognition dawned on him, sucking the energy from him. His head felt light and the room spun round.

Wellington was Archie. And had been with him all along. Every minute and second he'd spent at Tivoli Gardens he'd been watched by Wellington dressed up as a little character he'd invented called Archie.

Wellington clapped his hands and stomped his feet with glee, then removed his little disguise. "I got you. I got you good, didn't I. Didn't see that one coming, did you? I've been right across the hall from you all this time, and you never knew it."

"Why the hell did you do that?" Tannaz asked. "Just to keep an eye on him?"

"Sort of, all that keep your enemies close stuff. That wasn't the main reason. For a bet. A bet to myself. See, I always wanted to be an actor. Desperate, I was. Never got a part in my life, never got so much as a call back. I knew I was good. You know when you feel it deep down. Never got the chance to prove it, until now. So I had this little bet with myself when I saw Savage's name pop up on our system and found out who you were. If I could fool an ex-SAS man, it'd confirm what I knew all along. That I'm a great actor.

"I knew you were going to move in four weeks later. Got my room ready, made it look like I'd been there for years. Savage just assumed I'd been there as long as everybody else. Never thought to ask, did you?"

Savage snapped out of his daze. "That means you were never

there when Dave Mosely was there?" he said. "How come you knew so much about him?"

"Wasn't difficult, I just asked Truck and Vlad what he was like. Shy, awkward, kept himself to himself. Embellished the rest—that's acting, darling." Wellington gave a cheesy smile and made jazz hands.

"But you gave him money for the Nembutal," said Tannaz.

"Not in person, you fool. I just supplied the cash. Did all that through Truck and Vlad. Kept out of the loop, so if anything did come back on me it just looks like a case of a couple of dodgy employees dealing drugs with two potheads in Tivoli Gardens. Nothing to do with me."

Wellington's smug grin grew larger, almost splitting his face, like a Cheshire cat in a wind tunnel. "Never thought to suspect anyone around you. Did you like my little story about Archie's daughter, drowning in a scalding hot bath? The crocodile tears down my face, crying at the loss of an imaginary daughter. And the fresh Elastoplasts on my head." Wellington pointed to his forehead. "Made you think I'd been falling over drunk, added to the authenticity—I was particularly proud of that one."

"Ah, so that wasn't from running around in the forest at night, blindfolded," said Savage.

The smug grin dropped from Wellington's face. "How did you know about that?"

"We followed you into the forest one night," said Tannaz. "Saw your little *Intacto* re-enactment."

"Well, I'm impressed," said Wellington, his vile grin reappearing. "That, I didn't know about. You both followed me. Well, done. The pair of you."

There was nothing for Savage or Tannaz to be happy about. It was a small consolation. A bit like England scoring a goal against Brazil with one minute left, and Brazil seven goals up.

Wellington turned to Bluetooth. "Why didn't I know about these two following us into the forest?"

Bluetooth shifted uncomfortably. "Sorry, Mr Wellington. I slipped up."

"Yes you did," Wellington replied. For a moment he looked vulnerable, just a second and it was gone. Savage made a mental note of it. This guy liked being in control, liked to know the outcome of everything, and when he didn't it made him insecure.

"So all those nights you kept disappearing for days on end," said Savage. "That was to oversee your betting games."

"Occasionally," replied Wellington. "Mostly to go home and sleep in a nice bed. I could only take so much of Tivoli Gardens. How do you stand it? It's like living in a hovel in the seventeen hundreds. Animals live better than that."

"But it's your place," said, Tannaz. "You make people live like that. How does that make you feel?"

"Rich. It makes me feel very rich. And that's the problem, see. Being rich can get a bit boring. I mean, I have seven supercars—but I can only drive one at a time. I can have anything I want, which makes life a little dull. I can control everything, apart from chance. Of course, betting on the usual stuff is boring too. I like to get creative, as you know, turns out there are quite a few people just like me across the world. That's why I created my network."

"We found your little basement torture chamber, by the way," said Savage. "The old B&B in Sutton Road."

"Ah, yes. First property I ever bought. That was where it all started. Both my property empire and later on, my betting network. I can see you're dying to know what went on in there. Well, seeing as you're not going to be walking out of here alive, I'll tell you about that particular scenario."

"We saw the marks on the floor," said Savage. "A cage was set into the floor, wasn't it? One of the ones from Nortoft & Sons. And a CCTV camera on the wall."

"Yes and yes. A very simple betting game. Put a man in a cage, gave him water but no food. We bet on how many days he would last. Surprisingly, it was a lot longer than we thought; twenty-nine days. My network loved it, couldn't get enough, and I kind of got addicted to creating more and more outlandish scenarios to bet on."

Tannaz winced with sickness. "Don't you feel remorse for exploiting and killing these desperate people?"

"They aren't people," Wellington replied. "They're vermin, animals. Watch, this was the next scenario I created in the basement."

Wellington held up his phone and played them a noisy video of CCTV footage.

"I call this one The Hunger Games. Starved seven men for a week."

On the phone's screen, a line of sorry-looking bare-chested men stood with numbers marker-penned on their naked torsos, swaying unsteadily. They salivated while a huge fry up was brought in, piles of eggs, bacon, sausages and toast. The plate was locked in the small, ornate, heavy-duty cage set into the floor. The key was hung high up a wall on a hook. The door was closed and locked. Next second the men started fighting. Slaughtering each other to get the key, men ripping each other to shreds; biting, gouging, kicking, doing anything to have the food. The final frame showed the last man standing taking the key in his blood-soaked hands while bodies were left strewn everywhere. Hands shaking with hunger, he was barely able to open the lock. The footage ended with the man shoving the food in his mouth like a dog.

"We placed bets on who would get the key," said Wellington. "You see, they could've been civilised, shared out the food equally, like human beings. Instead they turned on each other, like animals."

"You starved them for a week," Savaged remarked. "What did you expect?"

"I didn't win by the way," Wellington said, disappointed. "The guy I bet on got taken out within the first few seconds, lost ten grand on that one. You see, Mr Savage, this just comes down to good old-fashioned betting—with a more interesting, creative twist, but good old-fashioned betting, just the same. I'm just carrying on the tradition of putting on wagers, just like the members of this club hundreds of years ago. Now, it really is time for me to say goodbye and for you two to disappear."

Bluetooth pulled back the slide on his gun, pointed it at the side of Savage's head. "There's a dead idiot at the end of this gun," Bluetooth said.

Savage swivelled around in his seat to look at him. "Oh yeah, which end are we talking about?" He turned back to Wellington. "You're going to kill us in a gentlemen's club?"

"That's the good thing about paying a fortune in membership fees to an age-old club where many a scandal has taken place— they're very good at keeping secrets. Covering things up. If these walls could talk."

"Is that why there's red carpet everywhere, so the blood doesn't show up?"

"I'll just pay for a new one, after you're gone."

Savage leant forward, casually lifted the gleaming stainless-steel teapot on the tray in front of him and poured the steaming hot beverage into one of the cups. "Oh, well. Better make the most of this tea, then."

Wellington laughed. "Typical Englishman. Tell him he's about to be executed and he pours himself a cup of tea."

Savage lifted the cup to his lips then suddenly flung it at Bluetooth's hand, the one that held the gun. The scalding hot liquid forced him to drop the weapon immediately. Before Savage had a chance to grab it, Bluetooth kicked away the gun. Instead, Savage snatched up the metal teapot and swung it in Bluetooth's face. The hot metal made a dull clang as it connected with his cheekbone, putting him on the floor. The henchman nearest came between Savage and the gun, blocking his way. Holding the pot in his fist like a knuckleduster, Savage punched him in the face, once then twice. He went down on his back.

Tannaz followed Savage's lead and threw her black coffee at the man nearest her. He was wise to the move and ducked. Didn't matter. It served as a distraction, giving Tannaz enough time to snatch up the tongs from the sugar bowl and stab him in the hand. Then she elbowed him in the face, smashing his nose.

The fourth man grabbed her around the neck. Before he could fully tighten his arms, Tannaz opened her jaws and bit down hard on the guy's forearm. The guy still held on so, Tannaz, still gripping the sugar tongs, gouged him repeatedly in the thigh, until he let go.

Savage turned to see Bluetooth on the floor reaching for the gun. Savage threw the metal teapot at his hand. It collided with his knuckles. Bluetooth snatched back his burnt and now bruised hand, buying Savage a couple of precious seconds.

"Run!" he said, grabbing Tannaz by the hand.

CHAPTER 49

THEY MADE IT OUT OF the library, expecting the subdued thud of a silencer round to whizz past their ears. Maybe Bluetooth couldn't shoot with his left hand. Maybe Wellington didn't want to risk firing a weapon out in the hallway. It didn't matter. They weren't safe until they were out on the street, and in public.

They thundered down the wide stairs, past the men sitting at the reception desk, alarm on their faces as Tannaz and Savage hurried past.

Out on St James's Street, Savage flagged down a black cab and got in. "Victoria station," he said to the driver.

As the cab sped off, Savage and Tannaz looked out of the back window, expecting one of Wellington's men to come bundling out of the club, gun blazing. No one came.

"Do you think Wellington would have really shot us in there? In the middle of a gentlemen's club?" asked Tannaz.

"Like he said, I'm sure it's not the first murder that's got covered up in that club."

"What do we do now?" asked Tannaz. "We're screwed. Nearly got ourselves killed back there."

"I am a bit disappointed," said Savage, gazing out the window.

"A bit? That's the understatement of the year."

"Yeah, I never got to try that posh tea they served. Bet it was something special."

"You're kidding me?" said Tannaz. "What about Wellington? He's been onto us all along. Got us on the run. Aren't you worried about him?"

"No, not really."

Tannaz grabbed him by the arm to get his attention. "Savage, he's either going to kill us or get us put away. He's got footage of you. And he's got evidence of me hacking into his account and systems. Savage, I could go away for a couple of years. And you could be put away for life, doesn't that bother you?"

Just then Savage's phone buzzed. He looked at the screen. "It's a text from Wellington: 'I'm coming to get you.' Smiley face."

Tannaz swore. "We need to get away from here double quick. And we need to ditch our phones. Stop him tracking us."

Savage nodded, spoke to the driver, "Can you go via the Embankment?"

"That's a big detour," said the driver.

"Don't care," Savage replied.

The driver shrugged. "It's your money."

"That reminds me," said Tannaz. "Just before that guy with the Bluetooth headset took Wellington's phone off me, a text popped up on his screen."

"What did it say?"

"It was odd. I think it was one of the tree-preservation numbers. I recognised the format, three numbers, forward slash, then four numbers. Someone wanted to put a bet on it. It said twenty thousand in Bitcoin on, then the tree-preservation-order number. I couldn't remember which one. Definitely one of the ones from Dead Maids. Like someone was betting on a tree."

"Why would anyone bet on a tree? That's a pretty dull betting game."

At Piccadilly, the driver turned right instead of left and drove through Trafalgar Square, clogged up with hordes of tourists and sightseeing buses. They passed Charing Cross Station and turned onto the Embankment where a slow-moving river Thames sloshed its way to the sea. "Pull over," said Savage to the driver. Then to Tannaz, "Give me your phone." Tannaz obeyed without hesitation.

Savage climbed out of the taxi, strolled over to the wall beside the embankment and the river beyond, and threw in both phones, then returned to the taxi, which continued its journey to Victoria station. Savage stared out the window, deep in thought.

"Savage, are you okay?"

"Never better," Savage grinned. "We've got Wellington right where we want him."

Tannaz slapped her head. "Am I missing something, Savage? We just got our asses handed to us. Barely got out of their alive. Are you saying you knew that would happen?"

"No, of course not. I was just as surprised as you were. Man, that business with him being Archie, didn't see that coming."

The taxi rattled its way through the burgeoning afternoon rush hour.

"You're surprisingly calm. He's been onto us ever since you called his office and demanded Dave's stuff back."

"Yes, but nothing's changed, has it? So he knows we're onto him and has done for a long time, so what? Do you want to wallow in self-pity or do you want to get him?"

"Want to get him, of course."

"Glad to hear it because we have the advantage now."

Tannaz snorted a laugh. "How have we got the advantage?"

"He thinks he's got us on the run. Thinks we're scared just like every other person he's come into contact with. He's over confident. He thinks he's just outmanoeuvred one of the best hackers in the country and an ex-Gulf War member of the SAS, even disguised as a down and out called Archie. His ego couldn't be any bigger right now. He's on cloud nine, probably celebrating with a brandy or a whisky—you spotted that, right from the start, sort of."

"I did?"

"Archie, or Wellington, as we know now, used to slip notes under my door asking if I'd like a whisky. He used to spell it with an 'e'. I thought he just couldn't spell, but as you quite rightly pointed out he was spelling it the Irish way, because he's from Ireland."

"What are we going to do?"

"Go back to Southampton. There's something I need to pick up from Tivoli Gardens."

"Isn't that dangerous?"

"No, that's the last place he'd expect us to be. He thinks we're running scared. Besides, we'll only be there for a minute or two."

"I need to get my stuff from the hotel."

"No, we can't. Too dangerous."

"You just said he won't be expecting us to go back to Tivoli Gardens. Surely that includes the hotel."

"Okay, fair enough."

They went to the hotel first. Tannaz unplugged various bits of computer equipment and shoved them in her bag. Savage turned his back while she got out of her business clothes and changed into her civvies, including her beloved DMs. "Ah, that is so much better," she said. Tannaz stood up and immediately began tearing down their little evidence wall, peeling off the printouts one by one.

"We haven't got time for that. Let's go," said Savage.

"Alright fine." Tannaz left them and slung a couple of bags over her shoulder and made for the door. "Well, are you coming?"

Savage stood statue-still. Mesmerised by the three printouts still stuck on the wall. The GPS map of all the trees at Dead Maids, the roulette table and the man with the pixelated face hanging from a branch in the Sea of Trees in Japan.

"I thought you were in a hurry," Tannaz huffed. "What is it?"

Savage didn't say anything.

Tannaz clicked her fingers. "Savage. Come on. We can't hang around."

"Might be something. Might be nothing," he muttered.

"Stop being cryptic. What is it?"

Savage shook his head. "It's far too twisted even by Wellington's standards."

"Why don't you let me be the judge of that."

Savage turned away from the wall and shook his head again,

as if disagreeing with himself. He halted, then turned back and said, "Okay, here goes. Wellington obviously has something big going on at Dead Maids. Didn't want to tell use because he's sadistic and liked seeing us squirm. You can be sure it's another gambling game, we know that from the text you saw, someone betting on a tree, okay?"

"Okay."

"Right, hold that thought." Savage pointed at the GPS printout on the wall. "Remember Goth-guy and his girlfriend, taking shots of all the trees? They weren't doing it for fun, they said it was for work, remember? Let's assume he was doing that for Wellington, taking shots of every tree, matching it to each tree preservation order, and therefore each GPS location."

"Apart from Dave's one, the one that got cut down."

"Now look at what's happened at Dead Maids. Three people have supposedly committed suicide who had a connection with Wellington. However, the fourth, the hiker, Samuel Thwaite, had no connection to him. Came all the way down from Doncaster to commit suicide. He was drawn there, just like people are drawn to the Sea of Trees in Japan to commit suicide. It's a mecca for taking your own life. We thought Wellington might be trying to create his own Sea of Trees right here in the UK at Dead Maids. We couldn't figure out why."

"Yes, I remember."

"So let's assume he *is* trying to recreate the Sea of Trees in the New Forest. To do that, he'd need to start a trend of suicides to establish the place so it gets a reputation, get the ball rolling. What if Dave was the first? What if Wellington heard from his men about Dave's plan to die up a tree? What if that gave Wellington an idea, a diabolical idea?"

"That's a lot of what ifs, and what idea?"

"I'm coming to that. Let's assume it's true. To turn Dead Maids into the UK equivalent of Japan's Sea of Trees, he'd need to cause a big splash, get it in the headlines. A normal suicide wouldn't do that. They happen all the time, nobody bats an eyelid. But a dead body falling out of a tree would get headlines. So Wellington's men give Dave the rest of the money he needs for the Nembutal. In return they tell him he has to use a specific tree."

"They give him the printout with the ringed number," said Tannaz.

"Exactly. Dave agrees. Does the horrible deed, and Wellington gets his son Ben to bribe Joel Diplock to cut it down. Dead man falls out of tree. The story is all over the papers, in the news, everywhere. That gets Dead Maids noticed. His PR stunt works. The place and that name— for crying out loud, Dead Maids—so memorable, it's a perfect news story. But it's still not enough to get the place established as suicide central. He needs more bodies hanging from trees. He picks on Dave's son, Luke. It's plausible, he's just lost his father so why wouldn't he commit suicide. We know better than that but the police buy it. Then there's Sylvia Sanchez. Just lost her patient Jenny Hopkins at the care home, also plausible reason for suicide, but we know better. Now Wellington has to be careful, he's sailing close to the wind here. Three deaths, all loosely connected with him. He can't afford another one. He doesn't have to. The trend has taken hold. The fourth person to commit suicide is genuine—the hiker, Samuel Thwaite, has no connection to Wellington, drives all the way down from Doncaster to hang himself from a Dead Maids' tree. And now that's happened, the game can begin properly. I think you saw one of the first bets being taken."

Tannaz shook her head in confusion. "What game?"

Savage pointed to the wall, at the two printouts side by side, the GPS location map of the trees and the roulette table. "Think of Dead Maids as a giant roulette table. In roulette, people place bets on which number they think the ball is going to land on. Dead Maids is just the same. People put their bets on trees, using the corresponding tree preservation order number. But instead of a ball landing on the number..."

"It's the next person to hang themselves," Tannaz said quietly.

"Exactly. They're placing bets on the tree they think will be used for the next suicide."

Tannaz collapsed on the bed. Hand clamped over her mouth, she swore. "How can someone be so vile, so heartless?"

"We already knew he was heartless. It's just the depths to which he's prepared to go, all for, what did he call it? Good old-fashioned betting."

Tannaz clenched her jaw. "He needs to pay for what he's done."

CHAPTER 50

THE LITTLE VW PULLED UP outside Tivoli Gardens. The cold, grey morning did nothing for the building's appearance, a crumbling monument to poverty.

"What are we doing here again?" asked Tannaz.

"We need some muscle power."

"Are you sure this is safe? What if Wellington's men are watching the place?"

"It's a risk, but like I said, it's the last place Wellington will expect us to be. And we're not going to be long. Plus, he's so cocksure of himself I doubt he's worried in the slightest about us. Probably imagining us scuttling away, like little ants."

"If you say so."

"Have you got the present?"

"Sure have."

Tannaz and Savage exited the car, walked up to the front door, unlocked it and went in. Tannaz looked around cautiously, expecting Wellington and his men to leap out at any minute.

Inside the dingy hallway they went straight to Dink's bedroom door and knocked. Seconds later, Dink appeared. The friendly giant beamed brightly at the sight of Savage. "John!" he cried, bear-hugging him tightly in his massive arms.

Savage struggled for breath, just about managing to get a few words out. "Hey, Dink. Can you loosen your grip a little?"

"Sure," said Dink, letting go of Savage.

Savage groaned with relief. "This is my friend Tannaz."

"Hi, Tannaz," said Dink. He turned to Savage. "I thought you'd left for good."

"Sort of. I don't think I'll be coming back here after this."

The smile evaporated from Dink's face, reminding Savage that he was just a youngster at heart. "Archie's disappeared too," he said. "Haven't seen him since you left."

"Oh, I wouldn't worry about, Archie. We'll keep in touch, I promise. Listen, Dink, have any of Wellington's men been hanging around the house, keeping an eye on the place?"

Dink shook his head. "Nobody's been here since you kicked Vlad and Truck out."

"Good to know," Savage replied. "Hey, I've got a present for you."

Tannaz handed over a large boxlike parcel, covered in bright yellow paper.

Dink's smile returned. "Can I open it?"

"Sure."

Dink's giant hands tore the paper to shreds, like a kid on Christmas day, revealing a traditional woven-wicker picnic hamper, complete with carrying handle and two buckled fastening straps.

Dink gasped with delight, then fumbled with the straps, desperate to see what was inside. The opened lid exposed its contents—a full plate and cutlery set fastened against the inside, together with four plastic glasses. What really caught Dink's attention was the food. A huge smoked salmon with cream cheese, fresh bread rolls and a bottle of chilled non-alcoholic sparkling wine.

"As I promised when I first met you," said Savage. "A smoked-salmon picnic."

Dink hugged Savage, nearly cracking his ribs. "You're the best, John." Then he turned his attention to Tannaz who held up her hands.

"No, I'm good," she said. "I don't do hugs."

Dink ignored her and gave her a bone-crushing embrace. Then he bounced up and down excitedly. "Can we have it now?"

"Of course," Savage replied.

They sat on the floor in Dink's room, which was surprisingly clean, having an indoor picnic, letting Dink take the lion's share of food and drink. It disappeared quite rapidly.

"That was amazing," Dink said, picking crumbs off his plate.

"Are you still making your soup, like I showed you?" asked Savage.

"Every day," he replied, getting up to take a book off the mantelpiece, entitled *The Best Soups Are The Ones You Make Yourself*. "Got myself a book and everything."

"That's great, Dink. Are you trying to stay off the junk food?"

Dink looked away guiltily. "I still like eating crisps."

"How many bags do you eat a day?" asked Savage.

"Just the one."

"That's not so bad," said Tannaz.

"Yeah but it's these bags." Dink held up a discarded crisp packet from his wastepaper bin. It was family-sized, made for sharing.

"Hey, don't worry," said Savage. "You're doing good. Got to have a few indulgences now and again. Listen, Dink. I need to ask you a favour."

"Yes, anything," Dink replied.

"I need your strength."

Out on the road in front of Tivoli Gardens the three of them stared down at the storm-drain grate. A couple of feet long by about a foot wide, it was an old, dull-brown cast-iron model with six thick bars across it like fat sausages. Designed in an era when things were built to last, the grate looked like it hadn't moved for over seventy years.

"You know," said Savage. "There are people that go around collecting shots of drains and manhole covers like this."

"Really?" said Tannaz.

"Yeah, they're called drain spotters."

Tannaz winced in disbelief. "Shut up."

"I'm not joking, it's true. Sounds like a nice way of spending your time."

"You need to get a life, Savage."

Savage turned to Dink. "Think you can lift it?"

Dink looked worried. "I don't know. I won't get in trouble, will I?"

"No, course not. I'll take the blame if anyone says anything."

"Well okay, then."

"Now be careful, Dink. That thing's solid iron. Make sure you..."

Before Savage had a chance to finish his little health-and-safety speech, Dink had bent over, grabbed the grate with both fists and tore it from its mounting, scattering years of collected dirt and debris onto the pavement.

Dink gently placed the drain cover next to the hole. "Wow," said Savage. "That was easy."

Dink smiled, happy to be helping. Savage rolled up his sleeves, lay down on the pavement, flat on his front. With his head and arms reaching down into the open drain, he fished about in the swirling murky water.

"You okay, Savage?" asked Tannaz.

"Never better," came his echoey voice. "Dink, could you hold onto my feet? Have to reach a bit deeper." Dink obliged, clamping his hands around Savage's ankles.

Moments later Savage's right hand came up out of the drain and dropped a filthy wet tube-like piece of dark metal onto the pavement. He reached in again and pulled out a thick rusty spring about the same length. Next to emerge from the drain was a slim rectangle of metal, blackened with dirty mud. Finally, Savage pulled his head and shoulders out of the storm drain, his face red where the blood had rushed to his head. In his hand he held the last piece of the puzzle, the handgrip and frame of the Baikal handgun he'd taken off the two heavyweight drug dealers months ago.

"Is that a gun?" asked Dink.

"Yes, parts of a gun, a very dirty gun."

"Are you going to shoot someone?"

"No, we're just going to scare a friend, Dink. Nothing to worry about. Could you put the drain cover back for me?"

Dink lifted the metal grille and slotted it back into place. Savage pulled a small hand towel from his pocket and wrapped up the pieces of the gun, then got to his feet. "Thank you, Dink. I couldn't have done that without you."

"You're welcome," said Dink. "What are we doing now?"

"Well, me and Tannaz are going to clean this lot up and get out of here."

"Can I come?" asked Dink.

"Best not," said Savage. "When we've done this little thing we need to do, me and Tannaz will come back and visit you properly, okay?"

"Okay. I'll make you some soup."

"That would be perfect, Dink. We'll look forward to it."

Tannaz and Savage watched Dink shrink in the rearview mirror as he waved them goodbye. "He's such a sweetheart," said Tannaz.

"He is. You know, Wellington swindled him out of his mother's house."

"He did what?"

"Took his dead mother's five-bedroom luxury house in Chilworth, made him swap it for that grotty little room he lives in."

Tannaz's voice dropped, became low and mean. "Now we've got the Baikal can I shoot Wellington in the head? Actually, forget that. Too good for him. I've got a better idea."

Forty-five minutes later they had parked up at Dead Maids.

"Does it have to be here?" asked Tannaz.

"This is the most isolated part of the forest. I can't think of anywhere better." Savage climbed over the driver's seat into the back of the van. He carefully unfurled the damp towel and laid it on the payload floor, revealing the grubby, dismantled handgun. From a holdall in the back, he took out an array of tools and liquids, including solvents, lubricants, abrasive materials, bore brushes, cleaning swabs and nylon brushes, and set to work restoring the Baikal back to life. He handed the slide of the gun to Tannaz, together with a can of WD40, a small bottle and a dry cloth. "Can you clean off any dirt with the WD40 and then apply a thin coat of rust remover?"

"Sure."

They sat rubbing, scrubbing, cleaning, sanding and oiling until all parts of the Baikal shone like new. Savage fitted them back together, testing the slide several times, cleaning and reloading the bullets into the magazine.

"Right, just one more thing we need," said Savage.

From the holdall he removed a thick cylinder, covered in lengths of black electrical tape, with two small holes either end.

"What's that?" asked Tannaz.

"This is a homemade silencer. It's pretty simple. One PVC pipe inside another. Sandwiched in the space between is builder's expanding foam, with a plastic cap on either end to hold it all together. The small pipe has loads of holes drilled in it, so when the bullet passes through it, the heat and sound is absorbed by the builder's foam, well, some of it. Not as good as a manufactured silencer, but good enough."

He stuffed both the gun and the makeshift silencer into his jacket.

"Shall we give it a test drive?" he asked.

"This, I'd like to see," said Tannaz grinning.

They left the VW van and trekked into Dead Maids, hopefully for the last time, seeking out the most isolated spot they could find. After an hour and a half of walking, Savage said, "This will do." He found a tree stump and placed a tin can on it, walked back thirty paces, took out the Baikal, turned, aimed and fired.

The tin can pinged up into the air, the loud crack from the gun dislodging any birds in the vicinity from their perches. "Gun works fine," said Savage, resetting his target. "Let's see how it fares with the silencer." He took thirty steps back, pulled the homemade silencer from his jacket and fitted it on the muzzle, took aim and fired. Rather than a crack, the gun made a dull, wet thud. A fraction of the volume of the first shot.

The tin can remained where it was, the shot disappearing into the ground next to the stump. "Okay," said Savage. "Accuracy at a distance is a bit off. It'll be fine for what we have in mind. Right. Let's pay Simon Wellington an unexpected visit."

CHAPTER 51

I F SOMEONE WERE TO DESIGN the quintessential English town, or what they thought the quintessential English town should look like, they'd probably end up with Esher in Surrey.

Nestled to the east of the River Mole and within easy commute to London, Esher was rich. Very rich. Wealthy and pretty, it was populated with nice people from nice backgrounds and nice families, everything about it was nice. The roads were leafy, wide and uncongested, travelled by cars no older than a year, mostly ship-sized SUVs and luxury sedans. Children were beautiful, healthy and happy, fed on a diet of organic couscous, olives and sourdough bread bought not from a supermarket, but delivered from a wonderful deli that had been recommended by a friend. Children grew up to be teenagers with good prospects who were groomed to take jobs in important positions who would then have more beautiful children, and so the cycle of wonderful privilege would continue. Homes ranged from the expensive to the ridiculously expensive—the massive price tag of even the most minuscule flat, a massive comfort to the residents of Esher, not so much for the investment potential. Mostly because it kept the riff-raff out.

All except one.

Simon Wellington.

On one of the most expensive roads in one of the most expensive areas of Esher, he'd bought a sprawling sixteen-bedroom mansion in an area called Claremont Park. Twelve-million-pounds' worth of house set in four acres of landscaped lawns and woodlands. In fact, all the houses along this road were so big and in such vast plots that it was impossible for neighbour to glimpse neighbour.

The only evidence that there were houses along this road were the occasional driveways, disappearing off into some rural idyll. No houses were visible, they were set so far back behind electric gates and high, well-kept hedges and topiary. Privacy and seclusion cost money in this country. It was also precarious. In the half hour Savage had been parked up an access lane in the cab of a long-wheel-base, bland white van he'd borrowed from Harry Preston, he'd only seen one other car go past. It was the least busy road he'd ever seen, so much so that he felt like the world had ended and he was the last man on earth.

No passers-by meant no witnesses and no alarms raised. Conditions couldn't be more perfect.

Tannaz was parked further down the road in a similar van, hidden from view behind a large holly bush.

They knew Wellington was a creature of habit. He still frequented the Cygnet Club, week in, week out. Every Monday, Tuesday and Wednesday he sat in the back of his handsome Bentley Flying Spur and made the trip to London and back with Bluetooth and his driver, who Savage assumed was also a bodyguard, up front.

Not nearly enough protection, thought Savage. Further proof that he was overconfident. It was no wonder he was so self-assured. The guy had spent weeks in Tivoli Gardens alone without any security whatsoever in a highly hostile environment. He was either fearless or reckless. Savage guessed it was the former. Wellington thought he was untouchable; the extra security at the Cygnet Club when they tried to snatch his phone, just a one-off event. He'd needed more boots on the ground to take care of Tannaz and Savage, and make their bodies disappear. Well, that hadn't gone to plan, and neither would his plans for today.

At three forty-five p.m., with OCD-like regularity Wellington was picked up from his London club, to avoid the rush hour, and would head back home. Fifty minutes later, the majestic Bentley would sweep along the tree-lined avenues of Esher and into his endless driveway.

Today was no different. Right on time, the luxury metallic-blue sedan glided past Savage's position. He clocked Bluetooth in the passenger seat, Wellington in the back and another guy driving. He called Tannaz and said, "Showtime." Then pulled out, following the Bentley at a distance.

Up ahead, Tannaz's identical large white van emerged from its hiding place and came to a stop across the full width of the road, blocking the Bentley's path. The driver had no choice but to slow to a standstill. Savage hit the accelerator, gunned the engine, closing the distance in a second or two, and rammed the back of the pristine sedan. Nothing like a good shunt in the rear to cause a bit of shock and disorientation. Slowed the mind of even the most professional and experienced bodyguards.

Savage leapt out of the cab, the Russian Baikal in his hand, improvised silencer fitted on the end.

Savage took aim and shot out the tyres on the left-hand side, just in case the driver tried something stupid, like a three-point turn or driving up onto the well-manicured verges to make a getaway. It also served as a warning to the men inside that he had a real gun and was prepared to use it. They'd certainly be armed, but after giving them a good bit of whiplash from ramming the car, he had the jump on them.

Savage tapped on the front passenger-side window with the butt of the gun, not to get Bluetooth's attention, he'd already done that. It was a simple test to see if it was bulletproof. The gun made the usual clack-clack sound of normal glass. If it had been bulletproof it would have been dull, almost inaudible.

Bluetooth was rubbing his neck.

"Out!" shouted Savage. "Now!"

Bluetooth moved slowly, far too slowly for Savage's liking. He was being a prick, buying time, stalling so he could plan a retaliation. Savage took a step back, aimed at the door, right where Bluetooth's thigh would be, and fired. The door would have taken some of the sting out of the bullet's velocity. Unlike most Hollywood movies that would have you believe car doors could protect someone from gunfire, the round had no trouble passing through the thin metal and plush interior panelling, and onwards, burying itself in Bluetooth's leg. At that range, even with the silencer's dodgy accuracy, he couldn't miss.

Through the window, Savage could see and hear him screaming.

The driver got out, hands up. Savage recognised him from the club and kept his gun on him.

"Tannaz," he said. "Take his keys, pat him down. Get his phone and any weapons. Get Wellington's phone off him too."

While she was doing that, Savage opened the passenger door and reached in to search Bluetooth. Savage pulled the guy's phone from his jacket and a small Glock twenty-six handgun, holstered under his arm. Blood was pooling all over the nice leather seat. The guy was breathing hard, panicking, clutching his leg. "You shot me," he gasped.

"Nothing gets past you does it?" Savage straightened up. "How are we doing Tannaz?"

Tannaz held up a phone and a small sidearm. Savage recognised it as a Walther PPK, favoured by James Bond. "You, 007," said Savage to the driver. "Come round here."

The guy hurried around the front of the car.

"Give your mate a hand, you're both going in the boot."

"We are?" he said.

"Actually, I've changed my mind," said Savage. "I think I'll let you go, you look like nice lads."

"Really?"

"Course not. Get in the boot now!"

The guy lifted Bluetooth out of his seat, hooked an arm around his shoulders and helped him hobble round to the back of the mangled car. The bumper had crumpled and the light clusters had both smashed. The boot was dented but still serviceable. Tannaz clicked the button on the key fob, and it rose like magic.

"Both of you get in," said Savage.

Bluetooth went first, resting his backside on the tailgate in an attempt to swing both legs in, taking far too long.

"Be quicker," Savage commanded, "or I'll shoot your other leg, then I'll shoot your friend."

The driver, clearly not wanting to get shot, grabbed both of Bluetooth's legs and shoved them in. Bluetooth yelped in pain. The driver climbed in after him, the vast boot easily accommodating both of them. Tannaz clicked the button and the boot lid slowly descended, muffling the sound of Bluetooth's agony.

Savage opened one of the rear doors. Wellington sat there calm and unworried.

"My phone will do you no good," he said. "It's highly encrypted and rigged to delete if anyone tampers with it, even someone as good as Miss Darvish."

"Get out," said Savage.

Wellington jutted out his chin in defiance. Probably the first time in decades anyone had told him what to do. He slid out of the car and straightened up his suit and adjusted his tie. "This is all very amateurish, Mr Savage. Do you have any idea what you're doing?"

"Yes. It's just a good old-fashioned kidnapping. Now get in the back of the van."

CHAPTER 52

TANNAZ DROVE THE DAMAGED VAN, the one Savage had shunted the Bentley with, to a body shop in nearby Sunbury that would ask no questions. They'd booked in advance to get the front end fixed before they handed it back to Harry Preston. They'd informed him of their plan to grab a scumbag landlord who needed taking down a peg or two. Harry, who had been ripped off by several landlords who'd charged him ever-increasing rents for his business premises merely replied, "Knock yourself out."

After dropping off the damaged van, Tannaz joined Savage in the passenger seat of the second van. He pulled off the body-shop forecourt and into traffic. They'd chosen Sunbury because it was where the M3 motorway began, taking them directly south-west.

Tannaz glanced over the seat at their passenger in the back, lying on the metal floor, his hands and feet zip-tied, and his mouth gagged.

"Comfy?" asked Tannaz.

Wellington said nothing. His enraged eyes said it all.

"You're going to love the little game we've got lined up for you," said Tannaz. "You like a good game, don't you?"

Garbled words forced their way out through Wellington's gag.

"We can probably take the gag off him now," said Savage. "We're on the motorway. No one will hear him."

Tannaz climbed into the back and sat down beside Wellington, loosening the gag from his mouth. She put a bottle of water to his lips. He drank greedily.

"So you're going to kill me," Wellington gasped.

"No, whatever gave you that idea," said Tannaz, mock outrage in her voice.

"I have friends. Important friends. Friends you wouldn't want to mess with. Big, powerful people."

"That's what we're counting on," Tannaz added.

Wellington laughed, rather too spiritedly to be genuine. "Ah, so you're going to hold me to ransom. You're nothing but a pair of third-rate criminals." He spat on the floor.

"Wrong again," said Tannaz. "A ransom never even crossed our minds."

"No, we've taken a leaf out of your book. Got creative," said Savage.

"What are you going to do?" asked Wellington. A tinge of worry creeping into his voice.

"Well let's see," said Savage. "Where are we now, junction two of the M3, you've got until junction fourteen to work it out. That's about fifty miles."

"You're taking me to Southampton."

"Clever boy," said Tannaz. "Oh, that reminds me," she said, rifling through her pockets. She fished out a pound coin and handed it to Savage in the front. "Savage and I are having a bet."

"What are you betting on?" asked Wellington.

"You," said Savage. "We've each bet a pound on you."

"What's the bet?"

"You'll have to wait and see," said Tannaz.

Before Wellington had a chance to digest this new information, Tannaz grabbed one of his zip-tied hands. "What are you doing?" he asked.

"I need your thumb."

Wellington struggled, assuming Tannaz was going to cut it off.

"Relax," she said. With her free hand she reached into her jacket and pulled out Wellington's phone and pressed his thumb against the home button so it would scan his print. She let go of him.

Wellington straightened up. Tried to assume a more dignified posture, which was pretty impossible with his hands tied, sitting on the floor in the back of a hired van. "Okay, so you've got into the phone's home screen," he said. "You won't get any further without the encryption key. And if you try without it, everything on that phone is set to delete."

"Yes, I know," said Tannaz. "You keep telling me. Maybe you could just give me the key now, save me loads of bother."

"Never," Wellington replied.

"Well, maybe I'll cut off your thumbs and see if that works."

Wellington pressed his back against the wall, his frame shrinking slightly.

"We'll see what happens, eh?" said Tannaz. "Right now I'd be praying that I get in, otherwise you'll lose your thumbs."

Ten minutes later Tannaz punched the air repeatedly. "I'm in!"

"What!" Wellington struggled against his bindings, unable to contain himself. "That's impossible. Impossible. The encryption is like nothing you've seen before. I made sure of it. No one can get into it without my authorisation! No one!"

"Well, I'm in your phone and, oh, guess what? I'm on your little network now. This is where the fun starts. All your secret millionaire gamblers across the world are going to be treated to one hell of a show."

"What are you doing? Tell me!" Wellington's rage swept over him like a dose of fever. He managed a wriggling sort of shuffle, attempting to get over to the opposite side of the van where Tannaz had his phone. She planted a boot on his chest and shoved him back, winding him against the side of the van.

"Do that again and I'll pull all your fingernails out," Tannaz said with such ferocity it even made Savage wince.

Wellington remained silent for the rest of the journey. A simmering, brooding anger bubbling under the surface. As they reached the outskirts of Southampton, Tannaz replaced the gag around his mouth.

Ten minutes later, Savage pulled on the handbrake and killed the engine. "Well, here we are, your final destination. We were going to take you to Dead Maids but we thought it would be more poetic to come full circle, back to where it all began. That humble little B&B in Shirley, which you later used to torture and murder people just so you could gamble."

Thrashing around in the back, Wellington's muffled moans filled the van. Savage pulled out the gun and pointed it at him. "Don't make me use this. Now shut up."

Wellington quieted down at the sight of the Baikal with its Frankenstein silencer.

The road outside was dark, deserted and cold, everyone at home hunkered down in front of the TV or online. Savage backed the van up onto the paved front garden, only feet from the front door, then snapped on a pair of nitrile gloves. Tannaz did the same. No one saw the briefest glimpse of a man in a suit dragged out of the back of the van and shoved into the house. Savage had been there earlier and unlocked the security shutter, leaving it open to allow them quick access.

Closing the door behind them, Savage held Wellington by the scruff of his jacket and guided him to the secret door under the stairs. He stumbled his way down into the basement where Savage hauled him into the little cement room with its strong metal door.

When he saw what waited for him there, Wellington trembled, tried breaking free of Savage's grip. Savage was too strong for him.

In the middle of the little room, bolted to the concrete floor, was a plain metal cage, measuring one and a half metres cubed.

"Sorry it's not as fancy as the one you had here before," said Savage. "This is just a bog-standard one we got off the Internet, but it'll do."

Wellington's gagged mouth chomped up and down, eager speak. Savage removed it.

"What is this?" he demanded. "What are you going to do? Do you know who I am? You'll be dead within a week. My men will find you and execute you. They've seen your faces, know who you are, you stupid amateurs."

"Yeah, they probably would. Except Tannaz has been in your payroll software and I'm afraid there's been a glitch."

"What have you done?"

Tannaz bent down and opened the cage door. "Let's just say, they won't be getting their wages this week, or the next, or the week after that. Actually, I think all the money allocated for your wages bill for the next few months, which is quite a hefty one—you must employ a lot of assholes—has wound up in the accounts of several homeless charities. So generous of you, Mr Wellington."

"See, even the most committed, loyal men lose interest when you don't pay them," Savage added.

Wellington's shoulders dropped in defeat, all fight had gone out of him. "Okay," he said. "What do you want?"

"Want?" asked Savage. "What I want, you can't give us. I want my friend Dave back."

"I told you, I didn't kill him. He committed suicide of his own free will."

"And what about Dave's son, Luke?" Tannaz held Wellington by the lapels of his finely tailored suit and pushed him against the wall. "You killed him, then you killed Sylvia Sanchez just so you could kick-start your stupid betting game at Dead Maids. Not to mention killing Jenny Hopkins *and* your own daughter. And the hundreds of others you've murdered for sport."

Wellington's back slid down the wall until he slumped to the floor. He looked a sorry mess of a man. Defeated and remorseful, Savage assumed he was about to admit his guilt and apologise for what he'd done. For all the lives he'd ruined. He couldn't have been more wrong.

"I'm never going to see my wonderful game come to life, am I?" he said forlornly. "That was going to be my Sistine Chapel. Create a mecca for suicide, a betting game like no other. It was an ambitious idea. Inspired and unique. Without equal. And you've ruined it!"

Tannaz swore and kicked him in the ribs. "You're encouraging people to hang themselves so you can bet on them, and that's what you're worried about?"

Wellington smiled sadistically. "Well, the game may not

continue but my legacy will. People will keep killing themselves there because of what I did, what I created."

Tannaz went to kick him again. Savage held her back.

"Come on, Tannaz," he said. "We've got our own game to play, remember."

Tannaz's anger simmered down.

Together they heaved Wellington across the floor and into the cage, while he thrashed and struggled to break free. Before shoving him in, they cut his zip-tied hands and feet. After he was safely inside, Savage shut the door and secured it with a hefty padlock.

"So that's it," said Wellington. "You're just going to leave me here?"

"Oh, no," said Tannaz. "We wouldn't do that. We're not monsters. This is where our little game begins." Having made certain their gloves could be used on a touch screen, Tannaz held up Wellington's phone, and began filming him as he squatted in the metal cage. "Okay, fellow online gamblers. We have a very special bet for you today, involving our very own Simon Wellington."

"Help me!" shouted Wellington, rattling the bars of the cage. "I've been kidnapped. Help!"

"That's right," said Tannaz. "Simon Wellington, the creator of your little betting ring has been kidnapped and is being held in the basement of twenty-seven Sutton Road, Shirley, Southampton. I'm posting the GPS co-ordinates right now."

Wellington's mouth hinged open in shock as he tried to figure out what was going on. The idea of a kidnapping where the kidnappers gave away the location of the victim clearly had him baffled.

Tannaz continued filming him. "So today we're betting on whether anyone will come to Simon Wellington's rescue. Just bet either yes or no. It's that simple. If one of you comes to free him, then 'yes' wins, if no one comes then 'no' wins. You have three days, that's usually how long a human being can last without water. Happy betting." She clicked off the video. "Right, I'll just upload that onto your network. Okay, that's up there now."

Wellington cackled loudly. "What kind of dumb kidnappers are you? You've just given away my location. People will be here within the hour to free me. Honestly, you people. You've just signed your own death warrant. I'll get out of here and then I'll make you wish you'd never been born."

Savage squatted down next to the cage, his face level with Wellington's. "See, here's the thing. Are the guys on your network thinking, 'Oh no, Wellington's being held prisoner, I better send someone over there right away to rescue him.' Or are they thinking, 'Oh no, someone's busted into our highly secret and illegal betting network, where we murder and starve people for fun. I better delete everything so I can deny all knowledge of Simon Wellington.' Which do you think is more likely?"

"Someone will come for me," Wellington said, gripping the bars. "Then you'll be sorry."

Savage straightened up and stood beside Tannaz.

"Don't worry, Simon..." said Tannaz.

"... It's just good old-fashioned betting," Savage added.

They turned and headed towards the large metal door to the sound of Wellington shaking the cage bars and spouting all sorts of profanity. Just before Savage closed the door behind him, he turned to Wellington and said, "I'll leave you with one of my favourite sayings about life—when one door closes... so do all the others." Shutting the large metal door behind him, Savage secured it with another substantial padlock. They could still hear Wellington's muffled protestations, threatening them one second, promising to give them everything the next. At the foot of the narrow stairs, Savage closed the second door, the one that was heavily soundproofed, completely drowning Wellington out.

They made their way up the stairs, replacing the false wooden wall and screwing it back into place. Outside of the old abandoned B&B, Savage locked up the front door then closed and locked the security shutters. He joined Tannaz in the cab of the big white van, started the engine and backed out.

"Did you actually manage to break the encryption on Wellington's phone?" he asked.

"No, no way," Tannaz replied. "Like he said, the encryption was unbreakable. And if I'd tried it would've deleted everything. He was right about that, no one could have hacked it."

"So with our little pantomime back there he still thinks there's a chance someone's coming for him."

"Yep. It'll give him false hope. Then he'll start having doubts. He'll think maybe no one's coming. That they've all abandoned him to save their own skins. That will turn to bitterness. Eat him alive. All these scenarios playing out in his head will send him into a rage. With all that whisky he drinks, he'll probably have a heart attack before he dies of dehydration."

Savage threaded the van through the streets of Shirley, not saying anything.

"You've gone quiet, Savage. What's up?" Tannaz asked.

"Nothing."

Tannaz shifted in her seat. "I hope you're not regretting what we just did, because that asshole deserved it."

"Yeah, I know, but..."

"But nothing. We had no choice. No evidence to go to the police. And if we did, it could be years before it went to trial. More time for him to exploit and kill more innocent people. He'd probably get off anyway. Those kind of people always do."

Savage sucked in air through his teeth. "Yes, but leaving him in a cage to die. Isn't that sinking to his level?" Savage wasn't really worried about Wellington. He was more worried about himself. Was he becoming like Wellington? A sadistic killer? Especially as this wasn't the first person Savage had locked up and left for dead. He cast his mind back to Minchie, the south London thug he'd sealed into an empty warehouse. Was Savage acquiring a taste for making bad guys suffer? "We could've just put a bullet in Wellington's head. Ended it quick."

"Not good enough. Not by a long shot. Think of all the misery that guy has caused. A quick death is not justice. Makes a mockery of all the people he's tortured and murdered. He needs to experience some of the suffering he's created. Get a taste of his own medicine before his sordid little life ends. It's not about being sadistic. It's about making the punishment fit, that's all."

"Yeah, I guess you're right."

"Damn right I am," said Tannaz. "I don't want to hear any more about it. We've just done society a favour. I think what we did was far too good for him. So don't start getting all touchy-feely on me."

Savage envied her surety and conviction. Things weren't so simple for Savage. He carried a lot more mental baggage, acquired from a lifetime of killing. The conflict in his mind would only grow, not helped by Jeff Perkins who would remind him of his actions next time he had another PTSD episode. Jeff was bound to attack Savage's warped moral compass, calling him a stinking hypocrite and a merciless vigilante. No better than the scumbags he hunted down.

Savage pointed the van in the direction of the motorway, and prepared for the long drive back home.

CHAPTER 53

A RETICENT SUN FAILED TO MAKE an appearance. Though the temperature had risen and the evenings were stretching out into summer, sunshine was still in short supply.

Tannaz and Savage pulled up outside Tivoli Gardens. A Tivoli Gardens that bore no resemblance to the one Savage had stayed in several months ago. Gone were the dilapidated windows that didn't shut properly. They had been replaced by smart, energy-efficient plastic ones. The roof, once covered in shoddy tiles like badly shuffled playing cards, proudly showed off its new, smart slate covering.

"Wow," said Savage stepping out of his little VW van. "That's an improvement."

"Almost looks habitable," Tannaz added.

Last time they were here, the front of the house had been a barren wasteland of discarded bicycles, a rotten sofa, dirt and dirty needles. Now it was a vast expanse of elegant block paving.

The front door swung open before they even reached it. That too was new.

Slimmer and with trimmed hair and clean shaven, stood the friendly figure of Dink, sporting a bright, wide smile.

He rushed out and clamped Savage in his two massive arms. Then he did the same to Tannaz.

When Savage had regained his breath, he said, "Dink, it's so good to see you."

"You look good," said Tannaz.

"I feel good," he said. "I have a job now."

"That's great. What are you doing?" asked Savage.

"I'm a kitchen assistant. You know, it's mostly cleaning but sometimes I get to make simple stuff, prepare food. I want to be a chef. The restaurant said they'd help me train, as an apprentice."

"I'm really pleased for you."

"Come in, come in," Dink beckoned them eagerly.

Inside it was the same story as outside. The urine stained hall carpet had been replaced by wood-effect laminate flooring, and the walls had been given a lick of paint.

They followed Dink down into the basement kitchen, the smell of something wonderful wafting up the stairs.

The kitchen was still a bit of a mess, an unavoidable fact of life in a shared house. Savage noticed a new, large fridge and the cooker had been replaced; still basic, budget white goods, nothing fancy, but a definite improvement on what was there before. And there was now a line of four stools and a high counter to sit at. A bubbling pot sat on one of the cooker's rings, throwing whorls of steam into the air.

"Take a seat," said Dink.

"Is that fresh bread I can smell?" asked Tannaz.

"Yeah," said Dink. "We're having soup with it. I made the bread myself."

Dink put on a pair of oven gloves, opened the oven and slid out a steaming loaf. The aroma was heavenly. Lifting the pan off the stove with both hands, he then ladled the soup into three bowls. "It's a Jamie Oliver recipe. Roast carrot and fennel." He tore off a hunk of fresh bread and placed it beside each bowl with a spoon, then sat and joined them.

Savage and Tannaz lifted a spoon of soup, blew on it and took a sip.

Tannaz swore.

Dink panicked. "What's wrong? Is something wrong?"

She shook her head rapidly. "This is by far the best thing I have tasted all year."

"Really?" Dink shook with delight.

"Dink," said Savage. "This is the kind of quality you'd get in a Michelin restaurant."

"Is that one of those restaurants you get on the motorway?"

Savage smiled warmly. "No, nothing like that at all."

"Michelin restaurants are the best," said Tannaz, dunking her bread. "And where you're going to end up working, if you keep making food this good."

Dink couldn't contain his happiness, making him restless and fidgety. "Ever since you showed me how to make soup I've been obsessed with cooking. I make everything myself now, from scratch. I get a thrill out of it. I mean, I still eat crisps and chocolate..."

"Who doesn't?" said Tannaz.

"My appetite is better now. Not so hungry all the time."

"That's great news," said Savage.

"Have you heard anything of Archie?" Dink suddenly asked.

"No, nothing," Savage replied.

"Strange. He disappeared after you moved out. All his stuff was left in his room. Nobody knows what happened to him."

"That's weird," said Savage and then quickly changed the subject. "I was going to say, this place is looking loads better."

"Yeah, totally changed when Ben Wellington took over. You know, after his father died."

Tannaz and Savage exchanged glances. The story had been all over the papers of how millionaire gangster landlord Simon Wellington had been found dead in a secret basement in one of his properties, locked in a cage. The press and social media went wild with sensational theories from a bizarre sex act that had gone wrong, to Russian gangsters taking their revenge. Whatever explanation people believed, the whole of Southampton breathed a huge collective sigh of relief. As a result of his death, the vast Wellington empire went straight into the hands of his son Ben, who'd taken a decidedly more human approach.

Dink continued, "Ben put in new windows, new carpets, new roof. Ben's been fixing things everywhere, not just here. And he's looking into that stuff with my mum's house, you know, how I signed it over to his father, he thinks he might be able to reverse it."

"That's great to hear," said Savage. "Sounds like Ben Wellington is a decent sort of guy."

"Oh, he is. You know Rosie and Grace?"

Savage nodded.

"First thing he did was get them out of here. Said it was no place for a single mum to bring up her daughter. They're living in a little house in Swaythling near the University, and Rosie's got a job there as a secretary."

"Good for her," said Tannaz.

"So who's in Rosie's room now?" asked Savage.

"Oh, yes. I meant to tell you. There's a guy from London in there now. He looks like a bit of a hard case, you know, all shaved head and mean face, but he's okay. Said he came down here to get away from someone really nasty. Said the guy nearly killed him."

"Oh really." Savage took another mouthful of the delightful soup. "Poor guy. What's his name?"

"Minchie."

Savage nearly spat soup everywhere.

If you've enjoyed this novel, why not read the
first one in the series *SAVAGE LIES*.

There's also a FREE short-story prequel you can
download from Prolific Works called *SAVAGE*.

Thank you for reading Savage Games. I'd love it if you
could leave a review on Amazon and recommend it to
your friends. Your opinion makes a huge difference
helping readers discover my books for the first time.

You can also drop by for a chat on social media.

Facebook: PeterBolandWriter
Twitter: @PeterBoland19

OTHER BOOKS BY PETER BOLAND INCLUDE:

The Girl by the Thames

ACKNOWLEDGEMENTS

I don't think I've ever come across an author's acknowledgements that starts by thanking their car satnav. So this might be a first. We were on our way to Bath a couple of years ago, which at the time had terrible traffic jams due to roadworks. The satnav in its wisdom decided to spare us the misery of sitting in endless queues by taking us on a long meandering diversion through the wonderful Somerset countryside. I'm really glad it did, because we got to see some truly magical villages, one of which was called Dead Maids. What a name, I thought. As soon as I got home I Googled it and discovered the origin behind its sinister title—the highwayman and his two fated lovers. When I read that story, I had to get it into a novel somehow. The idea for *Savage Games* built from there, except I moved the story to my own neck of the woods, or more precisely, forest. The New Forest. So thank you satnav!

Next, I have to thank the amazing Lauren Finger, whose great editorial talent has helped make this book far better than it was before. I'd also like to thank my awesome proofreader Loma Halden and my team of beta readers who really do make one hell of a difference with their eagle eyes and attention to detail; they include Kath Middleton, Terry Harden, Deanna Finn and Suze Clarke-Morris. Big, big thanks must also go to David Gilchrist at the UK Crime Book Club and Helen Boyce at The Book Club.

I owe a big debt to real-life members of the SAS Anthony Middleton, Jason Fox, Matthew Ollerton and Colin Maclachlan whose book *Leadership Secrets from the Special Forces* was constantly at my side during the writing of this book. Thanks must also go to Paul Johnston at the Forestry Commission for his expert knowledge of tree felling, and Nik Gruber at the National Park Authority for helping with tree preservation orders and GIS records, although I did use a bit of artistic licence here!

Once more, Simon Tucker has done an incredible job on the cover, likewise Glendon Haddon from Streetlight Graphics for his lovely formatting.

Finally, thanks to my beloved wife for all her support, who always encourages me even when I doubt myself, which is quite a lot.

Lightning Source UK Ltd.
Milton Keynes UK
UKHW010654041220
374560UK00004B/614